Merry Christmas
to
Sidney 1939

from
"Perks"

# LIVE AND KICKING NED

THE MACMILLAN COMPANY
NEW YORK · BOSTON · CHICAGO · DALLAS
ATLANTA · SAN FRANCISCO

# LIVE AND KICKING NED

by

JOHN MASEFIELD

NEW YORK

THE MACMILLAN COMPANY

1939

# LIVE NED

While at sea, I noticed a fitting on a sail, and asked a seaman what it was.

He said, "A reef-tackle."

I asked, "What good is it?"

He said, "In reefing, it takes up the weight of the sail, so that you can pass your ear-rings."

I have called this volume of my story "The Reef-Tackle" because it takes up the weight of my life during a blowy and anxious time. How I passed my ear-rings will be matter for another tale.

I F YOU have not read my story, let me tell you that I am a doctor, the son of a famous London doctor. Just before I came of age, I was accused of the murder of my benefactor, old Admiral Topsle Cringle, of Hannibal House. I was innocent of the crime, but my luck was out; I was condemned and hanged for it.

On the dissecting table, my medical friends restored me to life. With some trouble, and with much danger to myself, they contrived to get me to Liverpool, as surgeon to the slave ship, *Albicore,* then bound for the Slave Coast in Africa. As something of my escape was suspected or surmised, this ship was beset, even in the act of sailing, by the thief-takers, who came just too late to be able to board and take me.

You must think of me now, as a few hours older, the surgeon of the ship *Albicore,* bound down the Channel, with my past behind me, and not too much of a future before.

Let me tell you of my ship and shipmates.

The *Albicore* was a small, full-rigged ship, well-known, so they told me, for her speed and success; but as I found, beginning to shew signs of strain. She was commanded by one whom I shall call Captain Paul. He was the youngest brother of the famous Captain Valentine, who had been hanged for piracy many years before. Paul, although not a pirate, was still a credit to the family stock. As I entered Newgate, I saw him discharged, for want of evidence, for the atrocious murder of a seaman. On the night before our

5

sailing, in the efforts of securing a crew, he had killed another man; for this murder a warrant had been issued against him and had nearly been served. His chief officer was a man named Pegg; his second mate was a Mr. Tulp. We were now at sea together, with a fair wind, and piling sail to make the most of it.

The sun set early that evening. I was on deck, watching the yellow sky all tossed about with menace, and wondering at my escape, when Mr. Pegg asked me if I would go to have a look at the Captain in the cabin.

"What is the matter with him?" I asked.

"The usual," he answered. "He's got the Wraith on him."

Now this was a phrase that I had learned in Newgate, where it was believed that murderers are beset, soon after their crimes, by the wraiths or angry spirits of those whom they have killed. The talk in Newgate ran much upon this point, and agreed, that while the Wraith is on a man he is incapable of wise decision. That it is so, I have no doubt.

I went at once to the cabin, where I found the Captain at table. On one side of him sat the Black Mantacaw, his negress; on the other sat Mr. Tulp, plainly much scared.

The Captain had his case of bottles before him, and clutched a pan containing rum. He was swathed up in rugs, although it was not a cold evening. In spite of the rugs, he was shivering; his teeth chattered and he was mumbling curses or snarling. It looked to me like a bout of fever, brought on by the excitement of the escape. Often a mental strain will light up a fever long supposed gone, but really only hidden.

"What do you want, Doctor?" he asked.

"I'd like to take your pulse and see if a dose of bark won't help matters," I said.

"It's not a case of bark," he answered. "It's a case of bite. It's that fellow's wraith on me. He's on me like irons. He says he won't let me set a course."

"Nonsense, sir," I said. "There is nobody here but ourselves."

"You can't see him," he answered. "He isn't on you. He's on me, with the side of his silly head bashed-in. Ah, you grinning devil, for all your speed, you did not get the beaks in time. And you say I can't set a course but will lead me to destruction?" He leaned forward as he said this and spoke across the table to Mr. Pegg's empty chair. While he spoke, the signs of fever were gone from him. I am sure that he did see the wraith and that the wraith was there. "You were a Popery man," the Captain continued, "and you wouldn't this and you wouldn't that. And now I've fixed you so you can't even if you want to. Don't think you'll stop me setting a course that'll be good. I've got ways of finding a course that'll be good." Here he turned to the Black Mantacaw. "Listen, you," he said. "You see that Popery Barney, there?" He clutched her black claw and made her look at the empty chair. "Well, you tell him, you know some stronger than he knows. You know Him Big Goat Boy . . . you know Him Big Leopard Boy . . . You know Old Master."

The Mantacaw was scared, but she answered, "I know um."

"Yes, you, Barney," the Captain said, still staring at the empty chair. "She know um. She bring um, too: she drive you some place. They'll tell me a course to set where there won't be destruction. Now, you, Judy; you go call um. You get um, all three. Drive this Barney right down into hell where he belongs."

She was scared. She said, "Him Leopard Boy, he no come, not here; too much water. Old Master, he not come."

The Captain took a gulp of rum and said, "Get to your den and put on your scarlet and your crown. You fetch um. Go on with you."

She would have argued, but the Captain's last words were not to be disobeyed. He had an inflection in some of his speeches which made everybody feel that any hesitation in obeying would be visited with death. She went into her den, for all her scare. The Captain said, "Hoodoo'll tell me a course to set. It'll take more than Barney to go against hoodoo."

Mr. Tulp, being only a junior officer, usually said nothing in the Captain's presence, unless he were spoken to. To my surprise he spoke now.

"It won't do you any good, sir, on the Coast, nor on board here, to work hoodoo. The hands'll know it, and the natives'll get to know of it, and they'll steer clear and ruin you. You'd best not try it, sir; it's a bad thing."

"Cock," said the Captain. "If he ain't a psalm-singer."

"No, I'm not a psalm-singer," Tulp said, and it was a gallant thing to stand up to the Captain in that mood, "but, bad as your luck may be, hoodoo is asking for worse, and so you'll find, sir."

"You are an ignorant common fool," the Captain said.

"I know I am, sir," Tulp answered.

"If you give me any insolence," the Captain said, "I'll cut your throat just like a pig's over a pig-bucket."

I said, "Sir, he has used no insolence. You are suffering from a strain and an overexcitement. Let me give you a sleeping draught. In the morning, after a night's rest, you'll be able to set any course with a clear head."

Perhaps he would after that have cut the throat of one or other of us, but at that instant the door of the den opened, and the Black Mantacaw came in, dressed in scarlet and wearing a gold crown. She had a mad look in her eyes and was swaying from side to side; plainly she was up to some devilry, which rather scared her, but to which she was much looking forward; she had trodden that path before.

The Captain took a glance at her, and said, "That is the way; you fetch um Old Master." Then he turned to us, and took a gulp of rum. "On deck with you," he said; he was talking hoarsely, and had to repeat it, "On deck with you. I've got to prepare here."

"Sir," Tulp said, "it'll be the ruin of you."

"I'll be the ruin of you, Tulp," the Captain said. He had seemed a sick man, just an instant before. Now he slid sideways from his chair to the pistol-rack in the bulkhead. He had two pistols out of it, with two swift clutches, and turned to threaten us with them. "Get on deck with you," he said, "or I'll shoot the pair of you."

Tulp, who knew the danger-signals better than myself, leaped for the ladder and went; I followed. I turned to watch the Captain, wondering, had he gone mad, and ought we to disarm him. I saw him lean across the table with his two pistols, and speak to the imagined wraith. "Will you threaten me?" he said, and fired both the pistols through Pegg's chair and the bulkhead beyond it. The cabin filled with drifting smoke. He stayed to charge his pistols, while I went on deck.

I found that Tulp had already told Pegg all the news. The helmsman was listening with all his ears; pistols in the cabin meant something stirring.

"What on earth is hoodoo?" I asked.

"Their sort of god," Pegg said. "They consult him when they want to know a thing."

"Does the god tell them?" I asked.

"Of course he tells them," Pegg said rudely. "Surely you know that. But it makes this ship a hoodoo ship."

"It's a shame," Tulp said; "it's a shame; that's what I call it; and the first night out, too."

"It's a damned shame," Pegg said. "The hands'll pitch her overboard, and I wouldn't wonder."

"Why not stop it, then?" I asked. "Why not take the Captain and give him a sleeping draught and lock him up till the morning?"

"If you talk like that in a ship," Pegg said, "you'll damn soon hang at a yard-arm. That's piracy, what you're talking."

Down below, by the sound, the Captain seemed to be bringing out metal pans. In the odd way by which news passes through a ship, this news had passed; the boatswains of the watch had come aft, and some of the hands of the watch had found jobs further aft than usual, all to listen and to watch. My nerves were not very steady after all that I had suffered. It flashed at once into my mind, that the crew might mutiny, carry the ship back to Liverpool, and give up the Captain as a madman. If they did that, I should be lost.

"If you can't stop a Captain, you must submit to him," I said.

"So we believe," Pegg said. "But now we'll have nothing but trouble, you'll see; trouble with the hands, foul winds, trouble with the Coast; and a lot of slaves with vomito. You'll see, Mister."

But at this point the Captain appeared on deck, breathing hard and beset by the wraith. He was bareheaded, and had slung on his pistol-slings, so that he had six pistols in quick reach, dangling down his chest. He was a terrible-looking man at all times, mad, dark, sideways and murderous, but he looked appalling at that moment. He snatched a pistol from the slings with each hand; he was always fatally swift, swift as a snake, in his actions. The pistols were out and pointed in the one turn of the wrists.

"Get you forward out of this," he shouted. "All the lot of you, get forward. You, too, Misters; I mean you, too. Don't any one of you come aft again till I call."

The officers had sailed with him before, and all hands now knew enough to obey when he bade them. They leaped to the order; I leaped, too; for one had not to know much to know that in that mood a murderer will murder. The Captain went to the helmsman, took the tiller from him, and told him to get out till he was called for. The man slid away, quaking, and joined our group in the waist, where I think we all quaked. My own mind was made up. I would submit to any madness in the Captain rather than go back to death in England. However, my shipmates were also clear, that they would submit to any madness rather than be shot out of hand. I heard the old sea-proverb quoted, "Growl you may, but go you must."

Pegg swung round on the hands and routed them to jobs.

I had once thought that the world was run by justice and reason. I had been run right out of it by injustice, and was now being led by madness. There behind me was a ship's company cowed to grovelling point. To the west lay a wild heaven, looking, as north-westerly wind-heavens always do look, a lot worse weather than it meant. To me, who did not then know this, it looked like God's judgment and tempest. There in the glare of the sky, our Captain stood and steered, now looking at the upper sails, now bowing from dread of the wraith and snarling. Below him, somewhere in the cabin, that black Witch of Endor in scarlet and gold was asking her god what our course was to be. To say that the seamen were scared is to put it too mildly; to them it meant destruction. They had shipped in one of Hell's packets, they knew that; but now, Satan was being called in to command.

I do not know the method by which the hoodoo was brought to speak. It was a noisy method, and took a long time, with the beating of drums, and barkings and howlings. I believe that Knowledge surrounds us, the vast Knowledge, the Wisdom of God, and that all can have access to it by breaking down their pride. The savage breaks down his savagery by savagery and reaches truth; the saint breaks up the pride of his humanity by humility, and reaches truth; both reach truth, according to their grasp, though the methods are so different.

After a long time, the Black Mantacaw crawled on deck in the last of the twilight. She was completely exhausted. Her face was all grey, and bitter smoke followed her through the hatch. She tottered towards the helm, where

Paul was steering. She no longer wore a crown; the odd hairdress which she always wore, of her frizzed black hair worked up to a cone with grease and wooden ornaments and then transfixed with daggers, had all fallen sideways; all her scarlet was now foul. She crawled up to Paul, holding on to anything that could support her. Tulp was at my side; he heard what I heard: there can be no doubt of it. We heard the Mantacaw speak in a cold, clear, man's voice, not her own voice at all. We heard her give a position in latitude and longitude and the course, by compass, that would bring us there. It was spoken very clearly, and beyond any possibility of mistaking. I have never heard any voice very like it until within these last weeks, when I heard a famous politician use just such a voice.

Tulp, who was crossing himself, whispered, "That's her hoodoo speaking; Big Master, as they call him. Now he'll tear her and go out of her."

And indeed, something seemed to bend the Black Mantacaw as though she were going to be snapped in two; she fell down with a cry and lay senseless. However, hoodoo had spoken; the Captain had learned what he wanted.

As a doctor, I had to get the Mantacaw to bed. The cabin was full of smoke from foul-smelling bitter gums burning in pans there. It was very hot, and gave me a sensation of being still dwelt in by evil. Tulp, who was with me, helped the steward to rig a wind-sail through the hatch and blow the darkness out. Still, it was a long time before the smell of those gums left our quarters. They are common gums on the Coast and are used by the natives for many things; sometimes I meet with them to this day, and then a pinch of one thrown onto a shovel and held over a fire will bring back to me that evening in the *Albicore,* when the whimpering half-corpse, who had had the Devil within her framework, had to be brought back into humanity. I kept thinking of the priestess who consulted the oracle at Delphi; she breathed in some poison which broke her pride and sometime killed her.

Tulp, who helped me, said, "She's brought the Devil on board. It won't be easy to get him away; you mark my words."

I have here in my study a fine globe of plaster shewing the oceans and the continents. Visitors sometimes look at it, for it is worth the study. In the blue expanse of the North Atlantic Ocean I have put a minute speck of red ink to shew the spot to which we were directed. Nobody so far has noticed the speck. I can give you the compass course to it from our position in the Channel on that wild afternoon. To that speck our ship's head was turned, and to that point we sailed, with a wind which took us at once away from England and arrest, and then gradually died, so that we crawled on a stagnant sea.

Well, let me not be unmindful of my luck. For the moment, my luck was beyond all hope good. Destiny had fallen heavily on me and unjustly caused me to be hanged. Miracle had restored me to life and given me another chance. How good was the chance?

Remember this, kind reader. Anyone who has been in Newgate, expecting Death, looks on a reprieve of even one day as a mercy untellable. In that day, so much may happen. Why, the world may end; Newgate may be burned in a final judgment and gaol-delivery. A reprieve of one week is almost an eternity. A reprieve of a month is almost the King's pardon, for in a month the sentence may be changed and mercy pleaded to transportation or quashing of the verdict.

What sort of a reprieve was mine likely to be?

How safe for me was this Coast likely to be?

Even at that time, the English maintained a Governor and a Naval Station upon the Coast, at Cabo Amarilho. It was common talk in the *Albicore* (where, of course, my own past was quite unknown) that word would be sent to these people, to stay the *Albicore* and arrest Captain Paul, for the murder of the man in Liverpool.

How soon would that word come? I knew, though mercifully the men in the *Albicore* did not, that those who sent for Captain Paul would also send for me. If he were taken, I should be taken, too. In those hopeless days I always reckoned the worst first, so as not to have false hope. The worst, as I reckoned it, was this: On our way to the Coast, that is, on almost any day of the voyage, we might be overhauled by the despatch-vessel with the thief-takers sent after us. If that happened, we should be arrested in mid-ocean, and be prisoners again. That would be the worst that might happen, no question. By putting out little cautious enquiries, I found that this particular worst was most unlikely, firstly, because we could not be outsailed, nor met with in the ocean; secondly, because Captain Paul, who knew what to expect, would never let any despatch-vessel or thief-taker arrest him while at sea.

On the whole, therefore, I was inclined to hope that I might reach the Coast unmolested; that I might escape the worst possible.

What was the best possible?

The ship bearing the fatal orders or thief-takers might be lost at sea, or forced to put back. We might not only reach the Coast safely, but fill up with slaves and get away to the Indies or the Americas before any word about us reached the Station. Of course, when we got to the Indies, we should find the police-agents waiting for us, but that would be a long time hence.

But something even better than that might happen to me. While on the Coast, I might escape, or even exchange from the *Albicore* into some foreign ship; all ships would be glad of a doctor and would take me in. In a foreign ship, I might go almost anywhere in the world, in Europe or the Americas, and begin again on a clean sheet. Or I might succeed in doing what the men of the romances did. I might join the Moors, or reach the service of some rajah in the East, become a famous healer, and die in a marble palace, with a harem and slaves, date-palms, fish-pools and a soothsayer. Those rosy dreams came into my head, but I said, "No. My miracle has happened. I am still alive. I need expect no second miracle. The essence of a miracle is, that it is not repeated."

I told myself that between the worst and the best lay the likely; and the likely was, that I should not be in great danger till we reached the Coast. It was likely that we should not be on the Coast for another six weeks. It was likely, too, on the whole, that messages about us would not come for a fortnight more, say eight weeks. It was likely, therefore, that there would be little danger for six weeks, but that after that the danger would increase daily. Ah, I remembered what six weeks would have seemed to me in Newgate; when there was no hope of it. Now that I had the almost certainty of it, I was sick at heart, that I was not to have more.

Between this sickness of heart, and a hope that I dared not cherish, I lived in a sort of stunned rebellion.

Hope sprang in me, I assure you, though as a seesaw springs, so as to go down almost at once as deeply as it had risen. I had felt the power of English law now. England may seem careless of the life within her borders, but let a man outrage her laws, or be said to outrage her laws, even a very little, and her care will become awful, and her hand heavy to the death, and so far-reaching that there will be no safety from it anywhere on earth.

Newgate may from time to time, conceivably, benefit a man; it is conceivable. It usually kills its visitors quickly and certainly; all others, I should say, it makes reckless. It had made me reckless. My main thought in the *Albicore,* as we set our course for that ink-spot on the chart, was that for six or eight weeks at any rate, no man could molest me, no man accuse or arrest me. And with that recklessness, that nothing much mattered for six weeks, was a hatred of the society that had hurt me, and a loathing of all those who might beset my way and take my blood.

When I was studying in London, under Dr. Copshrews, he had always urged me to get the utmost from the persons and events of each day. He had said that by thought, effort and sympathy a man could learn much in every day of life, not only of practical matters, every one of them likely to be useful at some time or another, but of my own dear profession of medicine. He had said, "It is only by winning confidence, and by the minutest observation of little things that men can become useful physicians; therefore, strive to win confidence, and obtain exact knowledge wherever you go."

I thought of this, now, on board the *Albicore* as we sped out of the Channel. I was in a world new to me; it was now my world, and it behoved me to become useful to it; to win the confidence of its citizens, and learn its ways. So, on the morning after the witchcraft, when we were out of sight of land, I rose up, determined to learn. I knew that I had little sickness on board to occupy me. The Mantacaw had recovered from her exhaustion; one man was still sick from some drug or drugged drink which had been given to him; five others had been cruelly hit, kicked or clubbed; still, all of these could make some shew of working. My day was like to be idle, unless I made occupation for myself. I had been expressly told, moreover, by Captain Paul, that my job was to watch the slaves, who were worth money, not to pamper the hands, who weren't. "No man goes sick aboard me," Captain Paul had told me, "not till he's dead, and then he won't need to." I had detected in Pegg a kind of dislike of myself and my office. To him, I could see, I was a sort of landsman and idler; a kind of passenger, who ate and was yet worthless and did not pay his passage. I thought, "Perhaps, if I turn to and learn to be of use, he may change this view." I had already surprised him by not being seasick; "Now," I thought, "I will surprise him more by becoming a sailor." It was a praiseworthy resolve, but in my ignorance I went the wrong way about it, and made matters worse for myself.

As soon as possible, the ship settled to her sea-routine;

all hands were put to quarters, and especially to the exercise of the guns, for the Channel was not safe then from privateers and worse. Both in the forenoon and in the afternoon, the watch on deck had to exercise at the guns under Captain Paul's supervision. We had a Gunner on board, but Captain Paul took the first drills. He was a grim teacher, impatient and very savage, with a blow, a kick or some other devilry for any stupidity or slowness in any man. In the forenoon, when the guns were first cast loose, I went to the Captain and asked if I might learn the exercise. I said that I knew that in action I should have to tend the wounded, but that if we were hard pressed I should like to know what to do. Pegg, who heard this, said, "There's some sense in that, sir; when we're hard pressed, it's a matter of all hands on deck and the cook to the fore-sheet." He had no wish to back my plea, but liked to think that the doctor would now be put to ship's work like any other.

"You can learn if you like," the Captain said. "Catch hold of that piece of string and heave on it."

Now, in London, I had often seen the Artillery Company at their exercise, and knew something about it; I was a willing pupil, and did not do badly. I knew, too, that I pleased the Captain, for he said, "It's something to have one of a gun's crew who knows what a thing is for. If you'll go to Puggy, the Gunner, after knock-off time, and take him a pannikin of rum, I daresay he'll tell you what you want. It's pointing and charging you ought to learn, not this handspike and tackle part of it."

I said I would try to learn both. Pegg said something about a new broom always sweeping clean, and that I might not be so ambitious by the time I reached the Coast. However, after dark that night, I did take some rum to Puggy the Gunner, and made my lot the worse by doing so.

Puggy lived with the Sailmaker in the 'tween-decks. He was a short, elderly, powerfully built man, with a nose flattened by a blow, and yet pierced right through from side to side. I supposed that he had had a bullet through it in some fight. He wore ear-rings, like so many of the men, and was very fond of rum.

"Guns?" he said to me. "You want to learn about guns? You come to the right shop, and I'll be proud to learn you. Guns are a great mystery, as great a mystery as women and pretty near as destructive.

"The gun, the powder and the ball
    When used by Puggy Crackers
Will make the foes attacked to fall,
    And blast away attackers.

"Come, sit you down, sir, and I'll be proud to teach you. Bullets and Christianity are the two great gifts we bring the blacks, if you ask me."

I learned something of the theory of gunnery from Mr. Puggy Crackers, as well as much of the world. He asked me to come again on the morrow, in the dog-watch, to learn some more of these things; I did so. No doubt, he was glad of the tot of rum that I provided, and also of a chance to talk. He had had extraordinary experiences. Like most sailors, he did not know that they were extraordinary. On our second evening, he told me that he had lived as a native at a place called Milindi on the Coast

for eleven years, and that the hole through his nose had
been pierced there for the skewer or nose-plate, which a
native always wears, from puberty till death. I asked him
at once, if he would teach me some of the native lan-
guages. This was a mistake.

"Oh, no, sir," he said. "I lived native; that's one thing.
I was married to Samba, and in business. But I had to keep
White Man's face. A white man doesn't lower his face by
learning the native gibberish. That would be pampering
them. That would be putting 'em above their boots. We've
not sunk so low as that, I hope. Besides, they haven't got
what you would call a tongue, not most of 'em. It's just
clicks in the throat, half the time. And every town of 'em
clicks different. Bullets, Christianity and language are
what we bring 'em. I don't know which they need the
most. No, sir, what I talk to them is Palaver, and that's
what you'll have to speak to them. I'll learn you that with
pleasure."

Now, I wanted to make myself indispensable to the
ship; I thought, "I had better take some lessons in Palaver, too," so I thanked him, and said I would be glad indeed of some lessons. So I sat on there for some half-hour
more, learning how to speak to natives without endanger-
ing the White Man's face. Now, Palaver is a jargon made
up of all the European tongues spoken on the Coast during the past three hundred years; in the main it is probably always the tongue of the speaker. It is spoken for-
cibly, so that there may be a minimum of doubt of what is
meant, and it is emphasised with signs and gestures. The
natives are naturally shrewd and have by this time clear
perceptions of the simple greeds of white men. English

Palaver is very easy to learn, for it is mainly English. It has a few foreign words in it, like *bong* or *bwar,* for "good"; all these are pronounced as sounded; all English words are mutilated and mispronounced as if they were being spoken to a mentally deficient child. I began upon this tongue with interest, for the simple sentences of the lesson taught me something of the Coast where it is spoken. I gathered from the talk that on the Coast life was easy, and death easier still; that life was the satisfaction of greeds, and death a dissolution by vultures, ants and crabs. Thirst was the enemy, and cruelty the occupation. "Yet you know," he went on, "it gets you. It's the palm-oil, they say. The smell of it gets you, and you have to go back." It did not sound to me as if the palm-oil had much to do with it. The attraction of the Coast seemed to be the absence of all civilised restraint; it was a kind of Abbey of Thelema, where the monks did what they would as long as they were at all.

From Palaver, we turned to some of the practical parts of gunnery. I had never seen gunpowder made. Puggy Crackers, like many of the older sea-gunners, still made at least his priming-powders. He told me that a gunner needed something he could depend on for that, and that he would be making some the next morning, if it were dry, on deck. He promised to shew me how to make it; I could help him, he said. I was much interested in this: who would not have been? Is there anything more interesting than the crafts of men? Is there any craft that you would not like to know? Who would not like to be able to make gunpowder, and cast bullets, back the bow and flight the arrows?

I mentioned these things to the mess at supper that evening. I noticed that Pegg seemed sour about it, but supposed that he despised me for wanting to know mechanical things instead of how to sail a ship. Captain Paul said that Puggy was the best gunner he had ever had, but that Billy, his brother, who still lived as a native on the Coast, had been a Master-Gunner in the Navy at one time.

"You will have seen Billy, Mister," he said to Pegg. "He came out to the Coast, oh, years and years ago, in the *Hannibal* frigate. He was a boy, then, but the Coast got him; he couldn't keep away from it. He got back to it, somehow, and has been there ever since. You'll see him, Doctor, at one of the Coast ports, if he's not died of rum."

The words were spoken carelessly; they had been suggested by the mention of Puggy, but they caused a strange confusion in me. That little chance mention of the *Hannibal* frigate brought back my past that was now dead. I, too, knew the *Hannibal* frigate, every plank and sail of her, as well as the names of many of her crew; but for that ship and her little, crotchety, valorous commander, I should not have been there in the *Albicore*. I did not blench, I hope, though the shot had come unexpectedly. I could not remember the name of Crackers in her Muster-Book. Captain Paul went on:

"You might think a man would have a better name than Crackers, wouldn't you? It's only a nickname. Seamen generally call a Gunner Crackers or Bangs."

"Yes, sir," Pegg said sourly and with meaning, "or Old Stink-Pots, often enough."

I was on the point of asking if they could tell me what

chemicals were put in those hand-grenades known as
Stink-Pots, when I saw that Pegg was staring at me with
a very unpleasant expression. I was not aware of having
done or said anything wrong, but I knew that something
was amiss.

"Mr. Pegg," I said, "I hope you will join me in a glass
of punch?"

He was very fond of punch; usually he was kind to such
invitations. This time, he snorted, and reached to the
stanchion peg for his hat. "I must be getting on deck," he
said, shortly, and went.

Well, I had offended him, so much was plain; I could
not think how, and nobody told me. He had his work to
do; I had something to read; I then turned in. In the
morning, after breakfast, when my examinations and reports had been made, I joined the Gunner on deck, to
make some priming-powder. He had rigged up a set of
screens of wetted canvas in a quiet part of the deck.
Within this shelter, with buckets of water beside us, he
set out his ingredients, blended them and milled them, a
little at a time. I had never done it before; it interested
me very much.

I was busy, thus, with the Gunner, thinking no evil and
enjoying myself, when I heard Pegg, whose watch it was,
say to one of the boatswains,

"He signed as Doctor, but he seems to be Gunner's Mate
by the look of things."

The boatswain sniggered. I knew, then, that I had committed a sin against sea-custom in working thus with the
Gunner. Still, I had done so with no ill intent, and with
the Captain's approval. A few minutes before noon, I

went below, to find Mr. Tulp, who was then dressing to take the afternoon watch.

"Mr. Tulp," I said, "tell me, have I done any wrong to Mr. Pegg in taking lessons from the Gunner?"

He was a secret, sad young man, Mr. Tulp. He always spoke in a whisper, after looking about for listeners. I judge that he had had a terrible life of suppression and tyranny from which rum and knowledge had been his sole ways of escape.

"Yes . . . No," he whispered. "But he thinks you do it to shew that you despise him."

"What rubbish!" I said. "What utter rubbish!"

"He says, 'A chief officer ain't good enough for my lord Doctor; none but a Stink-Pot Maker is good enough for him.' "

"But, good Lord," I said, "I'm only trying to make myself useful on board."

"That's what he says," Tulp whispered. "He thinks you may be starting a party against the officers."

Now, this seemed to me so crazy that it took my breath away, but I remembered how my old Master had always warned me against the enormous power for evil in injured vanity. I knew, too, now, that the sea is ruled by custom often foolish and very old, but still a guiding force. Shaken as I was, I knew that Tulp had taken a very bold course (for him) in warning me thus.

"Thank you," I said. "Do, please, always warn me, if I make more mistakes like this."

I knew that I must not be heard talking thus to Tulp, so I slipped away. If it were wrong to talk to the Gunner, it might be wrong to talk to the Second Mate. Eight bells were made at that instant. Mr. Tulp went on deck to relieve Mr. Pegg, and the boatswains piped to dinner.

Before I had left my cabin, Mr. Pegg came down to the saloon, pitched his hat upon the table and cried in a loud voice to the Captain. "Sir, it's not what I've been accustomed to. This Doctor of yours finds this mess not to his liking. Every word we say here gets reported to that Gunner. If we're not good enough company, let him mess with the Gunner. But we're the Deck Department, and in every ship I've been in, the Deck's been a lot more important than any Bangs. Yes, and a lot more important than a whipper-snapper sangrado, if it comes to that, what's just done drawing teeth at Bart's Fair. If this Doctor can't stomach us, but must have the Gunner, let him go there, or turn me forward where I won't have the gall of it."

All this was spoken in a loud voice under an open skylight. Every word was heard, not only by the steward, but by the helmsman at the tiller just above us, and by half-a-dozen men of Tulp's watch who were working on the mizen-rigging. It was, of course, meant that I should hear it. I came into the cabin at once and said,

"If there's any complaint against me, I ought to hear it."

"Listeners hear no good of themselves," Pegg said.

"Do not listen, then," I said.

When vexed, Pegg had a snorty way of puffing himself out and blowing with his lips; he did this now.

"Come on," I said, "what is the trouble? You don't like my going to the Gunner? I go to him with Captain Paul's

permission, in order to learn things which may be useful
for a ship's doctor."

"I ship's doctor minds the sick; that's his business,"
Pegg said.

"I do mind what sick there are," I said. "Why should I
not try to make use of my time, when that is done?"

"Because it lowers the cabin in the eyes of the men," he
answered. "Because the men see you go direct from the
cabin to consort with the Stink-Pot Maker; and gossip
with that damned Sails."

"What is done with the Captain's approval cannot
lower the cabin in any way," I said. "If Captain Ashplant
no longer approves, a word from him will suffice. But
come, Mr. Pegg, this is early in the voyage, and I am green
to the life of the sea; you must make allowances for me. I
want to learn how to take my part in the life of the ship,
and I hope that presently you will teach me some of your
mystery. If Captain Ashplant will permit, I will ask for a
punch to settle this matter. What do you say, Captain?"

The Captain was an odd savage; one could generally
count on a rough answer from him. To my astonishment,
he was helpful.

"The trouble on board this damned privateer," he said,
"is this damned leak that's coming in. I don't wonder
you're vexed, Mister. It's enough to send anyone to the
Gunner, or to Satan's self for that matter. Come on, now,
steward, fetch a punch, and let's hear no more of this.
Now, Mister, you and the Doc, there, drink."

We drank, and for the time that matter ended; but I
knew now that Pegg was a jealous and evil little man,
with a set against me. It was the first time that I had

heard of any leak. I asked about it, as soon as we had settled to our meal. It was coming in somewhere amidships,
Pegg said, somewhere right amidships, and on the port
side, which was perplexing, because she had been tight
enough in Liverpool. However, it was nothing yet; they
could clear it easily; perhaps the Carpenter's gang would
get at it. I knew nothing about ships, at that time. I had,
however, read of leaks, and of men pumping and pumping
to clear them, and yet failing. We were not yet far from
England. What if we had to turn back to England, to refit? That would put me into danger again, of a very deadly
kind. I might be caught and ended within a very few
days. However, I reflected that Captain Paul would
never turn back. He would not face a second trial just yet,
but drive on somehow, to refit as he could on the Coast.

In a ship, you are one of a little community, so hedged
together that each man in her is to some degree a thought
or series of thoughts contained in a mind. I was aware,
now, that all hands were feeling that we had brought the
Devil aboard and had begun to suffer from his presence.
The leak had begun. They had found water in the well
early that morning, and though they had soon pumped it
clear, it was still coming in. The Carpenter had found it
to be somewhere amidships; he, Pegg and the Captain
had heard it loitering and trickling in; but they had not
yet been able to come at it to stop it. The pumps had to be
rigged every watch, and though they soon sucked, the
men already saying, "This is what comes of bringing the
Devil on board. It's all right, now; but soon, when we are
in the hot weather and the seams are widened, we shall
tell another tale."

That evening, the wind which had brought us so proudly and swiftly clear of the Channel and Soundings fell light and became flighty. However, it was still fair for us. We went on slowly towards that red speck or given point upon the chart to which some evil power had directed the Mantacaw. Presently, when we were thereabouts, the wind drew ahead, and settled. It was not bad weather. It was settled fair weather, miles from the usual course of the slavers bound to the Coast. There we slowly beat and floundered, against a light, hostile wind, which the seamen said was a dead muzzler. We beat against it for a week, and at the end of it had gone no further on our way; the drift was against us, and wiped out what we made. After a time, the wind failed—we were becalmed—then gave us a brief lift and died away. All said that they had never before known calms like that in that season. They said that that came of bringing the Devil on board, yes, and having him on board, too, for who could doubt that he was now within the Black Mantacaw, living in the cabin? She came on deck sometimes. When she did, the men made the sign of the cross upon themselves. I heard men muttering on deck in the night watches that they would get no fair wind nor come at the leak till that Black Judy was put over the side. It was hot, fair, hazy weather, with multitudes of flying-fish all about us.

When the calm set in, the Captain tried to find the leak. We shifted the weights to one side and worked very hard to come at the place. I worked with the others and enjoyed the effort and the hope of success. After a time, we did find whereabouts it was: I heard it. All the space of the hold was full of gurglings and complainings; odd,

stretching creaks and whickering cracks went across
slowly from side to side as the ship gently rolled back and
to. Water washed and whimpered away from her bows
outside and clucked and splashed in the bilges. Among
all these noises was a noise as of a small steady teapot
being poured; this was the leak.

"It sounds like a trunnel," the Captain said.

"Either that or a bolt, sir," the Carpenter said.

"It's not likely to get any worse," the Captain said.

"No, sir," the Carpenter said. "But it's best to keep the
sea on its own side the fence; I'll hope to get at it tomorrow."

As there was a dead calm on the morrow, they tried.
They took a lot of trouble, and hove the ship well up, but
the place was not to be reached. The verdict of the Carpenter was that it was coming in below where it came
through. They gave it up, after that, saying that on the
Coast they could heave the ship right down, and strip her
copper off. It was not yet a serious leak; still, it added to
the work and to the worry.

I continued to take lessons from the Gunner. I learned
to mill priming-powder and to handle big guns, and could
recite the charges for all known shot. Pegg growled and
was rude about it. I told him that it was no concern of his,
how I passed my time, and that he might take notice that
I did not interfere with him as Mate.

"No," he said, "and you'd best not try, neither."

"I have no intention of trying," I said. "I keep to my
own business."

"You don't," he answered hotly. "Gunning ain't your

business. Keep to your flapdoodle and rags and that—them's your business."

"Not altogether," I said. "As a member of a ship's company, I may have to do many things besides doctoring, and intend to learn them while I have the time."

"It's letting the cabin down," he said angrily. "It drags the cabin down to the level of the Gunner's berth. You belong in the cabin and are a Mister. He belongs in his berth and ain't. Let him come to you, not you go to him."

"You know very well," I answered, "that the Gunner cannot come to the cabin; I have to go to him. You'd be the first to stop him, if he were to come aft here to teach me."

"You're right in that," he answered.

We had many petty bickerings of this sort: usually we patched them up over some rum-punch, which we drew now as a daily ration. All slavers, I had learned, took in great quantities of rum in the West Indies, where nearly every planter made rum. I suppose that a third of the death and half of the cruelty usual in the trade was due to the rum. Rum only made a truce between Pegg and myself. After drinking, he would go off, snorting and vexed, to mutter against me to all and sundry. "There goes our precious Doctor, to his crony the Stink-Pot. If he'd tried currying favour with a Stink-Pot under old Captain Gorsuch, he'd have been made to toe the line." However, I learned that, on the whole, I was liked and Pegg disliked; and that sea-custom prescribed that the Doctor was not under the Mate, and could do pretty much what he chose, provided he did his doctoring. What doctoring I had to do, I did successfully.

Then chance brought Pegg to me as a patient. He was at work on deck with his watch, shifting a heavy spare spar. Being one who fancied his strength, he was helping to lift this great weight, and had his long arms round it. Through some folly or misunderstanding, his men suddenly let go and left him to support the weight, so that he had a severe strain. He was carried below, and I had to treat him. Like most sailors, he attempted to keep to his work, but this I forbade for a day or two. I told him the truth, that he had the finest torso I had ever seen. His arms were too long and his legs too short for beauty; but his chest was superb. He snorted at my praise, saying that his chest was as good as another's; but like many somewhat deformed men, he was very vain and took my praise kindly. After that, we were better friends; when he got better he taught me to take the ship's position by the quadrant and the chronometer. He told me something of sea-affairs. He shewed me how to steer, encouraged me to go aloft, and asked one of the boatswains to shew me how to knot and splice, as well as the uses of the different ropes. All these things added much to the interest of my life on board, which in many ways was not a life, for the gallows loomed up beyond, whenever I began to think myself safe. Soon we should be on the Coast, where men would be waiting for our coming, with warrants for me and the Captain. Well, I had my poison prepared for myself. I was not going back to Newgate.

Yet should we be soon on the Coast? The wind had died again; we drifted to and fro in a patch of weather which some sport of the seasons had filled with south-easterly airs and calms. None of our men had known anything like it. We lay and jangled and rolled, sometimes just steering, sometimes becalmed, in hot, fine, hazy weather, among the flying-fish, with the gear flogging and the leak running, and the temper of the men growing worse each day. I had hoped that we might make a swift passage to the Coast, so as to fill with slaves and be away on our Middle Passage before any letter about us could come from England. This hope was now gone; no ship could have made a worse passage than we were making. We had done what the Devil had bidden, and here we were, lost in the mid-sea, where we might perhaps stay for days to come. By this time, it was plain that even a slow ship with an average passage, standing on the usual courses, might have reached the Coast in spite of sailing a fortnight or three weeks after us. The men growled that it was the Captain's fault. This was what came of bringing the Devil aboard; this was the foretaste and the earnest of it; presently we should have the full due paid. As the days passed, it began to be said that we should lose our season. We should come to the Coast too late, and find all the slaves already shipped. It was always good to reach and leave the Coast early, so as to arrive in the Indies in early spring. If a ship did that, she could land her slaves and fill up with sugars, rum and so forth before the hurricane season (which was also the yellow fever season) set in. I heard a man say, "Here we are; here we shall rot, and the Devil will have his own. That's what we asked for."

It was true, we had asked the Devil. But it was the Captain, the man responsible for the asking, who cursed our fortune loudest. Like most captains, he was proud of his ship's speed, and had made famous passages in her.

Now he would walk the poop, snapping his fingers and rolling his grim yellow eyes. "See, now," he would cry to me, or Pegg, or the helmsman, "see, now. I stood to the West, as this damned Witch of Endor told me from her obi or her hoodoo; and here I am in a calm, which won't even give her steerage way." Then, in his rage, he would go to windward, or to whichever side happened to be northerly, and whistle for a wind. This, to myself, seemed only silly; to the crew, it was like tempting God. They all crossed themselves when he did it, and turned quite white.

"You must never whistle for a wind, sir," the Gunner told me, when I asked about it. "I don't know why, so don't ask me; I only know you mustn't. Only Finns and damned fools whistle at sea."

All this was many years ago; perhaps time has mellowed my memory of the Captain. I know that, at first, I was shocked by his appalling presence, and by the knowledge that he had murdered two seamen. After a few days, I found myself admiring some of his qualities; and I admire them still, though I say now, at the end of a long life, that he was quite the murkiest savage I have ever met.

Let me state his qualities. Pegg had described him as the finest captain in the trade, bear none. He was certainly that. He was at all times diligent in his business, if ever man was; no man could have served his owners with more zeal, nor with shrewder brain. He had affections, of a kind. He loved the *Albicore;* he was sometimes gentle to the Mantacaw; and he was devotedly fond of his father, now a very old man, who kept a little shop and

repaired boats upon the Mersey shore. He often talked
of this father, who suffered much, it seemed, from swollen
legs. Often the Captain would tell me of these swollen
legs and ask me about possible causes and remedies. He
would listen to me with deep attention; finding that I had
knowledge and sympathy in these matters, he was very
civil to me.

His appearance was frightful. In the slave trade, perhaps, his face was his fortune; it struck terror wherever
he came. He was a fine, big, strong man; the seamen always mentioned his strength as an excuse for his other
failings. I suppose that he had some devilish or criminal
taint in him, which had been encouraged in the slave
trade, where all was either devilish or criminal. Then, on
the top of this predisposition, he had had fever and other
tropical diseases, which had left him with a yellow tinge.
I suppose bile, gall and liver were all affected in him. To
this day, I cannot think of his face without a shudder. It
was pale, and tinged with yellow. The whites of the eyes
were injected as well as yellow. He looked at you down-
ways and sideways, with a lifting upper lip that shewed
his yellow hyaena teeth. He had a way of snarling before
speaking; his words followed on the snarl like a bite.
This habit he had cultivated, to terrify his crew. They
were very rightly terrified of him, because as the bite followed the snarl, so the blow followed the bite; and this
often with little or no cause. If the man answered a question, he might be beaten or half choked, for what the Captain called "coming the old soldier on me." If the man
were too terrified to answer, he might be half choked or
beaten for what he called "coming the sullens." The men

knew him very well, you must remember. They had not sailed with him before, but his name was infamous throughout the seafaring world; now that they were with him for a round voyage, they trembled, and were wise to tremble. If he were on deck when anything went wrong, those nearest were hit for not doing it right; if anything went right, those nearest were hit to make them not do it wrong another time. "I'll learn you dogs a little discipline," he would say. "I'm master here." Pegg said that that was the only way to maintain discipline—to let them see who was master. When Captain Paul was in a really bad mood, sitting at table in the cabin, we all quaked for what might come. Once, he seized the carving-knife and he chased the steward on deck with it, swearing that he would cut his heart out and make us all eat it raw; this because the poor man spilled some soup on a clean canvas tablecloth. Three times, he knocked the Black Mantacaw off her chair and beat her during the meal, for looking, as he called it, "old-fashioned." Indeed, to look old-fashioned was a crime aboard the *Albicore*. When human stupidity or frailty failed to provide a victim for him, he would say that such an one looked old-fashioned, and would go for him with the end of a brace. We in the cabin were usually free from personal violence from him. I was always free, because I told him at the beginning that I had letters to the Governors in the Indies, and would not tolerate any insolence of the kind, so let him beware, since the Governors should surely call him to a strict account. Still, Pegg and Tulp were not free. I saw him cast a rope round Pegg's throat and threaten to choke him dead, and once he beat poor Tulp grievously. Pegg admired the Captain for all this violence. In his opinion, that was the way a Coast captain ought to behave, to impress the natives, "keep up the White Man's face," and terrify the hands from trying to turn pirate.

He was all that is evil, yet I think of him always with some tenderness, because of his father's legs, and because of his liver, which was the cause of half his crime, I suppose; I might perhaps have treated that liver and left him almost human; but he was not one to submit to medical treatments.

He became worse, more cruel, and by much more dangerous as the passage lengthened, because it was now certain that word for his arrest must have reached the Coast. He punished the unhappy hands for this. He said that it would not be safe to make for any well-known port, and cursed his luck for it. I, who had my own reasons for fear, was thankful for it; but I was full of dread. I thought that they might have sent a cruiser to watch for us as we made the land. I should hear perhaps the oars of a boat, and the hail of some official voice. "You have on board an escaped felon under the name of Edward Torrance. In the King's name, deliver him."

These thoughts filled my mind as we stood in to make our landfall.

Though Captain Paul was not a communicative man, he had let it be known that he was going to avoid the used tracks and frequented ports. "I've got to be as coy as a damned virgin," he said. Still, even the coyest virgin in the trade had to approach the public once, at the landfall, the Cape of the Requines, where all ships picked up their position and put in, for news.

Just within the Cape, there is the fine "gumwood port"
of Monos Grandes. In the old Portuguese days, aromatic
wood from the lagoon was shipped there. The wood was
cut out long ago, and no more is to be had; but the port
was then, and is still, a place of some trade for basts,
dates, dragon's blood, gold-dust, and, especially, old ivory.
What made it important to the slavers was this. All slave
ships passed it, on their way, and all, by halting there for
even an hour, could learn where slaves might be had. The
merchants of Monos Grandes never dealt in slaves. They
were too far to the windward of the slave country proper
for them to do that with profit; but they had trade dealings with many of the slave-dealing Kings, and knew,
roughly, which of them held slaves. The ships coming to
the Coast used always to heave to, and send a boat in to
Monos Grandes, to ask the state of the market.

Remember that the Coast of Dead Ned is a peculiar
place, easy to get into, for the wind blows you in; difficult
to get out of, for the wind still tries to blow you in. As the
wind there blows from west to east all the year round, the
westward end is called the "windward"; the eastward,
the "leeward." No ship-captain goes to leeward if he can
help it because of the difficulty of getting back. It was,
therefore, the practice of the slavers to ask at Monos
Grandes if it would be possible to avoid going to the leeward. A pause for an hour or two might save a weary
beating back in the heat.

Now, Captain Paul had told us that he was going to a
little-frequented place rather far to leeward, called Great
Momboe. That place in most seasons would have been as

safe as Alsatia to him; but we had been so long at sea that he was now afraid of going there. He let it be known that he meant to ask at Monos Grandes if even secluded Momboe would be safe. If word had come that the *Albicore* was to be stayed, it would be talked of at Monos Grandes, and with a warning, Paul would go still further to leeward for slaves, where he would be safe indeed.

It had sounded perfectly safe, to go to a Portuguese port, to ask for news; but as we drew nearer to Monos Grandes, it sounded less safe to me. I began to dread again. Still, Captain Paul proceeded like the coy virgin; he went with caution, keeping far out to sea, and avoiding every sail. When we stood in, to make the land, I stayed on deck, staring, watching and scared.

The boatswain of the watch thought that I was waiting on deck to have a look at Africa. "Ah, sir," he said, "Africa's no different from any other country. You'll get nothing for nothing, and damn little for a plug of tobacco there, same as in a Christian land. I'd give all Africa twice over for a cask of rum, so long as I'd a spile for it. You'll soon see all the Africa you'll want."

Presently, we saw the Cape, and stood on towards it. We were in steaming heat now, which I enjoyed. We wetted the decks ten times a day, and had the wind-sails rigged. We had also picked up the following sharks, which swarm about that Cape and give it its name.

Now that we were there, we became very coy. Paul said that he would sail to the port entrance after dark and send Pegg ashore in a boat. Pegg would go to a certain agent known either as Perheira or as Old Gutsache, well-known to both of them, and find out very privately, yet exactly, what was known about the *Albicore,* and how hot a search was being made for her.

You may imagine how my heart sank at all this.

Pegg shewed some hesitation at the task set for him. "What are you growling at?" Paul asked. "Monos is Portugee. You're English. You aren't in any trouble. There's no danger to you, just going ashore and asking a question. You get an evening ashore and supper with Gutsache. What more do you ask?"

"I like that," Pegg said. "Probably they've got thief-takers waiting for us there, and they'll take me, instead; you'll see. I like my freedom as well as another man. I'm not going to be a chopping block for your meat."

This was sound sense in Pegg, but as like to mutiny as the Captain wanted. He leaped at Pegg, tripped him and flung him, then dragged him along the deck and bent his head over a bucket. "Not go?" he said. "If you won't go, I'll cut your throat right now, just like a pig's over this bucket."

Pegg exclaimed that there was no need to talk like that; of course he would go. On being allowed to stand, he put on an air of injured pride. "Come, Captain," he said, "there's no sense in talking like that. That's not decency nor manners, nor what I'm accustomed to."

"Right, then," the Captain said. "I'll send you in to-night, and with a case of claret for the Governor. But you won't meet with any trouble."

However, it was quite clear that both he and Pegg expected trouble, and I knew too well that I should share in any that was coming. But what I dreaded most, I must confess, was Pegg's going ashore and learning that I was only an escaping felon, and coming back quietly, dissembling, and doing nothing openly, but all the time helping to betray me to the thief-takers. There is nothing like dread for making men believe evil. I believed any evil of Pegg. I remember quaking in my very soul with the thought, "If there be any thief-taker ashore, Pegg will betray Captain Paul to him, so that Paul may be taken, and he, Pegg, left with the command." I was judging Pegg's heart by the evil in my own.

It was at about nine at night when we came off Monos Grandes, and lay by, while the boat made ready to go in. It was there that I first heard the noise that I must always associate with Africa, the solemn, long, lapsing and rising roar of a great surf. It was always the voice of the Coast. It was sometimes lulled, sometimes louder, but never silent. At night, it spoke like the lamentation of the Continent for the curse that man had brought upon it. By day, it was full of threat.

> Beware, beware, the Bight of Benin.
> Few come out whoever go in.

Paul made no farewell, except, "Well, Mister, you know what you have to do. Don't stay long."

Pegg said, meaningly, "I hope I shan't be made to," and went down the side and shoved off. I watched the boat for a long time.

The current set us a little to the southward as I watched, so as to open the port to me. I could see the lights, and hear the bells of a church and a noise of singing, I think from some anchored ship. Paul had the nettings rigged in case any officer came out to serve a warrant. He also had the guns loaded and pointed, and after giving the hands a dram, made them lie down by their guns. He explained that for all we knew England might have gone to war while we had been at sea, and that we might be attacked by an enemy. I knew very well that it was nothing of all that, but a determination to kill anyone who tried to take him, and then to turn to the seas, like his brother, as a pirate from that time forward.

It was a long wait. To begin with, the boat had to row in; and as Paul said, "It may be that you'll find police-boats inside, rowing harbour-guard, in which case, you may be taken first to the Governor." Even if there were no harbour-guard, it was getting to be late at night; Pegg did not know the city, and might find our factor away, or sick, or dead. I told Paul that, as Pegg did not know Portuguese, he might find it hard to explain himself or ask his way. Paul did not allow this as an excuse. "He knows the Palaver," he said.

We waited for a long time, watching the Coast, listening to the surf, and seeing the gleams in the water as swells lifted or sharks rose. The ship lay by idly, with creakings and tuggings of her gear. Paul talked about the surf. "It's a grand noise," he said. "I never tire of hearing it; but I wish this Mate of mine would come. It's not being certain that I dislike."

I said that we should soon know. Mr. Pegg must be coming soon.

"He's a damned vain man, Pegg," Paul said. "He is always shewing off before these ladies. If old Gutsache has had in the girls for him, we'll be all night here. I can't go without the boat and the boat's crew. I wish I'd sent Tulp. What do you think a judge counts as evidence?"

I said that a judge counted as evidence whatever is sworn from personal knowledge, but that he often made mistakes. I had reason enough to think so, God knows.

"Would he go by heads?" he asked. "I mean, if five said they saw me hit that man in Liverpool, and you and Pegg and Tulp swore I was never out of the ship that night, would the judge go by the five or by the three?"

I said I thought that most judges would test the three and the five, to try to find if either spoke the truth.

"Ah," he said, "well, I could bring in the steward and the boatswains, as well as Sails, and the Gunner. With all those, it would have to be brought in 'Mistaken Identity.' "

I said that he could never be sure, because judges went very much by what was probable, in any doubtful case, and would examine into the past records of all concerned and mark carefully all that might be most likely. I said that in most cases it was easier for the judge to be right, but that all judges knew that sometimes they went wrong and misdirected the jury.

We saw a boat at this time.

I said, "There they come."

His eyes were more used than mine to searching dark waters at night. "That's a fishing canoe," he said.

Indeed, in a few moments, I saw that she was. We heard the bells of the Portuguese church from time to time.

"It's close to the church that Gutsache lives," Captain Paul said. "Gutsache has given him a dram and had in these girls, and the fool has stopped to dance."

I said that very likely Pegg had found it difficult to get away. Sometimes you cannot get away from a foreigner without giving great offence.

"No," he said, "I never feel that a foreigner feels anything in the way we would. If foreigners had any sense, the same as we, they'd know we want to get away from 'em just as soon as we can hoof it. This Pegg's lost his head to one of these black girls, that's what happened here."

He named one or two bright stars to me, and said, "There was a black girl down the Coast at Milindi when I was young . . . I'd have married her if it hadn't been for losing face. You lose face with both sides if you do a thing like that. Still, I've often wished I'd married her and gone bush. She was a Mata, too; a proud judy; not like that black hag in the cabin. I'd ought to have married her."

He fell silent, thinking of his wasted life.

"What became of her?" I asked.

He did not answer. I could not see his face, but I do believe that he was weeping. The church bells ashore struck and chimed here, in a very sweet peal; after that, he said suddenly, "There are oars; that's a ship's boat. On deck there, stand by your guns. Blow on your matches, there."

The men sprang to their feet and stood by their guns. I saw the gun-captains blow on the smouldering matches, so that face after face along the deck glowed red for an instant. I heard the grunt of rowlocks, and soon saw a boat advancing from the harbour.

"That's Pegg," the Captain said. "He'd be well advised to come slow."

He went to the fife rail for a blue light, and with some little trouble, for the dew had damped it, got it to light at the binnacle. It burned blue, and gave an unearthly beauty to the ship. I saw that the boat was heading directly for us. I thought, "Now for it. Has Pegg betrayed Paul? Has word come that we are to be stayed? Is there a thief-taker in the boat?"

Paul handed the flare to a seaman and turned his night-glass on the boat. After a long time, he swore, and said to me in a low voice, "There's another man in the stern-sheets. Pegg's got somebody with him."

We watched and listened till the boat was within hail. Pegg had been warned that he would be fired at if he tried to board us without hailing. He now rounded the boat to, so that she lay broadside on some fifteen yards from us. I could see the second man. Was it a thief-taker, sent out from England for Paul and myself? It might well be. There had been time enough for one to come out; and with two birds to catch, the Law might well have taken the trouble, or if not the Law, someone with an interest in our two necks, the Friends of the African and perhaps Dennis.

"Ahoy, the *Albicore*. Is Captain Ashplant there?" Pegg hailed.

"Who's that you've got with you?" the Captain answered. "Who is he? What does he want?"

"He's all right, sir," Pegg shouted. "He's a dealer who wants a passage. He's Perheira's son-in-law, sir. He's given ten pieces for the passage to Momboe."

I did not like this story of the dealer wanting a passage; it sounded like a pretext to me.

"Is he English?" Paul asked.

"No, sir; doesn't speak any English; he knows the Palaver."

"Well," the Captain said, "trice those nettings clear. Secure your guns. Come alongside, Mister."

During the talk, he had had a good look through his night-glass and seemed satisfied: all the same, he drew his pistol. The boat drew alongside and Pegg jumped aboard.

"He's quite all right, sir," he said to the Captain in a low voice. "He's perfectly all right, and Perheira sends a dozen of port with him. He's a sort of a white nigger, sir, and won't give any trouble. He can mess with the Gunner."

At this, the passenger came aboard. He was a slim, well-made, youngish man, white, as far as I could see, rather good-looking and with charming manners. He bowed low to the Captain and to myself, and spoke to us in Portuguese. I answered for us both in French. The man at once spoke French, and asked if he might express his thanks to the Captain for permitting him to come with us. He said that he much wished to get to Momboe. Since we were going there he hoped that he might come, too. He added that he was expecting to find his venture in Momboe, of old ivory. As he seemed a much more civilised being than anybody now in the ship, I asked the Captain if he might not mess in the cabin? The Captain said, "Yes, but he must sling in the 'tween-decks." His goods were passed up out of the boat. The boat was hooked on and hoisted; in a minute more, we were under way again.

I heard Pegg say, "They have had no word here about

you, sir. It has been a bad season, in all these windward places, not a slave in any of 'em, but they are said to be coming in to Momboe. Old Gutsache thought we should do nicely there. He said that King Jelly Belly made a great raid to leeward and took a lot of people."

Paul looked at the passenger, turned to me, and asked, "What the hell does he call himself?"

I asked the passenger if the Captain might know his name. He said "Kamansh" or something like that. At first I thought he said *"Comment?"* but it was his name, Kamansh. I have since thought that it was the name of the poet Camoëns taken by him as a good Portuguese name.

"Perhaps, Doctor," the Captain said, "you'll see to Mr. Smask and tell the steward to fix him a berth."

He then turned to Pegg and said, "So Gutsache had heard nothing of the Liverpool trouble?"

"Not a word, sir."

"That's the best news," the Captain said. "I can drink on that. I was anxious about it."

The next day, when I saw Kamansh in the light, I found him a good deal older than I had thought. He was over thirty-five, he said. I asked him if he had been to France and had learned the language there.

He said, "No, I have never been in France; I am not Portuguese."

Presently, when I asked him what he was, he said, *"Je suis Kranois;* or as you might say, Kranish. We are a white race who live in the interior; some say that we are Greeks, but I do not think that, because of the language."

All through the voyage, the officers had spoken with

contempt of a mixed set of men to be found all over the Coast. They had always called these men of mixed races "Portuguese Drummers"; I never could discover why. But it was plain, from what they had said, that white men on the Coast were very eager to save what they called their "face," or prestige. A white man "lost face" by consorting with a man not wholly white; and a black or mongrel man "got face" by consorting with a white. Now I knew that our officers would never have taken a Portuguese drummer as a passenger; it would have lost them too much face everywhere. This man was telling the truth; he was a white of pure stock. It flashed into my mind at once, that perhaps the Admiral had been right, not out of his mind from fever or sunstroke, as I had often thought. Possibly, there was a white race somewhere in the interior. Possibly, this was one of them. Possibly, there was still some Frenchman of genius like that Edmond Quichet who had been so often in my thoughts. I looked at this Kamansh with the keenest interest.

He was of European stock, certainly; he had straight hair, a fully formed nose, and thin lips; he was a white man, with sallow skin and black hair. I had seen no Greeks to speak of, save a few sailors who had come for ointment in London. He did not seem to come of any of that stock; to me, he looked more like a Spaniard.

I said, "I heard once in London of a white race in Africa; a race which builds cities and boats in the European ways. I heard that the race had as many as seven cities."

"We say that we had seven once," he said, "but now we have two: a big one and a little one."

"And are they far from here?" I asked. "Could I go to them?"

"They are far from here," he said; "far to the east, and far inland. Many days. You could never get to them; nor will any white man get to them, ever again."

"Yet you go there?" I asked.

"No. I do not go there," he said. "I am exile. I have not been there for nine years. I shall not go there again. They are stupid, ignorant people." As he saw upon my face that this remark might be taken as evidence against himself (for who condemns, save the condemned?), he smiled and added, "So says the stupid man who was too ignorant to get on well at home."

"Tell me," I said, "if it be not a rude question: did you learn French in your city?"

"Yes," he said, with a change of face, which shewed that the question was resented. "Oh, yes; the French have penetrated there." He looked at me with a certain anger. I saw that the topic was distasteful, and asked him no more.

He smiled, and said with winning grace, "Tell me, then, in your great city of London, is it often mentioned that our race exists?"

"No," I said, "I have never heard it mentioned by name, your people, the Kranois. But once, a long time ago, I met a sailor who said something about there being a race of white men in Africa, who built cities, and had straight hair and claimed to be descended from the Greeks. There can hardly be two such races."

"No," he said. "Your sailor may well have heard of us."

We talked then of other things. He had a low opinion

of the Coast natives, and felt that they all should be enslaved, but not exported to the Indies or the Americas.
"That is folly," he said. "Why send them all those thousands of miles away, losing from a third to a half in the
process, when the land here will grow all that they will
be set to growing there? It is not sense. What can the
Indies or the Americas grow that cannot be better grown
here? We unpeople this land in order to till a more distant one. You say your business men are practical men;
they are fools."

He had a clear (and to me very awful) hope of a vast
slave dominion along the Coast, ruled by white men, with
lots of face, for the benefit of whites in Europe. After
some years, he thought that slaves might be bred there in
large numbers, for export to the Indies and the Americas.
"There is no reason," he said, "why this should not be
done. The mortality in slaves on arrival is due to the Middle Passage and to the seasoning, as they call it, on arrival
in the west. If we had brood-mare women-slaves and good
buck stallion-slaves, we should soon find a strain that
would export well. It is a well-known fact that children
stand the Middle Passage better than adults. It stands to
reason that they must. The tender and the young do not
have to be packed and chained. You can allow children
liberty on board. They arrive in good health, and do not
fall sick and die of the sullens as so many adults do. Very
well, then, let us breed thousands of good children here,
and ship them west as soon as they are fit to travel. It is
simple sense. Sooner or later, you will have to do it. It
will pay hand over fist. It will make the fortune of any
man who first does it."

It seemed almost too fair a prospect for mortal man. I confess that it made me sick to think of it, so I strove to turn to other matters.

"Sir," I said, "it is most interesting to me to think of descendants of the Greeks in Africa. You said that the language is against their being Greeks. I know not very much Greek; just enough to enjoy Homer very much. Would it be too much to ask of you, that you should teach me some of your tongue, so that I might perhaps resolve the point, or at least be able to submit it to the learned?"

He had a most winning charm, although he gave me the impression of being a very hateful creature. "Sir," he said, "I will most gladly teach you the Kranish speech. But I am sure that it is not Greek. People are apt to choose the wonderful and to claim the glorious, to hide the obvious or the distasteful. I have been in these years to Lisbon and elsewhere. I have traded to the Mediterranean. All along the sea there, are races that must have traded or gone exploring to Africa, and sent forth strong stocks into this continent. Some have died, others perhaps mingled with natives, but some must have maintained themselves. What of your Carthage? She and her allies? What were her allies? The Kranois are nothing save the remnant of one such stock; the once prosperous remnant. Lately, of course, Europeans have come in, to cause, as always, rivalry and clash. In Africa there should be only one rivalry and clash, of White with Black."

As it was plain that he wished to teach me, I gladly set to work to learn. It was a part of his charm that he loved to give, and to give delightfully of all that he wished to impart. He made me feel, however, that beyond this was

another self, with a very evil past, kept strictly hidden
and never imparted.

Well, there was the like evil in my own past; I don't
doubt that he saw that I, too, was hiding a good deal.
Captain Paul had said somewhere in my hearing, "Every
man on the Coast has something he doesn't want to talk
about. You don't ask questions on the Coast unless you
can stand a rough answer, or don't mind a knife in your
guts."

So, with much respect for each other's pasts, we set to
work upon the tongue of the Kranois. I remember that I
began by summoning up all the simple Homeric nouns
within my memory in the hope that he would light up at
their mention. I tried him with man, woman, child, king,
crown, gold, spear, helmet, crest, arrow, drug, horse, car,
chariot-driver, ship, wind, god, goddess, sea, river, city,
mountain, bread, barley, wine, cup, hawk, dove, oar and
cloud. All was useless; he did not recognize the words. I
began to fear that this white race might prove in the end
to be some mongrel generation of drummers very unlike
the long-haired Achaeans.

As I knew that the Captain and Pegg resented any
question that tended to give romance to Africa I did not
ask them about any supposed white race in the interior.
To them, Mr. Kamansh was old Gutsache's son-in-law, a
white man with some sort of face, but only a Dago, when
all was said. I asked Tulp if he had ever heard of white
people in the interior. He said, yes; he had heard it, but
it might be only a yarn. He could not remember where he
had heard it; perhaps away down to leeward, at Little

Massa. Later, he said that he thought he might have heard it from Billy Crackers, the Gunner's brother.

The Gunner, on being asked, said that when he and Billy had lived native he had heard that there was a white race somewhere far inland, and that they had tried to stop slaving, but hadn't done so. "It would take more than them to stop British commerce," he said. "We're free; we're not going to have free-trade interfered with by a lot of white niggers, I hope."

Well, the ship went slowly on, in light airs. When my work gave me leisure, I spent my time with Mr. Kamansh sitting in the draught of a sail trying to learn his tongue, which was unlike any tongue known to me. At first, I wondered if Mr. Kamansh were not making it all up; but no; that was not possible; it was a language. It had no literature other than some songs and genealogies; it had no alphabet, and no native system of writing. A certain number spoke French and wrote in the European fashion, so he said. They had a religion, too, so he said, but very stupid and ignorant, well worthy of them, in fact. What they were, I could not guess. Were they Phoenicians, Philistines, Carthaginians, Iberians, Macedonians, Maltese, Albanians, Etruscans, Lusitanians, Saguntines, Trojans? I have elsewhere set down all that I have learned of their origin, language and manners; from these things the learned may perhaps resolve what I cannot.

On leaving Monos Grandes, we had hauled well out to sea, and went slowly down to the leeward out of sight of land. The Captain made no secret of his reason. He feared lest the frigates at Cabo should have put out fly-boats to watch for us, and was determined to give them the slip, and to avoid being reported by any passing ship. So we leisurely dragged along, in great heat, in a good deal of anxiety, and with a leak which varied very little, yet tended, as a leak usually will, to increase as time went on.

Sometimes we saw Africa as a haze or cloud away to the north, sometimes we were right out of sight of land. We stole on, in sweltering heat, through a grey and steaming sea. In addition to my sea-companions, I had two intimates, ever with me, my past and my future. My past was grim enough with fact and with surmise. I had been hanged for a crime; who had done the crime? Had anyone been hanged since for saving me? Who had murdered that old Admiral for whom I had been hanged? My future was grim enough with the same two figures. The Law was after me: would the Law catch me? And if it did not so catch me, what were my prospects? I was an unvouched-for doctor in a slave ship, a man, that is, almost beyond the human pale and tinged with the infamy of the traffic. If I were lucky and escaped the Law, what future should I have? I might land and live native like the Crackers brothers, and perhaps marry a black woman with a skewer through her nose; or if I escaped into the Indies or the Americas, I might live secluded in some glen and come to town for market days to let blood and draw teeth at sixpence a patient. That seemed a poor life to one who had hoped to be famous through Europe, with half-a-dozen books to his credit, and perhaps a treatment or an operation known for a century to come as the "Edward Mansell." I had loved my profession and had hoped to shine in it: what sort of light should I be now? It was a hateful thought. I suppose I was half mad throughout that voyage from fear and from rage at the injustice of it.

And yet, I knew that I had been plucked from the grave, even after death, and the thought came to me time after time, that perhaps this had been because Fate held something for me. I remembered a man whom Dr. Copshrews had saved from death, when all other doctors had given him up for dead. The case had been spoken of all over England, but Dr. Copshrews, who had done the miracle, had said, simply, "God must have some special purpose in him; he must be reserved for something great." Might it be that I was reserved for something? I was still very young, and life was strong in me in spite of my hatred of it. Often I asked myself that question, "Am I reserved for something?" and hope would leap as I asked; and then I would answer, "Why cheat yourself? You do not yet know that you have been reserved, nor will know yet awhile."

Presently, as slowly as we sailed, we drew abreast of Cabo Amarilho, where we might look to be spoken with by fly-boats from the naval station. We had hauled well away from the land the day before and so lost the benefit of the land and sea breezes; we were becalmed there, or almost becalmed; we crawled there a sea-mile in the hour. I could not bear to go below in all the hours of our passing Cabo, lest the bearer of Fate for me should take me unawares. I stayed on deck, very foolishly, day and night, staring at heat haze, a brassy sky and grey sea. In the night, huddled in the draught of a sail, and often maddened by its jangle, I heard two old seamen of the watch (whom I knew by their nicknames, Morphew and Bilges) talking of Valentine the pirate. I knew that this Valentine had been our Captain's brother, who had been in hot ferocity what Paul now was in cold.

"I saw Valentine only that one time," Morphew repeated. "He came down to his boat at the Stairs at Port Royal, where I was waiting for my captain. He was a fine, big figure of a man ; open and hearty, not like this one at all. He had not gone on the account, then."

"Ah," Bilges said, "I saw him after, when he took Secoondee. It makes me quake even now. I watched him from under some mats in the house as he killed the prisoners, and wondered if I'd be the next."

"What ship was he in, then?" Morphew asked. "Was that the *Fair Maid?*"

"No," Bilges said. "He'd sunk the *Fair Maid* the cruise before. He was in a big Bristol ship, which he called the *Traveller's Joy;* she'd been the *William and Mary* before that. He *was* the traveller's joy, I reckon. He took a good twenty or thirty ships in her along this Coast. I reckon we're going over the bones of their seamen right where we are. He never spared anyone, man, woman or child, black, yellow or white."

"I heard he was a cruel dog," Morphew said, "or if not cruel, careless ; just didn't mind."

"No, he didn't mind," Bilges said. "But I saw the *Hannibal,* Captain Cringle, come into Cabo Road, with him a prisoner aboard and forty-seven of his crew. I was witness against him at the trial, next day. All the forty-seven were tried as pirates ; and Valentine and nineteen of them hanged the next day on the rocks between the tidemarks. I saw it. Careless he'd lived and careless died. But

I tell you there was a joy along the Coast when the news spread that he was gone."

"If I'm not mistaken," Morphew said, "some other of the family'll go the same road, in the same place. How was it Valentine was taken?"

"By a wise strategy," Bilges said. But here the watch were roused to trim the yards, and I heard no more.

I lay awake all the rest of the night, thinking that a few miles from me was a gallows between the tide-marks, where for all that I knew I might be strung up as a warning.

As we were now upon the Coast, we had prepared for the trade there. We had rigged up a trade-room below; and had set out in it the brightly coloured beads, pots and copper-pans which the Captain traded for what little gold or old ivory the natives might have to sell. We had also prepared the chains and shackles with which our Captain hoped to secure some hundreds of victims presently. Slaves were not paid for with beads, pots or pans, but with other currencies, such as rum, gunpowder, and what were called trade-guns; but the main coin paid for slaves by men of our race was bar-metal. We had on board what the natives would have counted a great treasure of small bars of iron and copper. Flesh and blood was reckoned with great exactness in these things; and as little else was discussed at meals, I had come to know how much to offer or to abate for the stalwart or infirm man, woman or child. I was also well-advised as to the diseases to look out for in the offered wares.

Presently, we had crawled well to leeward of the Cabo Amarilho. We had not been challenged by any fly-boat;

we had seen no sail, and reckoned that we could not have been seen, lying so far from the land, and shewing no light after dark. Presently, we began to draw near to our port of Great Momboe. Pegg was busy preparing his anchors and mooring ropes, for the word passed that we should be in the port on the morrow. However, the wind died and left us twenty miles from it, becalmed in the great heat, with the gear all flogging, and the night made hideous by the noise *turrug, turrug,* up and down, of the pumps. We always pumped at night, for the sake of the coolness.

Then, at dawn one morning, a little breeze came upon us and gave the ship life. We rippled forward and quickened, till we were all almost glad; this was the real *Albicore* again, moving like a spirit of the winds. I had been on deck all night. I now borrowed Pegg's glass and looked ahead towards the Coast. There was the land, still swathed in the heat haze but with clearly defined hills above the cloud. Presently, the haze went; I could see low-lying land with curls of white roller running along it. Soon I made out that the trees were of a rank, harsh green, and seemingly closely packed. They looked like a kind of green sheep gathered to oppose our passage, but indeed, we seemed to have no passage, only a green hill barring our way. I was so intent with the shore, wondering if they meant to wreck the ship, that I had not noticed other matters. Pegg suddenly asked me for the glass. I saw then that the Captain had come on deck; someone had reported a sail in sight.

I looked in the direction in which the Captain looked. With my unaided eyes I saw only a tiny smudge, dark

grey against the paleness of the mingling of sea and sky.
I saw that the Captain's face changed as he looked at her
through the glass. Presently, he shut the telescope, gave
it to Pegg, went below, and returned with his own much
better glass. He looked anxiously for a time, then slung
the glass behind his back and said to me and to those
within hearing, "In these waters it is always well to know
who your next neighbour is." He slowly went aloft to the
main-topmast cross-trees, where he looked long at the
Coast to which we drove, and a lot longer at the distant
ship. When he came down, he seemed relieved, as though
that particular danger were over. I had shared his fear all
through this time; now I shared his relief. In another
way, he was a changed man that morning; he loved action.
After the long inaction of the voyage, so full of calms and
setbacks, he was about to be busy, bartering for slaves and
seeing them on board. It is said that the devils in hell can
never be glad; but perhaps they feel as the Captain felt
that morning, rather proud, that a lot of new damned
may soon be under hatches.

I asked him what the distant ship was. He said, "The
Station frigate, bound to the windward; she won't trouble
us now." I did not share his faith, not knowing on what it
could be based. He rubbed his hands and said, "I believe,
Doctor, the heat would do my father's legs good. What do
you think?"

I said that it would be a great change of climate, and
that old plants were difficult to transplant. I added that
if I could see his father, I would be better able to advise.

As we were now within four miles of the Coast, the
hands roused up from below two breakers or casks of what

they called dolly. It was the custom to give a drink of
dolly to all natives who came on board to trade. I had
seen this poison brewed the day before by Pegg, who was
a master-maker of it. The foundation of it was bad ship's
beer touched up with rum and rinsings; the whole flavoured with the juice of boiled rank tobacco leaf and
seasoned with red pepper, to make it fiery. I had seen
Pegg taste it and spit it out, with the remark, "The best
dolly I ever made. Kicks like a mule and leaves a scar all
the way down; something as'll take the paint all off; and
cheap, too. No man could drink more'n fourpence worth
and keep his reason."

But by this time the Coast that had seemed to have no
passage had opened up. In front of us was a river-mouth
all whitening and rolling for half-a-mile and more. To the
left of this was a wooded hill, giving shelter; to the right
was a shallow bay in which a multitude of birds, nearly
all white, fished and clamoured, in a beauty unspeakable
of light and grace. And now, as we headed for the river,
at least thirty canoes shot out to reach us. In front of them
came one with a lugsail, going very fast; she had on board
a big black buck with a scarlet handkerchief about his
brow. After him came all the rest with straining, shining
bodies and flashing paddles and rags of sail of all the
colours of the rainbow. There were shouts and cries and
the shining of enormous teeth, with cries of, "You gib him
dolly. You gib him nicee dolly. Dolly for de black, he
makee jumpy-jack." In a minute the canoe with the big
black buck had run alongside, and the buck was on our
quarter-deck, saying, "Good day to Capn Ashyplank. Me
pilot take you to de pool." The other canoes boarded us as

they came up; all there were slavers or slave-guards; all demanded dolly; all cried that Capn Ashyplank was de good boy, we lub him. With shouting, swearing, yells, blows and muddling, we shot across the bar and slowly stood on to the pool, with our upper sails hanging in their gear and sail after sail coming off her. Some of our men had by this time got hold of some of the dolly. They were acting as though the paint had come off. Canoes ahead of us beckoned us the way. Women ashore held up their children to see us. All the port seemed awake to welcome us in. They were all singing by a sort of instinct a paean:

"Ho, de Capn Ashyplank, him come in de *Albicore*.
Yah. Yah.
Ho, he gib um plenty dolly, oh, so we lub him.
Yah. Yah.
Dolly, oh, de dolly, dolly; we lub de dolly.
Yah. Yah."

To this song, we came into the pool of Great Momboe, and at the word of our Captain let go the anchor, and fired a gun in honour of the local King. I asked Tulp the name of the King. He said, "Old Full-Bottomed Wig-Wig," and pointed out the royal palace, a big open hut thatched with palm-leaf. Almost at once the pipes sounded as Captain Paul went down into his boat to wait upon His Majesty with a gift of dolly, to ask about the prospects of slaves. We were in Africa.

In all the noise, drunkenness and yelling, the pilots and their friends had been able to give us news. The Station frigate had been visiting the leeward ports and had called at Great Momboe only three days before; we had just missed her, and need not expect her again, for she had lost many of her hands from the fever and was bound back to Cabo to refit. This was good news, to us, who had reason to dread her visits. There was no new war, as far as was known. But as for slaves; well, the season was one of the worst known. There were slaves in the slave-sheds ashore, oh, yes, but the pilots let us see that they were not quite the kind we were accustomed to.

"Dey not so good," the pilot said. "Dey not so good. Him die. Him go cluck-cluck."

All the shore swarmed with the subjects of King Wig-Wig, black, yellow and brown, according to their degree of mongrelism. The place was pretty big; there were many huts. About a hundred canoes lay about upon the beach. The town swarmed with skinny fowls, long-legged pigs, mangy goats and odd dogs. We were the only ship in the port. A schooner lay on her side in the mud not far from us. I could read her name, *Two Brothers,* Bristol, painted on her transom. Her crew had all died of "the fever" some years before; Wig-Wig had then sold her masts to a Dane, and nobody since had bothered about her. All this Tulp told me.

It was a savage-looking place, perhaps, but full of interest and beauty. The land on our western side was steepish red hill—mostly red rock, so Tulp said. The town lay to the eastward, and beyond that was the shallow bay with the birds. Wherever I looked, I was amazed by the energy of the life. All the natives, if they were doing anything at all were doing it with zest and shouting; they had a song for everything. Most of them were fishing now. They brought piles of fish aboard for us, in the hope of getting dolly for them, but the free dolly had now claimed its tribute of human membranes; no dolly was left for trade. Besides, as Pegg said, "Dolly is the only hold we've got on these fellows; it doesn't do to let 'em think they can always get it, especially for little things like fish. Dolly gets as dolly does, that's my motto."

However, I had not much time for thinking of these things; the boat came alongside with word for the Doctor to come ashore in her, since the Captain wanted me in the palace. I took my bag of instruments and was soon at the beach, where a big negro carried me out of the boat to a litter. The palace was only a bare thirty yards from where we landed, but we had to save the White Man's face there; it would have lost us face had I walked. At the palace, Captain Paul said that he wanted me to come with him to the slave-sheds.

"There are slaves," he said, "but something's wrong with them. Perhaps you can tell me how bad they are, and whether they can be shipped. Have they told you anything about them?"

"Yes," I said, "they say they are dying and going cluck-cluck."

"What disease would that be?" he asked.

"It sounds like some kind of cough," I said, "but one little look is better than any description; one man said, 'the fever.' Is there only one fever?"

"All fevers seem alike to me," he said, "only sometimes you get worse doses than usual. They tell me that this that these slaves have is just newcomers' fever, which everybody gets. You'll get it during the week. It's often nothing at all."

As he finished speaking, our bearers stopped outside some long open huts thatched with palm-leaf. There were eight of these, each being about twenty yards long by four broad. Each hut had the same simple design. The thatch sloped down on each side from a central ridge so as to screen a long, double, raised shelf on which the slaves were lying. The place stank intolerably, with the stink of Christian Newgate. Any doctor within scent of it could tell that here were plague, pestilence, famine, poverty and cruelty. The air was rank with disease and the smell of death, not the smell of death past or present so much as the warning smell of death coming, such as I had known dogs to howl at in England. These were the slave sheds, where the victims lay till some ship's captain bought them. Only one of them seemed to be full. I judged that when full each shed would hold a hundred slaves. A good deal of noise came from them; the jangling of chains, the moaning of misery, a lot of monotonous singing, in which three or four voices would join and then tail off from weariness, a lot of excited, silly jabber and even more foolish muttering, which came from delirium, and above all, a persistent, dry, hacking hiccough, from at least twenty patients. I knew from the sound that those who went cluck-cluck on that note, day in, day out, would very likely die.

"These men are very ill," I said. "Will you come in?"

"How ill are they?" he asked.

"Very ill; but I will see. Come in."

"Not I," he said. "I'll keep to windward here, thanky."

He swore in the Palaver at his bearers, who sheered away from the sheds to a tree with a dark bole and foliage some dozen yards away. Here they halted. The Captain, with some trouble, lit himself a roll of tobacco-leaf.

"I'll keep the infection off here," he said. "Be as quick as you like, and let's be away."

He called something in Palaver to the agents of King Wig-Wig, who were at the sheds, waiting to shew their wares.

The chief agent was a playful mongrel, who began thus : "Him a fine lot of boys, only dey got de cold, see? Him got cold in de head; make him cough. It go in one day, two day."

"Let me see this cold in the head," I said.

We went under the thatch together.

Now, I had seen some dreadful sights; a doctor has to see them. I had seen the Christian charity of Bedlam, and the Christian justice of Newgate. Now I saw the Christian commerce of Great Momboe, and a dreadful sight it was. In that shed, chained and tightly packed together, in the frightful heat and filth and stench, amid clouds of flies, were eighty-seven men, women and children, prone on the benches, some of them not visibly infected, some of them perhaps recovering, but most of them in high fever and visible agony. Some were dead, one was dying as I entered; and those who were ill were frightfully ill, and some few of them delirious to the point of mania, in a bodily anguish that made them scream. The chief symptom, however, was the hiccough which tore their poor bodies and took away their strength; it was a very distressing symptom. What was wrong with them, I did not know; but a glance told me that it was a malignant fever of an appalling kind. The Captain had mentioned a newcomers' fever, which was another name for yellow fever. I knew little about yellow fever, but this looked like what I had read. By this time, I had noted that the slaves were of four or five different stocks, all different from the subjects of King Wig-Wig; they were all probably newcomers. It flashed through my mind that I, too, was a newcomer, and that this might be my own initiation to the Coast. However, my task was to do what I could to alleviate suffering.

"Him got cold in de head," the agent said. "But him be well in one day, two day. Him a fine lot of boys, him buckra boys, good for dig in de ground, oh, so strong! Oh, how him lub to dig de ground for white mans!"

"These men will die," I said. "Who is looking after them? Who is here to give them water? Fetch plenty water quick. Give um drink."

He looked at me with a kind of wonder. I repeated that the men must have water; that they had fire in them, and that water might put it out. He stared stupidly. I said, "They are dying for water, for drink. Give um drink."

He laughed and spat. "Not such damn fool," he said. "Dey get de good drink when him go to bed."

"They'll die, can you not see that?" I said.

He repeated, "Him a cold in de head; him good boys; soon be well. Now, see, you tell de Capn dey soon be well; you make de Capn buy dem, we be your very good friend, see, gib you a wife while you here; she lub you dear."

As he saw that this did not win me, he raised his price to a barrica of palm-wine, oh, so good! I told him to stop trying to bribe me, and to try to help to make the men well; then I would tell the Captain to buy them.

He spat again and said, "Dey get well by deirself."

I had by this time taken a pulse or two and seen evidence that some at least of these sufferers had yellow fever; two symptoms, which I had read of, were plainly present on them. I went out into the air, for although the sheds were open, any place away from them seemed airy.

I called to the Captain, "Sir, half these men are down with yellow fever as far as I can tell. Will you send me a couple of hands ashore, so that I can set to work to try to cure them?"

"Yellow fever," the Captain said. "Send hands ashore? Are the slaves fit to ship?"

"Sir," I said, "they are desperately ill, but we could save some of them, perhaps most, for they have good bodies and may throw it off."

"You're not a slave doctor, but my ship's doctor," he said. "If they're not fit to ship, that's enough. We'll get back aboard."

"But, sir, we could save these lives—"

"I'm not here to doctor niggers," he said, "nor did I ship hands to nurse 'em. We will get back aboard. But don't come any nearer, thanky—I don't want the infection. Keep your distance, and when you come aboard, keep clear."

We went back aboard, but I was not allowed to sit with the Captain in the boat. He went aboard and sent the gig back for me; when I reached the deck, I was told that I should have to live on deck for the next three days, as I had been exposed to the infection. I heard the Captain swearing that the damned doctor had "asked me to send hands ashore to nurse 'em"—which was a good joke to all who heard; nursing slaves who weren't even well enough to be slaves was not how our commerce was fostered, by a long way.

When I came on board, I found that Mr. Kamansh had gone; I saw him from time to time ashore, no doubt on his obscure business of procuring "old" ivory. The elephants in those parts had long since been killed or driven away; there was no new ivory to be had there. Natives sometimes found places where tusks had been shed, or where elephants had died; this "old" ivory was collected by agents at different ports, and at last shipped to Europe, generally from Monos Grandes. I missed Mr. Kamansh and his lessons in Kranish; and I also missed my position in the cabin. I lived now as a pariah under the awning on deck, thinking of those afflicted and dying men ashore.

However, I was not shut from the knowledge of what was happening. It appeared that the Captain had counted on finding an English agent named, or nicknamed, Peter, at Great Momboe. This agent was not there, but "up the river, at Bimbi." Peter was sorely wanted, for only through men like Peter could slaving captains learn of consignments of slaves. I could hear the matter being discussed below.

"This Wig-Wig has only got a set of corpses. I can't make out from him how soon Peter will be back. I'll have to go up to Bimbi and see Peter. I must find out if slaves are coming or can be expected."

Pegg said, "Peter won't have gone to Bimbi unless he's expecting a gang of slaves there from up Malondo way. He'd never leave here in the season except for that. That's what it must be, sir. He's gone up to dash the Kings for it."

"So I think," Paul said. "I'd better take some trade and go up there in the boat to help him."

"Won't you send me, sir? I'll go, if you like, Captain," Pegg said. "No need for you to sleep rough."

"No, I'll go," Paul said. "I like the Bimbi country, where it opens out."

They talked thus at dinner, while I ate my own dinner in my quarantine just above them. I gathered from what followed that Bimbi was an important place in the trade, because two much-used slave trails led there to the Momboe River. In the afternoon of that day, after a siesta, and the loading up of two big native dugouts with trade, Captain Paul set forth with native paddlers to talk with Peter at Bimbi.

Now, it may seem strange, but I had come to like Captain Paul; when I saw him setting forth, my heart sank. I wished that he would offer to take me with him, for I did not relish being left in the ship under Pegg. However, he called to me as he went to the waiting boat, "I'm sorry I can't take you along, Doctor, but a doctor must stay by the ship in all ports on the Coast. That's the rule of the trade. The men may fall sick at a moment's notice. This is Dead Ned, this place. I'll be back—let's see—not tomorrow, nor quite next day; say, the day after, to make sure. You'll oblige me by keeping aboard till then."

I said that I would obey orders, but that I thought it inhuman to let those unfortunates die in the shed ashore.

He seemed about to fly at me, but answered quietly that he had neither the men nor the drugs to start nursing niggers, and that in any case he had his orders and I mine. He went down the side, to the sound of the pipes of

both boatswains and their mates. In the boat, he called
up to Pegg, "No one is to go ashore, Mister, on any pretext
whatever."

Pegg replied, "Very good, Captain Ashplant."

The Black Mantacaw now went down into the boat.
She was dressed in a scarlet gown with purple trim-
mings, and wore a big hat with an orange plume. She
made a great impression on the natives, and no doubt
added to the Captain's face.

The boats shoved off. The paddlers bent to their thrust
and set forth. The Captain turned his head and called
back, "Have two night watchmen on deck all the time.
I'll deal with any man who tries to get ashore as soon as
I'm back. I'll skin him and make him eat it."

All hands heard this, and knew very well that it was
not an idle threat. I watched the boats dwindle up the
river, till at last they were round the red rock and out of
sight. You may not believe it, but my heart was doleful to
see him go. He was the nearest approach to a friend that I
had in that world, and now he would be away for three
days.

As soon as he was out of sight, Pegg assumed the airs
of a commander. As Captain, he meant to enjoy himself.
As soon as the sun declined behind the hill, he dressed
himself for the shore, ordered the gig to be ready with certain goods from the trade-room, and in the coolness that
followed sunset, he went ashore.

Before going, he said to me, "You know the Captain's
orders, Doctor; you will stay on board. You'll go into
irons, if you go ashore, doctor or no doctor."

I said that I took orders from the Captain, etc. He gave me a deadly look, and set forth upon his jaunt.

After he had gone, I watched the city of King Wig-Wig, which now took on a strange beauty, as the myriad little oil-lamps began to twinkle. Fireflies, which I had never before seen, flitted in thousands among the huts; the stars began to burn, and belts of mist, some grey, some white, almost like snow, formed and slowly glid about the hill. Against their dimness a few dark trees or parts of trees stood out, were merged, and then stood out again, almost as though they were living persons in a kind of dance. Presently, the sea-breeze set in. With it came coolness and a sudden end to the droning of insects. With it, too, came the voice of the surf, which filled all the anchorage and echoed from the red rocks. It filled the air, and stretched along the coast with a thunder and a muttering. I must say that I could have listened to that voice and watched that various beauty for hours. All was strange and terrible, yet alluring. I had a sense of the mystery and vastness of the land. This was Africa, the unknown, the untrodden; it stretched for thousands of miles from where I stood, in forest, mountain and river, full of savagery, full of life, containing, perhaps, the pygmies who fight with the cranes, and the giant snakes who killed the Romans. Perhaps, within a thousand miles of me, the cities of the Kranois still stood, with Edmond Quichet in command. I had so often thought of the African shore; now here I was, almost where the Admiral had been.

A lot of native drums had been beating, ever since the

sun went down. Now to their noise was added the banging of some guns. Tulp, who was on deck, called to me
that the guns were in honour of Pegg, who was being en-
tertained at Mother Jumbo's. "It's silly of him to go
there," Tulp added. "A buck nigger will waylay him coming back." He moved away forward, to see that the watchmen were looking out. Some men came out of the huts
together, singing a song which hadn't much tune, so that
anyone could join in it. They sat presently by a fire near
the beach, smoking tobacco in their little funny pipes,
and going on with their song. Sometimes it was the same
for a minute at a time; then one of the singers would invent something new, perhaps a funny thing, for they
would all laugh and repeat the successful line until somebody invented another. Tulp came back towards me, to
the point at which he thought it was safe. He, too, was
listening to the song, no doubt with envy, for who would
not rather be a happy savage than a miserable slaver's
second officer? I have seldom seen a man who hated life
more than Tulp with less power to change it. He had a
kind of dumb, hopeless endurance, shot with occasional
sorrowful drunkennesses. Yet he had so much interest in
native ways that his knowledge was considerable and
full of colour.

I called to him, "What is the song? Is it a story?"

"No," he said, "it's about us. They always sing like that
the first day or two. If another ship comes in, they'll sing
about her. It is only silly stuff."

"Can you understand it? Can you translate it?"

"Some of it," he said. He listened and then said, "This
is the kind of stuff it is:

"The Captain is a great man, he beat everybody on the
  head.
He beat everybody on the head, oh yes, on the head.
He is the Captain, he hit them on the head, *bang, bang.*
'Why you not bring me more slaves? I hit you,' *bang,
  bang.*
Now he goes up the river away to Bimbi.
'You row me well, you rowers, or I hit your head,'
  *bang, bang.*
Bimbi is very far away, oh, a long way, the rowers get
  very tired.
But the Captain he hit them on the head. He say, 'You
  row.'
By and by all come back from Bimbi, the Captain glad.
He give nicee dolly, oh, so good, and then we all be
  glad.'

"They always sing a lot about the Captain," Tulp
added. "You see, he's like one of their own chiefs. They
like him for that."

Tulp was right about Pegg; he was waylaid by a buck
soon after dawn, and had a job to get away. He came on
board in a dreadful state of sickness from native drinks,
and then fell foul of one of the hands for not getting out
of his way at the gangway. I was on deck at the time, and
saw the matter. The man was an ordinary seaman named
Harry; he was scrubbing the scuppers near the gangway
when Pegg came on board. Pegg had been drunk and
fighting; he was flustered, sick and half-drunk when he
came up the side. Harry, who heard him coming, stood
up and moved his bucket aside, to let him pass. Pegg, being unsteady on his feet, lurched into him, and then

struck him for not getting out of the way. That was the case; I saw it. Harry said, "I beg your pardon, I'm sure, sir," and at this Pegg struck him again and swore. "You give me any of your lip, I'll make you jump clear of the ship." He then went lurching and swearing to his berth, and soon after that came on deck to interfere with the work. It was easy to see that he had now a grudge against Harry and meant, as the seamen said, "to work his old iron up"; this phrase means, that he meant to make his life unbearable.

My fear of arrest became greater again. At any moment, a Liverpool ship might come in with the news that I was a felon sentenced for murder. What could I do, when that happened? This was the slave season. English ships were certain to come. I had not now the solace of examining the hands, for I had been exposed to this infection of fever, and was in quarantine. I caused them to parade before me; all were still well, except the few who had had some dolly or contrived to procure native drink, by lowering a bucket over the bows at night. It was a bad time for me, while I was in quarantine there, and Captain Paul was at Bimbi.

Now that Kamansh was gone, I regretted that I had not asked him to smuggle me ashore and help me to find something to do. I reflected later that I should have been pursued and brought back. The gift of a beakerful of dolly would have turned all the might, majesty and dominion of King Wig-Wig against me; all the King's horsemen and all the King's men would have been after me in no time. I could not have escaped. There was no foreign ship to take me away; even if there had been, where should I have been safe?

Another point that troubled me was this: What had happened to all the other doctors of the *Albicore?* They had died or run, so I was told. But it occurred to me in my uneasy state that some of them might well have been sold as slaves in the Indies. A white slave was very valuable. All the slave-talk in the cabin had shewn me that a white slave might fetch as much as a hundred pounds. A white slave who knew medicine might be worth double that to a slave-owner. Why should not Paul sell me as soon as we arrived in the Indies, when he no longer needed me to look after his cargo? I had these letters in my chest, true; but if once these slave-men had an inkling that I was a convicted felon those letters would not stand me in much stead. If they swore that I was a slave, I could only prove that I wasn't by shewing that I was really a convicted felon. Wherever I looked, I seemed to see nets drawing in upon me. Was I ever to be freed from nets? Was I ever again to breathe the quiet breath of safety? Had my friends done well to tear me from the peace of death? If this fear were to dog me always, would not the rage of the surf and the mercy of the shark be better?

Captain Paul did not come back on the promised day; he was a day late. He came alongside after sunset, and told me to come down into the cabin with him, as he wanted a dose. He was looking ill, indeed, his look was frightful; his eyes were scarlet and had a frantic, mad look. He complained of agonizing headache, like "some-

one driving a jemmy between my skull and the brain."
He was in considerable fever; and his skin had a most
strange tingling heat. As it was not ague, I said that he
should take a mixture of calomel, rest quietly and drink
all that he could of cold water or very weak lemonade.
I had in my cabin a native clay jar for water. I had been
shewn that water stored in such jars could be kept icy
cold, if the jar were swathed in wet covers. These jars
were in much use on the Coast and were precious indeed.
I gave him some calomel and a sweating draught, and
caused him to lie down and drink cold water in abundance. He would not have obeyed me had not the pain
in his head been so acute. He lay tossing for an hour or
two; then said that he was something better, and would
come to table. His walk to the table was that of a very
old, weak, tottering man. My quarantine, I may say, was
now reckoned to be ended.

At table, he said that Peter was down with fever at
Bimbi, and that the slave season was the worst ever
known. Some scoundrel or fool from "up Malondo way"
had had a lot of slaves and had sent them by malice or
mistake not to Bimbi or Momboe but to Little Massa;
and if we hurried to Little Massa we should get there
about the time they arrived, and have a chance of buying
them. "Apart from these," he added, "there isn't so much
as the smell of a slave in all Dead Ned."

For a few moments he seemed to throw off the disease.
Action was always a great spur to him. "It's no good staying here. Peter is sure there'll be no slaves here," he said.
"A big gang was to have been here, but that damned
knave down in Malondo has sent them to Massa. We'll un-

moor, if you please, Mister, and get down to Massa for them, *muy pronto*."

"Now, sir?" Pegg asked.

"Yes, now; this instant."

"Very good, sir," Pegg said, and left the cabin to give the orders. The boatswains of the watches at once called all hands to unmoor and had them at it within the minute. Pegg returned in a few minutes to say that he was sure that he could take her out without a native pilot. Paul's reply to this was, "I hope you can, since a suckling child could."

The pain returned upon him, suddenly, across his eyes, his loins and down his spine. He muttered something about "All these yarns are got foul of the sheave. The trade's stopped, like a foul block. It's a stopped clock, this slave trade, in this year of grace."

I rashly asked what had caused this interruption to the trade. He swore at me for a time, telling me that I could pass my time curing his head, not asking a lot of tomfool questions. After a while, he said, "My joints hurt as though I've been poisoned." He told the steward to boil him some camomile, which is a very harmless, refreshing drink. As the ship's fire was long since out, the steward had to rouse the cook, to relight it. Meanwhile, the Captain said, "If you ask me, this slave business is finished all along the Coast; it won't recover this." After a long silence, during which I saw that he was suffering atrocious pain and mastering it down, in his grim way, he said, "The cause of this business is the Matablancos."

Often the Admiral had told me of that savage tribe,

the Kill-the-Whites; now I had them as neighbours, it seemed.

Pegg said, "But they're a leeward tribe; they don't interfere here."

Paul glared at him and with some effort said, "If you can only use your throat to talk punk, cut it." He glowered again, breathing hard from the agony in his head and joints. At last he said, in the Palaver, "Peter he a sick feller at Bimbi; him go cluck-cluck." After another long pause, he added, "Paul a sick feller; a damsick feller." Presently, he said, "The Matas have done what I always said they would do; they've come west, into the windward. All their old lands are threatened by the M'gai." He glared at us, ready, in his usual way, to swear at anyone who spoke; then, as no one spoke, he said, "The M'gai are moving. They mean to kill the Matas and kill the Whites, and have Africa for the black man."

We looked at each other and said nothing. We all judged, very rightly, that the M'gai were some conquering tribe, who had come out of the darkness killing and killing and would presently die by the spears of others or of themselves.

He waited in silence, almost groaning at each breath. He then said, "Spears; it is all in the spears—a short, broad blade, very broad, very sharp on both sides. If it goes in even one inch anywhere in the body, him finish. That is the M'gai talk. Him sabe mucho; white mans him finish, you see."

After a while, the steward brought the pot of hot camomile infusion. He had forgotten that he had ordered it, and asked what it was. I begged him to drink it, as it would refresh him and help the pain in his head. He slipped from his chair to the deck as I spoke, babbling something that I could not understand about rigging, and writhing from the pain. As he was no longer conscious, I was able to take charge of him as a patient, and had him to his berth. Pegg had to leave me in charge, for he had to be on deck; the ship was already out of her berth and slipping down the stream. I asked the steward for the Black Mantacaw. The steward said that she had not come aboard with the Captain; she had gone to see friends at the palace. He added that she would come off in a canoe before we left the river. I believed this, but perhaps she or her friends were too merry and missed their chance. When I left the Captain and came on deck, we were over the bar and at sea, bound for Little Massa; the Black Mantacaw had been left behind.

I had no doubt that the Captain had a fever far worse than the usual intermittent fever of the tropics; he was frightfully ill, of something that I had never seen and did not know how to treat. I told myself that it was neither typhus nor plague. Could it be yellow fever? I found that I could allay his agonizing pain with cold compresses, and lessen his fever with a cold sponge. There was no thought of feeding him; he was violently and frequently sick; abundant cold water was his food. Perhaps ship's water was not too wholesome, but we had no rain during his days of sickness.

Pegg assumed command, of course, and now shewed that he wished to keep it. If Paul had been well, he would have stood out to sea, to avoid any meeting with a Government vessel sent to ask about us. Pegg stood along the shore. He said that we must lose no time, but drive her all the way, so as to have a chance of these slaves. I knew very well that he did not care twopence about the slaves, but that he hoped to meet some Government vessel and have Paul removed from our midst, so that he, Pegg, might be confirmed in the command.

The wind was very light inshore; we went slowly, in stifling heat. I fell very foul of Pegg on the first day out.

On the Coast of Dead Ned, a ship's surgeon surveys the whole company every morning. We had no men really sick, but half-a-dozen were ailing; I judged that they could not stand the intense heat. I, therefore, suggested to Pegg that these sick might, at least, be kept out of the sun for a few days, and given some quiet work under the awnings till they settled down to the climate.

He said, "The best cure for sickness is work, to work it out of you."

He promptly gave orders for stages to be rigged over the sides, and turned my half-dozen into them with orders to scrape and paint the topsides in the full blaze of the midday. As he plainly did this to shew that he was furious at the suggestion that a doctor's opinion might be wiser than the practice of a brute and a bully, I spoke up to him; we had a hateful dispute in public on the poop. I said that, if the men died as a result of his orders, he should be made responsible in any port we came to. He won the dispute by saying that he was in command, and would put me in irons if I said another word. There was no doubt that he won. Unfortunately, my speaking proved to be fatal.

I mentioned the man Harry, who was in Pegg's displeasure. After I had left the deck to attend the Captain, Pegg saw the man Harry doing some sheltered job about decks, and at once turned him over the side, to scrape paint from a stage. Harry at once obeyed the order, and went. He was a quiet, decent man, not very bright in his wits, but a fair seaman and sober. I had plenty to do in the cabin; I heard the order and Harry's quiet reply, and thought no more of it. By and by, I went to my cabin for something and heard a man just outside the cabin say, "Lend us your wisp of yarns, Harry," and knew that he was working just outside my cabin, abaft the main rigging.

Almost at once, Pegg's voice rang out. "Put your back into it there. Do your work."

There was a moment's hesitation, then Harry answered, very gently and honestly, as I will swear, "I'm doing it, sir."

I will make oath that the words were uttered with no taint of insolence, by a gentle, quiet and rather stupid man who always did his best. It was, of course, ill-advised of him to utter them. Sailors usually stand mute to abuse, and let the storm blow over. They know, too well, that "answering back" may be called mutiny and punished as such.

Now, I had often noticed, that Paul and Pegg believed that discipline could only be maintained by the savagest possible attack on the slightest possible excuse. To Pegg, now, Harry's quiet remark was "answering back," and the very chance he had longed for. He swore at him, and bade him, "Get off that stage and come on deck."

There was utter silence throughout the ship as Harry

clambered up the side. I feared that Pegg meant to murder him, so I ran up on deck to stop him. Perhaps by
doing so I let poor Harry in for much cruel misery. Pegg
saw me come on deck, and did not commit that savage
assault for which he had prepared. Instead, he said,
"I'll teach you to answer back when I bid you mind your
job. I'll teach you manners, my fine lad. Get forward
there."

When forward, he bade Harry take two of the wind-
lass-bars, put one on each shoulder and then march up
and down for a while. Harry shouldered the bars, not
without difficulty, for he was rather clumsy with his
hands, and such bars are clumsy things.

"Not like that," Pegg cried. "You're not going to rest
the bars on your shoulders that way. Hold them upright,
like a soldier does a musket. Now march, like a soldier.
Quicker nor that. March. You always were a damn sight
liker a soldier than a sailor. March."

I felt the indignation of the crew all about me. The
ship was soundless. I knew how near the men came to
rising and flinging Pegg overboard; however, law and
long obedience triumphed; the boatswains' mates and
other warrant officers suddenly damned them for not
bending to their work; they ceased to listen, and bent to
their painting, while poor Harry trod up and down with
the heavy bars at his shoulders.

"Now march," Pegg cried. "You'll be sorry you answered back before I've done with you. March, my British
Grenadier. Right. Left. Right. Left. That's about all
you're fit for, to march with the rogues' battalion."

All this was on the hottest day of which I had any experience.

Knowing that my presence would exasperate Pegg to greater savagery, I went below, wondering how I could save the man. Marching up and down, with those heavy, clumsy bars, in that appalling heat would soon kill any white man. It was almost noon: I resolved to speak to Pegg when he came down to dinner.

In a few minutes he came down, saying that he was as hot as hell; he pitched his hat into his berth, dipped his hands in a pan of water and wiped them on an old sail. He took the Captain's place at table, and as the steward lifted the lid from the pot, said, "I'll make that man sick that ever he answered me back."

"Mr. Pegg," I said, "you be careful that you don't kill him."

"Kill him, be damned," he said.

"If you do kill him, you will be damned," I said. "Come, sir, I speak as a doctor. To march a white man in the sun like that, bearing those weights, is a certain way to kill him."

"I'm in command here; not you," he said.

"I'm responsible for the health of the crew," I said. "It's my duty to warn you that if you're not careful you'll kill that man; and that'll be murder."

He looked at me very evilly.

"Come, sir," I said. "If your office and custom demand that the man be punished, even more than he has been already, I beg you to find some other way."

"You doctors from college talk a lot of wisdom," he

said, "but if you think you can run a ship by softness you'll find your error."

"Are you giving the poor man a chance to drink?" I asked.

"Drink?" he asked. "Drink? No."

"You must, sir," I said. "Come, I will not see murder done. Give him a caution and let him go, to drink and rest."

"I'll give him a caution, all right," he said, and went on deck. We heard him call one of the boatswains and give an order. After a few minutes, he came below again. "Well, there you are, Doc," he said; "that's that. I've sent him below, and now I hope you're satisfied."

"That is well done of you, Mr. Pegg,' I said. "I am grateful to you. Let us shake hands."

We shook hands, without any enthusiasm from him, however. The meal was over, and Pegg went to turn in, but paused to ask, "How's the Cap?"

I said, "Desperately ill, still. You can see." I shewed him the sick man, who was delirious and babbling. "He's in high fever still."

"Is it catching?" he asked.

"You know as much as I do," I answered. "I believe this is yellow fever; no man knows how it spreads, but it seems to come from places more than people."

"I'll run no risk with yellow fever," he said, and moved away from the door.

During that afternoon, I ordered the Carpenter to get a scuttle opened in the deck above the Captain, so that a small ventilator could be rigged to blow a draught down upon him. But for that, I do believe he would have died of a heat-stroke. As the Carpenter worked, I kept sponging the burning, dry skin, with a cold sponge. I wished that the Mantacaw were on board; she might have helped a little; and in any case, the patient's rage on hearing that she had been left at Momboe could only be bad for him. I was with the Captain all the rest of the day, unable to think of anything else. All my faculties were bent to that one thing, to save him, if he could be saved. I knew little enough of fevers, and had never seen anything like this fever. I remembered old Copshrews' quiet remark, "We fight fire with water. Nothing can be better." I sponged the dry, hot, restless, moaning, babbling body and devised a way of getting him to swallow water. When the air began to blow down upon us, I felt for the first time that I might save him. Mind, he was a cruel, terrible savage who had murdered two men, one of them in cold blood. I didn't care about that. I know that I would have given my life to save him. There was something about that fearful creature that I could love and pity. I watched by his cot all through the evening and then far into the night. Sometimes, when my patient drowsed, and lapsed into muttering and restless tossing, I, too, drowsed, and had some confused muttering, restless sleep. At other times, I was at work, and often at desperate work, for my patient, whatever his weakness, was often violent. In his paroxysms, he was always leaping up from bed, and flinging away his bedclothes, or trying to tear them. I had not much light, save the battle-lantern. I would see the restless, moaning, swearing, puking figure gathering for an outburst and be ready. However, the outburst always came unexpectedly, without warning. When he was up, it was fairly easy to get him down, but he was a heavy man, and it was very hot. One very marked symptom in the sickness made me long for my father; it would have interested him, and I would have given my right hand to discuss it with him. I would have given my left hand to have had Dr. Copshrews with me. At intervals, the patient seemed to know who I was, yet would address me as Moctezuma, Bloody Bill, Titus Oates, Sir Friendly Pogg, or Jane Shore. Then he would weep and swear, and burst out singing, usually a metrical version of a psalm to the tune of some low ditty, or the low ditty to a psalm tune.

All the time, I was partly aware of what was going on above me; the men were at work on deck; the watches changed, and certainly the wind freshened and made the ship go faster. I was well convinced that I was with a yellow fever case. I was not sure if the disease were contagious; no man seemed to know; but if it had been variola or plague, with a risk as great or greater, I would have stayed. I meant to save him, if any man could.

After two in the morning, he was quieter; and this quiet presently turned into what seemed a restfulness. He was less burning hot; there was even a moisture on his wrists. The pulse was weaker. In another hour, he was fairly asleep; in a good, quiet sleep, which I should have welcomed, but for the marked drop in the pulse. I watched him quietly for a time, hoping that the rest would last for some hours. I was tense enough at first. I expected more paroxysms and hurling of the bedding. None came; he slept.

It must have been a little before dawn when I fell into

a deep sleep. I was awakened by the steward creeping in
with some hot infusion of camomile. It was light but not
yet broad morning. I knew that the steward must have
been up long before, to get the fire lit and this infusion
boiled up. He was a cowed, broken, pathetic man, who
had lived so long in fear of blows that he no longer dared
to speak without looking around, to see who might be listening. Indeed, in that cabin space any conversation
could be plainly heard, and was listened to, without
shame, by everybody, and usually repeated, with distor-
tions.

I said, "That is good of you, steward; well done. You
must have lost your beauty-sleep, to brew him this."

I took the tisane, and contrived to get the Captain to
drink some of it. I noticed, on turning round, that the
steward was shaking.

I said in a low voice, "Do not be afraid, steward. If
this is yellow fever, as I believe, it probably is not catching from the patient."

He looked at me piteously; then he whispered, "Harry's
dead, sir. Mr. Pegg killed him this morning."

"What?" I said.

He repeated his words, shuddered hard, with chatter-
ing teeth, and then began to cry.

"Now, come, steward," I said. "Help me to get the Captain into clean things; you can talk as you work."

I did not get the whole story from him; it reached me in
pieces at odd times, in the course of the day. It was the
most dreadful thing.

When Pegg went on deck, as I thought to release Harry,
he did not release him, but sent him to march with his bars

in the heat of the 'tween-decks, which are always so much hotter and closer than the open deck. He made him march there, without rest or drink, till he prayed for mercy. Pegg had then gone to him, and asked, would he sing, to be released? Harry, who had a sweet tenor voice, as all on board knew, said, "Yes, sir; gladly." Pegg, therefore, made him sing, and this without the refreshment of a drink of water, till he could sing no more. You must remember that this was at four in the afternoon, and that Harry had been on deck, doing hard work, with no food, since eight that morning. When from thirst and exhaustion he could sing no more, Pegg had said, "I'm not going to let you off for a song like that. A sick cow could sing better. Pick up them bars and march again." He had obeyed and had marched till perhaps five o'clock, when he had knelt to Pegg and begged to be spared, saying that he couldn't march or carry the bars unless he were allowed to lie down for only twenty minutes. Pegg told him to "pick up those bars when he was told": he had chosen to give his officer a back-answer, and now he should find his error. Harry had picked up the bars and had tottered up and down with them, while Pegg mocked and imitated him, calling to any who were near to see what a fine soldier they had on board.

At last, Harry begged Captain Pegg to flog him, or anything, but let him rest, even for five minutes. "Ah, so you'd rather be flogged?" Pegg had said. "Well, you shall be." He then ordered the boatswains' mates to lash him to the windlass and beat him with the ends of ropes, which they did. Harry had expected that he would be set free after the beating, but Pegg made him pick up the bars and go up and down again, till at last he fell. "Ha," Pegg said, "would you rather have another beating than walk?"

Harry answered, "I can do no more, sir."

"You shall have another beating, then," Pegg said. "Seize him up again, you." This time they beat him till he was senseless and did not release him. They left him lashed to the windlass, and Pegg said he would like to see the man who would presume to let him go. He would shew them what mutiny led to aboard a ship like the *Albicore*. No more back-answers or they would know what they would get. He then strutted up and down, just abaft the windlass, defying the crew to come up and try to cheer the mutineer. "He's got his just deserts," he kept saying, "what all of you'll get, if you try to befriend him." From time to time he struck and kicked his victim. The crew, cowed as all slavers' crews were, by constant tyranny and brutality, did nothing. What could they have done? The officers and petty officers were ready for them, and had the law on their side; any protest was mutiny; any effective action, piracy. They just had to watch and listen. When they were knocked off from work after pumping, and went below to their supper, two of them did come aft with the request that Harry be allowed to come below to his supper, since he had eaten nothing since his breakfast of biscuit at dawn. Pegg told them to cut forward, quick, since Harry was going to get rope for supper. And at this, Pegg picked up a rope's-end and beat the poor thing a third time.

Harry was kept seized to the windlass during the night. In the middle watch, one of the boatswains told Pegg that he thought the bastard was dying, so Pegg went to him, spoke, and getting no answer, kicked him "for being sullen." Harry roused a little at this and asked for his mother. "He asks for his mammy," Pegg said. "A little cold water will serve as mammy for you, my lad." He had then dashed a bucket of salt water over him. However, this gentle treatment came too late; Harry quivered a little and died.

Pegg then told the watch to bring the body on deck, and warned them they had better learn that lesson or he would repeat it; he was quite ready to teach them. He then ordered them to throw the body overboard, which the boatswains' mates did. There was no prayer, no word of burial, though some of the men wept openly. "Now," Pegg said, "now you'll know what you'll come to, if you set up for captains and answer back."

That is the story of Harry's killing; I have omitted some details, which I disdain to write. Judge of our feelings, cooped up in the ship in which those things were done.

You will not believe how deeply I loathed my life and my race. I had had a glimpse of the blacks, now. I had not seen them uncontaminated by the whites, it is true; but even so, those whom I had seen at Momboe were healthier and happier than any people whom I had seen in Europe. Yet savages like Paul and Pegg were driving poor men like Harry to misery and death so that those blacks might be driven to misery and death. Paul and Pegg were guilty, no doubt; but what of the proud and grasping soul behind them, who urged them on, who stayed at home and bribed Parliament to support him? His emissaries bore the heat, did the sin, shed the blood and broke the soul; he took the rich reward. He did not see, as I saw, the poor men of the crew, in the mercy of a brute like Pegg, creeping about their work with bent heads, some of them weeping. I knew now to the full why Dick had called the men in the African trade devils from hell, and why Sokdollijer and his brother thieves and cheats found it hard to find crews. This service in a hot and stinking ship in the command of devils, in the doing of devilry, was what fat and false Parliament members called "the nursery of British seamen." Do not imagine that deaths like Harry's were rare. Only the voyage before, Captain Paul had beaten the man Maggot Williams to death in that very ship, with similar callousness.

What with this misery, the heat, my restless night, and my anxiety, I was nearly exhausted. But I had some consolation. Paul had come very much to himself. He looked, and said that he felt, much better. The fever seemed gone, though it had left many marks on him. His pulse was bad, and his weakness was dreadful. His tongue when he put it forth had a strange wavering motion which shocked me. I contrived a wash for his mouth, which refreshed him very much. His eyes and skin were tinged with yellow. His pain, in head and joints, was gone; his thirst was gone; his skin had lost that tingling heat which had so impressed me; it was now cool and moist, though it had come out in tiny red spots on arms and chest. The wild, anxious, bright, hard, mad look was gone from his eyes, which were now yellow, not scarlet, and the distressing hiccough and sickness had gone. I made him as comfortable and cool as our means allowed, and noted that a soft pillow gave him intense pleasure—this in a man who was as indifferent to bodily ease as man can well be. He asked for food.

I said, "No; no food; try to sleep. You must not have food yet."

He said, "Why not? I'm as empty as a shell."

"It is wise not to feed a fever," I said. "We fight fire with water."

"I'm all water already," he said. "Let me have some brandy."

I said, "No. Your stomach is in a very tender state; it has been rejecting everything. You must not think of inflaming it with spirits. Let it have some rest, while nature restores its tone. You try to sleep a little."

He growled that food would restore his tone, but that he would like to sleep, as he had been very uneasy. I left him composing himself to sleep, and being deadly weary myself should have done the same, had not one of the boatswains' mates asked to see me, complaining of pain and fever. I saw the man, and noticed at once that his eyes, which were slightly tinged with yellow, had the bright, mad look that had been so marked a symptom in the Captain. The man had often had fever; he asked for bark.

I said, "I'm going to give you some calomel; it's better than bark."

He seemed uneasy, and said that he had been one employed to beat Harry, and was afraid that Harry was after him. I told him to put any such thought from his mind, to take the calomel, and go to his berth. I would see that Mr. Tulp excused him.

He said he was sure Harry was after him. I told him not to think of such folly any more.

He said, "Ah, sir, what's folly in England isn't folly here. Harry has done his juju on me."

I said, "Get you below to your berth and say your prayers. They'll put your fancies out of your head, and the calomel will put the fever out of your guts."

He went away a few paces, then returned, to ask what prayer might be best. I said that the Lord's own prayer was the best. He asked which Lord, and what prayer that was? I took him forward, to explain, and on deck passed the murderer, Pegg, who glared at me, as I at him. I took the sick man to his berth, taught him what few words of prayer his racking head could retain, and saw him into bed. I told the other petty officers that he would need looking after. I stayed by him for some time, arranging for his drink and sweats. I did not at all like the look of the case. I had read of yellow fever killing more than half of a ship's company; we had it on board us now; who would tell when it would go? After a time, I felt that I could go back to my berth. As I went, I took a good look at the poor cowed watch going like ghosts about the deck. How many of them would have that hard, mad look in the eye? I was thankful to see none. I was very careful to say nothing to anybody about my fears. One or two men, wishing me good morning, asked if Doggy, the boatswain's mate, were very bad? I said, "I've dosed him; I think he'll be better when the medicine has had time."

I suppose that by this time it was ten in the forenoon. I was so very weary that I did but glance into the Captain's cabin. He was sleeping quietly, which seemed by much the best thing he could do. Having crept from his door, I went to my own berth and was almost instantly asleep. I was awakened at about three in the afternoon by the steward, who asked me to come at once to the Captain. I turned out as I was, and reached his cabin in an instant. I found him in a state of desperate sickness, his face dusky, yet suffused with yellow, his chest speckled with tiny red spots, his consciousness gone, and all the fatal symptoms hung out like death's flag upon him. He was dying.

"How long has he been like this?" I asked. "He was asleep at ten."

"Yes, sir," the steward said. "He was very well at dinner-time. He woke and said he felt quite well. He asked for food."

"You did not give him any, I hope?"

"Yes, sir; he made me fetch him food."

"What food?"

"A soft boiled egg, sir; one of the eggs we bought at Momboe."

"Any drink?"

"Yes, sir; some brandy."

"There it is," I said. "I told him that he was not to have food or brandy."

"Yes, sir. I heard you tell him, sir. But I have to obey the Captain's orders, sir. He said he was well, and only needed a little food to get his strength."

"Live and learn," I said. "Nothing can save him now. I wish you had called me instead of letting me sleep. Why wasn't I called?"

"Mr. Pegg said he called you, sir."

"Called me? But I wasn't called."

"He said he called you, sir."

I knew something of the heavy sleep of the sea. It was well possible that Pegg had called me, and that I had answered, yet not roused. It was also well possible that Pegg had not called me, hoping that the Captain would die. I knew that no patient recovered from the symptoms shewn by the Captain. He was doomed; nothing could save him. He fought on, in an unconscious gabbling way till sunset, then died quietly; just as men came aft to ask me to come to Doggy, who was now desperately and ragingly ill, in acute pain, and saying that Harry was waiting for him.

I went forward to Doggy. On my way one of the men stopped me gently, and asked me to have a look at Buddy there, who wasn't feeling too well. I shall ever remember my relief when Buddy told me that his complaint was not a fever, but a springing of boils, to which he was subject, and to which he owed his nickname. Doggy, however, was frightfully ill, with a symptom which I know now to be a bad one in this disease; he was talking or yelling wild folly, knew that it was folly, yet could not control it and utter sense.

By midnight that night, we had buried the Captain, and come to know that Doggy would not survive. The yellow fever had two of us; who would be the next to sicken?

And now I knew something of the powers of the un-taught, brutal despot. There was a general feeling among the crew that yellow fever is a contagious disease. After all, they had seen it before, on other voyages, and had some grounds for their beliefs. I can understand their believing this and dreading the contagion. As soon as the Captain was over the side, Pegg said that he wasn't going to have me in the cabin again, infecting everybody. I should keep on deck, and deal only with the sick. He ordered all the Captain's bedding and clothes to be flung overboard. This was done by the boatswain, who, however, tied a line to the bundle in the dark, let it tow overboard and later re-trieved it. For myself, I went back into my quarantine; I lived again behind a screen of canvas rigged for me under the awning, and all my things were placed there. In a way, I was thankful for this; it saved me from contact with the appalling Pegg.

The man Doggy, before going onto the sick-list, had had a very evil influence upon the crew. In his babbling he had impressed them with the belief that the wraith of poor Harry had "worked a juju," as they called it, upon him which would not be satisfied till vengeance was ex-acted. This belief was now held by everybody. It was no good saying, "That is all nonsense." They replied, "Harry'll come for him. Harry'll come for all who killed him; you'll see; you mark my words."

I had not much doubt that Doggy would die. He was quite desperately ill, and more violent than the Captain. He had a way of shouting, "Harry's waiting by the wind-lass," which rang through the ship and terrified every-body. Pegg was terrified, as he plainly shewed. He even asked me if I could not give Doggy something which would "put him out of pain like that." I said that he must know that in such a disease the stomach brooked no remedies.

It was a hot doldrummy night, with violent rain-squalls. Sleeping under my awning, I was frequently wetted and wakened by the rain, which I did not mind; it was so fair a refreshment in the heat. I slept ill, and often in my worry and misery wondered if the seamen were not right. Why should they be wrong? Why should not poor Harry's wraith wait by the windlass, calling for vengeance upon his killers? A frightful deed had been done against an in-offensive man : why should not judgment follow?

In the last day I had heard a great deal about this native custom of working an evil spell or juju. I told the men that Harry would have been quite the last person to work such a spell. They did not believe me. They said that Harry knew very well that the blacks worked evil upon others by wishing it and "pointing" it intently upon their victims, and that Harry had done it upon the ship. "Look at the Captain," they said. "Look at Doggy. They've both been smitten down already."

In my worry, I began to think that on the Coast of Dead Ned, where so much was savage, the savage thing might be the true thing. Somewhere forward by the windlass there might be drops of man's blood, crying with their sub-tle tongues for hounds to pursue and harpies to tear the shedders. All along that frightful Coast of Dead Ned and Sin millions of wild black men must have wished evil in-tently upon their wrongers, the whites. Surely, all that mass of hatred must now be almost a living thing, an army of hounds with dripping fangs, going out against the white man. The soul of poor Harry had but to cry, to turn all that mass of hatred against us.

I suppose that the heat, the worry and the misery had almost made me light-headed. From the present, I turned to the past, and to those two problems : who had killed the Admiral, and what was now happening at Hannibal House? "By this time," I said to myself, "Dennis will have bought the House from the Crown ; there he will be, probing in the plaster, pulling down the wainscot. Perhaps, by this time, he will have stricken some lucky blow and found all the Admiral's treasure tumbling about him, in deeds and gold and precious stones." With these thoughts I bothered myself to sleep.

I roused at about half-past three in the morning. I can not say why I roused, but I started up, thinking, suddenly, that I had heard Doggy cry, "Harry'll come for me at four, he says." This I had heard him babble several times during the afternoon, and had thought it only nonsense. I did not think it nonsense now. "I'll go down to Doggy," I said to myself, "so as to be near him before four." On my way, I met one of the better seamen, to whom I mentioned what I was going to do.

"That's kind of you, sir," he said. "If you bring him past four, he'll be all right, no doubt. It's fancies and giving way to them that kills folk on the Coast here. When he finds it's fancy, he'll be ashamed."

I stood talking with this man for some minutes. The ship was slipping along quietly in the hot, hazy night. We seemed to be shearing through swaths of wool which, as we drove into them, streamed aside into rolls of flame, that broke into spangles and died again into wool. I could hear the sick man on the deck below babbling and muttering.

"You hear him, sir?" the man said. "He's a lot better now."

I asked, "Has Captain Pegg chosen another officer?"

He said, with some surprise at my not having heard, "Yes, sir. Mr. Staggers."

Staggers was known to me as a young, truculent boxer

of great physical beauty; he had been in the ship in the previous voyage; during this present voyage, he had been Sailmaker's mate. I had seen him about the decks and had disliked his look.

At this moment, there came cries from below, with a noise of scuffling; the man, Doggy, came rushing up the hatch, tearing off his clothes. He fell exhausted on the deck close to me. Even in that light, I could see that he had become dusky in the face, like a mulatto. He babbled, "Leave me. The boat's coming at four. Harry's sending the boat for me at four. Eight bells. And there'll be a man in the boat I won't want to see."

I tried to raise him, but he struck at me.

"Come, Doggy," I said, "let us get you back to bed."

"Leave me in the cool," he said. "For God's sake, leave me in the cool."

The watch gathered about, coming not too near, but gazing with fascination and terror. It seemed to me that Doggy was at the point of death. I said to the men, "I believe he's dying: do not touch him." They would not have touched him. Doggy was babbling something. I knelt just over him, knowing that he might say something coherent of importance to someone in far-away England. He began to mutter the compass, "North quarter east; north half east; north three-quarter east, nor' by east." This became muddled at once into nonsense like "three-quarters south a half west; south east by north a quarter west, live dead by dead three-quarter dead, dead live dead." After a minute of this, he said solemnly, in a little voice which only two or three could have heard:

"Dead by live three-quarters live.
Dead by live half live.
Dead by live one-quarter live.
Dead by live.
Dead three-quarters live.
Dead half live.
Dead one-quarter live.
Dead."

When he had reached this East Point, he said, "There's the boat hooked on, and there's Harry. Oh, Harry, don't go against a shipmate. Tell the gentleman, I had to do what I was told." Then he cried, "The gentleman's got his bonnet over his face. Oh, keep him off, Doctor." He struggled a little faintly and died, just as the helmsman made a long arm and struck the bell eight for four o'clock.

So Doggy died, and was promptly buried, without any prayer. One of the men began to sing a hymn, which began, as I well remember,

Sweetly sleep, dear saint, in Jesus.

He stopped after this line as he could not remember what followed. Long afterwards, I found the whole hymn in an old book, and read it through with thoughts of Doggy, whose real name I never knew.

Presently, the wind freshened and cleared away the heat haze. We were running not more than a couple of miles from the land, as the shore was bold and the water deep. When the sun rose, we saw the surf running, dying, and again rising; its voice came to us continually in a melancholy increasing, lapsing roar, most mournful yet very beautiful. At places, the surf must have been terrible, for clouds of spray rose high and dissolved slowly.

"A good boiling today," Tulp said, as he passed me, nodding at one such place. "A good bubble on the pot. But bad as it looks from here, it's nothing to what it is close to."

Some time later, I saw that they were rousing out cable and mooring-ropes, as we were nearing Little Massa.

I remember that at one point of the voyage we passed a wooded, bold cape, with a ruined white image on it. A seaman told me that the mark was "Our Lady of Matapanga," that the Portuguese had put it there three hundred years before. "They had a settlement in the gully there," he added, pointing. "But they all died of the fever; it's a bad coast for fever, Dead Ned."

At the moment, we had no other fever case on board, worth calling a case. Three men had had rigors, and a fourth man who had had a fever had a yellow tinge in his eyes. I judged that all these had had the disease in a mild form.

The man Buddy was ill. He had been crazed, I suppose, with the heat and the pain of his boils, into trying to cure himself. His theory was that, since Africa had given him the boils, Africa might cure him. He had, therefore, "eaten a hair of the dog that had bitten him." He had gnawed and swallowed down a piece of African wood from the arm of an idol, which one of the men had bought at Momboe. He was now very sick and in grievous pain.

The night before he reached Little Massa, I had a perplexing time with Buddy, trying to give him some relief, and not succeeding very far. When I had done what I could by him, I went aft to my screen, to sleep, thinking that he would probably die of perforation. He had a good watcher by him, who would call me in any emergency. The cabin skylight was open. I could hear Pegg and Staggers in the cabin playing a simple card-game, of which they were very fond. It is the game called by children "Beggar-My-Neighbour"; they called it "Check." I heard them crying, "Check," continually, and then fell asleep.

I did not sleep long. I was wakened by hearing them creep cautiously on deck, as I supposed in the hope of catching someone asleep in his watch on deck. I heard Pegg say in a low voice, "Is the Doc asleep there?"

Staggers tiptoed close to me. I lay still, for I did not wish to talk with them. He said, "Yes; dead-oh. He can do with his all-night-in, the Doc."

They moved aft a few feet from me. I heard Pegg repeat, "You're sure he's asleep?" and Staggers repeated, "Dead-oh."

They stayed there only about five feet from me. They could hear that the watch was busy at a job forward, and see that the helmsman was wide awake. Pegg had a look at the compass and returned to Staggers, who began at once thus:

"In the *Almeria*," he said, "under old Cap Scratch Toes, the Doc kept watch and watch, all the time, when no slaves were aboard."

I knew that this was designed to suggest to the Captain that I, too, should keep watch and watch. Any reply to it would also shew to Staggers just how Pegg regarded me.

"And a very good way, too," Pegg answered. "Why

should a Doc live easier than any, when no sick are aboard? I've half a mind to try the same here."

"Why not?" Staggers asked. "You're Captain."

Pegg muttered in a low voice, "He may not be quite safe."

"How d'ye mean? You're Captain."

"Yes, I am Captain. But he's got letters in his chest to the Governors of Jamaica and Carolina. He may be a bigger dog than he seems."

It is said that listeners hear no good of themselves. It would be odd as well as most unjust, if they did.

"He don't seem much of a big dog to me," Staggers said. "He wouldn't come in a slaver if he were much of a big dog. He came like all the other docs in the trade come, because he wanted to lie low a bit."

"How d'ye mean, lie low?"

"Docs get into trouble by giving the wrong dose and that. This man came aboard at the last minute, with a lot of ready-made slops. All his things were new and marked new. They've been forward to be washed, and we talked of it there. He didn't bring one old thing to sea. That's odd to begin with. Generally, when a man comes to sea, he brings the oldest he has. Even this man's trunk was new. And that's odd, too, for one who says he was brought up in France, as they all say he says he was. I mean, you'd expect he'd have a trunk that had batted about a bit and shewn the marks of travel and that."

"Yes, he says he was brought up in France," Pegg said, "and he has a French book or two. And it is odd, now you mention it—"

"What is odd?" Staggers asked.

"He's got no papers to shew he's a doctor: no parchment; no licence. I've been through his things to see, and can't see one anywhere."

"Maybe he's got it on him," Staggers said. "He very likely keeps it on him."

"I suppose it would be small," Pegg said. "It would go into a pocket-case, folded up. But it's odd you should mention what you do."

"Mention what?"

"About all his things being new, yet coming as Doc to the Coast. If he were hard-pressed, like most of 'em, he wouldn't have had new things, that's sure. Are you sure he's asleep?"

Though he trod softly as a cat, I heard Staggers creep to me and examine me. I am not much of an actor, but I can act being asleep with anyone. Staggers looked and crept back.

"Dead-oh," he said. "It's what he's best at."

"There's a mystery about him, that's sure," Pegg said, "but there can't be any doubt of his being a doc, because he cured the steward's leg, and he sets about anyone the right way. He set about Paul; a London surgeon couldn't have done him better; give the devil his due. He's a doc, all right. And old Sokdollijer shipped him and brought him on board. He must be a doc. But, God, don't he make me sick, with his airs and college-talk. And he's only a kid, when all's said. I'll tell you my view of him. Mind, I don't want Tulp to know or to suspect."

"I won't moot it to Tulp, nor anyone else," Staggers said.

"Well, my belief is, he's a spy. There's lots of talk in England now by cranks and that, about this trade. It's being enquired about. Our old friend Paul, who's gone to play his harp, set a lot of tongues wagging, about that useless specimen Maggot, and so forth. A lot of sky-pilots were up and down Liverpool, you'll remember, asking about how the poor slaves are packed. My brother says they're at the same game in Bristol, all prying and peeking in anybody's business but their own. They've got men to ask about it in Parliament, too. The trade's a lawful trade, and it's best done by men who understand it, whose business it is. Now, we got out of Paul's trouble very well, considering; and my brother tells me they beat these spies at Bristol in the same way; they just spirited all evidence out of the way by shipping 'em foreign at once. But there's a lot of money behind these spies. It may be French or it may be religious money. They want to find out what goes on out here and in these ships. It's my belief they got this kid, who's very likely a French spy when all's said, to come out here to report. That's what my belief is. There's something odd about him. His name's a purser's name, I do believe. Torrance ain't English by the sound. It's the French name Torrong, what means a waterspout. And when he's been the Middle Passage to Jamaica or the Carolines, he'll hand in those letters to the Governors and make his reports, and then there'll be all hell to pay."

"God, that's a dirty trick, ain't it," Staggers said, "to eat the trade's bread and then complain of the flour?"

"I'm not quite blind," Pegg said. "I've seen him close to and had time to figure on it. If he ain't that, what is he,

this French lad? But I've made up my mind that he don't
get past Captain Pegg. Paul wouldn't believe me when I
talked all this to him. He said that the kid had been very
strongly recommended from London, and that old Sokdollijer knew what he was about. So do I, if it comes to
that. He ain't going to issue a report."

"What d'ye mean to do, then, Captain Pegg?"

"I'll just have a look-see if he's as asleep as he gives
out."

Pegg came quietly to me, and in a low voice said, "Are
you awake, Doc?" I moved in my sleep and flung myself
over, as though about to wake, then settled to rest on my
other side.

"He's asleep all right," Pegg said. "Well, what I'm
going to do is to sell him the day we make Jamaica or the
Carolines. You may have heard what Paul did the other
time with Doctor Tim? Hey? As a white slave with no
papers and a knowledge of medicine this man or any
other doctor'll fetch seventy-five to a hundred pounds
on any big estate. He'd be worth more than that; double
that."

"But with those letters to the Governors," Staggers
said, "there'd be trouble; big trouble. It don't do, to stir
up Governors."

"There won't be any letters to Governors by the time
we make Jamaica," Pegg said. "There won't be any letter
to anyone, nor any certificate round his neck, nor anything else. You mark my words, that kid is not Edward
Torrance. He's here under an assumed name. He's here
under false pretences. He'll be sold as a creole slave with
a knowledge of medicine, and of the name of Edward. If

he's not a creole slave, let him prove it. He'll find it hard enough to prove, when once he's become it. But it's my belief he's too plumb scared of being found for what he is, to make much of a struggle. If I let it be thought that he's a spy, the planters would waft him away by next morning. They'll get some black dame like the Mantacaw to rub a little bamboo in his slabber. Now I've opened my mind to you, Staggers, I shall look to you to bear a hand when the time comes. You shall not be a loser by it. He may make us sick enough with his airs at table and that, but he's a living bank-note for a hundred plunk."

Staggers said that he would bear a hand when the time came, but that a kid like me wouldn't give trouble. I was only a kid and had never done any work.

"He'll do some soon, then," Pegg said. "Were you ever at Bluefields Creek out at Lagarta?"

"No," Staggers said.

"Well, I know the overseer there. He was saying only last voyage, how they ought to have a slave doctor; only they can't send a slave to learn doctoring in London, because of these cranks who say a slave's free when he lands in England. Besides, he'd learn a lot too much besides doctoring. He might start wafting folk away: 'send him home to him he lub.' However, this Doctor Torrong what means a waterspout'll do fine. It's anything from sixty to a hundred plunk, just put in our pockets."

After this, they talked a little of the whites all dying in Matapanga, and then a little about Paul. One or two of the cold-blooded devilries of Paul were told with admiration. "You can't help laughing when you think," Pegg said, "he was up to every trick the trade has."

After this, Staggers said he reckoned he would turn in.
"I would," Pegg said. "I'm glad I've had this talk.
Now we know how we stand as to Waterspout. If you
stand in with me, you'll find there's a good deal to be made
in this trade on the side. We'll talk of another matter
later."

Staggers went below. Pegg stayed awhile creeping
softly about, probably to spy upon Tulp, or to hear what
the watch on deck were saying. He looked closely at me,
to make sure that I was asleep. I judged that he was going below to my berth to have another look for my certificate, which I was now carrying, much as they had
surmised, in a little oilskin case hung round my neck.
My letters of introduction were in this case with it.

After he had gone below, I did not sleep too well. I now
knew what Pegg had planned for me; I must say that it
terrified me. He was so frightfully right in his guess: I
was "too plumb scared of being found" for what I was to
make much of a struggle. It was true. And Dick had said,
"They'll sell you, if they get half a chance." They would
have a chance. What was to stop their chance, when we
came to Bluefields Creek out at Lagarta?

I was not sold yet, but I found no answer to the question. And another question also ran in my head: how
many of the *Albicore's* surgeons had already been sold?
What had Paul done with Doctor Tim?

Well, in time, we drew in to make the port of Little
Massa about which I had so often thought. Edmond Quichet was famed to have burned it; now here I was, about
to enter it. From the talk that had gone about the decks,
I knew that it was a safe harbour, but dangerous above

most ports at the coming in and going out. I came up
from my examination of Buddy, to find Pegg and the
other officers all staring at the surf ahead. To me, it
seemed to boil and spout; these experienced men seemed
to think it nothing.

"It can't be bad," Staggers was saying. "They'd burn
us off else."

"What is 'burn you off'?" I asked.

Staggers looked at me with pity. Tulp said, "They raise
a smoke to keep you from trying it."

They had sent a hand aloft with a glass, to see if there
were other ships in the port. Up aloft, a man could see
over the outlying rocky islets which broke the water.
This man hailed, "One ship in the port, sir."

"Just our luck," Pegg said, with an oath. "She'll have
got that gang. We're too late."

"What is she?" Staggers called.

"Foreigner of some sort, sir; looks like a Portugee
pink."

Pegg rubbed his hands. "Ah, well, we'll have some of
them."

He ran up the rigging to the top, took the glass and had
a look. He came down in a few minutes to say that the
ship was only a Portugee pink, partly dismantled, and
that the *Albicore* would get any slaves that were going.
We stood on towards the row of spouting and up-cata-
racting islets which fringed the harbour.

At Momboe our approach had been the signal for a
race of eager blacks, in canoes, dugouts, rafts and other
contrivances. We had been cheered by a hundred glad
savages, and piloted in by a master pilot. At Little Massa,

nobody put out to us. I could see black people on the beach ashore; not one was going to venture out, nor was I surprised, for the surf in front of us was frightful and seemed to worsen as we neared it.

I said, "The surf looks pretty bad."

Pegg snorted and said, "Surf's nothing, so long as you know the marks and keep your head. That ain't a bad surf; not what I call bad."

However, Staggers and the boatswain did not like the look of it; plainly they did call it bad; the boatswain asked, "Shall I signal for a pilot, sir?"

"Pilot? For Little Massa?" Pegg said. "I can take her in, I hope: a place as easy as this."

Like many vain men, he was ready to do a desperately silly thing to attract attention to himself. I took some of the despair from the faces near me. I could see into the lagoon or harbour now. It was exquisitely still and blue; so blue that I have seen nothing bluer. It was bluer than any flower or jewel or sky. It was one great placid flower, one burning jewel, or the sky of a dream. It was so blue that it made one cry aloud from delight. But to get to it, the way to it was through the Clashing Rocks and a rage like Brynhild's fire. Pegg had been in and out of it before; he knew, what I did not, that the entrance, though narrow, was well-defined, well-marked by guiding-marks, and without bends or any sunken rocks. If you aimed straight and had wind enough you got through.

By this time, he was taking her in, and we had a nearer view of the surf, which had a rage and a roaring that would have frightened a saint. It broke with an untellable fury on a big rock to the west of the passage we had to make. As we were coming close to this violence the wind began to fail; I saw the sails crumple and empty, steady to the full, then crumple and flog. I knew that without power we were ruined. I gave the ship up as lost, for we were in the catch of the outer rollers and seemed to have lost all power of independent movement. The weight of the Atlantic Ocean seemed behind us; some of it was running under us and rising and rising, and hurling itself into indescribable ruin high over our masts and then right under our noses. I could see that the crew expected the ship to strike. I saw them get over to the starboard side, to be away from the shock. Then suddenly, before Pegg, who was as white as a sheet, had found any order to give, if any order would have been of use to us, we felt the ship plucked, as though by a terrific force, and spun away in the backwash, in a current that ran us as a mill-race runs a forget-me-not blossom. We went spinning away in the rush of this current, a nine-knot current, so one of the men said, without any means of helping ourselves, for the sails were flogging loose, and we had no sweeps out. To be brief, we went smash into a rock, which flung us for an instant on our side. Something crashed and ground below me, and certain light things came down from aloft. Then we were clear of whatever we had hit and were swimming gently in to shelter, across that exquisite blue calm, where we anchored near the town.

"Just where I was in the *Jonas and Silas*," Pegg said. "Just the very same berth. What were you dogs quitting station for, just now? Have you never seen surf before? If we'd had to go about, then, with you off your stations, we might well a gone ashore. What is it, Carpenter?"

The Carpenter and his mates had gone below at the first crash of our hitting. They came up, now, to say that she'd been hit pretty hard in the old place, and that the water was coming into her; not much, but you could not tell yet.

Little Massa was a pleasanter place than Momboe, being so much more open. There was no sinister bush; there were no brooding hills. The town was on both sides of a river, which was nearly as blue as the harbour. It had an aspect almost gay from the profusion of scarlet flowers growing there. When I wearied of the glare of these, I had but to turn to the blueness of the harbour. I have never seen a blue to equal it. I cannot describe it, nor give you any effective simile; but if I were treating any melancholy case, I would try to send him to Little Massa, to gaze on the blueness of the sea. If that could not cure him, what would? All colour must proceed from light; all light must proceed from the Source of light, Who is the only cure of our darkness.

When we had entered the harbour, the native canoes rushed out to greet us, as at Momboe. However, Pegg called to the hands to rig out boarding nettings, as he wasn't going to dash a lot of good dolly till he knew what he'd get by it. He was going to see what slaves there might be, first of all. If there were slaves, then dolly. If no slaves, not a drop of dolly. It was strange to see what a change for the worse power had made in Pegg. Well, it is as searching a test as helplessness, perhaps. A change from generosity to meanness is a sad and bad sign. It was a bad sign here, and bad for us, for the blacks were furious at not being treated, and held up the fish and fruit

which they had brought for us, so that our men might
see what we were losing. However, a Captain commands,
and hands obey. Pegg and Staggers went ashore to see
about the slaves, while we remained on board, with orders to let no black aboard. This order was obeyed, but
the canoes were soon under our bows and a trade of a
meagre kind was done for fish and fruit and tobacco leaf.

The Portuguese vessel lay about a quarter-of-a-mile
from us. She looked in a sad way, partly dismantled
aloft. Two melancholy men were on her deck; they waved
to us from time to time, and seemed to invite us aboard.

Down below, our carpenters worked at the new leak,
and presently called to Tulp to rig the pumps and free
her, so that they might know what the new leak amounted
to. The men pumped the ship free. After this, the carpenters came on deck completely exhausted and said
that they couldn't come at the injury without shifting
the water-casks, which would need the Captain's orders.
They said that the ship had probably been holed, and had
broken off the rock that holed her. They advised Tulp to
try to get a mat or, as they called it, a thrumming ready,
and then to get some blacks to dive down to see what and
where the trouble was. But by this time, the few blacks
who had dealt with us had abandoned us, calling us various things in songs. Tulp translated some of them to me:

"They do not give their friends anything,
    They are like dog with bone; they say, 'I eat this. No
        other have some.'
    They are like the mangy buffalo. They smell and not
        know how bad they smell."

We had lost face.

Pegg and Staggers came back hot and cross for dinner. Both were cursing their luck, and let it be known that the slaves of whom Peter had told us had been at Little Massa only two days before, and that the agent had sent them back to Bimbi and Momboe, thinking that a mistake had been made.

"They've sent them back, if you please," Pegg snorted. "Four hundred Samboes and Talliks; enough to make our voyage. They've sent 'em back, all that way by road, where a hundred of 'em'll die. Now they're forty mile upcountry, and we won't get 'em at all."

"You could send a runner or a galloper after them," I suggested.

"And a fat lot of good that'll do," Pegg said. "The man in charge of them is Billy Pock-mark. He knew at Bimbi that there was some mistake, but that fool Peter insisted he should bring 'em here. Nothing'll make him turn back here."

"Have you tried?" I asked.

"Tried? Of course, I have. I've sent the runners after him from the King."

"And are there no slaves here, then, at all?" I asked.

"Yes, there are; but that damned black King is sour because I haven't crossed his palm. He asks forty-five pound a man. He'll not get that from me; never."

It was the custom of the Coast to bribe the Kings before trading. The Kings expected it and exacted it. Pegg knew this very well; but, having made up his mind not to pay the toll, he was stubborn on the point. He had now angered the entire black population. I judged that he would get very scant consideration while at Little Massa.

The talk ran about the slaves and the Portuguese ship. There was something about that ship which had haunted me. Her name was the *Virgin of Busaco;* so much I had seen through Tulp's glass. Now I learned that she had been away down to leeward, "away south, beyond the Sixteen Peaks," where her Captain had sold guns and powder to the M'gai, for gold dust. The M'gai were the coming Nation, so the tale went. This Captain had then persuaded the M'gai to invite a hunting party of Matablancos to a feast; it was a large party of Matas, more than a hundred, all men. At the feast, this Captain, who was a mulatto, bribed the M'gai to drug the Matas' drink with what they call "bwala" or sleep-drink. This the M'gai did; nearly all the Matas were stupefied, and taken as slaves aboard the *Virgin of Busaco,* which put to sea at once while they were still unconscious. It had been a sudden idea of this mulatto; he had neither the food nor the drink for nearly a hundred men beside his crew. He had to put in to Little Massa for yams and water. Here, he died, being poisoned, as was thought, by his officer, who later in the same day was killed by a Mata. As the ship was now without an officer, the King of Massa took the slaves ashore to his own slave-sheds, "to see they no die." A Danish ship had called there a day or two later. The King had offered the Danes the slaves, but the Danes had refused; "they would never buy Matas, who would never submit to slavery, and would infallibly, sooner or later, kill their masters."

The Danes had, however, bought some of the Portuguese ship's rigging from her crew, and had then, being short-handed, offered this crew a passage to windward; all, except the unhappy two whom I had seen on the *Virgin's* deck, had taken the chance and had gone.

So the story went. The talk now turned on what was to be done. It was siesta time, during which no native would lift a finger. After siesta time, Pegg hoped to get native divers down to examine the damage to the ship's side. He planned to hear their report, and perhaps lay the ship upon her side while the carpenters repaired her. During the few days which this would take, the runners might reach the marching slave-gangs, and cause them to turn back. I said that a good present to the King might cause the slaves to appear at once. I said that the natives were very shrewd, and might well have the slaves waiting near by, in which case a barrel of dolly and five pounds' worth of tinsel would be money well spent. Pegg snorted and said that that might be a doctor's way of doing business; it wasn't his. The King might whistle for a present.

Well, the Doctor was right. The natives were now furious with Pegg for his meanness, and the King gave orders that we were not to be served. The divers would not examine the ship's side, the fishermen and fruit-sellers would not trade with us. We stayed there day after day, waiting for reports from the runners. Pegg went ashore daily, to speak with the King. He was insulted, kept waiting, and put off with lies. All the time, the ship lay in the port, leaking from both leaks, neither of which could be reached by the carpenters. The two Portuguese men in the *Virgin* begged to be taken into our crew. Pegg refused, saying that he wasn't going to have papists in a Christian ship, thank you.

After some days of this, a big Guadeloupean ship came into the harbour, with a salute to the King, of flags, guns and trumpets. The King came off to her in her barge, and went ashore from her dressed in a new scarlet coat with a cocked hat. He had been treated as he thought fitting. The next morning, that ship received the four hundred slaves which Pegg had been told were on their way to Bimbi. The next morning, having filled her water and loaded yams for the passage, she went off upon her way, leaving us in rage and despair. Pegg had missed his market and lost his voyage.

The only consolation was the very poor one, that the Guadeloupean had refused to ship the Matas. They were still to be had, some seventy-odd, but it was not to be denied that two shrewd slave-captains had refused to have anything to do with them. The Matas had a bad name. Nobody had enslaved them yet; they died rather than submit. Still, there they were, and no other slaves were being offered or were likely to come in. Pegg now talked of getting out of the place and going to Cabo Amarilho, the naval station. "Now that Paul's with the angels," he said, "there's no need to avoid Cabo. We'd get slaves there, sure." I had every need to avoid Cabo, and you may be sure that my heart sank. Staggers said that you only got a poor type of slave at Cabo; the district had been gone through too thoroughly; all the good ones had long since been taken. He added, "I'd take those Matas, if it was me. I never saw a slave yet a white man couldn't tame, one way or another."

"I'm not going to pay forty-five pounds a man for a slave," Pegg said. "What with the passage, and losses and the seasoning, and they're a sullen lot who'll season bad, they'd come to double that to make a profit. Who'd pay ninety pounds for a man?"

"Any planter," Staggers said. "They're short; they've had almost none for three seasons."

Staggers had his way, of course. It was decided that I should come ashore next morning, to have a look at these men. Pegg judged that they might be a sickly lot, as well as sullen; I had better have a look at them. If I approved them as healthy, he would buy them. I believe that Staggers was right, and that the planters would have paid almost any price that season for a strong man-slave. One strong man's work would have paid his purchase price in one season. These were said to be very strong men, in appearance; real Matas. Well, I had heard all about the Matas; now I was to see them.

Just as we were deciding this matter, there came a hail from the port:

"Ho, the *Albicore*. Is Captain Ashplant aboard?"

Tulp, who was on deck, in charge, called, "No; he's dead," and a minute later came down and said, "It's old Billy Crackers, sir; Puggy's brother. He'd like to come aboard, if he may."

"That old fraud," Pegg said. "Yes, let him come aboard. He may know of slaves."

"He's just come from the leeward, sir," Tulp said.

"Well, he will know what's doing there, at least," Pegg said.

We all went on deck to see Billy Crackers. I had heard

of him often enough, of course, and was glad to see him in
the flesh. There he was on deck, talking to Puggy. He was
dressed as a native. He was burned and stained almost
black from exposure to the sun and the constant use of oil
in which nut-ash had been mixed. He wore a sort of
feather-kilt, no other garment. His hair had grown long
and had been worked up with clay and oil, into a headdress which served instead of a hat. He had a long ivory
skewer thrust through his nose. It was sharp at both ends
and stained scarlet. He looked extremely healthy and
cheerful. He was the only white man present who seemed
to be either.

"Why, why, if I don't see Captain Pegg," he began.
"Well, sir, welcome to the Coast and congratulations on
the command. Here we are again, you see. Good old Billy
Crackers; you can't kill him with an axe. And now, Captain, will you taste some of my chee-chee? Boy, go. You
bring him chee-chee. De Cap him drink."

He had a sloop alongside; he had built and rigged her
himself; she made his home most of the time, as he went
about the Coast, peddling, fishing and doing odd jobs of
trade and barter. His two boys, or black servants, who
sailed everywhere with him, brought up a gourd of a sour-
sweet native drink flavoured with gin; we all drank to
the trade from it.

"And now, Cap," Billy said, "what's the cruel trouble?
Your brow is in the mists of care. That's a mistake in this
climate and in any other. Why aren't you slaved? I can
smell you ain't."

"No slaves to be had," Pegg said shortly. "They're very
few and dear as love."

"Not to be had?" Billy said. "Well, that's a state of things'll soon be cured. The M'gai are moving. You go along to Sixteen Peaks and that place Tsika south of it, you'll get all the slaves you want, and dirt-cheap. Hundreds of 'em. The M'gai are going to root out all the Coast tribes and live there. Slaves? You will bless the name of William Crackers when you see the cargo you'll get there. And you'll be the first to open trade with the M'gai. They'll give you any slaves you want for powder. What's this old thief here in Little Massa asking for slaves, cock and hen?"

"Forty-five pounds for a cock; he hasn't any hens in store," Staggers said.

Billy whistled. "Never knew prices like that," he said. "But you get along to the M'gai, and you'll get your account. They'll give you any cock you like for two pounds of powder; and a hen for a half-a-pound of bullets. They'll ask you to take the slaves as a gift, they've got so many."

"Look here, Billy," Pegg said, "is this the truth?"

"Of course it's the truth; the truth and me's brothers born. I've been in Tsika, and seen 'em. But it's no good your going there. That was twelve days ago; no; I lie; it was a week more. You go to Sixteen Peaks; that is where they'll be by the time you get there. Then, if you don't slave right up to the hatch, you call me the son of an unmarried merry female, what liked her own way best."

"Have you been in Sixteen Peaks? Did you put in there, coming here?"

"No, I've been in the islands. I've been there, of course."

"What sort of a place is it?"

"Very good. It's deserted; has been for years. There

were French pirates there once; not now. The M'gai are going there now, and that's where you'll find 'em."

"Yes," Pegg said. "But will they trade?"

"Boy, they're panting for trade. What they want is powder. Powder, rum and Christianity are what they want from us. You give 'em powder and they'll lick your boots. On that I swop my solemn sam. I see you won't believe me; well, have it your own way. I've told you."

He turned to his boy for confirmation. "Say, you boy," he cried. "Don' I tell him tlue? M'gai hab plenty slave? Him dash de slave for bang bang?"

His boy grinned and said, "M'gai got slave, oh, like de waves of de sea."

After this, Pegg and Staggers took Billy below, to give him a drink and also to trade beads and small wares for some of the gold dust, which he carried in a gourd in the sloop. I do not doubt that Billy held his own in the bargaining with them. During their talk, it was arranged that Billy and I should go ashore the next morning. I was to look over the Matas who were for sale; Billy would bargain with the King for them. If Billy could beat down the King's price, and I could pass them as healthy, Pegg would buy them, ship them, and sail for the Sixteen Peaks. There, he would probably find a big settlement of M'gai, with hordes of slaves. He would be able to careen the *Albicore* in the harbour, find and stop the leaks, ship the slaves and make a fortune.

At least, this was what Billy foretold. There was a genial warmth of happy hope in Billy; it is a rare quality in white men, and very rare in the old. Billy had it as though from a kind of inner sun. I must say that I did not and do not wish to have that kind of old age myself, going about three-quarters naked, peddling goods to savages; yet I liked the old man, and looked forward to hearing from him about the *Hannibal*.

I went ashore with him the next morning; the ship's boat took us in. I had a sort of—what shall I say?—oddness of feeling, about sitting next to a nearly naked savage, with tusks in his nose. It was an odd feeling, in one who had been in Newgate Hold, and in the hangman's cart, yet I had it. There was no trace of unease in Billy. His eye was bright and his wicked old mouth merry. He made me remember a remark made by a Frenchman to my father: "So you ask the good God for wisdom and for guidance? Perhaps. But I ask him only for a good digestion and no memory." Billy had a good digestion and no memory at all for anything unpleasant. He talked all the time. As the boat took us in, a shark drew up to look at us. Billy said, "That's a slave-shark. You can tell 'em by the white snout. He knows your ship's a slaver, even though she's got no slaves aboard. The smell stays. They've got the noses of bloodhounds, sharks; they smell Death coming, days before. They won't look at fish after tasting man; cannibals won't, either. Old Captain Voyal said he often had sharks follow him all the Middle Passage just for the slaves that went overboard; he would get to know them by sight, and always knew from them when a slave was going to die. They knew, just as they say a wolf knows; there they were. They could only know that from smell. Away south of Tsika there, all the Coast men are cannibals. They like white man better than black; him good chop, all better as pig."

As we were carried to the slave-sheds in litters (Billy had a way of getting this done for us, which Pegg would certainly not have done), I asked him why he took to the Coast, which most white men hated.

"I like it," he said. "I did from the first, when I came here in the *Hannibal,* Captain Cringle. I said, 'This is the life for William Crackers,' and it has been. I like the sun, I like the life. Where would I get the sun and the life in England? No place. In England, you're always doing this or that because it's done, or because if you don't, you're marked at once. Here I do what I please, which is what I always wanted to do. I like natives. They're a great deal better lot than white men, take them on the whole; and man for man, there's no question. It's my belief, they'll boot us out of the Coast, and that within the next twenty years, no, in the next ten. The M'gai won't have the white man here, depeopling the whole land. They'll boot the white man out, and a good job, too; it's a dirty job, this slaving."

I said that I agreed, and asked about the M'gai.

"They're one of these warrior tribes," he said. "My son, when you see the M'gai, you'll know what a man can be. I'm strong myself, few white men stronger, but I'm short. There's no man in the M'gai less than six feet. They're coming north and west, and they'll put some sense in the Kings here. They'll stop the slaving; they've got some sense. They won't let a lot of dirty traders poison all the young men for miles round with doctored dolly, and sell all the strong men oversea. You fine fellows, the slavers, 'll have to shut up shop. Not but what the M'gai may be a problem in themselves," he added.

"They're very free with their spears; him likee blood too much."

But by this time, we were at the sheds, where the King's slave-master was waiting for us. He was spoken of by Pegg as "Old Pilly Pepper-Pot," goodness knows why. He was a short, squat, fat, pock-marked savage, grey in the face, being some kind of a mongrel, and walking with a waddle. His greyness made his face like a mask, in which his little astute eyes were the only living things. His nose had a golden moon hanging from it. He wore an old scarlet uniform coat over his loin-cloth, and had a cutlass at his side.

"Ha," he said, with insolence. "Why not Pegg come? You only common mans. I not show good slaves to common mans. I save my face."

"Don't try it," Billy said, "or you'll get it trodden on. None of that with me. Let's see these boys, and less talk about it."

I have described the slave-sheds of Momboe. These were much the same, except that here there was no fever. There were many bold brown hawks cruising about for garbage. The slave-smell, of dirt, poverty, and misery, which clung about the hold of the *Albicore,* was sickeningly strong all about the place.

"That's the house-flag of the trade, that stink," Billy said. "And 'Handsome is as flowerlike smells' is my motto."

We ducked under the eaves with Pilly and entered the shed.

I had been told that about a hundred of these men had been taken. There were not nearly that number there now; not more than seventy-five, I judged. As we came into the shed, every man turned to us, and fixed us with a stare. I knew from the quality of the look that these men were very different men from the wrecks who had lain dying at Momboe. These men were warriors, with hard, clean-cut faces. They had been trained to be indifferent to suffering, to endure all things and to shew no trace. I knew, too, that they summed us all up as we entered. Pilly, I could see, they meant some day to torture to death in the savagest way they could devise; Pilly they knew and despised; myself they saw to be useless to them. The light of scrutiny died out of their eyes; they lapsed into apathy. I looked along the chained rows for any sick or dying men. They were not sick; the flies swarmed about them; they must have been in desperate discomfort, but not a sign shewed on any face that they felt anything but at peace. These were the Matablancos of whom I had been told. I must say that my heart went out to them, not in pity so much as in admiration.

"Dey fine boys," said Pilly Pepper-Pot. "Dey work, oh, how dey work! De best boys ever to work. Dey worth any money. What you gib? Hey? What you gib?"

"These are Matas," said Billy Crackers. "Dey no good. Dey bad boys. Dey go killy killy. You take shoot dis lot. You give him sharkee; you bury. Dese not work. No can make work. Too bad boy. No white mans gib penny piece for all him." He turned to me, and said in a low voice, "Just go over 'em, Doctor. A lot of 'em must have died, but that bwala they gave them is a poison. Askanie-root in their grog, was what did for them. Askanie's ticklish stuff and not all men can stand it. I guess that twenty of 'em died of it."

He turned to Pilly, and asked, "Him go die? Him drink bwala and go cluck-cluck?"

"Some of him," Pilly said. "Some got away. Not any more get away."

I turned to look at the slaves in turn. They were magnificent men; they had no fever, nor any visible infection. I went down the line slowly, then slowly returned, gazing hard at each man. At my first coming into the shed, I had noticed a man about halfway down the line. He sat or reclined in a way unlike the posture of any other. Dr. Copshrews had always urged me to look with attention at that person who was at all or in any way unlike his fellows; I, therefore, had noticed this man.

When I had gone down the line and returned, I went to this man, whose eyes were steadfast upon mine. I had made up my mind that he sat or lay in an odd position not from genius, but because his irons had chafed him and the chafe had ulcerated. This I found to be the case.

"Mr. Crackers," I said, "get some brandy for me. This man must have this chafe washed and bandaged, or he'll have a fearful place here, which may suppurate and kill him."

Crackers came forward, examined the chafe, and spoke to the man in Mata; the man replied in Palaver that the sore would surely kill him, but what matter? If he died, he would die.

Finding that he spoke the Palaver, I spoke to him, and told him that I could ease his suffering. With Crackers' help, I was able to wash and dress not only his chafes but those of a dozen others. I found that the unusual man, the man who had drawn my attention, was a lesser chieftain of the Matas. In the Palaver, which most of them used, he was called "Deray" or "de Ray," which meant, roughly, "the King," the leader of the party. He was a young man, but was no doubt a fine fellow. Nearly all the party had one or more white, raised scars at the sides of their brows. Billy told me that this was their "man-tally,' and that a warrior put one such mark on himself for each man he had killed in battle. Now Deray had seven of these, although I suppose he was only about twenty-three.

When I had finished washing and dressing the chafes, this Deray spoke to me in the Palaver, using a kind more full of French than our sort. He asked me, "What will they do to us?"

I told him, "They send you in ship far to the west. Perhaps sell you, and try to make you dig."

About a dozen of the slaves asked him what I had said. When he explained, a kind of derisive laugh passed along the benches. They were laughing at the thought of being put to dig, they, the warriors of the Matablancos, whose women dug for them. The very thought of being put to dig was joy to them. A spade was some sort of weapon, and to use it they would have to have their hands free. Let them but be put to dig, and somebody's skull would be the first thing dug. These men were going to be dangerous till they were dead. Surely Pegg would not buy them. If he did, what sane planter in the west would buy them? These were terrible fellows, hard, scarred, tattooed and awful. Every man of them had more than one white "man-tally"; one man had nineteen. I looked at old Billy Crackers, who was considering them with thought.

I said to him, "Surely these men will never be slaves."

"So they say Britons won't be," Billy answered, "but a lot of 'em are, and damned unhappy ones."

Pepper-pot, who had been listening with much acuteness, said, "Dey make de best slaves, dese boys. You gib him big tick, go bang-bang, beatee beatee, he very good boy; oh, he dig so good."

I did not agree with him. When we were out of the shed, I said to Billy, "You won't advise Pegg to buy these?"

"I never knew men buy Matas before, or have the chance to," Billy said. "If once it's known that Englishmen have bought Matas——" He shook his head, leaving the sentence unfinished.

We went back aboard with our report. I said that the men were seemingly sound, without visible infection. Billy said that it would be not only money thrown away, but just wicked foolishness to buy Matas. It would be known all over the Coast at once. The Matas would never forgive it; they would at once join the M'gai and wipe out every factory from Cabo to Tsika, and cook and eat every white man in the trade. "No man buys Matas," he said. "You take a wise man's advice; have nothing to do with it."

"I'm not going to leave seventy able-bodied men to be bought by the next comer," Pegg said, "in a bad season like this, with all the West Indies just rotting for the want of slaves. I'm going to take what offers."

"God help you, then," Billy said.

"He helps those who help themselves," Pegg said.

"I'll tell you a thing," Billy answered. "You're a business man. You understand your business best, no doubt. I'm only one who goes around and sees things. It would pay you a thousand times over, to buy these Matas, and take 'em straight to leeward, to somewheres near their people; Sixteeen Peaks or so. Tell 'em from the first that you're going to take 'em home. Treat 'em good and take 'em home. Let 'em go scot-free; even if you pay fifty pounds a man for 'em. If you make friends with the Matas, you'll get all the slaves you'll want till the day you die. If you try to slave these boys, you'll pay according, and white men for a hundred years'll pay. I've been among Matas; and I know how to deal with 'em. I tell you true."

"Well, now you tell us something else," Pegg said.

Billy was vexed at being insulted by one whom he considered as a foolish boy; he went aboard his sloop and shoved off, and we saw him no more. Pegg bargained all the afternoon with the King for these Matas, and at last bought them and paid for them. They were, no doubt, hoping to escape while being brought on board, but great pains were used to check them. Only one man got away; and though they put dogs upon his trail at once, he was not recaptured. The seventy-three others were brought in bonds on board, and laid on the shelves in the lower hold in the airless, stinking heat, in heavy irons. Newgate Hold was fairyland to that hold. What Pegg paid for them in the end we never knew. Probably it was some big price which he felt ashamed to speak of.

He was uneasy about the purchase after the men were

aboard. Billy Crackers was known to have great knowledge of all the tribes; Billy's advice was not to be quite
set aside. Yet greed was strong in Pegg. He hoped to
profit by Billy's advice, to make friends with the M'gai,
and buy their slaves cheap, and at the same time, to dis-
regard his advice and take these Matas to the Indies.

"Any man with legs and arms'll fetch his weight in
gold this year," he said. "And you, Doc, understand that
these blacks aren't like white patients, to be fawned on
and pampered. They're property, to be kept marketable,
whether they like it or don't."

"If you wish them to be kept marketable," I said,
"you'd better have them out of the hold to begin with.
They're used to the free air."

"They're used to murder and plenty else they won't
get again," Pegg said. "They are blacks; they'll stand
the hold very well. Some'll die, of course; some always
do; they wouldn't be human if they didn't. Your job is
to watch 'em. When any of 'em comes out sick and spotty,
say so; and we'll have him overboard before he infects
the rest. That's the doctor's job; stop the infection."

We were getting ready to sail from Massa, in fact were
preparing to sail the next day, when a small incident occurred, which had its effects upon our fortunes. At
supper, Staggers was called on deck, to see some native,
who had come off in a canoe to see him. Staggers went
on deck, and presently returned, looking a little askance
and odd. About half-an-hour later, when we had turned
in to sleep, we were roused by a persistent shrill yapping
from somewhere on deck. It was at first plaintive; then
it became querulous and broken-hearted. It was impossi-

ble to sleep through it. Pegg came from his cabin swearing. "Where is that damn dog? It seems on deck there." He slipped up to the deck and called, "Watchman, there; what is that infernal dog?"

"It's Mr. Staggers' dogs, sir," the watchman said.

"What Mr. Staggers' dogs?"

"Two dogs Mr. Staggers bought, sir; they're in the pigsty."

Staggers by this time had reached the deck. "They're two dogs I bought, sir, to hunt the slaves with, in case they get away."

"They ain't going to get away. What dogs? You never said nothing to me about no dogs. Who said you could have dogs? I hate dogs anywhere. It's a woman's habit to have dogs. Nasty, messy, stinking things what spreads leprosy. Hark at the yap they make. I could as soon sleep through earthquake. I'll not have the damn things. Overboard with 'em."

"But, sir, I paid for 'em."

"More fool you. Where are they?"

He came aft in a few minutes; the watchman had produced the two dogs. They were odd little things, with long noses and very long ears. They are common enough in all the Coast, and I believe Staggers was right in saying that they would serve to hunt escaped slaves with; their noses are said to be very delicate.

"Pitch them overboard," Pegg said. "Perhaps then we'll get some sleep."

Staggers protested, but overboard the dogs went. It did not harm the dogs at all; it was what they wanted; they swam ashore and ran home. But it did harm our

society. Staggers swore to get his own back, on a man
who had tried to drown his "pore little pets." "A man
who would drown dogs would drown his grandmother—
pore little things. And I give a new pair of duck breeches
for them, too, what I'd hardly worn at all."

Well . . . we sailed from Little Massa, despised and
mocked by the blacks, to whom we seemed stingy and
without face, for giving so little "dash," and also crazy,
for shipping Matas as slaves. Our crew was scared of our
cargo; the Matas were dreaded everywhere. Still, when
men are chained prone upon shelves, so that they can
barely turn over, and are then battened and barred in
for the night, and the only possible exits are two narrow,
closely guarded holes down which loaded swivel-guns
are pointing, their chance of being terrible is dimin-
ished.

"There's nothing like good chain," one of the boatswains said to me. "And you need it with these fellows;
they're so artful. It's these first days are the dangerous
ones. After a week on the shelves, they aren't quite so
uppish."

We were bound now for the Sixteen Peaks, of which
I had so often thought. In a few days, I might expect
to see them. I say a few days, for we were now well to
leeward, in waters where the winds died out, and left
only a few stagnant draughts.

On leaving Massa, with great difficulty, I got the
slaves the afternoon privilege of a quarter-pint of water,
and begged that this mercy might be continued every
afternoon, in the worst of the heat. It was only granted
when I said that the men would surely die of heat-stroke
without it, and then only on the condition that I myself

pumped the water and served it. Pegg thought that I should be too proud to do this, but I did it. He mocked me for doing it.

"Here's one of these Friends of Africa, going round bottle-holding to a lot of stinking savages. This is the way to keep the white man's face, I must say."

However, on the next day, the slave-guards, the trusty, tough boatswains' mates, reported while we were at breakfast, that the slaves had got the "sullens"; that is, they were in a conspiracy not to eat or drink.

Pegg asked, "Are you sure? It ain't their religion coming out?"

"No," the mates replied, "it's the sullens. They took their chop and slabber last night; but this morning we found it all spat out."

I said, "Very likely they're seasick."

"Seasick," Pegg said with much contempt. "We know when a slave's seasick, I hope. No. It's the sullens; their cursed black froward natures."

"It's certainly the sullens," one of the mates said. "I seen 'em doing it; spitting it out; we tried 'em with some slabber just now; just to see."

"Right," Pegg said, "that'll be their chief. He sends round the word and they all take it from him, and starve 'emselves dead. Never neglect sullens. You get up the three who seem to be chiefs; we'll start Jouncer on 'em at once. Christianity says you ain't to kill yourself, nor let another kill hisself. I'll give 'em good Christianity from Jouncer."

He went to a locker and produced some grim iron appliances.

"These are Jouncers," Pegg explained. "Put one of

them in Juba's mouth, with the spikes and that, then
you've only to turn this screw to heave his jaws apart,
and then the chop has to go down and the slabber on the
top. If they don't know their good, I do. We'll have up
the two or three what get the respect. When they've
had nice chop, we'll see if we can't persuade 'em to dance
a little to shew they like it." He was watching me, and
saw my disgust. "We don't go to college," he said, "to
learn how to doctor slaves. If they lose appetite with us,
we make 'em eat, and if we find 'em sullen, we make 'em
dance. A good cut or two with a cat'll make a big black
Mantacaw dance like Harriet Lane, and a turn with the
Jouncer'll make a rabbit eat like a wolf. Sense is what we
go by, here, let me tell you."

I said that, from what I had seen of the men in the
hold, his methods wouldn't succeed. "They'll die," I
said. "Those men are a tough lot. You won't bend them;
they'll die."

"You'd like 'em to die, wouldn't you?" he said.

"Yes," I answered, "I'd rather they died than live to
be slaves."

"They're not going to die, nor are you going to let
'em die," he said.

"I am under medical oath," I said, "not to let anyone
die if I can prevent it. I warn you that those men'll die,
if you try your methods with them. They've got something in them that's stronger than you."

"We'll see that," Pegg said. "I rather think we'll win.
Iron is stronger than most things. Iron and pain'll make
a lot of difference to even the proudest Juba. You might
remember that, too, for your own good."

"If that be a threat," I said, "let me warn you, for your own good, not to threaten me. I have some very good friends who may make it exceedingly uncomfortable for you."

He knew that I referred to the Governors to whom I had letters, and to those unknown, but doubtless powerful friends who had caused me to be received at a moment's notice.

"I can't stay jawing here," he said. "I've got my duty to do."

I, too, had my duty to do. I had to examine every member of the crew for marks of fever or disease. While I was doing this (and there were four in need of treatment), Pegg applied his methods to three who the mates said were the chiefs. They were not the chiefs: they were the three most easily brought on deck. After this was over (and I saw nothing of it, or I would have protested), it fell to me to make my first examination of the slaves in the shelves. One of the boatswains' mates attended me with a lantern. I may say that, after my little tussle with Pegg, I had some fear that he might chain me with the slaves, for sale later. However, I judged that he needed me as a surgeon at present; my turn would come later.

I went with my lantern-bearer along the 'tween-decks to the little manhole which led to the tiers. The 'tween-decks was as hot as any closed space under a wooden roof in the tropics can be. But when I came to the manhole to the hold the heat of that lower place was something that one could lean against. It had been shut in all night, save for the slender pipe of one windsail and two little barred holes.

The heat was but a small part of the terror of that darkness.

I had often been told in conversation round the cabin table, that all ships stank below the water, even in the colder climates. They said that water would seep in, by one way or another, and accumulate below, and swiftly rot into something that stank like skunks, the "bilge-water" which so many have mentioned. This smell hung about the lower parts of the ship at all times, and mixed with other smells, of dry-rot, and wet-rot, ship's canvas new, tar, not very fresh provisions, cargo, paint, rope and the presence of rats and mice. Now to all these rank and rancid stinks was added the reek of seventy prisoners, chained prone upon the shelves. The boatswain's mate noticed that the smell affected me.

"It come up very ripe this morning, sir," he said. "You'll get used to it. Use is second nature. It gets thicker than this in a busy season. This is nothing. I've known men faint, going round with the chow; but that was in the lower tiers, when we were running full."

"How can men live in air worse than this?" I asked.

"Why," he said, "they do live, the most of 'em. The aim of most folk is to live; even though it mayn't be fun, they'd rather live than not live. But these fellas aren't like Christians. They get something like this from their own choice in the villages where they're at home. If you'll let me go first, sir, I'll hand you down; this ladder is very steep. Hold the lantern, will you, Bill?"

Bill held the lantern, and I came down into the space of the hold, in a heat and stench such as made even Newgate seem a Paradise.

"It's these lads we believed were the ringleaders," the man explained. "They seem took very bad."

I could not at once make out where I was, for the hold was very dark. Bill's lantern cast a yellowish glow about the place. I could see gleams upon chains and upon stanchions. I did not see the slaves at the first look, only stood, trying not to be sick in the fog of stench in which I was. Bill's lantern burned dimly unless he held it up. The place was full of noises, mostly uncanny, as a ship's hold always must be. The water went lamenting past as we slipped along; down below me, the water gurgled and splashed in the bilges; the planks creaked and whined; little slow, stripping, progressing crackings ran along the beams as she rolled now one way, then back; there was a kind of drumming noise of wind coming down the wind-sail, flapping the edge which secured it. Above all these noises, I was aware of the presence of the misery of many men, who were lying close to me, breathing heavily, moaning now and then, in rage or stupor, and shifting about, with many clinkings of chain. Gradually, I came to see in the darkness a sort of long, low shelf or slab on which dark figures were packed, heads towards me. A long line of heads was on each side of my ankles. The men had been packed there as close as they would lie.

"We put 'em low down," Bill explained, "for if we have a good buy down Coast, we'll have room for two or three tiers above these. And we stick them heads nearest so as they can't kick, and we can drag 'em out easier if they up and die on us."

"Let me see the men who are sick," I said. "Hold the lantern so that I can see."

He held the lantern in turn over three faces; all three were close to the hatchway. Being the easiest to come at, they had been chosen for Jouncer. The three men had all been cut with the cat-of-nine-tails, and all three mouths were bloody from the Jouncer. The three presented the same symptoms, which were new to me. They were unconscious; they did not respond to voice or touch; their eyes were inverted, and their pulses very slight, so slight that I knew that they were in an extreme of weakness. I did not understand it. I asked the men if they had been flogged with great severity. "No," they said, "they only give 'em a dozen or so, more in fun than anything, just to make 'em dance. We always touch 'em up to make 'em dance. It was nothing." I said that they were scored and cut with the lashes, and that didn't look like fun. To this they repeated that "a seaman would have thought nothing of it; just nothing at all."

However, these men were not seamen, and did think of it. For all that I could do, all three died before noon, and were flung overboard.

"That's one of their tricks," Pegg said. "That's their sullen spite."

I said, "I told you that these men would die, if you tried your methods on them. They have died. These men have something in them that will beat you every time you pit yourself against them."

To my astonishment, Tulp spoke up. He was a little drunk, having somehow found some rum. Whenever he was a little drunk, strange knowledge shone from Tulp; it shone now. "The Doctor's right, sir," he said. "These leeward warrior tribes can all will themselves dead.

They're taught the trick young, in case they're caught in battle. Old Captain Quoin told me he'd seen a hundred will themselves dead at once, 'all to be dead by daybreak'; and they were. They just settle down and die. You'll have all these Matas dead the same way, if you try."

"I'll give 'em something to die for," Pegg said savagely.

"Wait a moment, Captain," I said. "Let me try speaking a little to these Matas. They're wild savages and cannot know what is being done to them. Let me tell them and see if I can't persuade them to food and so forth. Since force won't work with them, let me try persuasion."

"Try it and be damned," he said, "and you'll soon see where you get."

I lost no time in trying it. I slipped down into that hell upon sea, the lower hold, and spent all the afternoon there talking to Deray and the others. I was worn out at the end of my time there, but came away knowing that I had given them hope. I tried not to give too much hope, knowing how frightful the disappointment might be. I tried not to betray that trust which all white men feel in the presence of a multitude of black men, that they belong to the whites and must maintain the white cause. I know that I did give them hope, and that I did betray the whites; at one time these things troubled me, now they do not. I told them that we were going to Sixteen Peaks, and should be there for some days. It was that which betrayed the white men and gave the Matas hope. I did not see things very clearly in that sweltering, smelly dungeon. I only knew, from what Deray and the others said, that the orders to refuse all food and drink, which had gone abroad among them, were now withdrawn. I knew that every man among them had shed human blood in battle; they were mankillers to a man. Yet as I went about among them, I felt a kind of power of gratitude all about me, for my talk and the little cup of water which I could give to each. I knew, then, why the clergyman in Newgate had refused preferment, so that he might stay with the lost, the despairing and the mad in the condemned holds.

I went on deck, nearly dead from the heat and want of air, to tell Pegg that the men would take their food and drink thenceforth. I had talked them out of their resolves, I said (I had done nothing of the kind, of course). Pegg stared at me. I was white and sick.

"They'll die, if you don't rig another wind-sail," I said. "The man, Bill, fainted twice there."

He did not answer, but seemed to think that if Bill fainted the air might be coming up rather ripe. At any rate, as I sat on a hatch and gulped the air, he gave word for a second wind-sail to be rigged. As one was on deck, all ready, it was soon set; air and coolness in some measure did go down to that lower hell.

We loitered on towards our port, in light airs, in sweltering heat, with the leaks gaining. By now, we were in the leeward seas, in the deadest of the land of Dead Ned, further to leeward than the crew liked, in a part where slavers seldom came. We were going into the almost unknown, from which few indeed came out, whoever went in. In that leeward sea, the savages were cannibals, and death lurked in every port. We had had the Devil aboard us, the Devil and Death and Murder; now we were going on, to our dooms, so the men believed, to have our bones picked at a feast, and our skulls polished for a black King's drinking-cups.

One great boon blessed us; it rained daily. We had such an abundance of rain that I persuaded Pegg to double that little tot of afternoon water to the Matas. In the Bible there is a text, "The clouds drop fatness." Here, on the Coast of Dead Ned, the clouds dropped life itself.

We hauled a little away from the land, as that part of the Coast is little known. Indeed, the crew talked as though it were the Coast of Death himself. "A many ships have gone down to the leeward," they said, "and never returned." I asked Tulp about it; he always knew the truth of these things.

He said, "Yes; I believe it is so, but less so than it was. All down to the leeward was once a great place for pirates, Valentine and the rest. Pirates took a good many ships, at one time and another. Then all down the Coast to leeward the natives are savages and cannibals; they've taken a lot of ships, first and last, and ate the crews. And then, in many ports there is fever; ships have gone in for water and lost all their hands, and just stayed and rotted there. Then there is always a surf, and quite a lot of unknown rocks; and always this light air coming in flaws; a ship coming along here comes onto these dangers, and in the light air she can't always get away; so then she goes ashore; and if the hands get ashore the blacks eat them or the fever kills them. I wouldn't be a bit surprised to find three or four wrecks in the Sixteen Peaks."

At that moment, a man who was aloft, working on the rigging high up, gave the hail of "Land—Ooooo." He pointed to the north-eastward away on our port bow, where the heat-haze was moving away like the smoke of an autumn bonfire.

"That'll be the Sixteen Peaks," Tulp said. "I'll fetch my glass."

On the instant, it seemed to me that the heat sensibly lessened, something of a freshness seemed to come into the air. I remembered how the Admiral had said that it was always cool at the Peaks. Now here was proof; the dream was proving to be true. I gazed and gazed, seeing only the heat-haze slowly shifting. Mr. Tulp came down from aloft with his glass, and said, "If you go up into the top you'll see the tops of the Peaks quite clearly." I was sailor enough for that by this time; I borrowed his glass, went up into the mizen-top; and there, holding on tightly and steadying the glass on the rigging, I took my first look at that shore.

At first, I saw only high rolls of forest with the smoke or haze upon them. Then, rather to the eastward from these, I saw what I had so often seen in my mind, a bunch or cluster of spires bright at their spiky summits with the last of the light. Some were red, some grey; they were the Peaks of Quichet's drawing. Under them, somewhere, lay the river-mouths and the forts, and on one of those red peaks was a little cave, with a brook running through it, perhaps a King-snake on guard, and perhaps, somewhere under the floor, a King's ransom in jewels. I stood there watching and watching. All the points were tiny and distant, but very clear. They reminded me, as they had from the first, of drawings of minarets in a city of the East. I was now looking at the very Peaks themselves. Old

Admiral Cringle, then Captain, had looked at them from the *Hannibal* in just that way from perhaps that very point, and had stood on to his fate from where I then was. It thrilled me to the bone to see them thus. Then, quite suddenly, the light passed off the Peaks, and a smoke of haze drifted over the sea between me and them.

Early the next morning, when I came on deck, I saw all the Sixteen Peaks shining in the morning sun a few short miles away. I gazed at them intently, as though they were old friends given back from the grave. I decided for myself which red one held Edmond Quichet's cave. We were standing in to the shore. I could see, from the changed colours in the water, that a great river emptied there by various channels; this river had formed islets at its mouths; all were overgrown with jungle. There was no sign of man there; no settlement, no smoke; no crowds of natives leaping into canoes to race out to us for dolly. Billy Crackers had been wrong about the M'gai with their hundreds of cheap slaves. Well, here we were, away to leeward at Sixteen Peaks, and in that harbour, if we could get into it, we should have to find our leak or leave our bones there. I gazed and gazed at the place which I knew so well. It was plain to me that floods had much changed the channels since the Admiral had been there. Pegg was cursing, because he had counted on a multitude of slaves here, and native divers to help him career; now there were neither slaves nor so much as a pilot to bring him into the river.

"This is another of these sepulchres," he was saying. "Fever under every tree and not another soul in sight. Which the devil is the channel?"

He ordered a gun to be fired, hoping that the natives would answer the signal; there was no answer of any kind.

I said that I had heard that the western channel was the good one, that I had heard this from a naval officer. Pegg snorted, and seemed inclined to try one towards the centre; but he had had a little lesson from his rashness in the other channel at Massa; he bit his finger-tips and swore. Staggers suggested that they had better have a look at the channels in the boats; so two boats were lowered, and Tulp and Staggers went in them to have a look. They left nothing to chance. They knew that in islets like those in front of us a thousand savages might be lying in ambush; the boats were, therefore, well-armed. We in the ship loaded our guns, and lay with backed main-topsail for the boats to return.

Presently, the boats passed out of sight. We stayed on deck, listening for some sound from them. The ship rolled and jangled. Plainly, there was a good volume of water coming down the river. It stretched in a great, reddish fan, almost into the blue water where we were. Just where the discoloration ceased, swarms of fish were leaping, as they struggled for what the river brought them. All along the harbour entrance, the surf was silent, but the roar and the flash of it were to the east and to the west.

The boats did not return till ten or so. They came back, laden with fruits, to say that they had found a very good channel with plenty of water in it, and that inside there was a great anchorage, big enough for a fleet. They said they they had been up and down, and had seen no sign of any men; certainly no one was camped there with slaves for sale. They added that there was one good berth on the westward side of the harbour, which was the very place for putting the *Albicore* on her side. Of fresh water there was an abundance.

There was a general growling against Pegg at having brought the ship away down into this cannibal country, and all for nothing, since there were no slaves to be had there. The hands growled and cursed, saying, with perfect truth, that if he had only got on the right side of the blacks at Massa, the slaves could have been bought, the leaks could have been repaired, and they could now be on their way to the Indies. However, growling was their only solace. However much they growled, there we were, with work to be done.

We stood in to the river mouth; the boats went ahead and bore out lines to the trees ashore; by means of these we were presently drawn into a turbid, reddish river, with forest on one side, and wooded islands on the other. Then, presently, we were out of sight and sound of the sea, in a great lagoon or bay, several miles long. This I knew was the anchorage where Edmond Quichet had had his settlement. There was no sign of any settlement now. All seemed savage forest, with a few birds and a few animals, who paid no heed to our coming. Men seemed to be strangers there. The flood of the last few days was fast falling. I noticed that flowers had already sprung up among the flood-wrack; but flowers were everywhere there, in great swaths and heaps of white, purple and blue.

In one part of the lagoon or lake, near our berth, the flood had swept an islet bare. This had not yet sprouted much. The rush of the water had laid bare what seemed to be the burnt bows of a wooden vessel; it lay on its side, with the timber ends starting from its planks; black as coal. Perhaps, the wood was only water-logged, but I thought at once of Edmond Quichet's settlement which had been burned, somewhere near that point. Could that have been one of his ships?

You may ask if I saw the red peak with Edmond Quichet's cave upon it. We came into the lagoon from the west; his peak lay to the east, some miles from us. As we came in, we were shut from the Peaks by the great trees on the islands to our right. When we were fairly in the lagoon, I did for a brief while see them, but only for a brief while, for I had so much to admire near at hand. We were now heaving with song and fiddle to the berth which Tulp had chosen. We passed out of the lagoon proper into a bay or bend on its western side. I knew, directly the hawsers tautened to drag us into it, that it was the very place which the *Hannibal* had moored in years before.

The years had not altered its main features, as the Admiral had described them to me. There was a patch of sandy and stony beach, much strewn with dead branches all barkless and white as bone. Beyond the beach was the character-mark, "a bank or little cliff, perhaps twenty feet high, over which a stream fell into a rocky basin." Towards this place of laughing bright water our men were heaving the *Albicore* by lines passed to the trees. It seemed a very heaven on earth, with the brook, the many flowers, the fruits and berries on the trees, and bright birds pecking at them. Soon, when Pegg judged fitting, our anchor was let go; we moored there. When we were moored, I looked to the westward across the lagoon. From where we lay, I could see only six of the Sixteen Peaks; I know not which. Four of them were grey, two red. Their strangeness made my heart beat fast. Sometimes, as I looked, those peaks were like living things. Were they not alive? Had they not somehow wanted me and called me thither? Had they not contrived that I should come there, through all the trouble and shame of these last months? Now they had me there; I was arrived.

I stared at those peaks, till my duty wrenched me away. I went below to look at the slaves in the lower tier.

I had noticed an excitement among them, ever since I had told them that we were going to the Peaks. I knew, of course, that they had lived in (or, at least, roved over) a vast range of that part of the Coast. I supposed that even if these conquering M'gai had now ousted their tribe, they would still be glad to see those scenes. It crossed my mind that perhaps they hoped to be rescued there. I had done my best to check this hope. They would have no chance of rescue, I said. They would be too well guarded, and would be shot if they made the least attempt. I said that we should be there only to mend the leaks, to load more tiers of slaves above them, and then to sail for the Indies.

Now, when I went below, I found that in some way they already knew that we were berthed to the west of the lagoon. Deray told me; he described the place to me. We were to the west of the big lake, near a waterfall. I thought that Bill or one of the boatswains' mates had told them where we lay. It may have been so. I have sometimes thought that their acute senses, stretched to the utmost, had smelt the place and had at last heard the brabble of the brook. Deray had been there on hunting parties, he said.

When you have been in Newgate, you will know very acutely the acuteness of the senses of prisoners. I knew that I was in the presence of a terrible excitement among those shut-up men. It shocked me with pity for them. They would be landed while we mended the leak. They would see that old haunt of theirs (where they had moved as hunters), for the last time, as shackled slaves, and then would see Africa no more. I tried to tell them not to mind it too cruelly, that fate had dealt them a cruel turn, but that they were still alive. That was the comfort (my only one), that I used to give myself. I had lost all, as they had, but was still alive, which was somehow something; since I would rather have it than not. I did not get much comfort from it, nor did they get much from my halting version of it. Who gets comfort from another when the trouble is real? I came up from that awful den, shaken with the state of mind that I had found there. No man could go down to those shelves without feeling the tenseness of the mood. You have heard and seen bees swarming? Can you imagine being in the midst of a silent, invisible swarm that is yet overwhelming in its number and intensity? The minds of those slaves were swarming, as I could feel. I remember leaning on the rail to gulp the clean fresh air and thinking, "Poor fellows, poor wretched fellows, it can only make their misery the greater; for they have no chance; none; and when last they were here, they were free warriors at home."

I looked at the Peaks, I watched the lagoon, where some fishing-hawks struck fish, and some lovely grey birds flew slowly past in a line. Then I looked again at the waterfall near which we were moored. Beyond the cliff of the water-fall (and I should call it a bank with stone outcrops rather than a cliff), the bush or forest grew, with its vast trees, and mysterious grey-green undergrowth. It was strangely beautiful. Already the beach was busy with our crew. Most of the hands were ashore, under the carpen-ters, cutting uprights in the grove of spearwood near the water. Our plan was, to build huts ashore, to land every-one and much of the gear, lay the *Albicore* upon her side, find the leaks and mend them. Some men were already set-ting up stakes for the tents.

When you have many hands, you can get a great deal done in a short time. This work of securing poles and stretching canvas was that which the seamen had had much practice in. They were working well and cheerfully. They were ashore, which was a change to them. It was cool, which was another change. They were to sleep out of the ship, which was another change, and they had been told that, if they worked well, one watch at a time might go fishing later, in the lagoon. Besides all this, they had all the water they could drink, and as much ripe fruit as they cared to pick. Bushes full of samberry, as they called it, grew just up the bank. It was well-known to be safe, though the older seamen kept away from it. The crew had not been so cheerful since they joined the ship in Liver-pool.

As I could do little more on board, I went ashore and worked with the others at laying out the huts and tents. The plan of the camp was simple. The tents were to run in a line along the beach. At the north end there would be a

big tent for Staggers' watch (the port watch). In one end
of this a canvas screen shut off a berth for warrant-
officers. In the midst of the settlement the main hut or
tent, roofed with two mainsails, would contain the slaves.
Further to the south, nearer to the sea, a third big tent
would hold the starboard watch, with a berth screened off
in it by canvas for the idlers. Still further south, nearest
to the sea, was a fourth tent for the officers, including
myself. There were forty men at work on this place, all
working with a will, and enjoying it. I can honestly and
truly say, it was the only time that I saw the crew of the
*Albicore* enjoying anything, except the little ration of
rum on Sundays.

We did not finish it that night, but were ashore at it before daybreak. We fenced the outer line of it with stakes
and heaped driftwood. At the angles and in the centre we
mounted ship's guns. The space about the slaves' hut was
ditched, fenced and entangled. Above these checks, we
built two raised sentry-boxes, in which men with muskets
kept a lookout. I have often thought that most men have a
talent for making or building; if that talent be employed,
they will be happy and the state will prosper. If it be not
employed, they will becomes destroyers and cruel. Our
men were certainly happy in making that camp.

The slaves were brought ashore, two by two, heavily
chained, and watched by armed guards. Whatever hope of
escape they may have had was taken from them by our
precaution. Pegg was often rash, but in this matter he
took every care. He left nothing to chance. Any slave making even a gesture of trying to escape would have been
killed on the instant. They were watched till they were

shackled to the spare spars on which their platforms rested. Even when they were shackled, the chains were searched every half-hour. Yet, hopeless as their case seemed, I noticed and reported a great change in the slaves. There was no trace of the sullens among them now. They had lost the hopeless look which had so wrung my heart on board the *Albicore*. There was a gleam in their eyes, which came from an inner fire. I put the change down to their coming into the light and the clean air, and to the fact that they were given abundant fresh water and even some allowances of samberry. "It'll keep 'em from getting scurvy," Pegg had said. "It's a bastard when slaves get scurvy."

He was uneasy when I told him that the slaves were the better, even after four hours ashore. He said, "I'm sorry to hear it. I don't want these black dogs to be too uppish. I don't like having 'em ashore at all. I'll have a rowser stretched along 'em, in case they try to come it fresh."

He ordered a rowser, which is a cruelty I disdain to describe. I knew that if stretched it would be impossible for anyone even to try to escape. It made me sick, that I had reported their looking better.

"Now," Pegg said, giving his orders for the rowsers, "now, maybe, they won't try to come it fresh; they'll suffer if they do, at least. It's bad enough to have these black dogs right in our midst like this; in the very best place in camp. I'll see they don't enjoy it at least."

Even with the rowser, he was not satisfied. He told off another two men to do slave-guard, inside the slave-house.

Now this, coming in the heat of the day, after eight or nine hours of very hard continuous work of various kinds, was the beginning of a change of mind among the crew. Until that moment, they had enjoyed the novelty of work; now they were feeling the strain. For one thing, the work ashore, even the walking on shore, had used many little-used muscles, and used them hard. Then the work of the ship had not been neglected. She had to be pumped twice daily, for she leaked where she lay. In addition to this, all hands since dawn had been toiling to and fro, bringing the slaves ashore, unlading gear, provisions, arms, bedding, powder, piling driftwood into the fence, digging, carrying fresh water, unbending sails, taking them ashore and stretching them as awnings, as well as cutting firewood for the voyage to the Indies. It had been a full day's work for all hands, and this extra guard in the slave-shed was much resented. The men hated coming near to the slaves. It is seldom pleasant to come very close to misery; all not trained as ministers to the sick shrink from it naturally, with some old herd-instinct, which dreads a wounded fellow. They had reason to suspect that the slaves carried infection, which the slave-guards usually caught. Now four of them instead of the usual two had to watch in the presence of this infection, and this in the heat of the day when watching was most irksome, and infection (as they thought) strongest. They growled and cursed, but none the less had to do what they were told. Tulp told them very sensibly that if they were at sea they would have their turns of steering and looking out, etc., and that on shore they would have to expect extra watches; that in any case they would be able to go fishing after sunset and, even with the extra watching, would have more sleep at night than they would get at sea. However, the extra guard pressed heavily on them. They reckoned rightly that every man in the crew would have a turn of guard each day in a place of discomfort and danger. As sailors will, they growled, and with justice.

I mentioned the raised stands on which our sentries stood to watch the forest. The whole lagoon was so savage, so lonely, so without trace of man, save for that old wreck on the mudbank, that fear of attack had not entered my head. No men had frequented that place for years, so far as I could see. It was too far to leeward for slavers. As I was passing under these raised sentries, I heard one of them say to the other,

"It's not much good our being here. We can't see over that bank in front of us. If there were blacks there, they could be on us before we could fire a shot."

The other said, "It's the Old Man's perk to order some damned silly thing."

Now almost as he spoke, there came some sudden outcry from the men inside the slave-hut; a cry like "Stop him; quick; look out; he's free. Look out." One of the men who had been stretching the rowser rushed to the hut door, near me, and cried, "Quick; give me a musket; he's away. Dick. Bill. Shoot. Shoot, there."

It was a sudden alarm, when most of the hands were in siesta. I heard someone rushing away from the further end of the slave-hut. I could not see who it was since the hut was between us, but instantly the sentries fired; and with yells and curses all the camp sprang to life. I darted into the slave-shed, where I found three men, all much scared, telling the slaves not to try that again. I saw that Deray was gone.

"Has a man escaped?" I asked.

I got no answer, for the camp was now running to arms, finding a gun here, but no powder; or a horn there and no gun. However, a dozen shots were fired. Then, with a shattering bang, some bright spirit fired a cannon, point-blank, into a tree. I now caught sight of Deray. He was in the lagoon. He had plunged in, had swum under water, and was now up for a breath; he was swimming strongly and well, whatever chain he wore. He dived again, as the men got ready to shoot; and now Pegg came running, swearing, having woken from his nap.

"What are you playing at?" he screamed. "Get to the boats after him. Get the boats out. He's there. Don't shoot him. I won't have him shot. I'll teach him and the rest a lesson. Get to the boats."

He struck, kicked, swore and stamped. The men dropped their guns and ran to the boats; but here they were stopped by Staggers.

"Keep all fast with the boats," Staggers said. "No, Captain Peggs. No boats, please, till we've had a look at the irons here. We may have the whole seventy running, if we don't mind."

He set the tide flowing back to the slave-hut, where after much testing of irons, the frightened guards were told to tell their story. They were too scared to tell much, even if they knew much. Somehow, as they were loosing Deray a half-instant, to get the rowser fixed, he struck them, right and left, and was away. With one of his blows, he had cut one of the guards over the eye with a piece of his arm-chain, then he had been out and away, like light. They had yelled; the sentries had fired; but he had dived and swum under water, then gulped a breath and dived again. As far as men could tell, he had come ashore on the mainland among some bushes and was gone.

Pegg stamped and swore; he said he had a good mind to flog the guards for letting the man get away. "It was nothing but your carelessness; nothing but your tomfool, pigheaded imbecility and damslam carelessness. What d'ye mean by letting him go? No rum for you till we pay off. No rum, and no afternoon below. I'll work your old iron up, till you sweat blood. And I'll dock the man's worth off both your pays, mark that."

However, at this point Staggers came to say that no other would get away in a hurry.

"Don't talk to me," Pegg cried. "But for you stopping the hands at the boats, we'd have got that man and taught them all a lesson. Come on, now. Get the hands into the boats. He can't have got far with some of the iron still on him. We'll find his trail and follow him."

"Damn it, Captain Pegg," Staggers said sullenly, "we got no dogs. How'll we find him in a bush like that with no dogs? Dogs go overboard in this ship. Well, now the slaves go overboard."

"Don't answer me," Pegg said. "Do what you're told."

The point of the thrust about dogs was not lost on Pegg. Staggers took a dozen hands, armed with muskets, to the point where Deray had landed. They told us later that his tracks were plain in some soft earth; then they disappeared. The men poked about in the bush for an hour or two; they fired several shots; and at each shot I wondered if they had shot the poor man. I longed for him to escape. I had been a prisoner too recently, and had liked Deray too well. I prayed and prayed that he might get away. I dressed the cut over the eye of the guard; he was very sick from the shock; and perhaps this fact (though it seemed very natural to me) weighed with Pegg and spared the man a flogging.

The seekers came back presently, to say that the slave had got clear away; that they had found his ankle-clip, as they called it, about twenty yards from where he got ashore, and some few footprints in the mud. They had been very hot and rather scared of being lost, bitten by snakes, or speared. They were not blacks, they said. They couldn't tell which way that black devil had gone; he had just disappeared. "If we had had one of them two dogs," they said, "we'd have found him, then."

Pegg swore a little more and said that if he had been there he betted he would have found the trail; but that they were a lot of fools and slackers who didn't want to find him. This was no doubt true, but did not mend the matter. It was no good looking for Deray any more; the hunt stopped.

I had finished my work for the afternoon, and greatly longed for a walk, to see something of Africa and to stretch my legs. I was much too scared of being lost in the bush to venture far; still, a short walk would not lose me. I could keep beside the water all the way. I longed to get away from the company for a while and to be free from the tyranny of office.

I took a stick, as a guard against snakes, and went to the main gate, below the raised sentry-stand. I said to the sentries, "I am going out for a walk. I shall be back from this same direction, so don't shoot me as I come in."

"Never fear, sir," they said, "you go out; we'll watch out for you."

I went out; and on going forth noticed at once that the comment of the sentries some hours before had been just. It was easily possible for enemies to creep up to within thirty yards of the fence utterly out of sight of even the sentries on the stands. I walked up the slope in front of the fence to make sure. It was only too sure. Men could creep through the forest to the top of the slope and there (themselves unseen) observe all the camp and what was happening in it. And, if the creepers-up were marksmen, they would be able to pick off any man in sight. When I had seen this with my own eyes, I marvelled that no one had thought of it. It would have been so easy to camp on one of the islands, where we would have been secure from any possibility of surprise. Of course, the water had been the attraction; that running brook, so close to the anchorage, so easy for water-fillers—what seaman could have resisted it? Well, there we were, established now.

From the top of the little slope, after I had looked down at the view, I pushed into the bush for a short way. I had heard how easy it is for white men be lost in bush. I saw, then, why. Every yard of that mysterious wilderness was like every other yard of it. It was something endlessly repeated, a dark, thorny thing, a soft frondy thing, a green shiny thing, then another, then another, thorny, shiny or frondy, all a little taller than man, each a little confusing; all, together, baffling and fatal. I rattled with my stick among the bushes a good deal, from fear of snakes. I was now in the bush quite out of sight of the camp. Presently, I returned to the top of the slope and went back to the gate. I hailed the sentries, to ask, had they heard me rattling the scrub?

They said no, they had heard nothing.

This troubled me, for if our sentries could not hear a noise wilfully made, they would certainly not hear stealthy enemies. I met Tulp near the officers' quarters, and told him that the camp was badly placed.

He said, "I wouldn't worry. There's no one here. The beasts and the birds are just about as tame as if they'd never seen men. Besides, we shall be gone tomorrow with any luck. Even if we were attacked, we've got the cohorns mounted. No savage will face cohorns."

It was true that the murdering pieces and swivel guns had now been mounted all along our fence at intervals. They were loaded and primed. They contained scattering charges of pebbles, broken glass, old gun-flints, etc., etc. These and the bigger guns made a very strong defence. Still, I was uneasy. When I saw Pegg, I asked him if he felt anxious about the Matas. We were in their country; their hunting parties might well be near by, and would perhaps have heard or seen us. He said that he had heard no sound and seen no sight of any Matas; that all the stories went that the Matas were gone from those parts of the Coast, from dread of the M'gai; and that the next day, he was going to explore the eastern side of the harbour for the M'gai. They would be coming from that quarter with their slaves, and could not be long delayed.

He was always rashly confident; his confidence now did not reassure me. Still, the older seamen, who had been many times on the Coast, did not seem to dread any attack. I made my nightly visit to the slaves. In spite of the

rowser and the extra chaining, all were still better for the
coming ashore, and much the better from knowing that
Deray had escaped. I had some talk with them about the
Matas and that part of the Coast. They said that the
Matas did not much come there now. "It not good." They
pointed with fettered hands towards the west. "There,"
they said. "Two day from here; that where we go most."
Somewhere there (I gathered) there was another lagoon
where the Matas always found a fish which they much
esteemed both for its flavour and for an oil which they
got from it. I could not make out what the fish was; it was
not a shark, much smaller than shark; and "he come many
at once; him gobble mans."

One of the slave-guards said, "I guess he means barracuda; they get them devils along here sometimes."

When I came from the slave-shed, it was fast falling
dark. Our men were now back from their fishing and were
gathering to supper. They had builded big fires to the seaward of each hut, so that the sea-wind, now setting in,
might blow the smoke through the huts and keep away the
mosquitoes; though indeed the night was striking in too
cold for mosquitoes. A roll had been called. Just as the
men settled to supper, Pegg sent Staggers to them, to say
that one-half of one watch would stand guard till two in
the morning; and that then half the other watch would
relieve them till eight. They cursed, of course, for they had
expected more sleep than this; however, it was better than
watch and watch. Now that night was falling on the lagoon, the anxiety which had been on me all day increased;
I was glad indeed to hear that we should have ten men at
least awake all through the night. I have not told you that

it was a dead moon, in her last quarter; we should have no help from the moon until morning.

We supped in our tent to the seaward, with a sentry pacing outside. There was a novelty about it, which had a charm for me. We had a dinner of fresh fish and stewed samberries; a rare feast, in fact, however rudely served. After supper, our crew started singing their old country ballads and tales of pirates. They were fond of singing and sang well. We went out to listen to them.

I know not how long we listened; the time passed so sweetly, with song after song, usually full of feeling. One song there was about a great storm and the unhappy crew of the *Elizabeth;* it was very long, and had a chorus. It meant very much to our seamen. They sang it at the beginning and half-an-hour later sang it again. It made a great impression on me. I remember it to this day, it had such a strange, melancholy tune. Gradually the singers dropped away from the concert to turn in. The best of them stayed to sing love-songs and tender ditties about sailors' wives. I could have lingered to listen until morning, for after so many days of cruelty and brutality, the grace of even the rudest art seemed to come from another world.

It was dark all about us, with intensely bright stars in heaven. The noise of the distant surf had deepened with the darkness; its melancholy roar filled the seaward side of the night. Inland, strange owls were crying; and some unknown creature, bird or beast, made a chacking, shrill noise. In the trees, a kind of cricket was trilling. In the forest quite near us, twigs fell, with the sound of footsteps; creatures rustled, and sometimes cried. Our sentries paced to and fro, with occasional hails:

"Port watch hut. . . . Guard awake. . . . Matches burning. All's well." "Slave-house guard awake. . . . Matches burning. All's well," etc.

Presently, the remaining singers took up for the third time their song of the *Elizabeth,* and sang it through to the end. Then they broke up from their song. We saw their dark figures passing away to throw more wood on the fires and wrap their blankets round them. And now that the camp was silent save for the sentries, I heard a sad, low song, hummed rather than sung, among the slaves. I had heard this song before from them, for they crooned it in the hold sometimes. Now they took it up together, at first very gently, then in a pitch so strange that it seemed to fill the night. I could not help but listen. It was so sad, so plaintive, so uncanny. I stood listening to it for some time. Presently, I found that Tulp was beside me. He had been stealing round to see if the sentries were on their feet.

"What is that song?" I asked. "I've often heard them sing it. What does it mean?"

"It's only a silly native song," he said. "It is only:

> "No more, never any more, never again,
>   No more fish in the river."

Pegg came out from his berth and walked across to the slave-shed. "Stop him damn noise," he called.

They stopped, then, for a little while, but they soon be-

gan again. Quite suddenly, they stopped on the words "no
more fish," or the words which Tulp said meant "no more
fish." It was just as though all the strings of the instru-
ment had snapped; they broke off, and there was silence.
As I was made uneasy about this, I went to the slave-shed,
which was lit by two candle-lanterns and by the fitful
firelight. I saw that all the slaves were awake and in a
state of great excitement. A long row of eyes gleamed at
me. I asked one of my friends if anything were wrong; if
I could perhaps do anything for them. He said no, unless
I could tell him how long they would be there. I said I did
not know; it depended on the sailors. I asked the guards
if anything had disturbed the slaves. He said he judged
they were all upset, at being on the shore again and having their friend get away and singing their komisaa song.
"But *they* can't get away," he said. "I've been over their
shackles twice. What with them and the rowser they'll lie
where they're put. Children act the same way sometimes,
when they get excited. I wish I'd half their chance to
sleep. But these lads, doing nothing all day, haven't the
same wish to sleep as we have."

"Neither the wish, nor perhaps the power," I said.
"They aren't on a bed of ease."

I went back into the shed, and talked a little with my
chief friends. I asked them about the song, and whether
it was about there being no more fish. They said that that
was what it meant; but that it was not that at all. After a
time, I learned from them, or thought that I did, that it
was about a chief, who was turned into a fish by a wizard,
and lived as a fish for a long time, till he learned how to
break the spell, "He gobblem little gold-worm." As he left

the river, he sang from joy that he would be a fish no more.
I was glad of the talk and of the explanation; and wished
the slaves good night. It seemed to me that singing of the
breaking of the spell and getting away from the bondage
of the wizard had been quite enough tc excite them. I
knew from Newgate how hard it is for a prisoner to sleep
at any time. Singing of freedom there would have kept
the whole prison awake.

I, too, was a prisoner there, with little hope of release.
I was reasonably free from fear of arrest until we made
the Indies; say, two months or a little more. But when we
made the Indies the whole dreadful fear would have to be
faced again. Well, it was two months away. I might die
long before that time came.

And yet, much as I dreaded the future, I did not want
to die. I lay down in my hammock in my tent with a lively
fear upon me, of being killed quite soon where I was. I
was lying down to sleep in Africa, and did not feel at all
safe. I had heard of lions which would steal in to eat men
in their beds; of bats which sucked the blood of men, of
crocodiles which left the rivers at night and prowled
ashore, of hyaenas which bit away the faces of sleeping
men, of hunting dogs which ran men down, and of terrible
snakes which crushed or bit. All these were in Africa. Besides these were the savages, the Matas, who ate white
men, the M'gai who killed Matas, and tiny Bushmen who
shot darts from which none ever recovered. I felt again intensely how easy it would be for the savages to creep up
close to our camp unheard and unsuspected. Perhaps even
now a troop of blacks armed with great spears might be
within forty yards of me, ready to charge down upon us.

With this fear came a suspicion that clever savage fighters (and I knew that all savages had a cleverness) would choose my end of the camp for their attack. They would charge where the cohorns were the fewest, and where the resistance must be least. Then the thought came to me, had the slaves learned somehow, by some savage signal unperceived by us, that their friends were at hand? Had Deray got to their friends and sent in a message somehow? I was uneasy. It was foolish to hate life as I did and yet to dread death. Man is foolish in that way very often. I loathed, or felt that I loathed, everything in my life; yet here I was scared of being swiftly killed. I could not sleep for my anxieties and fears. Just when they were beginning to exhaust me into sleep, I began to feel the cold, which struck from underneath me into my back, so that I shivered and ached no matter how I crouched. At last, I turned out and went to the tent door.

In the stillness of the night, the noises of the river and the surf, the wash, gurgle and ripple, the great lapsing roar, were very near and plain. The old moon was aloft now, very bright. Owls were cruising near us. I had heard that natives imitate the cries of owls, and signal to their fellows with owls' cries. Were these owls birds or natives? Fish leaped and splashed in the lagoon. All the bush was alive with little patterings and scutterings. Away to the north, a company of bullfrogs was in croak. I did not know what the noise was. I feared that it was, perhaps, the roving crocodile seeking his meat. A sentry passing near, to see what I wanted, told me that the noise was made by frogs. Other creatures cried or yapped in the coverts near us; there were brayings, trumpetings and coughing low-ings as beasts came to drink or called their fellows. Wherever I looked, there were fireflies gleaming and fading; up above were great stars and what was left of the moon. I was comforted by the peace of the night and went back to my bed. I crouched shivering there till all the birds and monkeys in the forest, after shaking the sleep from them, began to cry and scream. In that execration, all savage Africa seemed to be cursing the white man. There was no chance of sleep after that.

All hands turned out, replenished the fires, and stamped their feet and flogged their arms from cold. Some of them went out of camp, launched our boats into the lagoon and caught fish for our breakfast. Till we had breakfasted we were all too cold for much speech. I remember suggesting that it might be a good thing to hang some of the copper and tin pans and pannikins, which we had brought for trade, onto tangles of spun yarn all about the camp, so that any enemy approaching would be sure to jangle them and rouse the watch. My suggestions were seldom welcome to Pegg, but Staggers backed this one. He said that it would be a very good thing. Pegg presently agreed, and a sort of network was spread, all hung with pots and pans, some of them partly filled with pebbles. It took a good time to do. It made yet another black mark against Pegg, for camping there instead of on one of the islands.

I had expected to find the slaves much the worse for the cold of the night; but they were still the better for being there. They took their food and drink. Not one of them was turning sick. I asked them if they did not find the night cold? They said, "No. Keep him warm inside." I believe that they had some power of mind that could order any part of them to feel warm. Perhaps we all have some such useful power and let it die in us from disuse. I reported that the slaves were bearing up well.

"Why shouldn't they?" Pegg asked. "They've nothing to do all day and plenty of good nourishing food, as well as all night in. Half the hands would be only too glad to change places with 'em. You ask 'em."

This next day was a hard day for the crew. They had the hard task of clearing all the weights in the *Albicore* to the side, so as to heave the injury out of water. I was ashore and had no part in the trouble. I knew that it *was* trouble, for when the work had been done, it proved to be useless; the carpenters could not reach the leak. When this was known, more weights were landed. The ship's berth was changed, and preparations made for heaving her right down upon her side. There was a very good place for this, close to where she lay. The preparations used nearly everybody all day long. When the hands came ashore for the night, it was already dark; they had been at it since before dawn, and were nearly worn out. Staggers had been in charge of the work. I gathered that he was not seaman enough for the task: others had had to make suggestions. Things had not gone smoothly and Staggers had hurt a man. Staggers was ever hated for his brutality, which would have been overlooked had he been a better seaman. There was no singing that second night. Indeed, it came on to blow and rain, so that we were all wet and wretched, as well as weary. The one good thing about the night was the storm. I had heard on board that savages never attack during a storm. I felt a kind of security from the statement, though I know now that it was false.

The next morning broke brightly and warmly, to bring us cheer. Tulp contrived to persuade Staggers to persuade Pegg to give all hands a two-hour siesta that day, for indeed the hands needed it. Pegg needed it himself, and, therefore, granted it. The promise made all hands turn to willingly again. I always had much to do in the forenoons, going over the slaves, and examining all the men of the crew. They were all keeping well, or pretty well. I had taken to giving the crew small doses of the Peruvian bark as prophylactic; this I advise to all surgeons staying on the Coast at all seasons. Some of the men were upset from eating certain of the fruits; four of them had ugly places on arms and faces, where they had been bitten by insects and had then scratched the irritation; still, we were well, and the slaves amazed me. They were patient and heroic. They were reminders to me daily of what is meant by virtue. I had been a prisoner unjustly. I had not behaved like these men; far from it. But all that I had seen of black peoples had tended to shew them to advantage. I liked them, more and more.

From our first coming to the lagoon, I had longed to see Edmond Quichet's cave up there in the red peak. I had had no chance yet of doing any exploring, for the boats were in constant use all day, going to and from the ship, or taking the fishers out to catch a supper for us. I feared that we might sail before I had a chance to explore the eastern side at all. However, Pegg said that if he did send over a fishing or shooting party, or go over himself to look

for the M'gai, I should go, too. I had no wish to enter the
bush beside us; in that grey-green mystery I should be lost
at once. Yet in the long siesta of that day, I thought that I
would walk down the river towards the sea, find a good
fishing-place and do a little fishing. I could not possibly
lose myself in that direction. The Sailmaker lent me a
frame and line with some hooks; I cut some salt beef for
bait, and set out. In the bright sunlight, let me say, one
had much less fear of the bush than after sunset. Still, I
took a stick against snakes.

After about ten minutes' walking, going leisurely, I
saw the sea blazing in front of me, with no sail in sight nor
any trace of man. After a minute or two more, I came to a
deep little gully or watercourse running directly across
my path between myself and the sea. It was a place of
great enchantment, covered with flowers over which bees
were busy. In the bottom, were many big tumbled rocks,
past which a little river ran. I went down to the river, and
found a pleasant coolness in a kind of cave among the
rocks, through which I could watch the water. I sat there
for a little, but soon thought that I had better get to fishing, and on coming out into the light saw on the mud of
the river-brim a little black dugout canoe upside down at
my feet. She was plainly not new. I poked her over with a
branch; she was half-full of red mud. I tipped her out and
scraped her, then lifted her to the water and washed her
clean. Here indeed was a treasure; here was a boat in
which I could explore where I wished. She had been skil-
fully hewn and then neatly burned from a trunk of light
hard wood. She had a little low thwart, and had been
smeared within and without with a black gum which had

hardened like cement. This was scratched and cracked in places, but in good order. Better still, her paddle was tightly lashed to her seat with a thong of hide.

Both at Momboe and at Massa I had seen many such little canoes, some of them well out at sea, under a rag of cloth set upon a stick and one tense native fishing. I wondered whence this one came. It might have been brought down the little river in the flood of a few days before, but it seemed to me more likely that it had come from a great distance down one of the main channels of the river, and had then been carried into this glen by the tides, for this gully was subject to the tide.

Perhaps nothing in my life had given me greater pleasure than this finding of the canoe. It made me in some sort a King over my destiny. With her, I could, if I wished, go off into the lagoon, up the rivers, or among the islands, and finish with the *Albicore* for ever. I could set up somewhere as a hermit, living alone on fish and fruits, perhaps more happily than I had been able to live with men. I had but to thrust into the reeds among the islands to be hidden from sight; they could never find me. If I were to be sold as a slave or taken as a felon directly I reached the Indies, might it not be wise to escape now? I might hide in Edmond Quichet's cave; presently I might perhaps meet the M'gai or the Matas. One white man with some little skill as a doctor might be received into the tribe. I might live as a savage thenceforth and marry a savage; go native like Billy and have a tusk through my nose. There was a fine end to my dreams of fame as a physician. I dallied with the thought awhile; and decided that I had pledged myself to be the doctor to the *Albicore;* it might

be that I might save many lives by staying with the slaves.
I could make their lot a very little lighter by staying; I
ought to stay. None the less, I picked up the boat, and hid
her carefully in a hole among the rocks. I meant to go
exploring in her.

After that, I went fishing near the beach and did well.
When a man is fishing with success, he pays little attention to the passing of time. I fished for a long time, much
longer than I thought. I returned to find Pegg furious
because I had gone from camp. He swore at me and asked
me where I had been. Here were two of the men nearly
dead, and the doctor gone traipsing away fishing.

I went at once to the two men, and very sick men they
were. They had been working on the damaged side of the
ship, putting in extra supports to the masts to help in the
heaving down. With the carelessness of their kind, they
had worn little or no head cover in the blazing sun of the
afternoon, so that after sickness and headache they had
every symptom of insulation. I treated them with cold
water, and worked at them for the rest of the afternoon,
and did in the end bring them to a safer state. I asked
Pegg if he would give the hands a warning, not to expose
themselves in this way, as it must lead to sunstroke. He
said, angrily, that if he went telling them that this or that
was dangerous they would never do a hand's turn. I said
that if they got struck by the sun they certainly would
not; so we went at it again, in public, and in the end, as
always, he asked if I commanded or he did? It was his
constant answer in all disputes. In fact, I believe that it is
the answer of every captain in the sea-service. Whenever
I heard it, I knew two things: firstly, that he knew that I

was right; secondly, that what I wanted and reason demanded would not be done. An answer very like it is sometimes given in Parliament, when a Government is asked a pertinent and troublesome question.

At this point, Pegg fell foul of the steward, to ask why supper was late. Picking up some rattans or canes that had been cut for breamers, be beat the poor creature.

"There," he said, "go tell the men that's what they'll get if they get sunstroke."

Sick at heart, I went out, determined to warn the hands myself. On going out, I was hailed by my friend the Sailmaker, who was looking very grave about something.

"I beg your pardon, Doctor," he said, "but may I ask if the Captain said anything to you about the warning?"

"Warning the hands about sunstroke?" I asked. "Yes, we've just been talking of that."

"No," he said, "not about sunstroke. I mean the *warning.*"

"I've been out of camp, fishing," I said. "What warning?"

He looked at me very closely. Three or four hands had gathered, each with an anxious face.

The Sailmaker said, "Did you not hear about the warning?"

"Do tell me what you are talking of," I said.

"Why, sir," he said, "after the knock-off time, this afternoon, some of us went for fresh water to the Spring; that would be about three o'clock or so. When we got there, we found what we didn't like."

"What was that?"

"You know, sir, we always keep fires burning at the

Spring, so we can scorch the insides of the casks with charcoals. When we got to the Spring after knock-off, the fire had burned low; so we went for the driftwood and that that lay about. We picked up this."

He handed to me something that I did not at first recognize. On taking it and shaking it clear, I saw that it was a much-used native sling. The pouch of it was of soft leather; the strings, as I judged, of gut. It had been kept soft with oil.

"That's one of their slings, sir. I picked it up here. Look, sir; if you will but step with me, I will shew you the place."

It was but a step. I went with him. He shewed me a place just above the Spring where a dead, fallen tree-top lay. In among the grass, flowers and decayed wood was a sort of form, where a man had lain for some little time.

"That's the place, sir," the Sailmaker said. "That's where the sling lay. If you will sniff the ground, sir, you'll sniff it was a native. The palm-oil's as strong as a badger, still. Ed was at this very place just before knock-off, and it wasn't there, then. When we got back, this hollow was warm from him, and it was lying in the midst. A savage was here, sir, looking right into the camp."

"You saw nothing of him, as he went?"

"No, sir. He took good care of that."

"Didn't the sentries in the boxes see him?"

The men looked uncomfortable and angry, as they always did, when they had cause to complain yet lacked the courage to do it. The Sailmaker fidgeted and then said, "Captain Pegg had the sentries at work, sir, most of the knock-off time. They weren't in the boxes, or they might have seen the man."

"What were they doing, then?" I asked.

"They were tidying up the Captain's tent, sir."

I bent down and sniffed the form where the man had lain. The smell of palm-oil, which all the natives use upon their bodies, with such advantage to their glorious skins, was unmistakable; certainly, a savage had lain there. It was a savage's sling, no doubt. It might have been one bought as a curiosity by a seaman, but then, this was freshly oiled; it had been in recent use; no sailor would have oiled a curiosity thus; it would have been hard had a sailor dropped it.

"What tribes use slings like this?" I asked.

"Why, a many do, sir," the man said.

"I shouldn't think he will come back for it," I said. All the same, I thought that he and his friends might well come back for a good many other things. "I was out of the camp during part of the knock-off," I said. "I was down towards the sea."

"Yes, we know you were, sir."

"I saw no one, while I was out. In the meantime, it is no good being scared."

"It's a warning, and in a foreign language," the Sail-maker said. "It's not a thing to neglect."

"Did you take it to the Captain?"

"Mr. Tulp did, sir."

"Do you know what the Captain said?"

"He said one of the hands had been trying to be funny."

"I don't think one of the hands left this," I said.

"We're very sure none did, sir. None could have."

"Who did then?"

"Somebody did, sir; a savage, who didn't want to be seen and left in a hurry."

"Has anybody heard or seen any savage at all, since we came to this place?"

"No, sir. Jenkin thought he saw a light the first night, away over yonder." He pointed across the lagoon towards the Peaks. "No one else saw it. It may have been a rising star."

"Strange," I said. "Well, it ought not to be neglected. I will speak of it. But first, I want to speak to the hands about working in the sun without hats. I'll talk to the Captain about it, later."

I spoke to the men about wearing hats in the hot sun. Some of them had big native grass hats which they had bought from the blacks at Momboe. I told them to wear these. They listened and smiled, but I could see that they never would. Either they had bought the hats as presents to friends in England or knew that such hats could never be worn aloft. I asked several of them about the sling. Some thought that it was somebody's joke; some thought that I had left it; some said they didn't like it; but it was what you might expect in a place like this. Two to my astonishment accused Pegg and Staggers of having put it there, as an excuse for giving everybody extra watches. I said that that was impossible; but they shook their heads. With some misgiving, lest this explanation should prove to be the right one, I asked Pegg what he thought about it.

"Think about it?" he said. "I think one of the hands slept there in the knock-off time, so as to have the fire-smoke over him, to keep away the flies. He had the sling all ready, in case he was caught. He was going to say, he'd seen a savage there, and took his sling away. He knows I've given strict orders, about not sleeping out of camp. That's all it was. He was nearly caught, so he left the sling and ran for it. Now, of course, he daren't own up. I know this Coast, and I know seamen. That's how the sling got there. But I'll see he nor no one else does that kind of thing again. And, as a matter of fact, I'm glad he's done it. With a bit of a scare, the sentries may be a bit more watchful."

I was not persuaded by his confidence; it seemed to me certain that a native had left the sling, and that he had come there solely to spy out the camp. Still, authority, however mad or wicked, has the last word in affairs, in this world.

I said that some of the men took it very seriously.

"They would," Pegg snorted. "They've been here all these days now, and everyone must know by this time that this lagoon is deserted; not a M'gai nor a Mata within a hundred miles."

For the moment the matter ended. The next trouble between us came a little later on, the question of my warning the hands about sunstroke.

I had given my talk quietly and, as I supposed, unseen by Pegg and Staggers. However, they had their spies everywhere. Someone, probably one of the boatswains' mates, a sullen-looking devil, one of the best seamen in the crew, who acted as a spy to keep the cabin informed of what the men said and did, soon let it be known, that I had been talking. I could see at supper-time that Pegg was furious. He snorted in silence through most of his meal, then at last, at the end, blurted forth furiously:

"Doctor, you take too much upon yourself. The hands say that you are always interfering and giving them orders. Understand, that I command this ship and no one shall give orders save me or through me."

"I do not give orders," I replied. "I give advice and, as a doctor, shall continue to give advice; and any interference with my advice, if it lead, as it must lead, to the death of men, shall be reported to the proper authorities when the time comes. The men ought not to expose themselves to equatorial sun in full blaze. If they do, in the hard work of heaving the ship, they will die. To prevent that, I shall give what advice I choose and think proper. You yourself are looking the worse for the afternoon sun; let me feel your pulse."

"To hell with my pulse!"

"Let me feel your pulse," I said. "No nonsense when your health is concerned." So at that he gave me his pulse, and I looked very wise. Then I asked to see his tongue; then I turned down the corners of his eyelids, and looked wiser than before. "Yes," I said, "not a doubt of it. You've got a touch of it, too."

"A touch of what?"

"Cerebral insulation. I am going to give you a dram, Captain, and ask you to get to bed till it works."

He was a very coward where his health was concerned, for all his boasting; he turned very white and said nothing. I would perhaps have given him a dram that he would have remembered; but at that instant the steward came in, all blubbered from his beating, to ask if the Doctor

would go to one of the slaves, who was choking. I ran out
at once. I found the man very sick. His neighbour slave
said that he must have been stung in the throat by a wasp
or bee that had got into his slabber, or evening mess. I
treated him for this, and stayed by him till I felt that he
was safe. The slaves told me that the wasps would get
into the food unless real care were taken. "It will happen
again," they said. "You tell him take care. Next time
man go for die I tink." I tinked so too, and went back to
the officers' tent to try to make Pegg tink so.

I found Pegg and Staggers sitting on their cots, talking. It needed no seer to divine that they were talking
about me, and against me. I saw them look evilly at me,
and glance evilly at each other. These were the two who
were going to sell me on my arrival at our port in the west.
I asked Pegg if he were feeling better; he growled something or other, and then snapped, "Why haven't you made
your report?"

I said, "My Captain is my chief patient. I have to ask
my Captain how he is first. The man nearly died but may
do well, now. There should be great care in mixing the
slaves' food. He seems to have swallowed a wasp and been
stung in the throat."

"He'll have done that on purpose," Pegg said. "I'll take
it out of him tomorrow, before the rest of 'em, to shew
them that no swallowing of wasps is going to be allowed
here. They don't get away with that on me. That was a
shot at suicide. He'll know better than to try suicide when
I've done with him."

Growling in this way, that he would teach them Christianity in a way that would stop 'em swallowing wasps,

he glared at me, and surlily turned in to his cot to sleep.
Staggers said it was a wonder anyone could be deceived by
the old wasp-trick, since it was as old as the hills. I said
that Death was older, and that most of his signs were
well-known to me. He said that it was an old woman's job
anyway, to look after sick people. With that, he swung
off to his sleep, and I went to mine. I found that, while
I had been with the sick man, someone had caused a great
heap of gear from the ship to be piled into my little
screened corner. I judged that Pegg had made the steward do this, to make me uncomfortable, and perhaps give
me a fall as I went in. He did not succeed, for by very good
luck, just as I plucked the screen to enter, the wind blew
up the bonfire to a flame, so that I was lighted to bed. I
slept in my clothes, for the greater warmth that night.

I have said that we were in the last of the moon. When
I woke, the moon was pretty bright, which told me that
it was near morning. I felt uneasy somehow and scared.
I thought at once of the warning, and wished that I had
not heard of it. I turned out and waited for the scare to
pass; but it did not pass. Hatred and scare had been constant inmates of my mind for a long time. I sat there,
listening for I knew not what, but repeating the French
phrase, *"Soyez en garde."* Some moonlight shone on the
gear on the bare ground of my berth. I saw chronometers,
boat-compasses, boxes of cartridges, and bundles of blocks
and fair-leads. Among them was a bright mahogany box
which I recognized as Captain Paul's duelling-pistol box.
I had often seen him cleaning these duelling-pistols, which
were a very fine pair. I leaned down and pressed the catch
of the lid. Inside were the two pistols with all their gear of

powder, bullets, caps and wads. I took them out and saw
that they were loaded. Having done that, I pocketed them
and took their gear. *"Je serai en garde, au moins,"* I said
to myself. Now it may have been a prompting, it may have
been my half-mad, nervous touchiness, but I felt too uneasy to stay where I was. I felt that something was wrong.
So I crept out into the camp and listened.

The fires were smouldering and gave out some warmth
still. I could hear the slow steps of the night-guards up
and down, the distant noise of the surf, the nearer gurgle
and whimper of the river; the cry of the owls and the occasional splash as a fish leaped. The forest wavered,
sighed and creaked a little, twigs fell and creatures scut-
tled, the fireflies shone out and disappeared. I heard
snores and heavy breathings from the sleeping watch.
Some of the slaves cried out a little and clinked their
irons as they shifted. I moved out a little towards the
slave-shed, and ran into Tulp, who was half asleep leaning against a post.

He said, "It's a cold morning. It might be January, at
home."

I asked if the slaves were all right. He said, "They were,
when I came on deck." I told him that I would just visit
them. He said, "Do," and lapsed into his huddled position again.

At the entrance to the slave-shed, I found one of the
guards fast asleep; the other was toasting himself a ship's
biscuit on which a piece of fat salt pork was melting.

He said, "They're all right, Doctor. They're all awake.
I've just been in."

I said, "I suppose it's the cold that wakes them?"

He said, "It is cold. But these black fellows always wake at this time. It's their danger time."

I went into the shed, and found that they were all awake. I spoke to them, and asked several if they were finding it very cold. They all laughed at the question. A warrior to feel cold; no, they were warm inside. "Him very warm." The man who had been stung in the throat was well, so he said.

"You watch him slabber no get sting," I said, and went out of the hut.

I could not think of going back to bed. I was too well awake. I went round the camp and spoke to some of the sentries. On the eastern side of the camp, I saw that the sky above the Peaks was beginning to shew colour; it would very soon be morning. I waited till it was rather lighter; then I thought that I would go down the river to my fishing-place, to catch fish for breakfast. So I took the fishing frame and bait, and told the sentries to let me out and not to shoot me on my return. They said they would not shoot if I would bring them some fish: I said I would certainly share what I caught with them. One of them said, "It's a lovely morning for a bit of fishing." It was. It may seem foolish of me to go out of camp at that hour; but recollect, the last of the moon was bright, the dawn had begun, and the work of the day was beginning. As I left camp, I heard the cook and cook's mates roused to prepare what our men called "Soup-o," a sort of hot drink given before they turned to. There was no sight nor sound anywhere that might have threatened or suggested danger: none. It was one of the most peaceful, lovely mornings I have seen.

I had some little anxiety, I admit, as the first part of
the way was dark with bush. However, I soon came into
sight of the sea, with lines of breakers away on my right
and the Peaks against coloured sky on my left. The marvel
and miracle of morning could never have been more glorious. Who could be afraid in the presence of such beauty
and such majesty? Birds were beginning to twitter a
little, and I could no longer see the fireflies. I know that
I saw one strange thing. Far out to the west a long roller
caught the light so that a kind of slow arrow of fire ran
right along it; that was very beautiful. At this moment,
the ghost-birds, as our men called them, a kind of big
white owl, began floating past me to their roosts. I think
that they had been getting shellfish or something of the
kind on the rocks by the sea.

As an idle man will, I turned to watch one of these birds
as it floated past me. It was making for the forest near the
camp. As I watched, it seemed to me that something
gleamed in the scrub in that direction. It was not a swarm
of fireflies, nor a blink of our campfire. It was too far to
the left to come from the camp. It looked to me not quite
like the flash of a lantern, but more like a mirror throwing back a ray. Bright metal might have done it. I thought,
too, that I had seen something very like it on bright moon-
lit nights in England, when a metallic leaf, such as a
laurel-leaf, had caught a moon-ray. It startled me at the
time, but it did not seem to startle the ghost-birds; they
kept their course and dived into the wood. "It was some
shiny leaf," I told myself, and went on to find and launch
my canoe.

I set forth in her, going cautiously, for I had not been

in a boat at all like her. Soon, I was in the big river, standing across to one of the big wooded islands. Waterways
stretched among these islands into romantic distances.
The great trees rose up, with their tops in colour and
often flaming with flowers. I was enchanted with what I
saw. I drove the canoe into a still alley of water between
great trees. Somewhere there, as I knew, the old Admiral
had come exploring. In that very island, or in one just
like it, Edmond Quichet had had a battery of guns near
the sea. "I'll set my lines and look for it," I said. So I did.

In that network of waterways leading hither and yon,
it was easier to go by boat than on foot. Presently, I came
to a place near the sea, where the foam of the big rollers
washed right up to me across a long shallow salt-pond.
There beside me among the jungle was a stone-wall, much
fallen and overgrown. "There it is," I cried to myself;
and on landing found that I was right; the place had been
built as a battery, and had guns in it still, all of small
calibre, from small ships, and rusted almost out of shape,
and, of course, long since without carriages. On one of the
guns' reinforce I could still trace a fleur de lys and "R.F.,"
for *Royaume de France.* Rusty little cannon-balls were
there, too. This was Quichet's port; all that the Admiral
had told me had been true, so far. What of the rest of his
tale, of the cave in the red north Peak, and the wealth
below the fireplace?

All the last half-hour had been noisy with the birds
and monkeys, who scream for joy of the morning with
shrill, harsh, exhilarating cries. Suddenly from the direction of the camp there came quite clearly across the water
the yell of savages, and shot after shot. The yell swelled up

at once into a rage and storm of battle, in the midst of
which there came shots, the loud bangs of cohorns and
many a scattered volley of muskets and small arms. "My
good Lord," I cried, "the slaves have risen, or the Matas
have come. I must get back."

But getting back was not so easy. I had come easily
to where I was, being helped by the set of the current and
guided by the breaking of the sea. But on trying to get
back I found a network of waterways, each exactly alike,
with the same red flood-wrack, the same mixture of giant
trees, soft brush, flaming flowers and tangled creepers
on its shores, nothing to shew me which was mine, and
each one with a current not easy to stem. I took two which
had little current, and soon found that each led nowhere.
All the time, as I paddled, I heard shouts, yells and shots,
now loud, now shut from me by jungle. I had hoped to
hear the roar of the ship's guns; I did not hear them. I did
not hear the cohorns banging again; I could not hear any
ordered cheer such as white men use. As I went, the shots
became fewer; such yells as came to me were those of
savages.

Sometimes in a dream I have tried to hurry and found
my feet tangled or glued or hobbled. In my paddling to
the battle I found my way checked. I had not got into the
way of paddling against a stream; the boat needed a rigid
paddler, and I had not that habit of rigidity. Then, the
recent flood had made many channels in that expanse. I
judged that before the floods, the many islands had been
two or three big islands; the flood had cut these up
afresh into an archipelago; often I took a turn which
took me from my way.

Still, I went on, and at last heard no more shots; only
yells; then a sudden sharp volley and a fearful yelling
and screeching; and now the smell of burnt powder came
down the wind to me; and I could smell the wafts of
camp-fire smoke and the slave-house. Then suddenly, I
heard a crackle of fire.

I was now, as I judged, near the camp, but shut from
it by a part of an island and the breadth of the river. I
drew my canoe ashore, and made my way through the
tangle across the island to find out what was happening.
The tangle was all crisscrossed with lianas, and I dreaded
to make much noise. All the time, the smell of burnt
powder drifted down upon me; presently, I saw driving
smoke and wafts of burning stuff blowing with it. There
was no more shooting, but the noise of rejoicing in the
camp was devilish. I had no doubt now that the camp had
been surprised and taken. What of the whites? Where
were they?

I said to myself, "If they were surprised in camp, they
will have fired, and then got to the boats and gone off to
the ship. It is true that the ship is on her side, but they can
easily right her. They will be doing that. When it is done,
they will open fire with the ship's guns and clear every
savage out of range." It was comforting to think thus, but
the other thought came back, "That is too good to be true.
In Life, it's the worst thing that happens." That was my
opinion at the time, remember; my Newgate opinion. "If
they were on board, they'd have fired by this time. These
sailors are stupid and unforeseeing to a degree, but when
they do act, they are swift beyond any men I have known
or read of." I must say, that I had not much liked the

*Albicore,* but they were my comrades, the only ones I had; my lot was their lot; I was in this adventure with them. My heart was sick for them.

There were some thorny bright bushes, very thick, with yellow flowers on them, very fragrant. They made a sort of wall to my island at one point, with a few little gaps through which I could peer. I was at one of these gaps when I saw savages moving on the opposite shore, down the river from the camp. A great many men were in the party; many had guns, spears and shields; but many were our naked slaves, some of them not yet wholly freed from wrist and ankle irons. All were in a state of savage glee; they yelled and hopped; some of them had the heads of white men in their hands; they played at catch with them and danced. I could recognize the heads; oh, horror and terror. And for all their glee they were intent on blood; they were searching and sometimes sniffing the ground for tracks; they knew that they had not killed all the whites and were looking for more. Then I saw that one of them saw a trail and pointed it to the rest. It was my trail, no doubt; I had gone to my canoe on just that line. Half-a-dozen of them gave tongue, like dogs, and leaped into a run along the tracks, straight to the rocks where I took the canoe. "Ah," I thought, "they'll know that I'm in a boat, and will search the islands for me. But they cannot have killed all hands. They had only half-a-dozen heads. The rest will be in the ship."

The party went on towards the sea, out of sight from where I was. After half-an-hour, they returned, going back to the camp. They were still looking for tracks. They were carefully looking for my tracks, to see where I had come ashore, and some of them eyed the island where I was, for tracks on the banks where some poor wretch might have clambered up after swimming the river. They were still dancing and shouting. One of them had two white heads, which he clashed together as cymbals while he danced. In the camp itself, the fire had smouldered down. I judged that it had been one of the sails over the huts. Plenty of people were yelling in the camp, but no gun was fired from the ship. I feared now that all the whites had been killed.

I lay where I was for some time, till I could stand the suspense no more. I crept from my cover back to my boat, in which I softly paddled away. After a while, I landed again, and crept under cover to a point from which I could see both the ship and the site of the camp. The ship lay on its side still; no men were on her; the camp was full of dark figures moving about; the huts had had their roofs burnt off; the smoke was still blowing about. Further up the shore, some more savages moved. What shocked me most was the fact that the *Albicore's* big boats were still on the beach, just where they had lain the night before. No man of them could have escaped by water. I could only conclude that a great might of Matablancos or M'gai had charged the camp while all hands were at "soup-o," and killed everybody before they could get to weapons or to the boats. The warning had been a real warning. Pegg had been a fool and had neglected it. I could see no white man anywhere. All that I could distinguish across the lagoon were savages.

Then I thought, "Some may have got into the water and escaped by swimming." If that were so, I might meet with them not far from where I was. I looked anxiously for some sign of someone moving on the islands, some sudden flight of birds or so forth; but knew very well that if I saw any such sign I should not dare to draw near to it. It might more probably be made by savages looking for me. I had had fine thoughts, as I have said, of joining the savages and becoming one of them. The memory of that warrior dancing to the clashing skulls put this kind of plan right out of my head. I was sick with terror, shocked with horror and blank with despair. Still, after a time, I said, "I must get away. I must down into the midst of these islands and hide." So I crept into my boat and put forth again away from those scenes. I paddled down strange channels, among the forest and the creepers, taking any turn which seemed to lead away from the savages, till at last I felt that I could do no more, but must lie up and think.

When I came to a stony place, where I could land, as I supposed, without leaving many traces, I crept ashore and carried my boat to a space under a tree. There I lay and quaked, a lot too scared even to think of fishing for my dinner. You will ask why Dead Ned's paltry half-hung life should be so precious to his silly soul. Often, in the past few weeks, I had longed and longed to die, and so be out of it. Now that I had an excellent chance of dying I shrank from it. Well, I was young, and most of us have hope in our souls, put there by the Maker of hope. Then, when a man "longs to die," as the phrase goes, he hopes to do it gently, without pain, from some quiet failure of the heart; he shrinks from being slowly cooked at a fire, with little bastings of palm-oil, and would rather not be eaten afterwards. Death might be all very well, but the excessive agony of the torture likely to be mine before death came, made me wish to avoid it if possible in that form and this place.

I know that I also said to myself, "Of course, this is fever; this is not real. I am Edward Mansell, a doctor. I am in delirium in a putrid fever. I caught it at Old Mother Hubbard's common lodging house when I set that simple fracture. I am now near the crisis. Soon I shall wake up into my real self, though very weak and silly, in a clean white bed at Dr. Copshrews' or perhaps at Hannibal House. Patty Morsoe will be there with a bunch of flowers for me, no, everlastings, for it will be winter now; or is it spring? She might have daffodils. Or good, kind Mrs. Will Coxwain will be there with lemonade."

Then I would wake up and say, "No, this is real. If those blacks come past in the ship's boat, they'll smell me out, as a dog might; for they have the noses of dogs. 'Fee. Fie. Foe. Fum. I smell the blood of an Englishman.' Then I shall be tortured and cooked and eaten."

Then I would say, "But they cannot have killed all the crew. In a day or two, I may meet the survivors, and perhaps we shall be able to take the ship back to Massa; or if not the ship, the boat."

Well, this was not very helpful. After a bout of it, I told myself that I was a lot too near the camp still, and had better find a covert further from it, and this at once before the savages came fishing in the boats. So I put forth in my boat, and with my pistols ready and terror in my heart I crept from waterway to waterway, till I found a place that seemed quiet enough. I put out my line and fished and caught some good fish. Then just as I was at point to eat one of these raw, a big bird flew up from her nest close to me with a cry that must have told any savage within half-a-mile that a white man was somewhere there. I was sick with the scare, and put forth away at once, by these alleys in the forest, so dripping and dark. It was like paddling in an endless Gothic cathedral, with the altar of hope ever further away. Often the awful flowers seemed faces leaning out to bite me; often what I took to be a dangling creeper turned out to be a waiting snake. Now that I was away from the nest, I told myself that I had been a fool not to take the bird's eggs. Then I came to a dark place in a gully of a backwater.

It was the best place that I had seen hitherto, and I took it, because I was too tired and scared and sick to go further. Where it was with regard to the Peaks or to the camp, I had no certain idea. It was a good two miles or more from the camp, I suppose, and rather to the south and the east from it, but I have not been there since, and could not hope to find it again. I pulled my boat ashore, and pushed her under cover. Then I hid myself as well as I could and ate some of my fish raw. It was not a dainty dish, but I was hungry and felt much better for the food. When I had drunken of the creek, I thought that I had strength for what might follow. After that, I fell asleep and slept like a dead log of a tree. It was coming to be dark when I woke. I heard a distant shot or two from where I judged the camp would be, but no other noise of men. Soon the gloom of the forest deepened, and with a roar and a whirr the birds began to come back to the tree-tops high above me. For half-an-hour the flights gathered among the island, and then their myriads settled and sparred, screamed, pecked, arranged themselves and then shook the whole colony out of arrangement, and at last fell silent, save where one or other lost balance and fell from perch.

I remembered that Robinson Crusoe had climbed a tree. I did not try that, having a poor opinion of trees as beds or seats. I muffled myself up in my coat as well as I could, with my pistols handy, and settled myself down to sleep. I had expected to be eaten alive by the mosquitoes; but with the sunset, it struck too cold for them to bite and for me to sleep. I had to sit up and chafe my limbs and fingers, all the time quaking at the noises round me, all the forest so stealthy, all the waters so full of threat. I had read in my medical books of men going mad in solitudes. There were strange things, owls or jackals, screaming in the night not very far from me. Sometimes, the note of the screech made me wonder if they were not some of the *Albicore's* crew gone mad from terror, and wandering there. It was bad enough when it was dark; but the last of the moon rose in her appointed time, with a white light which made the darkness uncertain; and terrifying. Homer speaks of the "swift, dark night." That night seemed to me to last a year; however, all things end; that ended; the treacherous beasts padded home, the birds woke, yelled, wrangled, flapped, and at last, with roar after roar of wings, went away into the light. Warmth came, to take the aches from my bones. I caught a fish and ate it raw; the world did not seem so full of evil.

Someone in the ship had said that no savage stays long in the place where he has slept. He moves off, spends his day elsewhere, and camps in a new place. It seemed to me to be a good doctrine, not to be too much in one place.

So, when I was a little thawed and unfrozen, I got into my canoe, and shoved off from my shelter to see what I could find. I went, generally speaking, into the darker channels. After a long time, I had the knowledge that I was wandering to and fro in a maze of stagnant alleys from which there was no outlet. I came to a splash of yellow fungi which made a sort of capital M upon a fallen tree. I had passed it twice before, and noticed the M. But this third time, I saw that beyond it was what looked like fruit upon a tree. I landed, and found that there were several trees growing there, bearing a copious fruit with hard rind. Many hundreds of the fruit lay on the ground, broken open. Birds had eaten and were eating these, so I ate, and found them very good. What birds may eat safely, man too can eat. I ate as many as I could, and was refreshed extremely. I then fished and caught a small snapper, which I ate as he was. As that place seemed as remote as any in the anchorage from any possible fishing parties from the camp, I stayed there all day, and heard no sound of man in all that time. At night, I slept there, if it can be called sleep. It was as wretched a watch as the night before. At an hour or two after midnight, I could endure it no more, but rose up and got to my canoe, and ate what was left of my fish for a breakfast.

I waited for the moon to rise, and then pushed on, to keep warm. This time, I took a careful note of where I went, or thought that I did, but presently found that I had lost the tree with the yellow M and thereby the plantation of fruit-trees. I had the uncertain moonlight to guide me

or mislead me, and the cold of the night to drive me. I paddled on till I was so weary that I had to stop. I landed,
drew my boat ashore, set my lines, and slept, or tried to.

In the morning, when it was light, I found that I was
about two miles from the camp, and able to see right
across the lagoon to it from where I was. The *Albicore* lay
on her side, hove down. A little wisp of smoke rose up
from her side. It thrilled me to see it. It looked as though
her men were burning the barnacles from her, which, of
course, would shew that they were back at work on her.
After long watching, longing for a glass, I judged that it
was nothing of the kind. Someone had set fire to her and
the fire was not doing well. I tried in vain to see if anyone
were in camp; it was too distant, and the bush made too
dark a background. I caught no fish that day.

Nearly all that day, I lay in cover watching the site of
the camp, seeing no sign of life there, and no boat plying.
The smoke, whatever it was, ceased to go up from the hull;
the fire was out. Late in the day, some great flights of
black-and-white birds, of the kind the Portuguese call
Dominicans, flew past me straight towards the camp. The
light was very good and strong. It seemed to me that the
birds went straight to the camp, lighted there, and after
a time rose thence; but it was too far away; I could not be
sure. What if the savages had gone? What if survivors
were there, creeping back? What if Tulp and the Sailmaker and Puggy Crackers were still alive there? What
if poor wounded men needing my help were there? The
last thought was almost more than I could bear.

From what I had seen of the savages, I did not think it
likely that any white man survived. I knew that the Matas

were a race of warriors and hunters, not likely to stay long
in one place. But would they not be staying here now?
Might they not be mustering near the lagoon in order to
fall on these M'gai, who were going to take their hunting-
grounds?

Far as the eye could see, it was their country. Their
settlements might be within half-a-mile of me, for all that
I could tell. The place was vast and blind; anything might
be round the corner. Imagine a stretch of water, broad
and deep, four or five miles across, with countless islands,
most of them covered with timber and tangle, and the
wreck and mess of flood. Directly one passed from the
main lagoon into a channel of river or sea, he was lost
completely, and knew not in what direction he headed.
Within those islands perhaps fifty thousand men could
have hidden unknown to people within a quarter-of-a-
mile of them. When I had left camp to go fishing, a war-
party, certainly two hundred strong, must have been lying almost within touch or scent of us, unsuspected by
anyone. Not unsuspected by the slaves, perhaps: no;
somehow the slaves knew; certainly they knew; why,
they were all awake. They may have been awake from
cold and misery, but who could doubt that word had come
to them that their friends were near? I had no doubt of
it. The Admiral always said that savages had some way
of speech which the whites have not. "They cry like birds,
or like bats, and understand what is meant; they send
out whispers across the jungle, and the whispers carry."
And at that moment, as I thought these things, I was
scared, because close to me as I lay I heard a voice whispering; someone was saying, "Hush, hush. Listen, listen,

never answer. Hush, hush, hush." It was quite close to
me, to my left. For an instant I was sure that one of the
crew had escaped and lay near me, and the joy of the
thought was terrible. I whispered back, and the noise
ceased for a few seconds, then began again just as before.
I knew soon that the noise was not someone whispering,
but might well be a savage cleaning a spear. What if it
were? What if I had whispered to a savage cleaning a
spear within ten yards of me? I drew out my pistol, and
crept towards the noise. It was no savage; it was a big
turtle covering a clutch of eggs with her flippers in the
hot lagoon sand.

From that point I could see the eastern lagoon, all
bright in the sun, with the strange Peaks above it, looking so like creatures of intelligence. I had seen strange de-
signs from China in some London houses; they were fashionable then. Somehow, these Peaks reminded me of
Chinese sages on a bowl in Patty Morsoe's home; they
looked unutterably wise. Do not think me too mad. Remember, that my recent life had given me odd fancies.

Still, at the moment, I had nothing but joy; my fear of
the savage was gone. The turtle eggs would give me food
perhaps for a week; and there was a chance that the Matas
were gone from the camp.

When the light died, I crept out and took some of the
eggs and ate them; I then burrowed myself a shelter in
the hot sand, and found comfort in it. I slept better than
I had slept since I left the ship.

When I woke, I looked towards the camp. It was now
black midnight, with starlight dancing in the lagoon.
In the camp there was a little red spark of fire, a one-man

fire. Might it be that one man had crept back, and now lived there? I remembered how Dr. Copshrews had said, "The healthiest place is where an epidemic has just ended." Possibly the safest place here was where the murder had ended. Possibly more than one man was there; half the crew, perhaps. I watched that tiny light with longing. It grew no bigger; now and again it seemed to go out, as though someone had put more wood upon it. What if it were some poor wounded or sick man, sorely needing help? Nothing was more likely. A survivor would probably have been hurt, I judged. I had not much loved the *Albicores,* but I knew their good points, and even the worst of them would be welcome to me now; he would be white; he would be a fellow Christian; he would be a comrade. But the thing that weighed with me most was that I was a physician, pledged to help the sufferer, and that the man yonder by the fire might be wounded or have a broken bone. In the end, I could not bear that thought; the darkness gave me a boldness that I lacked. I took my boat and drove forth in her. I meant to see what poor wretch it was that kept vigil there among the ruins.

Knowing that I might not find my nest again, for all the bearings I took, I loaded my boat with the turtle eggs, and made sure that my lines were safe. I stood out into the dark lagoon away from the shore, and crouched low as I paddled. It was the dark midnight, well before moonrise; I must have passed as a river-horse, or as one of those floating logs, of which the lagoon ever bore many. Even if the man were a sick slave, I thought, he will be a friend.

The voyage took me a long time, for my plan was to

work well away to the north, then to crouch down, and
let the current, aided by a judicious paddle, take me past
the camp slowly, within about a hundred yards of it. I
should drift past like a log, see everything, hail, if necessary, and land, if my hail were answered.

The moon rose before I started to drift; she gave some
light to me. You may be sure that I watched with all my
eyes as I began to loiter down with the current. I saw
now that the fire was not a campfire, no, but something
like a pile of logs, that had been fired and left to burn
itself out. One corner of it, or rather, one big log of it, was
now an ember, which glowed, and faded, smoked, and
then sparkled with little flames.

I could see and hear jackals or wild dogs all about the
camp; they were yapping and scratching; certainly no
man was there. I passed very close to the *Albicore;* she,
too, was deserted, lying on her side. I longed to board her
for some necessaries, but feared to do so. Some Matas
might be watching from the forest. I drifted past her,
quite close, with a pang in my heart.

After I had fallen well below the camp, I struck off
to the nearest island and drew ashore. I ate some eggs,
and took some sleep. When it was light, I found a place
from which I could see into the camp. The dogs or jackals
had gone, now, and the birds were feeding there without
fear.

The boldest course is often the best; I paddled to the
camp at once, and landed there. As I feared, the killing
there had been complete, though already the dogs, the
vultures and the ants had removed the traces of death.
The relics of the battle lay about; certain places had been

much trodden. I judged that the camp had been taken
by surprise and lost in a few minutes; and that then the
survivors had fallen back to the upturned longboat on
the beach, and had been killed there, in trying to launch
her or defend her. The place was littered with rags, bits
of clothing, and the loose grass slippers which the seamen plaited for themselves. I came upon a broken musket
with a burst barrel; it had been loaded with repeated
charges, full to the muzzle, by some crazy man. The
crammed barrel, with many unexploded charges in it,
had been blown from the stock. Part of a black-and-white
hide shield lay near it. It looked as though it had been
blown off at a gun-muzzle. Further up the beach I found
a spearhead bent double by a bullet. However, Europe
knows the wreck and mess of war too well for me to describe it further. With the wreck and the mess remained
the haunting that possessed the place, that terrible things
had been done there, and human life torn from its strength
too soon. I had no reason to suppose that many savages
had been killed in the attack; but whether or no, their
bodies were now scattered bones not to be told from those
of their victims.

The victors had plundered the camp for what they
valued, such as trade-goods and iron, especially those
things easily reached. All the slaves' shackles and irons
were gone. Many things remained untouched; a boat's
compass in brass, a quadrant, a case of charts, some boxes
and barrels of gear, and my own copy of Gay's *Fables*. The
sails that had roofed our huts had burned.

In the fighting, the longboat had been shot through
and through in twenty places; she had caught fire, from

a linstock which was still in her; and someone had staved her with an axe. She was useless to me. The second boat or cutter had had a fire lighted in her; she was burned through, beyond any repair that I could make. The little skiff was gone. I wondered if some man or men had got away with the skiff. I kept turning from the cutter to the longboat, wondering if I could patch either up, and make shift to sail to Massa. I could not launch the longboat by myself, that was sure. The cutter was too far gone. Yet I hated to admit it; I tried to think that I could mend her. She was ruined. I admitted it at last.

It had been home to us, that camp; it was a place of heart-break to me now.

I said, to myself, "Now I will go on board the ship. It is just possible that someone is aboard her and still alive."

The *Albicore* lay partly hove down upon her side. I had thought that I had seen her on fire; certainly, I had seen smoke coming from her. When I drew near her, I found that this fire had probably been accidental. She had had a mass of reed laid on her exposed side, ready for the burning off of her banacles. When the camp huts burned in the battle, some burning flakes from them blew over her, lodged in the reeds and set fire to them. Some of them had burned, but the rest, being damp, had presently smouldered themselves out. A plank or two had been charred a little; nothing to hurt. It had rained that morning, and after so much heavy rain, the ship had not been dry enough to catch.

I clambered up to her deck with some difficulty, after tying my canoe. You will not guess with what anguish I went to the hatchways, and called, "Is anyone below there" and waited for the reply which did not come. She was deserted, save for her rats, and silent, save for the gurgle of the water in her and the noise of creaking and moaning which no ship can ever be without.

I asked myself, "Why have not the Matas burned the ship?" I knew that some savages were afraid of ships; but as far as I could tell, the Matas were afraid of nothing. They may have thought that she was on fire, and been afraid of her blowing up. Or they may have thought that she was sinking. I then asked myself, "Even if they have not burned her, why have they not pillaged her? She has about her the only wealth they understand, much copper and abundant iron; and, of course, a great store of powder. In her fastenings, she is a mine of wealth. Why have they left her unsacked? There must be some overwhelming reason; what was it?"

Plainly, the warriors had been in a hurry to leave; they had snatched what booty lay to hand and then vanished. *Why?* Might it not be that the enemies of the Matas, those M'gai of whom the tales had gone, were already at their borders? Billy had said that the M'gai, those terrible men, were even now in the act of coming to the Peaks. Probably, the Matas had saved their friends and fled to avoid the M'gai. In any case, it seemed certain that the M'gai would be there at once. How would the M'gai treat Dead Ned when they came upon him? Would they welcome a doctor with a letter to the Governor of the Carolinas, or would they fatten him on yam for a week, and then cook him in a pot with pepper-pods? Which seemed the likelier? The more I thought of it, the surer I became that the Matas had gone because of danger. If there had been no danger they would at least have taken the ship's rum, and drunken themselves mad while it lasted. They had probably gone two days ago. If they had gone from danger then, the danger must now be two days nearer. If that were so, my position there was dangerous indeed.

I went down into the cabin for some clothes; my own were so foul and so torn. The ship lay so much on her side that there was no comfort below, but she was a palace to me, after the jungle.

I remembered a street preacher, or "enthusiast," as we called such, speaking in a London street from the text, "What shall I do to be saved?"

Well, what was I to do to be saved? I knew that the savages would soon be there, either Matas or M'gai, to both of whom the ship would be prize, and myself a sacrificial feast. If I stayed in the ship, I should be caught.

It seemed wise to take what I could from the ship and be gone from her. I could hope to take some things from her—enough, perhaps, to fit myself out as a sort of Robinson Crusoe. With such things, I might live in some fastness of the lagoon, in one of the inner islands, say, perhaps for years to come: if I could avoid the savages.

You need not think that I was gravely deliberating all these things thus. I was in a twitter of terror. I flung off most of my old clothes, and took new from my locker. After dressing, I had to go again on deck, to spy for enemies. I crept cautiously to a port, from which I could look out for the enemy. I was reassured by what I saw. The blue, still lagoon bore no sign of man upon it. The birds seemed feeding everywhere, among the beaches and the trees, undisturbed; no men were about there. Birds came from all directions, settled right and left, ate, pecked, fought and preened themselves, with never any alarm at all. My eyes went everywhere, and then rested on something white, among the bushes of the nearest island. The white was the bow portion of the *Albicore's* skiff. It was poking out of the thicket of water-brush, as though the rest of her had sunk. I could not understand how she could have got into that position. There she lay, seemingly tipped on her end, and held down by a weight in her stern, in quite shallow water. My heart leaped at the sight, for if I could salve the skiff, then I could, like Robinson Crusoe, take what I willed from the ship, and get away, perhaps even along the Coast to Massa. Paul's telescope was in the rack below. I went down for it, and gazed at the boat. I could make out that a body and the blackened branch of a snag, or drowned tree, held down the stern. It looked as though I might be able to free her.

I went off to her in my canoe. She lay in the outermost of the fringe of scrub which grew in the water near the island. In my unstable canoe, I could not shake her clear. I could see that she was held down by two or more bodies that lay across her stern-sheets, and that the weight of these had so pressed her down that she had caught as she drifted underneath a bough of a snag, which now held her. I thought that if I had an axe and some seamen's tackles, I might free her. After some search in the ship, I found these, a small boarding-axe, a block or two and a coil of light rope. With these I returned to the island. I landed, drew my canoe ashore, and began my task.

In those waters, you often meet the barracuda, which is

a small, greedy, fierce, swift fish, which hunts in packs and tears like sharks. I had to wade out to the skiff, through the thicket of water-bushes. These indeed gave me some stability of footing, for their roots made a tangle, but would have been no check to the barracuda. At the edge of the water-plants, I came to a softish mud; wading and slipping in this, and up to my thighs in water, I tried to free the skiff. A seaman had told me, that if ever I were trying to save anything from the sea I ought to begin by getting a line to it, "for then," he said, "it won't get away from you." I remembered this, and began by making fast my line to the exposed part of the boat. Then, drawing the axe from the rope about my waist, I turned to set her free. I cut the boughs that held her down; and saw, as I did so, the crew she carried; and having seen, had to come ashore, sit down and weep. There were three dead bodies lying across her. One was Tulp; I know not who the others had been. I saw too well what had happened to those ship-mates of mine.

In the confusion of surprise, they had run to the boat and got her into the water. They had not put in the plug; perhaps had not seen it; or had not had time to beat it in. They had been shot or speared in the water, while trying to get into the floating skiff, had fallen across her, and had drifted down in her into the brush, where the stern had sunk under them and caught in the bough. I had liked Tulp; and was sick with grief for these men. You will say that half the grief was for myself; grief often is; but it is none the less grief, and more than one can bear.

However, I had my line secure to her, and by arranging my blocks and doing everything wrong several times, and with the lines catching, and having to be cleared, and making enough noise to rouse all the blacks within a mile, as I supposed, I did suddenly succeed; I hove the boat free, and saw her grisly crew glide from her. I had then to wade out to her to tip her over and float her, and drag her ashore. I was a glad and a very weary man when I had her safe.

As I supposed, her plug was not in her. Some iron slugs had been shot into her from very close quarters; some of the paint was scorched. I cut new plugs for these holes. Her two oars were in their slings still, and her boathook was still under the thwarts. So far, all was very well; but I had made so much noise, trodden up so much mud, set floating so many chips and broken twigs, that I gave myself up for lost. However, as no one seemed to be coming to look for me, I determined to lose no time, but to pillage the ship at once. So, towing my canoe, I set forth and came alongside the *Albicore*.

Here, you will think that I had an easy task, since my wants were all simple: food, shelter, warmth, the means of making fire, some drugs, weapons, powder, tools, lines for fishing, a few pots, pans, a spar or two, a small cask or two for storing water and provisions, a small boat-sail, a little tar, light rope and so forth. I needed all these things, but how to find them and to get at them with the things all in unusual places, and the ship on her side, was less simple. Well, I began at the beginning, with lighting lanterns, and from light went on to food. I filled a bread-barge with biscuit. Captain Paul had what he called "his table" (or special provisions) in a locker in his cabin. I burst this with my axe, and took from it some Dutch cheeses and three bottles of botargos. For shelter, I got out a roll of canvas; for warmth, some blankets, a burning-glass, flints, steels and tow; for drugs and instruments, a packed tray from the medicine-chest. There was an after-magazine, but this I could not open. It had always been kept locked. Paul had worn the key round his neck; I did not doubt that Pegg had done the same. The Sailmaker had been the great fisherman among us. In his berth, I found some lines, especially those strong sea-lines, baited with spoons, and well weighted with bullets, which I had seen him use with such success, since we came to the Coast; these I took; I also took some of Puggy Crackers' priming-powder in its small, well-screwed-up iron case.

I loaded these things into the boat, after a long, steady look about the lagoon for signs of enemies. The birds were flying, swimming and feeding all about the ship and, indeed, as far as I could see. I then went to the galley for pots and pans. Most of the cook's kids and copper-pots had been landed; but the smaller things were still on board. I took some three things; a copper basin, a strong iron saucepan with lid, and a round small pot of iron, with long ears. A few of the crew's hook-pots were stuck on a batten there. I took two of them; they packed easily into the other pots. I loaded these things into my boat; again searched the shore for signs of foes, and then went swiftly to the carpenter's shop. It was near the galley, and had been padlocked, but I broke the hasp away with my axe and held up my lantern. It was very neat. All his shavings were swept up daily into a sack upon the bulkhead, which he had called his sack of shakings. The cook had come to it daily for stuff for the lighting of his fire. All the tools were in their racks and hold-fasts; all bright still, and smeared with oil against the rust of the Coast. I did not know too well what tools to take. However, his bag of daily tools was hung in its place; I judged that it would contain most things, and found that it did; as a saw, a tenon saw, a jig-saw, a bow-saw, a hammer, a wrench, a hard-wood mallet, a big and a little gouge, two chisels, a firmer chisel, a right-angle, a screever, as well as callipers, foot-rule. I took the bag; also a box of mixed nails into which I put some brads, screws, a screw-driver, pliers and a file. Be sure that I knew not the right use of all these things; it was likely that I might now have to learn the same. There were tar-pots and glue-pots. The glue I left, as I had heard Pegg say that no glue had "as much stick as spit" in that climate. The tar and the sack of shavings I took. On the bulkhead of the shop was a stretch of small chain which the carpenters' mates had been slushing, meaning to make a new rowser from it. I took it, thinking that it would make a rare boat-cable, if I had no anchor. I kept telling myself that I ought to hurry, since it could not be long before the enemy returned. This ship was a prize such as the savages could not neglect.

I did not see any small barrels likely to serve my turn, except the two small barricas or scuttle-butts, from which the crew drank when on deck. I could not prize one of these from its fittings. I took the other. For sails and spars I had to look about me. The skiff could only stand a tiny sail. I took for mast and spars a broken oar and a stretcher from the longboat. For sails, two spare hammocks seemed the best that I could see. I cut some coils of light rope from the pins, and took some line from the boatswains' lockers, especially tarry line, which I hoped might not tempt the ant. I felt, when I had loaded these on board, that I had taken most of the necessaries. I longed to stay longer and take more, for I told myself that this was my last chance of getting anything. After this I should be like the savage, who has to make what he needs for himself. But I had a terror of the blacks. At any moment, as I knew, they might come swarming down on me.

In racks on the forecastle and poop of the ship were what are called "boarding-pikes." These were very light, tough spears, with hafts of Spanish hickory and heads like the heads of lances. I took two of these. I had just cast loose to be gone, when I remembered Captain Paul's fowling-piece and musket. I went down to fetch these, with their shot and bag of bullets. I told myself that the sooner I made myself a bow and arrows and learned to use them, the better it would be. I dared not stay longer.

I had some scheme of watching the ship for some time, and coming again before dawn, or when the new moon had grown a little, and having another search in her. But as I blew out the candles in my lantern, I told myself that I should never have the courage to climb on board after nightfall, into that ship of cruelty, greed and madness, where the ghosts of so many fearful creatures must cling like bats all day, to come out at night.

I clambered into my loaded boat and shoved away, with my loaded canoe in tow. All the five miles of lagoon, all the forest, all the islands, and the great Peaks above them seemed to be full of eyes staring at me, to see which way I was going. My way was to a channel where I should no longer be seen. It was not far to that point; and certainly, as far as I could see, I was alone; utterly alone.

I had not rowed with my tow more than a hundred yards, when there came a loud snapping noise from the *Albicore*. I looked up at her, and saw the ends of her heaving-down ropes flying upwards into the air. An instant later, she righted herself in a violent roll. She rolled violently half-a-dozen times, then steadied to an even keel. "Now she will soon sink," I said to myself. "The plank has been partly stripped; I shall get nothing more from her at all, if I am not quick."

You might think that I should have been in a fervour to get my load unloaded so that I might hurry back for more. It was not so. My aim was to hide, before any savages came to find out what the noise of her righting might have been. It had been a noise like a shot, followed by two or three other shots. That should have warned any savage within a mile or two that there was trouble on the lagoon. I was all for discretion at that moment, and also for a rest. I had had a hard time, trying to salve the skiff. She was leaking badly, for my hasty repairs were not too good, now that she was loaded down. I had to find some place where I could unload her, repair her, and gather new strength for my next step.

Just before I pulled into the gloom of the channel which was to hide me, I noticed the Peaks away to the east of me. I thought, "Why not go to Edmond Quichet's cave? Why not make that my home? There is shelter and water there, so the Admiral always said." What if the Admiral had lived only to tell me of a shelter and had only died so that

I might go to it? With fishing lines and hooks, I knew that I should never lack food in that place. Fruit of sorts grew wild there in most of the year, I could maintain myself surely, alone.

I asked myself, was it not better to be alone than to be with men? What had I found among the whites, except monstrous injustice and cruelty? What should or could I expect from the blacks except the same? If I lived alone in the wilderness, it might not be much fun; nay, I knew now that it would be terrible; but better than anything that I could expect from men. I remembered so well how the Admiral had said to me, "The natives are afraid of the Peaks; they say that they are alive." Having seen them, I could well understand how simple minds might think this. Well, at least the blacks would leave me alone there.

You, who lead sheltered lives, may not know how exhausting terror is. It takes the life from a man.

When I had reached a seclusion in the heart of a cluster of islands, I drew ashore, unloaded and also beached my boats, then ate, drank, wrapped myself up and slept heavily.

I woke refreshed, and determined to go on to the cave, if indeed it existed, or ever had existed. First I had to patch the boat with rope-yarns and tar. And when I did start, I had to keep in the network of channels among the islands, going now north, now south, and only getting to the east at lucky times. Still, I dared not go openly by the lagoon. Even in my fear, the beauty of those water-channels touched me to the heart. It was strange to me that so marvellous a place was not inhabited, save by the fishing-birds and the fish and the snakes. Theirs were the only eyes that watched me, so far as I could tell. I rowed slowly on, with pads in my rowlocks to keep them from grunting to the stroke, and the westering sun sometimes glimpsed in the tree-tops to guide me.

A great many people write that suffering is good for people, that it strengthens their moral fibres and so forth. I never find that the writers of this rubbish seek out suffering for their own good, or relish it when it comes to them. As a doctor, I say that suffering is bad for people; when I find it I do my best to end it, and ever will. It is bad for the individual to suffer, and bad for the nation to have sufferers, and atrocious and damnable that nations and individuals should make others suffer. Any ill that diminishes the bodily or mental power of a man—and all suffering must do both—is hateful and of the devil. It is the Enemy that must be fought. Fight the Sins all you like and all you can; but fight suffering first.

Now I, at that time, was suffering and had been suffering for months. It had not been good for me; I was ill. As I rowed along the channels, edging my way through them towards the east, I was sure that a lot of people were on both shores of the stream, talking behind my back. They were all talking in a mutter about me, saying, "Here comes Dead Ned. This is the man who was hanged. Here he comes; he will soon be taken by the M'gai, who will skin him and rub lime-juice on him and eat him. But what matter? It is only Dead Ned."

I tell you that I was sure of these voices. Often, I turned round to see who was there; but I would only see the channel, with the trailers drooping; here and there a splash of light; here and there butterflies; sometimes dragonflies or

gaudy birds; and sometimes a fallen tree, which forced me
to go back to find a new way. As my eyes grew more used
to the forest tangle, I began to think that I saw figures in
the half-darkness flitting away whenever I turned my
head. When I became sure of these, I thought they were
M'gai. Of course, they were only birds; the matter of
their speech was the flutter of their wings; they were rising up and going twenty yards forward whenever I drew
near; little flocks of them on both sides. As they went,
incredible multitudes of little caterpillars dropped to the
earth or water to avoid them; and the fish rising at these
made a kind of whisper. Then at times I scared away
strange beasts, which looked at me and then seemed to
fade into the jungle.

Once, it seemed to me, from a certain ominous lower in
the light, that I was coming well under the Peaks; but the
channel was contrary, and I had to pull elsewhere, without even catching sight of them. Then, quite suddenly, my
channel ended in a forest of reeds. They were ten or
twelve feet tall, these reeds, and grew in water not less
than another ten feet deep—a crystal-clear water, quite
other than that river to the west. The stems of the reeds
were pale yellow, and built, as it were, in joints of about
a foot long. They threw out long spear-headed leaves of a
pale blue, a pale green, a bright silver-grey, or all these at
once. The leaves were all in movement like the leaves of
an aspen; they fluttered like myriads of butterflies. Little
birds ran about and flicked among them. The birds were
as exquisite as the leaves; for they were pale blue and
green and silver-grey, and had tiny scarlet topknots.
There were hundreds of them, and in the peace of the reeds

they twittered with tiny sweet cries, as though they were
lovely little women singing. They had no fear of me, but
I had some fear that I might scare them away in a flock
and betray my coming.

The reeds rustled, shivered, bent and closed in upon me,
so that their beauty made the entire world. I could not
row, and the water was too deep to pole. I laid in my oars
and very quietly and cautiously pulled the boat forward
by the reeds. We slid thus slowly along, till presently I
was aware that I was out of my channel between islands,
in a more open space, where the reeds were even taller
and thicker in the bright sunlight. I was shut in by them,
but knew that on my right hand I was under the Peaks.
After a time, I saw through the reed-stems a greater
brightness beyond me. Very quietly, I drew the boat towards it till I could see into a still, clear pond in which
some exquisite white cranes were wading. Just across the
pond the red Peak arose. It was the very Peak of the picture in the Admiral's room. There, just as the Admiral
had said, was a tiny natural boat-harbour of rocks. Beyond this was the scree of all the stone, earth and fallen
tree-trunk which had come from the odd red pinnacle up
in the light above it. Up there, looking most strange, still
liker an uncanny being than ever, was the red Peak; and
on it, just as the picture had shewn, was the natural butt
or lower slope that held it up, with a most strange formation along it, looking exactly as though man had once
builded a carriage road up the slope and hedged its southward side from the cliff with a great grassy rampart. This
was the place. The Admiral had come to this spot; now
here was I, his heir, succeeding to his inheritance.

I pulled my boat a little further forward, so that she slid out of the reeds into the clear water and light. The cranes were not afraid of me. They did not take flight; only like spirits surprised by a mortal, or like those swan-maidens in the tale, whose dance must not be watched by men, they moved slowly with the grace of spirits to the rocks of the harbour and thence away into the flowers. I have sometimes wondered whether they were not spirits.

In all that space of lagoon and islands I could see no mark of men. I drew out one oar, and using it as a paddle slowly moved into the harbour. Once the Admiral had landed there; now I landed. I drew the boat to the rocks and tied her fast. "Now," I said to myself, "now I will see Edmond Quichet's cave. If the King-snake is there, that the natives say lives forever, perhaps he will bite me and bring my troubles to an end." Yet, for all that, I was determined not to be put an end to if I could help it. I took out Paul's pistols and very carefully reloaded and primed them; and then slung them handily in the sea-fashion, so that I could snatch them with either hand. I took a boarding-pike against the snakes. It was drawing towards the last hour of the daylight when I set forth up the scree. If you ask what my feelings were, I should say a kind of mixture of stunned terror and stupid wonder. It was all something of a nightmare, that yet might become something of a dream.

I know that the landing-place was fragrant from aromatic bushes. The leaves of these bushes were oily and had a strong, sweet, pungent smell, which all insects avoid. I plucked some of the leaves and crushed them as I walked. Crumpling them and anon thrusting with my pike in front of me, for fear of snakes, I set forward up the slope.

In a little while, having climbed to a point of vantage, I stopped and looked behind me, over the lagoon, spread out like a mat. The *Albicore* was out of sight, behind an island. I could see the sea, now, clearly away to my left, beyond all the network of islands and channels. The birds were beginning to come in from the sea. In the west, the sky was reddening and the sun drooping down into the red. Away to the west and north, the forest spread in great rolls, with never any sight of man.

It was not wise to linger, for I felt that, if I could see all this expanse, a clear-sighted savage anywhere in that field might see me. I went on, therefore, and soon stepped out of the fragrant bush into a slope where the very grass was scanty and no bush grew. I was now well up, on that strange road or gully, which swerved round the Peak like a belt.

It was so odd a place that I must try to describe it. Up above me, very near me on my left, the Peak rose, much as a vast red spire might rise from a tower. Being so close, and so sheer, it was impressive, indeed, overpowering. It was made of a sort of red shale or rock. It looked scaly; it shone with wet and felt greasy. It was what clay might be before becoming rock, or what rock might be when changing into clay. It shot up a good two hundred feet above me, and was pretty steep; so steep, and of such a gliddery structure, that nothing would have tempted me to try to climb it. A hawk was cruising about the top. Something in the movement of the bird and the angle at which I had to hold my head, to look at it, made the Peak seem toppling, and toppling to the point of toppling over onto me. And when I looked from it to my right, there up above me were three other Peaks, each like a great alligator standing on its tail and looking at me with a smile. I tell you, they all seemed alive. I knew that in a moment, when I had gone a little higher, I should see the full tale of the Peaks, and should think them a synod of gods, not Greek gods, but African gods, who might find it fun to eat men. Remember, I was not too sane after my last few days.

The gully or roadlike formation on the side of the Peak suddenly deepened, so that I walked, as it were, in a trench, shut in by a great rampart, made of that red shale or clay (I know not what to call it), which glistened with wet and seemed to have the power to keep off any plant. It was liker a nearly dry red paint than anything else. Trickles of water made shiny tracks all over it.

Well, this gully went up, curving out towards the south; then in its curve it swept round towards the east. I followed along it, with my eyes alert for any snakes or tracks, and my ears keen for any noise of men. All the time, I had my stupid wonder that I was here, where the Admiral had been. It was not a long climb, though the slope was steep. For an instant, I thought I heard voices. I stopped, drew a pistol and cocked it. The noise was not speech, but running water just round the bend ahead. "I'm near," I said. "That's the brook the Admiral mentioned. It runs through the cave." I was very thirsty and longed for a drink of it.

Quite suddenly, the gully fell away. I was there. I was on a little level grassy court. On the right was a low earth bank, three or four feet high, with an amazing view over the sea and the Coast, and far-away islands. On my left was the Peak, towering up towards a blaze of little clouds in mid-heaven. The grassy court was full of flowers. A brook of abundant water flowed across it and through a gap in the bank down a sheer cliff to the lagoon. The brook ran from a cave, which made a tall triangular doorway into the red cliff of the Peak. I had no doubt that it was outside Edmond Quichet's cave. I stood still and called, "Is anyone there?"

On the instant, three white men, each carrying a spear, appeared at the cave-door and looked at me with wonder. The biggest and most stalwart of them, an old, erect, very noble-looking man, with long hair not yet much touched with grey, was Edmond Quichet; the others were young fellows. I would have known Quichet anywhere from that little portrait and the Admiral's description, "He was unlike anybody else."

All three were excited at my coming. Edmond Quichet called, *"C'est toi, donc, Raoul."* The others said, *"Mais non. Ce n'est pas Raoul."* One of them called, *"Qui êtes-vous?"*

The other ran to the bank, looked at the sea and the lagoon, and said, *"Non. Pas de vaisseau."*

*"Dites,"* said Edmond Quichet. *"Vous êtes de France?"*

*"Non,"* I said. *"Pas du tout."*

I dropped my pistol to the ground, and my pike also. I held up both my hands to shew that I meant no ill, and stood so for an instant, while the three looked at me. Then Edmond Quichet held out his hand to me, for me to shake. There never was anyone like him, surely, for swift decision. Not many men could have decided at so swift a glance that I was harmless. I was unwashed, unshaved, and had a look of having been in the jungle for some nights, and

of having been a felon for months. I went straight up to
him, shook his hand and said, *"M. Quichet, n'est-ce pas?"*

"Yes," he said, speaking good English, and looking at
me with a searching gaze and much bewilderment. "You
are not from France?"

"No," I said, "from England."

With some amazement and, as I thought, disappointment, he asked, "Where is your ship? What are you? Are
you in a slaver?"

"Yes," I said. "I am a doctor. The rest are all killed by
the Matas."

"Are you hurt, then?" he asked.

I said, "No. But I saw them dancing with the heads."

I began to weep at that, in a silly way. He was very gentle to me.

Presently, he asked, "How do you know me?"

"I come from Admiral Cringle," I said.

He looked at me with more bewilderment, and said,
"But come in, then." He took me by the arm to lead me
into the cave. As we entered, a big snake, with a kind of
knob upon his head, slid out of the door beside me. "Never
fear," Quichet said. "He is harmless. That is Hannibal.
We call him from Cringle's ship. He is invaluable here;
he keeps down our mice, which would otherwise plague
us."

I entered the cave with that same stupid wonder; here
I was, at that very cave from which the Admiral had
brought the painting. I had the feeling that I had been
there before, and that I knew it all from of old. So I had
and did, from the intensity of the Admiral's feeling about
it. It was just as I had imagined: big, cool, light (from

gashes in the rock), dry, too, in spite of the brook or perhaps because of it, since the brook's channel had been trimmed by man. It had a fire upon a hearth which had been built up of stones above a mass of red clay which had been cooked now to a kind of biscuit ware, like old Roman Samian. The wood upon the fire was oily and burned clearly, sending up into the cave a little very fragrant smoke. There were beds for four, slung, native-fashion, from frames and posts driven into the ground. They were strewn with blankets; woven. There was an arm-rack, with spears in it. One of the walls had been scraped or cut to a level face, and painted with some design, with what looked like verses beneath it. I took in all these things at once, with a swift look round. I had been there in mind, through the Admiral's mind; I did but confirm my knowledge.

"If you can talk," he said, "please answer me these things: they are very important. When did you come from England?" he asked. "When did you sail? What was the news from France when you sailed?"

I told him that we had had a very slow passage and could give him no recent news; but that all my latest news of France had been of great upheaval and disorder.

"When you left England," he said, "what was the opinion about the French trouble? That it would end?"

"No. That it would grow worse. 'The King is a lost man,' that was the opinion."

We had talked thus sometimes in English, sometimes in French; we were about equals in each other's tongue; my French was as good as his English. I could see that he was eager for news of France.

I said, "The report went at Monos Grandes that no French ships are on the Coast this season."

"I fear it," he said.

He walked swiftly to the door of the cave, and rapidly told the young men all that I had said, that no ship would be likely to come from France. He returned to me and asked my pardon for leaving me. He seemed much distressed by what I had said. He brooded over it for a minute, while I looked about me and marvelled. He rose and paced to and fro for a few moments. I thought, "Here I am in the cave. This is Edmond Quichet himself. I am here talking with him. Whatever it is that troubles him, it is something overwhelming."

However, he was one who rapidly judged of situations and of what could be done in them. He turned suddenly to me, with an infinite gentleness.

"Forgive me," he said, "I am not asking about you. You seem in sad distress. You say that all your crew have been killed by the Matas? When was this?"

"I can't think," I said miserably. "It was yesterday or the day before, or the day before that."

"Where? Here in the lagoon?"

"Yes; far over there to the west."

"What Matas killed your men?"

"Hundreds of them attacked us. We had some sixty Matas slaves. One of them got away and I suppose brought the others. I was out fishing at the time and so escaped. I've been hiding ever since."

"I do not understand," he said. "It is so perplexing. This is no slave-port. Where have you been upon this Coast?" he asked.

"Momboe and Massa," I said. "We came here from Massa."

"But what brought you to look for slaves at the Seize Pics?" he asked.

"We were told that the M'gai were bringing slaves here in numbers, and would be camped here with the slaves."

"Who told you that?"

"A white man, a trader, William Crackers. He may not have been telling the truth; but he had been somewhere down here to leeward, and we were all persuaded by what he said."

"Did he know the M'gai?"

"Yes. He said that they would certainly be here with slaves, because they wanted powder for one of their wars. As it happened, the Matas whom we had as slaves had all been drugged and captured by the M'gai, some little time ago."

He pondered this; it was plainly important news to him.

"Did this trader, Crackers, say that the M'gai were short of powder?"

"He said, 'They want all the powder they can get.' "

"No doubt they do," he said, "but I fear they have a great plenty."

He thought for a little while; then put his troubles from him to consider mine. He looked at me with the bewilderment that had been upon his face when he first saw me.

"Tell me," he said, "you say you come from Admiral Cringle. He was Captain when I knew him. How is the Admiral?"

"He is dead," I said.

"Generally," he said, "the slavers are shrewd. They do not try to enslave the Matas. But you bought sixty Matas, and then brought them here, where the Matas come for fishing sometimes, and within a day of many Matas."

"We were told that there would be slaves here, and besides, we knew we could mend our leaks here."

"Yes, but within a day of the Matas' spring camp."

"The English are said to be mad," I said.

"I don't think they are mad," he answered, "but they lack common sense, *bien sûr.*"

He looked at me with his look of whimsical gravity; again he seemed bewildered. "You will forgive all my rude questions," he said. "You say you come from the Admiral Cringle, who is dead. Yet you come as a doctor in a slaveship. That is strange to me. But perhaps you come as a student? Many young men seek to see the world; and young men of your profession seek the strange lands, where the terrible diseases and their remedies may be found. Are not you very young?"

"Yes," I said. "I am."

Plainly, I was a suspicious character. If I seemed so in Africa, surely my chance in the Indies would be slight. It is better to take the bull by the horns. The Admiral had said that Quichet had the two faculties of being able to persuade and to command. Now that I saw that face of goodness and gravity, I knew how truth will draw truth wherever it exists. I said, "I would like to tell you the truth about myself, however dangerous it is."

"The truth about one so young and so charming cannot be very terrible," he said.

"It is terrible and always will be terrible and dangerous."

"You are neither," he said gravely. "But continue."

The sun was going down, now, and had a great glow throughout the cave.

"I am a doctor, the son of a doctor," I said. "I was to have been Admiral Cringle's heir. He told me of you, and shewed me your paintings. He was murdered in October, by somebody. By unlucky chance there was much to connect me with the crime. All sorts of things were against me. I was tried and condemned and then hanged for the murder; but my friends brought me to life. But I was still under sentence, and people got to know that I had been saved. My friends got me a post as surgeon in the slaver there, the *Albicore*. My name in the ship was Edward Torrance. My real name is Edward Mansell. I did not kill the Admiral. I do not know who did. It was a man. And I even saw him leaving the garden and did not know it. If I am taken anywhere in the King's dominions, or anywhere else, I shall be hanged again, even if they have found the real murderer."

Remember that I was in a weak state of nerves, and had no great amount of control left; when once I had begun, I had to tell everything.

"Come," Edmond Quichet said. "It is well-known in my country that the English, with all their very great and remarkable qualities, are without common sense; without proper allowance of it. But I had not imagined that they would be so entirely without it as to think you a murderer, which you so visibly are not. This is absurd. This is unheard of. And now you have escaped the Matas. But come, we will talk tomorrow. You have been flying for your life. You must wash and feed and rest. So your name is Edward? Come in here, my grandsons, to meet Dr. Edward. These two are my grandsons, Charles Pierre, and Edmond the Young. They do not know English so well as I, but know a little."

The two came in and shook hands with me. They made me welcome there, and brought me hot water to wash with, clean linen clothes, and then prepared a supper of broth and meal-bread. I said that I had stores in the boat below the Peak. They said that those things could be fetched on the morrow. They had blankets enough in the cave. I could sleep there, and they could unload the boat by daylight. I was so very weary that I nearly fell asleep at supper. They got me to bed in one of the cots. I know that I said, "I must keep a fair watch with you; if you will call me, when it is my turn." Quichet said that they would keep no watch; no enemies were near. I was too tired to question this, or any other matter. I rolled over in the blankets and fell asleep at once. I woke, or half-woke, at times during the night; that is, I became sufficiently awake to know how very warm and snug it was. The firelight was dancing on the roof; some bats or big moths were flitting in and out; my three new friends were asleep in the cots near me, and the King-snake, Hannibal, was coiled up in a curl in front of the fire, so like a cat at home that I wondered he did not purr.

In the morning, I woke refreshed, and took more note of the three men.

"Will you tell me," I asked, "whether you are Kranois?"

"I am French," Quichet said. "These two are Kranois."

"I know a little Kranois," I said, and spoke a few sentences, learned from Mr. Kamansh.

"You have more gift for tongues than most English," Quichet said. "If it be not a rude question, may I ask if you learned your Kranois from a man with odd black specks in his left eye?"

"Yes," I said, with some surprise. "Do you know the man?"

"No; not now," he said, speaking with some distaste. "I did. Did he speak of wishing to return?"

"No," I said.

We went out into the flowery court, to see the great sea and all the shining lagoon.

"Sir," I said, "I can't thank you enough for believing that I did not kill the Admiral."

He looked at me with his strangely beautiful grey eyes, which had a look of great gravity and great sweetness mingled. "I have not yet been much mistaken in a face," he said. "Besides, who would kill Cringle, except for greed? You have no greed and no murder in your face. Forget it; begin again."

"I wish I could," I said.

"Do it, then," he said. "Let me help. Look at me, now: do I look like a pirate? You know, I was very nearly hanged as a pirate. Cringle could have had me hanged; would have, if he had done his duty. In fact, I believe I might be hanged now, on that old indictment, if it were proved that I was I. We are both under a cloud among your dear countrymen and ought to be friends. Would you care to come with us to our city when I return?"

"Indeed, indeed, I should," I said. "But what can I do there? I bring you nothing. I am a doctor, of sorts, it is true. I have a certificate here. Could you employ me as a doctor?"

"A doctor is one of the many things man always needs," he said. "But we are in sore need of many things at present; that is what brings us here; and I fear we are not going to get them."

"You, in sore need?" I said. "You have no enemies, you said. You have cities, so Mr. Kamansh told me; and all the natives think well of you."

"They have been friendly," he said; "but as your Cringle may have told you, even they sometimes turn against us. They drove us out of here long ago. The slavers bribed or tricked them into doing that. But as a rule we are very good friends with the Matas. It is the M'gai whom we dread. This land sometimes throws up a warrior king, who breeds a race of fighters. The M'gai are such. They have been coming in from the south and east for the last generation. Your Mr. Crackers expected them to be here. I believe that they spread that report, that they were coming here, to mask their real intention, which may be against us. I've been afraid of them for a long time, and have sent three times to France for weapons and powder. The last time, my son went. We have been expecting his ship daily for three or four months. But we are so far from France, and no letters come to us; we know not what is happening. I know not well what to do."

"Could you not buy guns and powder from the English at Cabo?" I asked.

"No," he said. "They would not sell to us. Your people know very well that the Kranois are against the entire slave-trade. Besides, you are too shrewd. You send weapons for sale on the Coast here, but what weapons? Things that explode and kill the shooter at the first shot. I want real weapons, not what your clever men call trade."

I asked him if he could tell me what the Kranois were, whether they come from Greece.

"I do not know what they are," he said. "Some Mediterranean race. They were more numerous once; 'seven cities'; now only two, twenty miles apart. I am in the smaller."

I asked how he came among them.

"I was sent by my rulers," he said, "to explore the land, and to discover if we might not plant the country and so end the depopulating by the slavers. I was the first white man to see the Kranois. I liked them and got on well with them. We thought that we could make all the land a great French state, with a port at Seize Pics here, and a French Governor among the Kranois. The slavers saw that that would ruin them. They charged me with piracy, and stirred up the Matas to attack me. Cringle will have told you all that. After that, the Kranois were not so friendly to me. There was no more talk of a French Governor. We lived as the Kranois had lived before. I stayed there, of course. It is my home. I had married a Kranish lady, you must understand."

"I know you have farms and herds," I said. "Mr.

Kamansh told me that you are rich in those. I could not quite learn from him what sciences you have."

"We are not so forward as we should be," he said. "Still, we are not backward. We have most things that men can want. Since my first venture, when I went rashly and tried to do too much at once, I have had to keep quiet. The rising of the Matas against us was a serious thing. We lost a lot of men, and I was blamed and unpopular. Then not many years ago, we had a pestilence in a hot summer and lost many. It sometimes happens that a disaster will take the best; that one did. Two or three of the little cities, if you can call them such, had to be abandoned and their people transferred. Then two years ago, a war-party of the M'gai raided and destroyed the last of the little cities and carried away many cattle. That was only a warning. It was then that I came again into favour. I was sent for and asked if I could obtain weapons from France, to prevent any other raid. You say, better late than never. I hope so. I thought that the weapons might come. It was late in the day, but I contrived to send messages, one after the other. Now it seems that no weapons will come."

"Will the M'gai come?"

"I fear it. In my bones, I know they will."

"Could you not stand against the M'gai, in your cities? It is said that no savages can conduct sieges."

"These savages can," he said.

"And you think they will move against you? How soon?"

"I fear very soon; and we have no real defence against them. Of course, it may be that your Mr. Crackers heard

the truth; these wandering traders sometimes do—
and even sometimes tell it. The M'gai may be coming
here."

"Sir," I said, "how did it happen that you did not see
our ship when she came in, or hear our guns? Could you
not hear the guns of the battle?"

"We have been inland, up the river, for some days, getting news of our people," he said. "We only returned
yesterday."

"I hope, sir, that you heard good news."

"There is no war yet," he said. "That is always good
news. It is a pity that we did not see you. We might have
bought some weapons and powder from you. But if we had
tried to buy, perhaps you would have seized us and sold us
as slaves. Such things happen on this Coast of Dead Ned.
Still, in our need, we might have tried."

"But, sir," I cried, "why not take what weapons and
powder there were in the ship?"

"But you said the ship was destroyed?"

"No, sir. We were camped ashore, while the ship was
repaired. The crew is destroyed."

"See how poor a guide reason may be, when we consider
the English," he said. "It never entered my head that
slavers would come with sixty Mata slaves into this
hunting-ground of the Matas, and then sleep on the shore.
It is so incredible. Then you have a ship still, with powder
and guns on board her?"

"Alas, no!" I said. "I fear she may have sunk by this.
She was laid on her side to be patched. She has broken her
bonds, and come upright. That means that her leak is
under water again; by this time, she may have filled."

"Come," he said. "Where is she? In the west channel, you say? Is she near a little waterfall?"

"Yes. They chose that berth for the sake of the clear spring so near the anchorage."

"But I know that channel," Quichet said. "Come. Quick. Tell me. What guns had your ship? What powder? What trading-powder?"

"No trading-powder," I said. "About one ton of ordinary powder; all stowed aft."

"How does the doctor know that?"

"I was friendly with the gunner. Besides, we were the only people carefully checked from smoking and carrying lights; I mean we who lived aft. Of course, some of the arms were landed for use in the camp. The powder that was landed is gone. But the guns and the cohorns are lying in the camp still; all that we took ashore. The Matas left them."

I then named the *Albicore's* armament which I knew with exactness. It was a heavy armament for a small ship: she was equipped as a privateer.

"Come," he said. "That is magnificent. And possibly half-a-ton of powder?"

"Three-quarters, at least," I said.

"But surely the Matas have plundered the ship?" he said.

"They had not yesterday. I was on board yesterday, plundering her myself. She will have sunk by now."

"Why did they not plunder her?" he asked.

"I cannot think. I felt sure that they would return to plunder her."

"The men who attacked you must have been a war-party," he said. "They must have gone on to some foray, or they would have plundered. We must get to your ship at once. Come down this way to the boats."

He was as active as a young man, when there was anything to be done. He said to me that time was always the first thing, in action; a thing done at once killed the dry-rot.

He called his grandsons, and rapidly explained what might be done. He then urged us out to the flowery court, and along a track as yet untrodden by me to the unseen side of the Peak. We passed between the northern Peaks, and down a slope, to an unsuspected, beautiful lake a mile long. On the shingly shore of this were some huts or shelters, thatched with palmetto, and beside these, drawn up, and thatched from the sun, were some large, neat, beautiful boats, all black, having been carefully pitched or painted with a very hard thin black gum, which had a glaze on it, like the black glaze sometimes set upon ancient pottery.

There were at least a dozen Kranois there; most of them youngish men. I have written elsewhere of the Kranois, their tongue, customs, laws and arts. I will not describe them now, except to say that they wore a good deal of silver, studded with amethysts, and that they all came to greet me with a ready charm and simple friendliness, which all their race at all times shewed to guests. I tried my Kranish on them, with tolerable success, as we ran the boats out and set forth to the *Albicore*.

We found her very low in the water, as I had expected, but luckily not lost, nor had she been ransacked. I suggested to Quichet that he should sail her to the next settlement, to sell her for powder and arms. He said very truly that he had no one with him who could sail her, and that he no longer had the time to spare. All that he could do would be to pump her clear, if possible, and then get at her stores and start at once for home.

While he rigged the pumps and set them going, I went with some others to take what stuff had been left upon the beach. We gathered the guns that lay ashore, and all the gunner's tools, such as sponges, worms, linstocks, prickers, wads and rammers. Of other goods unspoiled by fire we found few that were for our market.

I will not describe the various clever devices by which we freed the ship. We got pads over her wounds in the first day and had her clear in the second. We mended the ship's boats, also. I should remark that slave-ships are always well equipped with pumps. Slaves are packed low down in the hold; if water comes in at all, it affects the slaves at once, and as Pegg said, "It's bad for business when they get wet. They up and die on you with chest-cough."

We had loaded all our boats with gear, and had set off towards the cave, meaning to start at dawn up river towards the city, when I looked back and saw the last of the *Albicore*. We had stripped her hurriedly, but well; she looked like a hulk condemned. Just over her, however, I saw the sickle of the young moon bright in the green sky above the forest.

As we drew near to our landing-place, we were met by our camp-keepers, with two canoemen from the upper river. Word had come down to us that the M'gai would certainly attack the Kranois at full moon, if not before.

They had already held their war-feast, the messenger said; they were as the trees of the forest in number and threatened to come like the forest-fire.

"Right," Quichet said. "We must start at once, now. We may just get there before them."

He made some necessary changes in the equipment of the boats, so that their loads might sort better with their crews. This did not take more than half-an-hour, during which some gear was brought down from the cave, and a cup of broth given to all. After that, we took our places in the boats and set forth into the night, on and on, up the sometimes sluggish, sometimes whimpering river, under forest that sometimes hid the stars, then anon stealing out into lakes where we could set sail, under stars so bright that they were terrible. We took our turns at the rowing, but I could not row like those men. They endured in a rhythm as certain as clockwork. It never varied, and seemed not to tire them. They did not speak nor sing, only pulled tirelessly, with the great gluteal muscles and the will. I sat up and steered as Quichet told me, while the thought went in our minds, "To what are we returning? Shall we find a city of the Kranois, or will that all be smoking like a fallen Troy, with the M'gai dancing in the embers?"

Sometimes, we passed through almost a fiery mist of fireflies; I have never seen so many. Sometimes the watcher forward cried *"Ha,"* or *"Ho,"* to warn us of a danger to port or starboard. Then I would alter course, and soon would see a black antler drift by beside us, or more than that, an immense, black wallowing tree-head spanged with fireflies, slowly floundering down. Then at

times, the forest would draw in upon us, so that we moved
through a gully, and had to duck beneath the creepers.
Then the forest would give back into a distance hardly to
be scanned; we rowed through lakes and backwaters in
which the stars danced and the fish were leaping. We saw
no lights of men; all the vast land seemed uninhabited, or
given over to water, endless water, with forest and fireflies
and reflections of stars. I saw certainly no living thing
save the trees, the fireflies and leaping fish, save once, as
we drove near a shore, where something that may have
been a deer stood at a drinking-place to watch us, and slid
from us into the night.

I know not how Quichet found his way in those un-
marked channels. He said that he knew all that lower
river too well to be mistaken, having learned it when
young, in the hope that it should some day be his King's.
"It is easy, really," he told me. "Nearly all the first day is
eastward; nearly all the second, north of east. After that,
we come to the river-tribes, the Manira and the Tali-Mali,
who will give us rowers."

At two in the morning, we pulled in to a shore and made
fast for a while. The rowers ceased their clockwork; we all
came ashore, wrapped ourselves in sheepskin, in what
seemed to me atrocious cold, and slept upon a spread cloth
painted with a native tar which kept away insects and
snakes, so they said; also sleep—for me, at least, that first
night—for it had an acrid stink that sickened me. I lay
flat and rested my back, and relaxed utterly, so that I
might not feel the strain of the cramped boat any more
than these Kranois. Lying there, looking at the stars, I
thought that perhaps Ned was now dead forever; I should

be beginning again, now. I was reborn into life. What sort
of life was it to be?

We went up the great river for a long time, till it nar-
rowed and grew swifter. For one day, we went, as it were,
in the naves of endless, dark, green cathedrals, whose
clerestories flamed in the light and were glad with birds.
In places the forest was gone; it lay heaped and tossed
and tangled, as the tornado had left it; or blackened and
piked from some fire which had burned out the size of a
country. It was a silent voyage for the most part, save in
the mornings and evenings, when the birds and beasts
woke or came to roost. Twice in the forested parts, I
heard something very strange. We were then passing
through the Manira country. Manira boatmen paddled us
through all their reaches, so that we had nothing to do
but look and listen. As we went, from somewhere in the
forest, a deep musical cry rang out. It was not human, yet
not inhuman. It might conceivably have been made musi-
cally, by some string, over hollow dry wood. It was very
strangely moving. When it sounded, the Manira boatmen
sheered over the channel to the further side, and paddled
hard to get away. I asked Quichet what the men were
scared of. He said, "The gani." After we had heard the
gani for the second time, as we were going along, we
heard a slight movement in the bush and then a very
sweet, plaintive song, something like the linnet's song in
quality and the dove's coo in volume. Again our boatmen
blenched and sheered over the channel. Quichet told me
that that too was the gani, and that the gani is a sort of
female devil, who lures men to her "by the great song and
the little song," and then eats them in the forest.

At times, great beasts would rise in the river near us. Once we saw a serpent twenty feet long swimming with an erect head and open mouth across the river in front of us. He hissed at us; we were only too glad to let him go. The inside of his mouth was grey; this was very shocking to me. At times, we came to reaches where there were abundant fish. Here, there would be flights of exquisite ospreys and other fish-eating birds, plunging and taking, quarrelling over the catch and preening after eating. Then, in another reach, the trees would be hung with shrouds and streamers of many sorts, all covered with flowers of a beauty not to be told, and smelling of honey, so that all the reach was humming with the bees, the wasps, the hummingbirds and the butterflies. The river was all starred with dropped blossoms, and with insects stupefied with the honey, slowly struggling to death. Sometimes these reaches were so bright with the sun and so exquisite with colour that the Kranois seeing them would break into song. Then a darker reach would follow, with no sound at all, all still save for the deep note of the river. But we had to listen for that. When we had thought that all was still, we would listen and there was the note of the river, going on and on, with slippings of stuff from each bank and gurglings as it licked past the shallow and a deeper, more ominous note, of an enormous power set loose upon her path to the sea, and of a purpose that no man could deflect.

Then from time to time, often as though our passing in those still reaches had disturbed the balance of centuries, if not of thousands of years, there would come a sudden alteration in the peace and the stagnation; something would happen. A moment of suspense would change to a stripping and a ripping, and then a tree would totter and collapse, generally just behind us. The little wind or draught of our passing had disturbed it, so that the life, already held by a hair, could no longer endure. We would turn to see its fall, which sent up always a sort of smoke of insects and little birds.

We steered nearly always on the eastern or south-eastern shore of the river; Quichet said that sometimes a dwarf tribe of forest savages came birding on the other shore, and shot poisoned arrows at all who passed. They did not shoot at us. After some days of rowing up the stream, I felt that the river was a part of our days and of our lives. Its song was something to which we tuned our efforts, and by which we lived. For the rest we fished as we passed, we tied up to the bank when it seemed safe from ganis and snakes, we sometimes cooked and feasted; and sometimes even slept peacefully, in the smoke of fires lit to drive away the flies. Then we would re-embark and press on, up that mysterious stream, up that dim, drip-ping, dark nave towards the promised sanctuary. At nights, when beasts and birds had fallen still, some of the Manira sent out their cries, pitched in the age-old way so as to carry across the distance, and out of the unknown came answers not understood by myself, but audible as a murmuring in the air.

I was Dead Ned, brought all these miles to this, for what? Often as we went I would wonder, is this real, is not this all a dream? Soon, I kept thinking, I shall wake from all this strangeness of the forest and find the boat-men gone, and the river no longer curving on ahead. Or perhaps it will curve suddenly into a road at Cholsington leading back to Hannibal House.

I remember that at one point we passed through "the land of the Indoto," who had been attacked and destroyed some years before by the men of the slave-gangs, so that the Indoto were no more. They had had fish-weirs across the river; these were now broken. The huts and little landing-stages were broken and deserted, and the plantations were already gone back into the wild.

"They were gentle river people," Quichet told me. "Most of them killed themselves on the way to the Coast; they could not bear the thought of not getting back to the river."

Presently, we were out of all trace of the Indoto, going on, up the great stream, not sensibly less yet, but now trending more and more to the east, towards the land of the Kranois. Then came the grim day when we met a canoe with a message, "The M'gai are moving." The only counter to their moving was to move faster ourselves. We divided the men into three watches and gave up all rest beside the banks save in the heats of noon. We came out of the forest into a more open land, of what men call savannah, with rolls of grass and the trees in clumps and copses. Foliage there was of another colour from the dark, hard, metallic green of the forest, it had no blaze from flowers; all was of a dusty, faded green, with much yellow in it, yet the yellow toned down as though it were tired. All the landscape was of this colour. The river ran through it between banks which were usually high.

As we went on, we were presently hailed by another messenger, who called to us from the bank and asked to be taken on board. He said that no doubt the M'gai meant to attack the city; but they had not yet appeared before it. All their army was afoot, so the reports said. He thought that we might just reach the city before they came. We should meet a horse-train with carts and waggons at Five Men Bend in the river the next morning. We could load our stuff into the carts and come on with the carts. The upper river had fallen so much that we could never get to the town in time by water He told us all these things in our boat, as we rowed on upstream.

"You have the arms, I see," he said.

Quichet told him that they were not the arms he had hoped for, still they were arms.

The messenger said, that we had better keep well out in the midstream from that point onward, for the M'gai scouting parties were out, and might well shoot or spear us as we passed if we hugged a bank.

It was at this point that I began my new life.

I said to Quichet, "Sir, if we are likely to be attacked by scouting parties, let us be ready for them. One of our cohorns in the bows of each boat will settle any party that may try to stop us. Let us mount and load them; then we shall be ready."

It is a simple matter to mount a swivel-gun in the bows of a boat. When we had done it, in each boat, we arranged our gunners. The Kranois did not use guns; they knew nothing about them. I, therefore, took charge of the gun in the leading boat; Quichet's grandsons, who knew at least something about guns, had charge of the guns in the second and third boats; Quichet brought up the rear-guard.

After resting, eating, and seeing all ready if we were
attacked, we set forth for a hard night of rowing. We kept
the midstream, even though the current was strongest
there, and all night watched the bank on each side for the
heads of M'gai scouts waiting for us. It was a night of
needless alarm. If we had but thought, we should have
known that the M'gai could not know that we were coming, and would not have scouts out to watch the river.
This fine thought occurred to me just before dawn, as we
neared the Five Men Bend. I thought it so important,
that I pulled out of line and mentioned it to Quichet, who
said, "I have been thinking of that; but I am truly anxious about the convoy sent to meet us. A cart convoy is a
noisy thing, and leaves many tracks. These M'gai have
the eyes and ears of animals. If their scouts have been out
at all, they must have learned of the convoy; if they have,
be sure we shall be attacked on our march to the city."

"We shall find the convoy killed, then," I said.

"No," he answered. "Natives always let men pass, and
try to kill them as they go back. They will bid you welcome and feast you; then spear you as you leave. It will be
the march to the city that will be the difficulty."

"We can mount cohorns in the carts," I said.

"Yes," he said. "But the ponies have never heard a gun
fired. They will bolt directly we shoot."

"None the less," I said, "let them. We will mount the
cohorns in the carts and drag the carts by hand. If the
ponies bolt, let them go; we will rally round the guns and
defend them. If the enemy are in scouting-parties, the
chances are that they will not charge home; only dog us,
while they send back runners. We shall be safe."

It was just enough twilight for me to see that Quichet looked at me with approval.

"Good," he said. "And there are the Five Men ahead. Pull aside. I had better go first here, to hail."

We stood on, in line, with Quichet's boat leading. Presently I saw that the bank ahead was low, and that the main stream swerved off away to the westward; this was the bend. I saw then that the Five Men were knobs or butts of stone, too big to have been raised by man, not far from the bend itself. They looked too like devils to be quite canny to men who had been all night in fear of attack. We drew past the Five Men; then heard the whinny of horses ahead, and saw figures moving on the river-bank. Quichet hailed them in French and Kranish; and was answered in French. So far all was well. We drove in, to a beach of shingle, ran the boats up, and met there the men of the convoy, who backed their carts down, so that they might be loaded. All there were in a good and lively dread of the M'gai, who were spreading terror and death. If they were not there, they were thereabout, and had killed some outlying herders. They had sworn to level the city of the Kranois with the plain.

The sky in the east was now silvery with morning; it was acutely cold. Gleams of silver were on harness and armour, as the men backed down the carts. The horses were little, hard, active ponies, all kicking with the cold and catching something, no doubt, of the anxiety of their masters. Quichet and I took four of the light carts for the cohorns. My design was to use these as light artillery to protect the head and tail of our convoy. Each of the four carts was armed with two cohorns, and had in it a breaker of powder and box of bullet. I took charge of the match for two of the carts; Quichet took the match for the other two. He led the convoy now. I brought up the rear.

In the pallor of dawn we set forth from the Five Men Bend, with scouts riding out on our flanks and to our front; then Quichet and his guns, dragged by teams of young men; then the gun-convoy, horsed; and my own guns in the rear, guarded by horsemen riding well out on the flanks. We pressed on into a savannah land, which soon began to take on colour as the light grew. It was very beautiful, I thought; but so different from anything known to me; the scrub was so grey and the grass so pale. We kept a sharp lookout for the enemy. We saw nothing of moment, but often thought we did. Sometimes the outriders rode in to warn us that some place ahead was a good place for an ambush, and must be approached with caution. Once one of them brought in something which shewed that an enemy had been there within some hours. It was a little pot or bottle made of the joint of some plant like the bamboo; it was exactly stoppered with a plug of hard wood and was neatly slung with a strip of hide. It contained a wet white clay for the renewal of the stripes painted on the warrior's face. The scout, who brought it in, had been a tracker. He said that it had been left the night before, and that the man who left it had been in his hiding-place for at least an hour, and had then gone on to the north-west.

After some hours of marching, the clumps and copses became scarcer; we emerged suddenly upon a great open expanse of grass. It seemed to stretch on forever, in the deep, clear light. In its suddenness and sanity it struck me at once as the most beautiful place in the world. It gave an extraordinary impression of freedom and health. There it was rolling along as free as a wild horse, marked or lined in two places by watercourses where streams ran to the river away to our left. In the distance, possibly thirty miles from where we were, great masses of mountain rose up and shone with snows. Between us and the mountains, and away also upon our right, were pickets of horse driving cattle. All these trains and droves were converging, as we were, upon the common centre, now plainly to be seen. There ahead of us was our goal, the long looked-for, long hoped-for home, the City of the Kranois.

It stood upon a gentle rising of the plain; you could not call it a hill; and yet when you were at a distance, and when you were near it or in it, the city dominated the plain; there was the queen, enthroned.

Between us and the city was a small watercourse, marked with shrubs and reeds. Beyond the city was a second, much larger, watercourse. I saw that these two waters joined about a mile to the west of the town, and ran on into the west as one.

The city herself rose up before us with a style that took my breath away. I had been in untamed savagery for some weeks; I had seen nothing in Africa that was not savage; now here was a city, walled and builded, the sort of place from which we take our word "civilisation." The walls were a full eighteen or twenty feet high, ramped and battered back for two-thirds of their height and perpendicular at the top. Who had built such walls? Who were these Kranois? The walls were of well-laid, hewn

stones of hard white-grey. There was a gate in the wall in
the side of the city nearest to us; we were on a track
which led to it.

There were some biggish buildings within the walls;
some of the lesser buildings had been lime-washed white;
and the walls and the seven tall watchtowers were
crowded with people, among whom weapons flashed in
the light. I saw shutters open at the upper windows; banners were thrust forth to welcome us; all of them were
white and blue for the Kranish colours; we were seen.

Quichet came back to me from the front of the column,
and said, "Here is the City of the Kranois. What do you
think of her?"

I said, "She is just what I have always thought a city
ought to be."

He said, "Those are the outland herders bringing in the
droves. They have left it long, for see: out there are the
M'gai."

"Come on, then," I said at once. "Let us bring the cohorns out to that side; a shot or two may keep them off."

"You are right," he said.

He called to his grandsons. We drew out our armed
carts to the east from the column, so as to protect the
droves making for the city. I had spoken and acted instinctively. It seemed to leap into my mind that that was
the thing to do. I blew on my match to make it glow, and
kept my eyes on what Quichet said were the M'gai. He
was right; there they were; a group of a dozen men on
ponies and a party of about twenty braves on foot. They
were on a swell of the plain about half-a-mile from us. I
judged that they were debating if they could stampede

the droves before they reached the walls. It was plain to me that they could not, for if they tried it we should have a fair shot at them; but that was no reason why they should not try. I told Quichet to call out some of the spearmen of the convoy to line the intervals between our carts; he called, and they came. I wished that they had muskets instead of spears, and that they were the *Albicores* instead of the Kranois; still, they came out to us, as we took up position, and waited, while the slow, mooing, loitering, stupid cattle moved on to the gates. Meanwhile, the M'gai men rode nearer on their ponies; not very much nearer because, as they advanced, some horsemen rode out from the city towards us, and soon joined us. The M'gai were joined by their foot soldiers; and then both parties stared at each other, five hundred yards apart, and made no sign of attack; while the cattle slowly dragged on to the gates.

When at last the herds were entering the city, we had a chance to draw back. Very slowly, covered by the horse, and often turning to face the M'gai, who slowly advanced as we withdrew, keeping their distance, we also went towards the gates. Three more mounted M'gai cantered up to their friends from the northern parts; they all halted to watch but made no attempt to attack. In a little while, I found that I was right under the city walls, near the gate, and it was time for our party to enter in. "Come in, then," Quichet said to me.

I know that my heart beat when I saw those great walls, and the helmed and cuirassed guards inside the gate. It was a big, strong, wooden shield of a door, swinging on a central pivot, and all plated and knopped with heavy bronze gone green. We went in, last of all, after the carts had gone, and saw the guards heave the gate to, and lift up and ship the three great balks which served as bolts. I was shut into the City of the Kranois.

The cattle had been driven into the space below and just within the walls. They were lowing there, and nosing to some stalks which had been flung there. The carts had gone up the lane round a bend between walls out of sight into the city. I was standing with Quichet, looking about me, when someone came running and thrusting (a good many people were there, some citizens and men of our convoy), and called Quichet by name, asking him to come.

Quichet smiled and said, "I'm here; I'll come." He turned to me and said in English, "I shall only be a few minutes. Wait here for me. I'll show you to a shelter."

He went off hurriedly with the messenger, and left me to look about. His grandsons had gone somewhere; I could see nobody from the boats; all my friends had scattered. I felt very much alone. The drovers moved here and there, trying to keep the cattle from bunching and blocking the passageways; the men near me moved up onto the walls, to look about. I did not like to leave the place, lest I should miss Quichet when he came for me.

It was very plain to me that the Kranois, though they might have been expecting the M'gai for months, were quite unprepared for them. On every face, there was a look of doleful anxiety; and about the city there was a sort of flavour, or forefeeling, of disaster; the air seemed to say, "This place is doomed; these throats will be cut; these faces will soon be skulls, and their hair will theek the nests of the redbirds." The redbirds were the only cheerful things there. They were exquisite little birds, with long tails, and wings of scarlet; they were boldly plucking hairs from the cattle for their nests in the crannies of the walls.

I stayed there a long time, waiting for Quichet, and wishing that he would come. I wanted to get the guns mounted, at least, and to be up, on the walls, so that I might see what was happening. Half the citizens were up there on the walls, and were made dumb by what they saw. What was it that was daunting them?

As Quichet did not come, when I had loitered for more than an hour I went up to the walls, and up the stone stairs to the fighting platform. When I looked over the parapet, I saw what had stricken the people dumb, and was stricken fairly dumb myself.

We of the convoy had entered the city in front of some forty savages. Now, the M'gai army was in sight; they had taken position on the rising in the plain where we had seen them, and were settling into camp there, from the south-east to the north-east of the city. A good many who were mounted on ponies were now herding cattle into the Kranish farmers' cattle-pens behind their camp. I knew from what the Kranois said, that the cattle belonged to the city and had now been lost. I stared at this force, and tried to judge its strength; certainly, some thousands were there.

In their order, their certainty and quiet power, they gave me the sickened feeling that was in the hearts about me. I had been staring at the camp to the south-east. I now looked to the south, along the track by which we had come.

On that side, on the further side of the little river which we had crossed, an army was slowly marching in a column two abreast. They stretched in a narrow ribbon along the southern side of the stream, almost to where it joined the bigger river. These men were not five hundred yards from us. They halted, suddenly, and sat in rank, while two men upon ponies rode along the line and surveyed the city. After that, the sitting warriors rose, and gathered in groups. There was no doubt that these men felt themselves to be the owners of the land they trod. Something of their feeling roused acquiescence in the minds near me.

Nothing happened after that, for a long time. I was still near the gate by which we had come in. I still hoped for Quichet, who did not come. I stood and stared at these M'gai, and then looked, if Quichet might be there. I had often read of war; now here it was. I had often heard of destroying savages; now I saw them. I suppose that I waited on that wall, weary, anxious, hungry and not a little scared, until noon, when to my joy I saw Quichet coming down the lane for me. I called to him; he saw me and signed to me to stay on the wall, as he would join me there.

"It is hard to do one thing," he said, "when others want you to do ten. I could not get away, as I had planned. These are the M'gai. We are shut in to the north just as we are here; they are coming now to a parley."

Indeed, a movement among them had begun some minutes before; the army of the M'gai had formed and were advancing on us in line. I counted eight main divisions of them, and reckoned that each contained seven hundred men. The regiments or tribes were each readily distinguished; one wore tall plumes of birds, one the skins of spotted monkeys, one leopards' skins, and so forth. They marched silently and with speed, and halted about a hundred yards from the walls. As they halted, they grounded their spears and long narrow shields. Each man began very gently to tap his white hide shield with his spear hand, till a gentle drumming noise filled the plain. It grew louder and louder, till it rang and roared and echoed. Each drumming man, under his headdress, seemed not less than seven feet tall; each grinned as he drummed, so that the rows of teeth made a white streak down their line. The broad blades of their stabbing spears shone in the sun, and each man glistened with oil. They had a ripple in their walk, a sort of ease and insolence in their bearing. Perhaps few of them had ever seen a city before, and they knew not quite what sort of puzzle it might be. But it was plain that they judged that their spears would soon solve the puzzle. Their chieftains stood in advance of the line; and now, presently, the leaders rode up, dismounted, left their ponies with young bucks who wore scarlet birds as loincloths, and advanced to the parley. The main chief was a short, squat figure, seared all over his chest and arms with the weals of scars, and of enormous physical strength; he was very black. With him was a taller morose-looking savage, not nearly so dark, and certainly thirty years younger. He was the chief of a regiment who wore big green wooden rattles on their arms. Each man in moving made a sort of dry, threatening rattle like that of the rattlesnake. The two men were followed by a Kranish captive, led by two savages. He was to be the interpreter.

The two chiefs advanced towards the gate near which

we stood. They moved with insolent ease and mastery, as
though all the land belonged to them. While they advanced, and after they had halted, the M'gai beat their
shields and hissed. I know no more frightful sound than
the one they made, thus. We were joined at this point by a
Kranois, who had been in the M'gai lands, and spoke their
tongue.

The young chief called something thrice in a question-
ing tone, and at Quichet's bidding this Kranois replied, to
ask what was the reason of this coming of the M'gai into
the land of the Kranois?

I give the answers and the questions as they were afterwards translated to me. They follow the ritual in use
among the savages of Europe and elsewhere, thus:

THE M'GAI: I speak for the King of Kings, and Slaugh-
terer of Slaughterers, the King of the M'gai. At great in-
convenience to himself, and with enormous condescension,
he has come hither to make friends with the Kranois, of
whom the fame has come, even to the M'gai.

How can I describe the King, my Ruler? Behold him.
He is one before whom all tremble; his friendship is a
treasure above wives and cattle. He brings peace with
both hands.

Lo, now, you Kranois, how you reject his friendship. He
cannot understand why you citizens have retired within
your walls, instead of greeting so great a King with
feasts and the giving of wives. The King asks only friendship and a refreshment of cattle for his young men. Let
you, therefore, open all doors, bring forth fat cattle and

let us feast together. It is only by feasting and the inter-changing of wives that friendship between nations can be maintained. This, that the M'gai ask, they ask with con-descension, since many great nations have asked it of them with tears and prayers.

THE KRANOIS: We cannot understand such talk. This for centuries of moons has been the land of the Kranois and of their cattle. You, the M'gai, have come hither unin-vited and have killed our cattle and herdsmen, and this without provocation of any kind. We will not offer feast to such visitors. Rather, we say that we have sent for our friends, who are even now upon their way, to demand pay-ment for the men killed and cow for cow. Let your King, therefore, depart, and take with him his army.

THE M'GAI (*with amazement*) : This is not the way to speak to the King of the M'gai, before whom Kings trem-ble; nor will I repeat such words to him. It is plain that I am now speaking to a man bewitched or without sense. However, the King, my Master, loves peace, and brings it with both hands. He much would prefer that you open your doors and feast him as is fitting.

THE KRANOIS: It is for a host to choose his guests; none but the unmannerly invite themselves. We, the Kranois, do not intrude on the M'gai, nor do they invite them. Rather, they ask them to be gone.

At this point, the King of the M'gai came forward. He had great dignity, and spoke well. I was much impressed by him.

"Hear, you people of the Kranois," he cried. "For years, the cattle of the Kranois have been trespassing into the hunting-fields of the M'gai, so that our hunters have had their game disturbed, its food eaten, and its wells defiled, and this without redress, even after many complaints. Now we are come to demand a settlement, and to insist that the young men of our army be welcomed and feasted until a settlement is reached. Will you, therefore, open to us and be our friends?"

To this, the only possible answer was, "No."

"See, men of the M'gai," the King cried, "they reject our friendship. These Kranois are men of blood and war-mongers; they ever were. They scorn our offer of peace. What, then, shall we offer them, Men of the Broad Spear-heads?"

The Men of the Broad Spearheads, at this, suddenly flung up shields and spears and shouted, "War."

"So be it," the King cried to us. "We will give you war."

No act of war followed at that instant; he turned, mounted his pony and rode off. His regiments saluted his passing with lifted spears. When he was halfway to his camp, the regiments turned, moved from the city, reached their old positions and sat down.

I remembered reading in some history book of Louis Quatorze, how "the King's army sat down before a town." Here was another king's army sitting down before a town; and I was inside the town, and could see how ominous it was. We were shut in. How could we drive them away? And if we didn't drive them away, how long could we live, shut in?

Well, we watched them sit down before us, and set their

guards, then Quichet said, "But come, now; we are both tired out, and they expect you. Come along the wall; it is quicker, so."

He led me along the southern wall-top, right to the western end of the city, where there was a citadel of no great height, but very big. He lived in the southern end of the citadel. He led me across a paved court and into his house, which was lime-washed white, within and without, and smelt of that brisk djriza gum that, when burned, will keep all flies away. Coming out of the sunlight, it was dark and confusing at first, for the windows were small, and shuttered against any sling-shot from the enemy.

After some darkness of passage and corridor we came to an unshuttered room which faced west; I could see through the open window away over the plain. There was a cot-bed in it, and a big coarse basin of blue and white pottery, full of hot water.

"This will be your room," Quichet said. "You might like a wash. Food is ready for us, through the door there, in that second room."

I swilled some of the mud of the river from myself and went to the second room. It was small and faced west like the other. A girl was standing there, waiting by the spread table. She was dressed in a white linen and wore a little fillet of white in her hair. As I appeared, she moved swiftly over to welcome me; she shook my hand and said, in French, "Be welcome. You are tired and hungry. I am Monsieur Quichet's granddaughter, Yvonne." She had dark eyes, and very beautiful brown hair; the face was pale; it had a darling look of life and charm on it.

I said, "How do you do, Mademoiselle Yvonne?"

"We do not say Mademoiselle among the Kranois," she said.

"Yvonne, then," I said.

Quichet came in; we three sat to food, which two of us sorely needed.

"You will need rest, both of you," Yvonne said. "You have had no rest since you left the Coast."

Something in Yvonne made rest quite the last thing that I longed for. I had been sad and sick at heart till I had come into that room; now I was alive again. I was once more one of a home, a member of a community; these were friends; and there arose in me again a welling-up of feeling which had stirred me on the march: that this business of the war was one that I could do.

"No rest for me, thanks," I said. "I must get to those guns. I am a gunner, of a kind; we must get the guns mounted."

"Grandfather tells me that but for you we should have nothing," she said.

"I hope that your grandfather will tell you everything about me," I said.

I was sick at heart to think that when he did tell her everything perhaps she would not speak to me again; still, I was not going to pose as anything.

"Will you tell me everything?" she said to me.

"Everything."

"Then, what chance have we of ever driving off the M'gai?"

Now, I had read that savages do not undertake sieges. Yet here were savages who plainly did and could, as Quichet had said that they would. I, therefore, could not say that they would be gone in a day or two; they would not. I knew, from my talks on the way, that the other city of the Kranois twenty miles away might send help, of spearmen and bowmen, but that the force might not be strong enough to reach us. I could see that our city was not strong enough to sally out and fight the enemy; and that no other help was to be had.

I looked at Yvonne and said, "We have walls, which they cannot scale, and certainly cannot breach. We have some guns, which will cause them some damage. And we have ourselves, who are utterly unbeatable."

She smiled.

Quichet said, "That is the spirit."

"Come on, now," I said. "We must get the guns mounted. We will beat these M'gai back into the wilderness."

We had risen from our seats, to set about it, when something rushed over my shoulder and cracked a piece of plaster out of the wall. Another followed it, and took something out of the ceiling. "Sling-shot," I said. I leaped to the wooden shutter and jammed it to. A third stone struck it as I closed it. I had a glimpse of the western field before it closed. There, dancing with joy and hurling with exquisite grace, were some fifty M'gai slingers. Outside our southern wall, as I could hear, were others. The walls, shutters and towers of the Kranois were rattling under a hail of smooth pebbles from the brook.

"We must get the guns to these gentry," I said.

If we didn't, those gentry might get Yvonne.

# KICKING NED

I sometimes call this part of my tale "The Skysail" or, perhaps, after all, "The Trust-to-God."

Once, in the *Albicore,* as we ran in the Trade, and I admired the tower of sail upon the mainmast, a seaman said to me, "Ah, sir, but we ought to set a skysail, above the royal, there."

"But a little sail, so far up, cannot do much good," I said.

"No, sir," he answered, "but nothing sets a ship off like a skysail. It finishes her off."

"Do sailors ever set anything even above a skysail?" I asked.

"Some set a Trust-to-God," he said. "Not many have one; but it's a very fine thing, a Trust-to-God. It finishes a ship off, even better."

W E WENT out from the house, and presently reached the steps which led to the platform of the south wall. Here Quichet and his grandsons were stopped by some men who were coming along in search of them. I thought that the men were sergeants or minor officers of some sort; they had blue and white Kranish tassels on their chests. I was disposed to like all the Kranois, but I did not much like the looks of these two. They said, that the Quichets, grandfather and grandsons, were awaited at headquarters for their report.

"Right," Edmond Quichet said, "we will go there at once. You, Ned, will you go up to the wall there, and wait for us?"

"Yes," I said. "How long will you be?"

"Twenty minutes, or half-an-hour."

"Very good. I will see where we can mount the guns."

"Don't go far, or get yourself lost," Quichet said in French. "Besides, this is war, and you might unwittingly rouse suspicion. They are touchy about foreigners."

"I'll be careful," I said.

We waved to each other; they went off with the sergeants, and I, after seeing them away, went up to the wall.

Even in that short space of time, the slingers had done their task; they had caused all the dwellers near the walls to close their shutters. The slingers had not withdrawn

into their lines. I could lean upon the parapet and take
stock of this new phase of my dream.

Well, there we were, shut up within the City; it is true
that, at the moment, the M'gai could not get in to us, but
it was plain that they meant to try, and it was plain to me
that we could not get out, just yet. You have never been
shut up? I had been—in Newgate. Believe me, the knowledge that you can't get out is daunting to the soul. One of
the worst points of being shut up is that you take the
shut-up point of view, you lose your individual soul and
become a part of a herd in a pen whose shut-up soul is
half a soul. I stared at the positions of the M'gai; they
were making themselves snug in camp, with huts and
fires; they were penning the taken cattle, or whetting
their spears. They were settling in, till their task was
done and the City taken. Even now, those whetters of
spears would shake their spears at us, dance a few steps
towards us, and shout their threats. They looked like con-
querors. When I looked from them, so sure of their might,
to the faces of the Kranois, I felt that I might be in Newgate again, in a Hold big enough to contain thousands, all
of them 'going out on Monday'; they were awful faces.
They had the real Newgate look, of horror and terror,
with wandering eyes, a sort of weak smile ever giving way
to a savagery, and then the horror and terror again, with
the eyes unable to settle, and the mind ever on Monday
and eight o'clock. To look at them was to know that no
man there had any hope; despair was everywhere. Now
that is the most catching of all complaints. I took it. I
heard what they said, and took the sickness from them.
They had been asleep, while the M'gai had been active;

they had been fools (to put it mildly), while the M'gai had been devils of astucity and treachery; they had neglected warnings, while the M'gai had made even readier than before. Now, suddenly, the M'gai were there. Very quickly, as a stranger will in an intense time, I began to understand the folly of the Kranois. They had great estates away to the east, where the Plainsmen, or country-dwelling Kranois, bred cattle. These Plainsmen had warned them repeatedly that the M'gai meant to attack. But there was, as I now found, an intense antagonism between the city and the country dwellers; each thought the other inferior, and was partly right. These two parties of the Kranois had been jealous of each other, and had thwarted each other in all possible ways. Quichet had told me of this, but the passion of the reality startled me, now that I was there in the town. And now the Plainsmen were proven right. The city men, or Old Party, had disbelieved and were unprepared. Now war was on them, the spears were at their throats, and nothing was ready. The blow had come so suddenly that I believe the M'gai could have taken the city then by a resolute rush. The walls were manned by a lot of corpses, already killed, by the look of them, and almost without weapons. The Council was meeting (so men said); busy-looking, ineffective men of authority were bustling about, going from one place to another. I could see a lot of helpless people in the square, staring at some guarded doors, over which pennons fluttered. Within those doors the City Fathers sat, and I hope felt sorry for their follies. But what were the City Fathers doing? Why were they not doing something? What good was talk, at this stage? Why had they not sent

men with Quichet to get my guns mounted and put into
action? I could be training guns' crews, and putting long-
shots into the M'gai headquarters. Yet here were these
people talking in closed doors, while their flock, the citizens, were all about me in despair. This anger at the City
Fathers was increased as time went on and nothing happened. I was up there on the wall, waiting. I was not
rudely treated, but I was made to feel, as Quichet had
warned me I should be, that I was one of the foreign
party, ranked by the city people as only a shade less dangerous than Plainsmen. The men came past me and
stared, and asked who I was and then stared again. Quichet, of course, was somewhere down among those City
Fathers, telling them that he had some guns. I wished
that he would soon come up and help me to bring the guns
into action.

As Crackers had told me that a good gunner should, I
made careful estimates of the distances of the M'gai positions. I told myself that with certain charges of powder,
we could reach them and give the M'gai some surprises. I
watched carefully for some sign that the M'gai had guns.
As far as I could discover, they had perhaps half-a-dozen
trade-guns, as the trade called them, that is, cheap iron
tubes upon stocks, which were meant not to fire. Some
natives loved to buy these from the slavers, for the glory
of having what looked like a white man's weapon. Certainly, as yet, they had no powder, for they fired no shot
at us. I could see nothing like even the smallest cannon
among them. I was cheered by this fact, and needed cheer,
for there were a great many of these M'gai, and their insolence of bearing was much unlike the woe of the citi-

zens. Indeed, why should they not seem insolent? They had been promised victory, and had had it. They had won the white man's cattle and pasture, now they would take the white man's city. From time to time, savages would stroll out singly towards the walls. Always, these strollers were big, leading men, over six feet in height, magnificent in bearing and in build, with great plumes over their brows, and an array of bright bangles on their arms. They were almost naked. Most of them had long narrow shields, black and white; nearly all of them had two short spears with long, rather broad heads. These boasters would impudently stroll towards us, threaten us with their spears and shout insults. It was shocking to me that the Kranois made no attempt to shoot at them: not an arrow, not a slingstone was sent from the walls at them; and this in a city said to have many good bowmen. Well, it was galling to me and hard to bear; but what was harder to bear than this tacit surrender was the look upon the faces. When I looked at those faces, I raged.

Where was the commander? What was he thinking of, to let the citizens get into this state? Remember, I had seen active service. I had been in the great, never-ending war of Man against Disease. I had been a staff officer to the great and blessed general Josiah Copshrews, and I knew some of the rules of the war. Often in that war I had been puzzled, I had been hopeless; but it was a rule of the school never to shew it, never to admit it, never to let our side see anything but the hope of glorious victory. Our rule was to try on, and to try again, and if one remedy failed, to be ready with another, and if that failed, to be prepared to admit our error, and make some new ap-

proach. We were to give life and to be helpful; we were to
be helpful and to give hope; we were to give hope and
faith, so that those might remain when all else went.
What of all that was here? This was appalling. This was
nescience, accidia and paralysis. Nay, I thought, is not
this the sign that they are outworn? Have they not lost
the power to adapt themselves? Suddenness is the test.
Improvisation is the virtue; anyone can live by routine.
These are now shaken from routine and are lost. So I
thought, and feared and raged, while I waited for some
sign of leadership and hope. I waited, too, and in vain, for
my friends.

Up there on the wall, I had a fair view of the city. I had
felt its pulse, so to speak, and did not like what it told.
Its frame seemed to me to be pretty strong. I had been
told to stay where I was till Quichet or someone from
him came to fetch me. After waiting for an hour or more,
I got into the way of taking short walks now in one direction, now in another, on the walk on the wall-top behind
the parapet, always glancing back to see if someone had
come for me. I must say that I hoped on some of these ex-
cursions to have a glimpse of Yvonne. I did not succeed in
this. I went along the south wall and looked along the
east wall, then turned back and had a look along the west
wall. At last, feeling that no one was going to come for
me, I walked swiftly and boldly right up to the end of the
western wall and had a good look along the northern face
of the city. I saw it for what it was, a very strong, walled
city. Quichet had told me in the boats that most of it was
very old. The lower parts of most of the walls were built
of great stones. These may have been of almost any age. I

could see the huge blocks and marvelled how they had been put into place. They made me wonder if the city had not been raised by the Giants. In most places these rude Homeric walls were topped by a politer building of small, well-dressed stones. The north wall stood upon a succession of outcrops and little cliffs, I know not how to call them, of hard black rock. There were traces of ancient building among these outcrops. The rest of the city stood on the level plain. I had been told, and now saw for myself, that the walls were all pretty good, except at the southwestern angle. They had been going to repair this for many months, but had put it off and put it off. I will not say that it was dangerous, but it had a sort of bulge upon it, which I did not like the look of. To my medical eye, it was too like an abscess that might burst. I wondered if the shock of my guns, when fired near it, might bring it down and make a breach.

Someone had said to me that Troy could only have been taken by a stratagem, and that ancient legions were perfectly safe inside their camps, since no primitive race had siege equipment. These memories reassured me. Yet I wondered. These M'gai were warriors. They meant to conquer. They knew war. Surely, if they examined the walls, they would see that bulge and know its meaning, and do something to bring the wall down there. They had lots of men; all of whom had plenty of that destructive instinct which the world so oddly prefers to creative sense. It would come naturally to such men, I thought, to see how readily such a wall could be breached there. Twenty squads of twenty men apiece, each running at that weakened wall with small battering rams all night long might

well bring it down. It was not an easy point to defend;
there was no good flanking tower near it. Apart from that
one weakness the walls were sure; I wished that their de-
fenders were one-tenth as good.

The time dragged on, and nothing happened from
within the city. The debate at headquarters continued
and, as there was no decision there, the hearts of all the
city were as water within them. It was precious time
wasted and daylight thrown away. I chafed and was unhappy. From time to time a M'gai slinger came dancing
in, slung a stone or two over the parapet and danced back.
Nobody sent a stone back, and nobody seemed to think
that it was anybody's business to tell the commander that
every such insult unavenged made each M'gai feel ten
times the warrior that he had been. I ground my teeth at
the want of preparedness and decision. Meanwhile these
sick and scared citizens shuffled by, looking poison at me,
the foreigner, and plainly thinking, as men will in war,
that being a foreigner I was no doubt in league with the
enemy. At last a young man, whom I had noticed a little
while before for his fair hair, which was a rare thing
among the dark Kranois, drew near to me. He had a
charming, smiling, sun-tanned face, and moved with the
swing and distinction of a beautiful body. He wore a twist
of soft gold-leaf on his right chest; I judged this to be a
mark of distinction of some sort. He came up to me with
his smile, and said to me in odd French,

"You came with Quichet, I think?"

I said, "Yes."

"I am called King," he said. "You are Monsell Ned?"

That was near enough, so I said, "Yes."

"I am not a King," he explained. "We act old plays of ours after the spring rain; I played the King last year."

He did not look like a city-dweller. I asked, "Do you live in the city here?"

"I'm a Plainsman," he said. "My home's out there." He pointed to the east.

Seeing two Kranois at the parapet, leaning to see the view, two M'gai slingers danced out and slung some stones at us. They went either high or low.

"See," the King said; "they let these fellows do this. Why aren't they shooting these fellows?"

"That is what I ask," I said. "Who is in command?"

"An old soldier." He gave the man's Kranish nickname, which means Old Sword. Fifty years before, this Old Sword, then a very active young man, had done very well in a war with a warlike tribe called the Tali-Malis. He was one of the few city dwellers who had taken any part in a war. "He went too fast fifty years ago," the King said. "He has gone too slowly ever since."

I said, "I have guns and powder here. We might be scattering those fellows. I've been waiting for word to mount them ever since I came. Do you know about guns?"

"Not much," he said. "Raoul Quichet told me about them. We expected to have them a long time ago. Are they as terrible as he said?"

"Yes," I said. "If I could have parties of men to help me, I could put the fear of death into these fellows."

"They must have decided something soon," the King said. "I've been in the council till I could stand it no longer. Presently, they'll send heralds round to the different wards, no doubt, to tell them what to do."

"What will that be?" I asked. "To mount our guns and
fire at all their positions?"

"You won't get fire from those men," the King said.
"Cold water is more their mark. But here come the
heralds; there they are, sounding in the Square."

A noise of penetrating, melancholy horns, blowing wavering notes, came from the northern and central parts of
the city. At the same time, we saw some officers with their
heralds coming along to the southern wall close to where
we stood. Some of them turned east, some west; some advanced upon us. The herald blew his note for silence;
when silence had fallen on those gathered to hear, an
officer said that the city was besieged, and that it fell to
the citizens of each ward to defend the wall of that ward.
We, being in the southern ward, would have the wall in
front of us with its towers to defend. We should go at once
to the officer of the ward in the central square, who would
enrol us in our watches, give us weapons and explain our
duties. We were to listen, while he repeated. We were to
go to the officer of the southern ward in the central square.
We should go to him. We should know his office by a green
flag hung from it. We must give him our names and learn
from him our duties; he would see us equipped with weapons, and we should remember that we were now under his
command.

The King said, "I must be off to my own people; this
farce will be the death of us."

As he moved away, the herald officer, who had been
wondering at me, asked, "Who are you?"

I said, "A foreigner, who came this morning with weapons, with Edmond Quichet."

"A foreigner, you say. What foreigner?"

"English."

He had never heard of any such people; he looked at me with suspicion and dislike.

"You belong to this ward?" he asked.

"No, I belong to no ward. I have weapons here."

He looked at me with greater suspicion.

"If you are here you must belong to this ward," he said. "You had better go to the officer of your ward and enrol like the others."

"But I don't belong to any ward," I said. "I have only but now arrived in your city. I have weapons here, to mount on the walls. The terrible weapons, which Quichet wished to bring here."

"I cannot go into what you have or haven't," he said. "You are in this city and must take your share in its defence. This ward is as good as any other. You, there. Shew this foreigner the Square and see that he enrols in the south ward."

"Let me say again," I said, "that I am a friend of Edmond Quichet. He will tell you that I have a lot of guns and powder here for the defence of the city. Such things may be vital to your defence."

"I happen to be responsible for the employment of foreigners here," he said.

He turned from me; he was already off to spread his tidings elsewhere. It was my first taste of the Kranois city official. Two or three of his underlings shewed me that I was to go with them. Quichet was not anywhere about; no word had come from him; I had no place there, save at the city's good will. I asked one of the men if he could take me to Quichet.

"No," he said. "My orders are to take you to the Ward Commander."

"Can I see the Old Sword?" I asked.

"No; you certainly may not," he said.

Well, when you are in a Kranois or other city in time of war it is wiser not to rouse that hatred of a foreigner which slumbers in men's breasts.

"Come, lead me to the Ward Commander, then," I said.

They led me up the slope of the lane to the high open heart of the city. I had seen from parts of the western wall that there was a big square here. Now I came into it, from the south, and saw the singular beauty and strangeness of it. On my right, there was a biggish temple, built simply of stone, with a fine relievo carved upon it, of involved figures in a kind of dance; this was gaily painted in colours singularly bright. Beside this, on both sides of it, was an outcrop of the dark rock which supported the city's northern wall. Now it was a very strange thing. This square was at the top of the city. Yet from this rock four spouts of stone (two on each side of the temple) gushed clear abundant water into stone troughs. I suppose that the water came somehow underground from the distant mountains; anyhow, there it was, a joy to see. Water at least would not fail the city. Quichet had told me of these springs, and how the city held them sacred. Well, there was the divine fount, singing, abundant, crystal-clear and life-giving. Surely of all things on earth water is the best and the most beautiful. There it gushed, confident and bright; it did my heart good to see it, after those hours on the wall.

I took a swift look at that, then looked about. The Kranish city was bigger than I had thought. The Square was full of life and muddle; all the bigger and more important houses fronted on it; to the one side, there were many women and older boys going for water at the springs, with jars upon their shoulders. In the midst, near me, many pens of cattle had been hurdled in. Many of these were uneasy, for, as one could see, they wanted water. No one had yet made water-troughs for them; though some of them had had fodder tossed to them. A few Plainsmen Kranois were sitting on the ground beside these cattle. I could already tell the Plainsman by his look of the open air. These few men had a sullen and angry look; they had tried to get something done for their precious cattle and had been told that the commanders had something better to think of. There they sullenly waited, knowing that there in the pens was the food, very likely the only food, that the citizens would have to live upon; and yet these city dwellers said that they had better things to think of. A good many little children and women had come to look at the cattle. They were all subdued and scared; and the cattle moaned, pawed, moaned, and seeing the water strained to it. Some men were bringing up small waggon-loads of a yellowish-looking fodder; the cattle did not want that; they wanted drink.

All this scene was bright with light and colour: the sun shone, the gay little blue-wings, a bird like a wren, darted to peck. It would all have been lovely but for the strain of war upon all things.

On the western side of the Square were (perhaps) two
hundred horses, all picketed to pine. They were small, active little horses, full of spirit and kick. They had a certain amount of shade from the houses where they stood;
not quite enough for their comfort. The flies were worry-
ing them; they stamped, tossed and switched. With them
were a good many men wearing the light woollen yellowish shirt and short trousers which were the costume of the
Plainsmen. These men had lances of what looked like
light cane; they also carried bows. Some of these men
were talking with their fellows, the cattlemen, in what I
already recognized as the broad speech of the Plainsmen;
I made out that they looked upon the citizens as hens, and
that they were furious that the city had not provided
buckets or watering-troughs for the cattle. My guides,
or guards, stopped to hear their complaints. A leading
Plainsman said that the cattle had been brought in, just
before midday. Some official had then promised that the
troughs should be made at once, so that the beasts might
be watered. In the paralysis of war, this had not been done.
The man who had made the promises had disappeared;
other officials, when asked, had made similar promises
and then also disappeared; meanwhile the heat grew and
the cattle suffered. Now, you will wonder why these
Plainsmen did not at once take the cattle to the stone
troughs under the spouts. Those fountains in the Square
were sacred; their water was for the temple service and
for the citizens. The Plainsmen had respected the holy
water for some hours, though with a growing rage; now
the matter was coming to a head. At that moment, as I
watched, the young man, the King, came out towards us;

he looked very handsome and, as I thought, most indignant. He went straight to the group of men near us.

"What is it?" he asked. "What is the trouble?"

"King," the men answered, "these hens have brought
us no troughs, and the cattle suffer."

"What nonsense!" the King answered. He looked
swiftly at the cattle, and said, "You mean that they have
had no water yet?"

"Not a drop," they answered.

The King called to a squad of lancers who had grouped
about one who was shewing string figures, or cats'-cradles,
to the rest. These men at once leaped to attention and
came to him.

The King said, "Form a guard about those troughs. You
cattlemen, take the cattle to water, pen by pen. The
guards will see that they are not interfered with."

Instantly, the lancers ran. With their lances they made
lanes to the water, while others walking outside the lanes
kept back the citizens. The Plainsmen, who had been sullenly glowering, at once sprang up and took the cattle
from the nearest pens to water. My guards cried out
against this outrage; so did the citizens; the women
screamed; here was the holy water being defiled by cattle. How they were to live, if the cattle died of thirst,
had not entered their heads. However, my own personal
guards had their orders; though they were plainly fum-
ing with rage against these Plainsmen, they had to take
me to my ward : they motioned to me to come on.

On the western side of the Square some of the bigger
houses had banners at their doors, with the blue and white
stripes of the Kranish colours. These houses had sentries

in front of them, wearing blue and white. They looked,
perhaps, a little like harlequins, yet were not quite such
figures of fun as the European soldier is often made to
look. I judged that these were the headquarters or Old
Sword's offices; and so they were. I wished that Quichet
would come out of them, see me, and take me in to the
commander. However, he did not. My lot was to go to a
much meaner house on the south side of the Square. A
green flag hung from its window; a longish line of young
men stood outside the door, waiting their turn. From time
to time, a man was admitted; then the door was closed
and the whole line moved up one and waited again. Presently, the door opened and a man would come out. Generally, when this happened, another man would try to get
in; often, the door would be shut in his face before he
could do so; there the line waited, till the door opened and
another man was allowed inside. The men in the line had
been there some time, and were weary of being there. My
guards went straight to the door, and knocked in an authoritative manner. It opened at once an inch or two,
while the weary line of men called out complaints that the
newcomers ought to take their turn and not come thrusting in thus to the front. There were cries of "Thrust them
back to the end. We've been here all the afternoon." A
weary sentry inside the door (he had been holding the
door in the heat against perhaps fifty assaults) asked who
we were. The guard said,

"We've got a foreigner: the Chief says he's to be enrolled at once."

"Shove him in then," the sentry said, "and one of you
come with him."

The guard said, rather tartly, "Go on, then—you hear what he tells you," and gave me a sort of thrust towards the door.

At that instant, there came a great outcry from the crowd by the fountains. The women and citizens had tried to stop the cattle from licking the holy troughs, and the Plainsmen, in anger, had loosed some pens of cattle among them. I saw some surging cattle and flying women; then I was heaved into the door by the press behind me.

"Come on, then," my guard said. "We've other things to do than enrol foreigners."

With that, they thrust past some men who were waiting in the passage, and so brought me into an inner room where there was somewhat more light, and also a pleasant draught of air. Three young men sat at a table. One had a parchment before him, a saucer of red wet paint and a hair pencil. He was the keeper of the roll. Next to him was a man with a pile of red and a pile of plain counters. Next to him was a man with a duplicate parchment. Behind these scribes or clerks was the Ward Commander, a big, slow, elderly man with a kind and stupid face. As we entered, we saw the first scribe look up and ask a man's name. The man replied, giving a name; then the scribe looked for it on his parchment, could not find it, and asked the other scribe if he had such a name on his list. The man said, "No." The first scribe then asked the recruit if he belonged to the South Ward, and how it came that he was not on the list. He was then asked if he understood either the bow or the spear; he said no, he was a tailor. He was entered upon the lists, the second scribe then gave him a red disc and a plain disc, told him that the red disc would

get him a spear at the South Ward arms distribution centre below the temple, while the plain disc must be kept
and shewn when the food was brought round. He was then
told that he was enrolled and subject to military discipline. He was now to go to get his spear, and then report
to the tower captain at the south tower. I knew that our
guns and powder were at the south tower. I wondered if
anybody had left word that powder was dangerous stuff
to have about. The tailor soldier was not very quick in his
wits. Probably he had been waiting for four or five anxious
hours at the door, trying to enrol. The scribes repeated
their directions; the Ward Commander said kindly, "Just
below the temple, boy, for the spear; next door to pretty
Moon-blossom." The tailor gave a sort of sickly grin and
was about to shuffle away, when a new man entered by a
door at the back. He was a little, rather dapper man, wearing white clothes. On the right chest of his tunic or upper
garment, he wore two of those twists of soft gold leaf
which I had noticed on the King. He was not a young
man; his face was colourless and seemed an odd mixture
of the faces of sheep and snake, brainless and yet dangerous.

He said, "Here. Not quite so fast, my friend. Ward
Commander, this will not do. We shall never do anything
with these fellows if they go about their tasks like this.
You, my friend, are now sworn to serve this City." (This
last was to the recruit.) "You will just bear in mind another time to throw up your right hand to your commanders."

At this moment, he caught sight of me.

"What on earth is this thing?" he asked.

"A foreigner, Master," my guard said, saluting. "We were to see him enrolled in the South Ward."

"A foreigner, eh?" He turned to me. "One of the Quichet party, I suppose?"

I said, "I came with Edmond Quichet."

"With the foreign help that was promised, no doubt?"

I said, "We brought some excellent weapons, which are not yet unpacked."

He turned to the Ward Commander and said, "This Quichet has passed his whole life in trying to bring this country under foreign dominion. This is, no doubt, the spy who will report later how the land may be subdued. Who said that he was to be enrolled here?"

Now my guard had slipped out, to see the fun in the Square; there was none to answer.

The Ward Commander turned to me and said, "You speak Kranish. Who said that you were to be in the South Ward guard?"

"I do not know," I answered. "An officer who said that he was responsible for the employment of foreigners here. He came round with heralds, and said that I was to join the South Ward guard, since that was as good as any other. But I have these weapons below by the gate and know how to use them. It would be better that I should be using them now against the enemy."

"It is for us to judge of that," he said. "We belong to the city and are entrusted by the city with her care."

He rose slowly from his chair and asked Sheep-Snake to come with him into the other room. I did not know why they were keeping me thus, and did not hear what passed between them; they were away for more than twenty minutes. When they returned, Sheep-Snake said,

"There must be some mistake in saying that you are to go to the South Ward. The Central Ward is a much better place for you. You will go there."

I said that I did not know the way.

"Oh," he said, "you will not have to trouble about that. You will be taken there."

.I said, "You are keeping me from using the weapons against the city's enemies."

"Yes," he said, "no doubt we suffer. . . . Still—" He gave the word to some men who were in the inner room, who came in and threw out their hands in the way he seemed to enjoy. "Take this foreigner to the Central Ward," he said.

They closed in upon me, one on each arm. "No need to hold me," I said. However, it was just as well to keep close together, for we had to thrust all three like sheep at a gap to get past the mob at the door and so into the Square, where by this time, the cattle had drunken, and the Plainsmen had won. They sat by their pens now, calmly exulting over the angry citizens, who stood apart glowering at them. Some men were wiping clean the stone troughs, or bathing cuts and bruises; the tussle had been acute for a while.

"Plainsmen and foreigners," one of my guards said, "they always bring trouble; that's sure."

I had a neat retort upon my tongue, that their own rulers had brought a pretty peck of trouble on them, too. It is, however, sometimes prudent to reflect on what St.

James has said about the tongue. I kept my remark to myself, and looked about for Edmond Quichet, Charles Pierre, Yvonne, or some of those good fellows who had been in the boats with us. I saw no familiar face. I could not understand why Quichet had not sent for or come to me. I asked one of my guards where Quichet was; I was sure that everybody in the City would know Quichet.

"You mean the foreigner?" he said. "You'll find him where you're going, in the Central Ward."

This cheered me. It was not half-a-minute's walk to the office of the Central Ward. In front of it, a cobbler or cordwainer sat at work making sandals. He had a very sharp knife, with which he was slitting the soles ingeniously, so that the thongs might be passed. He was hailed by the guards in some dialect or patois which I did not understand. He looked at me, wiped his brow, and said something about being busy. He jerked his knife to them indicating the door of the house behind him; the guards thereupon led me in.

"This is the Central Ward," my guides said. You'll be dealt with before you're much older."

With that, and paying no attention to my questions, as to their finding Quichet for me, they pushed swiftly from me, and locked the door as they went out.

Being left alone, I called, "Quichet. Quichet." Nobody was there. I went round the room as soon as my eyes were used to its dimness. It was a big place, well painted over with a shiny white lime-wash. It was lit by high windows, well out of my reach. I went round the room, looking at the things. No doubt, for some days, men had brought all manner of gear to store there. At the end of the room there was a stone trough into which a stone pipe spouted cold water. I had been for days in boats. I felt that I had had no real sleep for months, so I drank of this water, and bathed my face and hands. Then I flung some skins on the floor, put the cleanest of the fleeces on the skins and stretched myself upon it. In one minute I was asleep, and what the M'gai did till the next day I do not know.

There were hours of oblivion which did me more good than anything that I had known since my downfall. When I woke, I knew that I was in prison in a strange city; but I knew, too, that Yvonne was somewhere there, not very far away, to the west. The Central Ward had not enrolled any new recruit since my coming in. Someone was outside the door, singing in a low voice as he beat on something; it was the cobbler batting down some leather. I beat on the door and asked if I might have some food. He unlocked to me and said he had been in with food twice but could not rouse me. Presently he brought me food; he was a kindly fellow, much perplexed by the war, and suspicious of foreigners. He had not seen Quichet, and did not wish to see him. He said that he thought it odd, to say the least of it, that Quichet had come back to the city with the M'gai. I tried to explain that we had just crept in before the M'gai stopped the entry, and that we had brought weapons which might blast the M'gai away. As he knew nothing of guns, he could not believe this.

"Do not tell me," he said. "There are no such weapons, outside the tales."

He seemed inclined to believe, after a time, that perhaps we were not leagued with the M'gai, for what could we hope to get by it? "Still," he said, "our governors, who are responsible for us, cannot run risks in a time of danger, like this. The Quichet men are under guard, and so are you. I'd put the girl there, too; but she belongs to the temple." As I saw that he would suspect Yvonne if I asked about her, and what "belonging to the temple" meant, I did not question him. He was kindly, on the whole, like most of the Kranois; still, he made me very uneasy with this talk of our being leagued with the M'gai. If he, who was kindly, believed that, what would men like Sheep-Snake believe?

I was asking him if I might go to make sure that the powder was in a safe place, when the officer of the day before came past with his heralds. He had been giving orders along the walls, I think. He stopped when he saw me.

"I thought I sent you to the South Ward," he said. "What brings you here? They tell me on the wall that you have not kept guard all night. Why have you not done what I ordered?"

I said that I had gone to enrol at the Ward office, and had there been arrested and locked up all night, as the cobbler could bear witness.

"Enjoying yourself in bed, no doubt," he said, "while the citizens watch for you. You foreigners act as though your friends were already in possession here. They are not yet, let me advise you, nor are going to be. You will go at once, now, to the wall where you belong."

I said that I was a stranger to the city and had certain means of helping her, and that all this bullying and threatening was silly; it was simply keeping me from being of use to people. He said that a Kranois needed no talk of the kind from a foreigner, and that he, who was

responsible for the employment of foreigners in the city,
meant that I should serve on the south wall, with the
guard. So with this I was marched off to the south wall.
He followed me there, and handed me over to the old commander of that section or ward, saying that it would be
best that I were kept from going too near to the gate.

I had thought the commander of the ward a simple, stupid man. His men called him Old Gah, I do not know why;
they liked him, and so did I.

He said, "You can take the spear there, then, and go up
onto the wall, till we do our drill. You are not to go down
to the gate, you understand. Have you practised with a
spear?"

I said no: we had given up the use of spears, having so
much better weapons, guns, and so forth.

"Well," he said, "take your spear, there, and go up onto
the wall, with the rest of the guard."

I did as I was bid. The spear was heavy, with a hard-
wood handle, and a short steel triangular head. It was
very like one of the boarding pikes kept in racks in the
*Albicore*. It was odd to be holding a spear on a city wall,
watching an enemy below me. Once again, I was struck
by the comfort in the M'gai camp. They had settled themselves in. Many little huts had been built; many more
were building. I saw little companies of M'gai drilling
together. Although it was hot, the smoke from many fires
blew about. I could see that these were forges. Many men
were making or mending weapons. I saw the smiths strike
on their anvils, and the bright iron flash under the hammers. As I looked, a train of perhaps a hundred laden
pack donkeys came up to their camp from the north-

eastward. They had a line of supply there, it seemed. "Why are they left like this, undisturbed?" I groaned. "These Kranois have done nothing against them, but let them settle down. Now is the time to drop some round-shot plump into their midst."

I saw that the men of my ward were watching me curiously. Presently one of them, a very friendly young man, came up and asked what I thought about it.

I said that with my weapons I could shift some of those fellows from where they camped. He did not know about gunpowder, so that this was lost on him. I asked if anything had been done to molest the M'gai during the past twenty-four hours.

He said, "No, nothing. The M'gai are too strong."

"But the Kranois are good bowmen, so people say. Have they not shot from the walls? The slingers must often have been within bowshot?"

"Yes, that is true; but we have very few arrows as yet."

"Are people making them?"

"The heralds this morning said that energetic measures have been taken to ensure a good supply of arrows."

"How long does it take to make an arrow?"

"Well, we have to straighten the shafts first; they were collecting the shafts yesterday. Then the heads take a good time. Then there is the nocking and the heading and letting the gum dry. Then you have to feather, haven't you? And you can't expect that to be done very quickly, or the arrow won't go true."

"Then we haven't any arrows?"

"Not enough to go shooting them off from the walls."

"Do you think I could find a lighter spear than this?"
I asked.

"No," he said. "We are rather short of spears at present, but the heralds said that energetic steps were being taken to ensure a supply of good spears."

"You won't have to feather spears," I said.

"No," he said, "but it takes a good time to make and fit a head."

"You think they are being made?"

"Yes, if they have the shafts and the steel for the heads; they were seeing what they could muster."

"Where are the smiths and armourers?"

He pointed towards the east of the city, where work was going on; smoke rose and hammers beat on metal there; there was a clink and clatter.

"Then just at present we cannot do much against the enemy?"

"No, but word has been sent to the Big City, of course, and the scheme is, to get weapons ready here; then, in a day or two, the army of the Big City will come down upon the M'gai, and we shall issue out at the same time and take them as between two jaws. We shall have weapons enough for that, by that time."

"Yes, but have you food enough in the city for those days before the army comes?"

"Well, that is what we don't yet know," he said. "We hope so; but most of our corn is in the granaries out towards the Big City, a good way from here. It was to have been brought in, but there has been so much to see to, in these last few days, nobody seems to know if it has been."

"Who was responsible for its coming?"

"Oh, nobody very much."

"Then perhaps it hasn't come?"

"Oh, I should think that some of it has come."

I had begun to see that the long ease had made the Kranois unforethoughtful. I wondered how much fodder had been brought in for the cows. The cows and water might be our only sustenance. I looked from my perch on the wall over the city. It was a fair sight, so trimly built, and so brightly lime-washed and painted. The Kranois delighted much in wind-vanes, which in so windy a city looked delightful, as they swung and flashed, each one of a new and gay design. Some pigeons were flying about in troops and flights of twenty or thirty, wheeling and flashing in the sun. These sudden changes of light and movement delighted all the Kranois at all times. I heard at various points the shouts of men who were drilling companies of spearmen. Three such companies were at drill in the space just below me; they had no spears, only sticks and tools, the shafts of scythes, three-pronged forks and so on. Some had not even these, and did nothing but change formation and remake it, as though the end of war is to make a sensible being no longer human. Well, often that is the result of war.

I could not see much of the Square. In one little gap, I could see the heads of cattle tossing above their hurdles, and two dour Plainsmen, in their blue and white blankets, sitting staring in front of them. In another gap, where a lane ran into the Square-end, I saw some of the ponies still tethered. I hoped that the King would be somewhere there, and that he might remember me and come to speak with me. I longed for Quichet or some word from one of

his family, or of my comrades in the boats. I had no sign
of them.

"Are the horsemen going to stay in the city?" I asked.

"Horsemen," the young man answered. "You mean
those fellows under the King? I am told that he has insulted the Old Sword, in the way those Plainsmen always
have. I should think he'll be under arrest by this time, and
his men put on to do wall guard. The horses will come in
handy for meat. The trouble about these Plainsmen is
that they think they rule the city; they're only a lot of
cattle-tenders and cowherds when all is said."

At this point something whizzed just beside my head
and struck the plaster on a wall in a near-by house; a
second thing followed fast, even nearer. "Slingers," I said.
"Duck down." We ducked down, and the stones kept us
down. Other stones began to pelt the line of the wall.
Creeping under cover to the parapet, I was able to peer
round a stone. The M'gai had suddenly sent out perhaps
two hundred slingers all along our wall. They were fine
young men, all almost naked, dancing about from place
to place, and putting in their shots with skill and force.
All along the wall the stones were knapping on the  wall
and bringing the plaster down. Not one bowman appeared
along the whole south wall. Not one shot, arrow or stone
was sent back from our side.

I said to my friend, "That is crazy. Here are the enemy
insulting us as they choose. They'll think us a lot of hens.
Why on earth don't some of our bowmen shoot some of
these?"

"We must be saving the arrows for a battle, when it will
be really worth while," he said.

"Yes; but half-a-dozen of these fellows' shot would save all this. See, they've killed a man there."

Indeed, a man going carelessly to the parapet away to our left was hit at that instant on the temple and fell dead. A Ward Commander blew a whistle; some men crawled up and drew him away. The M'gai had seen him fall; they sent several stones at the place where the body lay, and then went whooping off back to their lines. They had enjoyed themselves; they had killed a man and scared (as they thought) a city; they had shewn that the M'gai were men and the Kranois chickens; now they went back to say what fine fellows they were, while other companies came out and slung at the other walls. I said at the time,

"Those slingers came out very suddenly; no one saw them prepare to attack."

"The natives here never prepare," a man said. "They attack; that is the first thing you know about it."

It was now safe to look over the wall at the enemy lines; I stood up and gazed. It was as before; a few squadrons drilled; the smiths beat at their iron; some men were building huts; others mended shields or sharpened spearheads with little whetstones; otherwise, it seemed like a peaceful village with men strolling about. In one place, half-a-dozen of them chased a pony which had got away, with a pack twisted under its belly. Two or three other groups watched these fellows; they cheered and laughed and danced. It was a stolen pony: the M'gai knew little of horses.

I said to my friend, "I suppose they made no attempt to attack last night?"

"Oh, no," he said. "They never attack at night; or are

said not to. They were too busy besides, all last night, settling into their camp."

"And you let them settle?" I said. "Surely, you might have kept them from settling. If I had had my guns, I might have made them think twice about settling."

My guns, with all that we had brought from the boats, had lain in the waggons just under the wall when I first had gone up that morning. Now, as I mentioned them, I looked down and saw that they had gone.

"Hullo," I said, "the waggons with the guns are gone. Did you see who took them?"

"An officer from the Chief came with a team of men and wheeled them away."

"Where to?"

"I don't know; one of the storehouses, probably."

"They'd better keep them away from fire," I said.

"They will," he answered. "The heralds were giving orders against fire in the city. But, in God's name, what is this?"

Now only a minute before, or so it seemed, I had been looking at a peaceful camp in which no M'gai seemed bent on war. Outside the camp there were slinging parties, it is true; the camp itself had been quiet. Now I had the chance of seeing what the M'gai could do in the way of sudden movement. I had heard tales of it, while in the boats, and had discounted some of it as legend, or the result of fear. Now I saw. "Seeing," they say, "is believing; but feeling hath no fellow." This time I could both see and feel.

Even now, I do not know how it was done. There were, opposite the south wall, not less than twenty-five hundred

M'gai in camp. At some order or signal, not perceived
by us in the city, about fifteen hundred of these darted
into order of battle and rushed at the city, each man yelling and screaming in a way that made the blood run cold.
I had disbelieved in the "war-cry"; now I learned its
efficacy. They came at a speed which I had not believed to
be possible; and though the main body came fast, a van-
guard of slingers came faster. They rushed at us, let fly
each some half-dozen stones with the speed of lads drawing sticks along a paling, and were at once out of the
action, slipping back into intervals left for them in the
main body. As they withdrew through these intervals,
the main body seemed to surge forward. Then I saw that
the advanced parties carried scaling-ladders. I had an instant of horrid fear that now the time was come. We were
to be carried by assault. All along the wall, whistles were
blowing to call the guards, who came running from all
directions. The sling-stones came over in a hail. A stone
hit a man near me on the side of the jaw and made him
yell. I saw a man or two fall. I shouted to some bowmen,
"Shoot. Shoot them." But as they knew no English and
were staring at the sight of the charge, which was so
beautiful that it was difficult not to stare, they did not
shoot. In any case, they had been told to save their arrows
except in a case of emergency, and no one had yet told
them that this was an emergency. Suddenly, the slinging
stopped, for the M'gai were now just under us. The ladders came up against the wall, with a clack, and in an
instant the M'gai were rushing up them. Just near us,
the ladders were too short. I saw terrible, yelling faces
under plumes, eyes like the eyes of lions, teeth like the

teeth of tigers; a.man flung a short spear or javelin at me from just below me. I caught it as it went over me and flung it back at him. It missed, not only him, but everybody else—how, I cannot tell, except that in the fury and confusion, screaming and roar of an attack, man's effort is wild, and destiny decides. In an instant, I saw that the M'gai were aware that they could not scale at our part of the wall. Instantly, by some signal that none of us perceived, the word went or the thought passed, "This must stop. Get away." Instantly, the braves were down the ladders, the ladders whisked away into the rear; the slingers were back again sending stone after stone at us and at the sectors right and left of us. The stones whizzed, clacked and banged; men fell and wailed and died, great shards of old plaster fell.

Now on the wall just to the east of us, there came a rallying-cry. I could see that the M'gai there were up, disputing the parapet. I saw a knot of Kranois heaving and thrusting at them. At that instant, another ladder full of savages came up against the wall between us and them; no Kranois were there to check them. A surge of M'gai came rolling up over the parapet. One of the biggest of them leaped onto the platform, slipped, and recovered. There was no time to be lost. I called, "At them, quick," and charged this man before he was well on his feet. Old Gah was beside me; he speared this man at once just as he knocked my spear out of my hand. I stooped and got his spear from him, and in stooping was knocked down by the men behind me, and knocked down some M'gai who leaped onto me as I tried to get up. Both sides jabbed at me with spears, but war goes by destiny; they just missed me. I know I did not expect to get up again; and yet, in an instant, the fight was over and inaudibly the word had passed that the M'gai were to retire. The attack was called off. The M'gai were back over the wall; the ladders were all whisked away, and back came the slingers with the sling-stones, whish, crack, splitter-splatter, whack, whish, whish. This time two or three arrows went after them, and missed them. Once again, I had to admire the extraordinary precision of the M'gai. They had come at speed, tried their attack, seen at once that most of the ladders were too short, and even in the fury of the attack had been able to break off the battle and retire. We had killed some of them, and hurt a few, but only two of their bodies remained with us. These had fallen off the wall into the city; all the other dead and hurt they carried back. They had tried a rush and knew, now, that they could succeed if the ladders were lengthened. They knew, now, that we either had no arrows, or had no bows. Perhaps, too, in their shrewd way, they knew that we had no leaders.

Well, they went back, and we drew into groups out of sling shot to talk over the battle. Old Gah said a nice word to me about my charging the ladder. I said that if I had had my guns I could have broken the rush long before it reached the wall. I asked about the guns and powder, and said that I could shew what could be done with them, if permitted.

He said, "You young fellows, you think you know it all. You don't, you know. You are too impulsive, like all you foreigners. You only get us into trouble."

I said, "I want to get you out of trouble, as you, sir, got me out of very serious trouble, just now."

"Yes," he said, "but you foreigners always think that you can manage our lives for us. You know, we don't think you can. Your friend Quichet has been saying these same points; believe me, it doesn't do. No, it does not do."

I asked him if I could go to see Quichet. He said, "No," and added that he had other things to do than talk to a foreigner. However, I talked with the men in my watch. They were of all sorts and conditions, all city men, and all prejudiced against Quichet's party and the Plainsmen. They were frank in telling me that they had thought that I was in league with the M'gai, and had been surprised at my charging to attack them. Now, I declare that I charged on a sudden impulse, to run forward; courage was not concerned in it; if the impulse had been to run away, I should have obeyed it just as blindly.

As young fellows will, we became good friends, straight away; we talked of the M'gai and how skilled they had been, how quick to seize advantage, how quick and cunning to break off when the advantage turned ever so little the other way. We told each other that they would most certainly try again when they had made their ladders a little longer; then we argued how the attack should be met; some were for having grapnels, to hook and drag the ladders aside as they were planted; others said to have boiling water or oil handy, to pour, or great weights to heave over. I explained my guns, and what they could do. They did not much believe in my guns; but two young fellows who had talked with the Quichet grandsons, these said that they had heard that such things did wonders but were dangerous to the users. Some said, when we had plenty of arrows (and he was told that there would be

plenty in two or three days), the M'gai attacks would
have no success whatever; they would never reach within
fifty yards of the wall. Most of them said, "Well, it will
only be two days more, or perhaps three, then the Big
City people will be here; we shall have arrows enough by
that time. And the horse will be ready, then. I don't think
the M'gai will stand a charge of horse."

I was not of their way of thought. I saw the M'gai as
instinctive warriors, used and trained to war; these
Kranois were as yet hardly used to the cessation of peace;
they had no weapons, no skill in arms, no art, even, of
making the flank or moving to an order. The thought came
into my head, "What if the men of the Big City be like
these fellows, or worse? What if there be no arrows even
in the Big City?" I thought of what might have been, if
I had had even one gun mounted on that south tower
when the charge of the M'gai began. I could have sent
twenty or thirty pounds of scattering gravel straight into
the head of the charge, and broken it as it came. I could
not bear this thought at last. I went to Old Gah, who
seemed on the whole to be reasonable, if slow and stupid.

I said, "Sir, I seek only to help this city. Will you let
me only try one of my weapons, if only once?"

"See, Ned," he said. "We have heard of your weapons.
Years ago, when Quichet was young, he had some of them.
They burst up, and killed a very fine young man, of whom
we had the liveliest hope. I was a friend of his; and I've
never liked Quichet since. If you go bursting one of those
things on this wall, the wall will come down. There is a
bad bulge in it already, just a few feet west there. We
have our own views of how to fight the M'gai; and remem-

ber that we are not the main fighters of this war; we are
doing all things in union with the Big City, with whom
we keep in touch. They will march to fight the M'gai;
when they come, we shall march out to help them; until
then, our task is to make ready to help, first by drilling,
then by making weapons."

"My weapons are already made."

"So are our plans, Ned," he said.

He would have said more, but at that moment Sheep-
Snake appeared, with some of his minions.

"You have a foreigner in your ward, of the name of
Ned," he said, to Old Gah. "Where is the fellow?"

"You mean this man?" Old Gah said. "He's here."

"He ought not to be there," Sheep-Snake said. "The
orders are that foreigners are not to be allowed on the
wall. The foreigners are not to serve on the walls at all,
but to be cattle-tenders. His place is with the cattle in the
Square. I have sent three times, if not four, to find him,
in the Central Ward, and all the time he has been here."

"I know nothing about that, sir," Old Gah replied. "He
was sent to me by the staff, and has behaved very well in
the fighting."

"He had better behave well," Sheep-Snake said. "Come
down from the wall there, you. Put aside that spear. Adopt
a military attitude when you are addressed by your su-
perior."

I fear I did not. I pretended not to know what he was
saying. Old Gah said that I did not understand the language very well.

"He had better learn it, if he's to stay in the city of the
Kranois," he answered. "You are my prisoner, my mili-

tary prisoner, do you understand? If you mutiny, or try to escape, you will be speared."

So, as a prisoner again, I was marched to the Square by an escort, and handed over to a cattle foreman. He was one with whom I had talked the day before. He was a stern-looking man, burnt to the colour of a brazen image, with a broad face, a little pug nose, a slit for a mouth, and eyes like sparks of fire. His hair was bleached by the sun to a kind of pale dust-colour. He was wrapped in a blanket of dirty yellow wool, which he threw off to welcome me. My heart warmed to him, for as soon as the escort had gone, he said, "You are just to do what you please. Imagine making a man like you a cattle hand."

When one has been an outcast, a little recognition is like rain upon the desert : the flowers spring up.

"Indeed," I said, "I will do what you tell me to do."

"You are not a cattle hand," he said. "I saw you talking with the King last night."

"Where is the King?" I asked.

"Still talking to these debaters in the hen-run yonder."

"What happened last night?" I asked. "I see you have water-troughs now."

"We shouldn't have had, if we had not struck for them," he said.

"Please teach me what I am to do with the cattle."

"The less you bother cattle, the better. Give them food, water and sleep and a turn with the opposite sex at times, and they'll be less trouble than city dwellers, who don't know that war isn't foolery."

"Did you see anything of the M'gai attack just now?"

"No. I heard it. But I've seen the M'gai. I come from

out there away to the east, on the verge of the cattle country. I've been neighbours with them for years. It is only
since their present King came that they've been resty. I
am one who likes the M'gai very much. They are good
straight people; when they say a thing they do a thing.
It's only lately that they've got this idea of grab and kill.
That isn't the people; it's the brute who rules them, and
his little gang of murderers. But they're like children or
like sheep; they obey; they do just what they are told to
do, and believe every tale as true."

"They're extraordinarily fine fighters," I said.

"That was all the old King. He made the army. He made
the stabbing spear, with that broad double-edged head;
and it was his eldest son, whom the present King murdered, that made the way of fighting. You haven't seen
it yet, the thing they call the lion's jaws; you only saw
them rush and then retire through the intervals."

"Yes, but that was marvellous. It was done at such
a speed."

"It is marvellous, and it is done at speed; but the lion's
jaws is also done at speed, and they have never known it
fail, so they say. They come on, rushing like a fire on a
plain in a high wind. No Kranois could reach that speed.
Then, as they run, they get what they call 'Mimbo,' possessed by their God Mimbo, and in that state they'll go
through fire a mile thick and water going over a cataract;
then, as they run, their wings swing out at both sides and
make the jaws round the enemy; and as soon as they are
well round, they close, and no enemy yet has ever got out,
they say. I've seen them do it with lions on the plain. I

haven't seen them do it with Kranois yet. But when the Big City army comes I'll no doubt see it tried."

"And is there no defence?"

"Of course there is; but they've not met any tribe yet that has one."

"What defence is there?"

"Something that will keep the jaws from closing. Arrows will. Or there; all these horse, eating their corn here; a charge of those would stop them. When they are running Mimbo they fling away their shields, and keep only their spears. Arrows will stop them; if shot in plenty. Get your men into a triangle, with all the pikes pointing out, and let the archers shoot over the pikemen's shoulders. Arrows'll stop any men; a good arrow through the heart."

At this point, a man came up to him and said, "I want five men from you, to cut spearheads."

"What's the sense in that?" my new friend said. "I've just this moment received five men, to tend the cattle here; now you want them for spears."

"I've got to have them for spears," the newcomer said. "So hand them over."

"Well," my friend said to me, "you'll have to go; no doubt they'll send you to me again as soon as the light goes. We have to bed these cattle down before dark."

Four other cattle tenders, all of them Plainsmen who disliked the rule of the city men as much as my friend, rose up unwillingly from their blankets and followed to one of the workshops in the east end of the city, below the temple. Here about a hundred men were at work, some preparing spear-shafts, trimming the sticks so that the shafts were clean, and pointing them down with small axes. My task was to help at the pointing. Others dipped the points in hot liquid of some sort, and passed them to the nailers, who fitted the heads, and secured them. After this, they went on to be tested, finished, sharpened, and sent to the different wards. No one asked us which, if any, of the processes we could do, or felt a genius for. We were put to the work the last batch had left, and in my case these had been shaft-pointers. I had never had much work with a small axe, and now had no one to shew me what to do. A man said, "Take a look at the shaft on the wall in front of you. Make a tapering point like that."

Now, if you think that I was stupid at it, go you, and cut some stout ash-poles and take a small hatchet, not sharp, and with no grindstone handy, taper down the poles till you may use them for, shall we say, hop-poles. You will find it a very pleasant job, but not one that you will do easily. However, I went on at it, and spoiled a pole or two. I longed for a knife, or a chisel, or a spokeshave; anything but a hatchet. They say that a good workman does not quarrel with his tools. A good workman demands the work that he can do; then he will be known by his tools. I asked one of the men if they had anything like a vice, that would hold the poles while we worked. He said that all the vices were being used by the bowmen.

There was a good deal of singing. I enjoyed the job there; we were sheltered from the sun; we had abundant cold, clear running water to drink, for a brook ran by us from the springs. Another delight was the continual singing in the temple, where relays of women were singing psalms of intercession or prayers for help. Young

unmarried women "belong to the temple," I was told, and
always sang thus. They sang sweetly in the gentle Kranish
mode. I was cheered to think that among them probably
Yvonne was singing, perhaps with thoughts of me. The
Kranish smiths, who were making spearheads down the
road from us, struck into the singing sometimes, when
they knew the hymns, or when the hymns were not what
they called the women's hymns, which men were forbidden
to sing. Our men joined in less often, because we were
perplexed by our unfamiliar work.

I had worked at these spear-shafts for some hours, I
suppose, when the Sheep-Snake creature came round after
me. He had, I think, wanted to see me tending cattle, and
had not found me doing it; he now had come after me to
annoy me at some other angle.

"So," he said, "the foreigner whom I put to tending
cattle has come away to an easy task, shaping spearheads.
What do you know of shaping spearheads?"

As I had seen that it annoyed him, I pretended not to
know what he said; I looked at him and asked my neighbour what it was he said. He was furious.

"So you do not know the Kranish tongue, though you
can eat the Kranish bread," he said. "You guards, march
him to the defaulters' drill at once. He may learn there
something about spears before he has the pleasant task
of cutting them."

So, once again, I was taken under guard, this time to
a sad-faced, saturnine, black-haired man, who looked as
though his parents had not wished him to be born, and as
though ever since then he had shared their views. He was
known everywhere as Old Crow; for he was liker an old

derelict crow than anything. He was wearily taking a
party of bad lads and erring citizens in what he called
spear-drill. He had a short spear; the others had sticks,
or even reeds. He looked at me wearily, told me to take a
stick from a heap of wood, and fall in at the rear, and pay
attention to all that was said.

"This that I'm teaching you is the spear exercise," he
said. "I cannot go back to the beginning. We have come
now to the exercise known as Exalting Spears, which is
an exercise of ceremony number two, following on exercise one, ceremony and salute, which spearmen learn
after they have mastered field exercises one to five, on
the handling and use of spears in battle."

It is something to learn the exercise of the spear; but
to one who had learned gunnery under Crackers it was
something of a come-down. We were doing this exercise
in a clear corner of the Square, not twenty yards from the
temple entrance. As we listened to the Old Crow wearily
explaining for the tenth time that we were to wait for
the order, the complete order, and not to act on the first
word of an order, that the word Exalt meant nothing;
it was *not* an order; it was a caution. How could we tell,
till we were told, what it was that was to be exalted? But
when he said, "Exalt spears," why, then he wanted to see
all the spears go up as one. . . . While he was droning over
all this, and the sad dogs, the defaulters, were nudging
each other, and passing low remarks, I saw Yvonne come
down the temple steps with two other women. They all
wore the black cloaks of light silk which all Kranish
women wear in public; but I would have known Yvonne
through a mask. I was in the rear rank, and I feared that

she would not see me, but she did; she saw me and gave a
little quick nod and smile. I saw, too, after she had passed,
that she looked back, and smiled again, and then hurried.
She was on her way home from the singing, I had supposed. However, she did not go straight home; she parted
from her two companions and turned there in the Square
to one of the shops in the northern face of it. Almost as she
entered the door of it, Old Crow said:

"From this practice, we will proceed to theory. The
theory of the exercise of the spear is twofold. It is important that the twofold nature of all that he does be
properly grasped by every spearman. Silence there, you
in the rear rank. You will be named in my report, if I
hear your voice again. Now the theory of the first part ..."

His dry scraggly voice, so like his thin scraggly beard,
was beginning on the first part when there came from the
north-eastern angle of the city the appalling noise of a
M'gai attack, and the cries, whistles and alarm calls of
the garrison on the wall there. I said, "The M'gai again,"
and at once grabbed Old Crow's spear from him and ran
towards the wall there. Yvonne was in that part of the
city. I meant to be between her and the M'gai at least. I
know that I slipped as I ran and had a fall in the Square,
but picked myself up, and was just halfway up the steps
to the platform of the wall, when I saw M'gai in the Square
itself below me. "They are in, then," I said to myself.
"They've got us this time." However, just above me half-
a-dozen M'gai were clambering over the parapet. I flung
myself at these. I saw the King attacked by three braves,
and had a great towering warrior foaming at the mouth
with Mimbo overtopping myself. I stabbed at him, and hit

him somewhere, and he fell from the parapet into the
town. I saw the King swing left and kill one of his braves,
and by the very movement miss the spears of the other
two. He swung right and killed one of the other two. A
rush of Kranois drove me into the M'gai; and then we
were at the ladder heaving it over, all crowded with M'gai
coming up it; we edged it sideways with a bar, so that
it slithered over and fell. All the time, the slingstones
were whacking the walls, women were screaming, the
cattle were panicking, and the M'gai were yelling their
cry. Then, in another minute, this attack, too, was called
off; the M'gai had melted away. Looking down into the
city, I saw that three M'gai lay dead in the Square. One
of them had speared a cow, and had been killed as he tried
to withdraw the spear. Still, they had had a time of some
success. They had been inside the city; they had rushed
the walls, and gotten inside; they had killed a cow, a
woman and three men inside the Square, and four other
men on the wall; and this with a loss of only six of themselves. What I could not understand was how they had
taken the wall by surprise. I saw the King speaking to
some of the wall-guard there. He was asking about that
very point. I came up to the group to hear what was said.
It had been a surprise, and this after the surprise on the
south wall that morning. The wall-guard had been reduced to two or three sentries; the others had been sent
to various duties, some to straighten arrow shafts, or to
bind arrowheads; some to help the forges; some to grind
the city corn, so that the army of the Big City might have
bread when it arrived in two days' time; all that part of
the wall had been judged to be safe, since it was built on

the rough ground of rocky outcrops. The M'gai through
their spies had learned which walls were weakly held;
then they had suddenly made their rush and had been into
the city at once. The Commander of the Ward now came
up; the King went at him.

"Surely," he said, "you know that these M'gai have
the ears and the noses of dogs. They know which part of
a wall is weakly held. You were surprised here, with
nobody on guard but two unsupported sentries. You were
only saved by the fact that the ladders were too short.
If they had judged the height of the walls better, they'd
have cut the throats of half the city by this time."

The Commander knew that this was the truth. He was
scared at the narrowness of the escape.

"And even now," the King said, "even now, after the
lesson of this morning, there's no one ready to hurry them
back, after an attack. Not one archer on all the north wall;
and three and a child on the south. You have bows; why
don't you use them?"

"Sir," the Commander said, "we are saving all the
arrows for the battle when the army of the Big City
comes here."

"If you're not very careful," the King said, "if you
don't mend your ways, the Big City will find no city left
when it gets here. You've twice been within an ace of sack-
ing; you'll have no third luck."

He saw me and came towards me, to greet me in French.
"Well, Ned, I've been looking high and low for you. I
traced you to the Central Ward, then to the South Wall;
then to one of my cattle-herders. He did not know quite
where you had gone after that."

"First, to make shafts, then to the rogues' squad," I said.

"God's blue sky!" he said. "And, of course, you have not had your weapons unloaded from the waggons yet?"

"No."

"I'm weary of this," he said. "I've been talking to the Chief in there till I am tired. This is no way to check the M'gai. Anyhow, I'm not going to stay longer. I'm going out tonight with my men. With two hundred horse, I can make the M'gai very restive; not camped as you see, enjoying themselves."

I hoped that he would say, "I want you to come with me." As he did not, I was a little dashed from asking if he would take me; but, indeed, I was kept from asking by the thought that I ought to stay where Quichet (and Yvonne) were.

"Where is Edmond Quichet?" I asked.

"They've got him and his grandsons in what they call preventive hold, in the citadel yonder." He nodded to the double tower at the north-east corner of the city. It was close to us. It looked a forbidding place, being older, darker and rather sterner in its build than the other towers on the wall.

"Surely," I said, "they do not suspect him of bringing in the M'gai?"

"That's a story which they are not above spreading. They dread his getting control here; these old Kranois who can't act with sense themselves are scared of anyone who could do it for them; these old men, who only own. Owning is much, God knows, but compare it with doing. But I suppose you don't have such things in England."

"I suppose not," I said.

"The Old Sword was a bright fellow once," the King went on, "but he was the first to insist on Quichet's being shut up. There he comes, our Commander: that old man on the old white pony yonder. I must speak to him, and then I shall be going. But I'll have a word with you first. We shall be having our battle, probably, in about forty hours from now."

There were cheers from some of the citizens in the square as the Chief rode up to our corner. He rode an old white pony, which was one of the city pets; he had taken pleasure in fostering the city's interest in the pony, and had found that it repaid him; some of the women called him "Lillyboy" after the pony. Two orderlies followed him, each carrying a blue and white pennon. The Chief was an oldish man, with a look of authority and kidney trouble. He gave me the impression that he was at all times acting the part of the father of the city, the citizens' saviour, which indeed he had been some forty-five or fifty years before. He always seemed to be saying, "You Kranois know me. You know your Old Sword. Lillyboy will not fail you. You can trust Lillyboy, and Lillyboy knows that he can trust you. The Kranois can manage their own affairs without foreign interference, if they will but trust old Lillyboy, give him all that he asks, and do all that he bids them. He believes in you. You believe in him." And so forth. But his arrival, smiling, on his old pony, in the undress uniform or old woollen tunic that he affected, in a part of a city undefended by his negligence, and nearly lost through his incompetence, and this a few moments after a surprise attack, which he had not foreseen and had done nothing to counter, all this was bitter to the King, who had fought for his life in that space only a quarter-of-an-hour before.

"Sir," the King said, going up to him, "if you do not have one-third of all your spearmen on the wall, and another third just below it with their weapons, all the time, you'll lose this city. The third time they attack the ladders will be long enough. They were in here, as you can see."

"I see," he answered, smiling, not at the King, but at the citizens who were smiling at him. "I see; but they do not seem to have got out again."

He swept his hand towards the dead M'gai. I looked, too. One of the corpses was close to me; a fine big fellow, wearing black plumes. These had been the regimental badge of the attackers there. The citizens laughed and applauded at this. I noticed, now, how curiously bitter the citizens were against the Plainsman; they were going to support Lillyboy against the Plainsman, that was clear.

"Sir," the King said, "I am going out from here, as you know. I'll try certain schemes that occur to me, and you shall have word from me at the times arranged. But I do beg you to give attention to this young Englishman, Monsieur Ned, who has brought weapons that may make all the difference to the battle that has to be fought here."

"I do not know any foreign weapons that the Kranois cannot do without," the old Chief replied. "Even he, I see, has given up his weapons for the good Kranois spear. Is not that so, sir?" he asked turning to me.

"Sir," I said, "I am using a spear because the city has not let me try my own kind. I assure you that my own weapons are more effective than spears; more than ten times as effective, for the M'gai do not know them."

"I had some experience of that kind, when I was young," he said, "down by the sea at a place called Sixteen Peaks. We Kranois can do without such, I hope."

"Yes, indeed; we can do without them," the people answered.

"In war, you need all the help you can get," the King said.

"Ah," the old man answered, "that is just where we old men differ from you young ones. Remember, we too have known war. We were in war before you were born—or your father, for that matter. You are going out at sunset, or a little later. See you don't knock up all your horses before the fight. Send me word as arranged."

He lifted his hand to dismiss the King, nodded to me, touched his pony with a foot, and moved on with his following towards his quarters not far from us.

"There you have our leader," the King said. "Well, I hoped I might get you leave to use your guns. I must get my men and go, now. After the battle, we may have a more sensible city to welcome you to. Good-bye, Ned; we'll meet after the battle, I hope."

"I hope so, King."

"It is a general rule that the M'gai don't attack at night; they sleep. However, since they think that the Kranois sleep, they may change their ways. This King of theirs is likely to do what you least like."

"So I expect," I said.

"What would you least like him to do?" the King asked suddenly.

"Bring battering rams at the bad place on the wall to the west of the south tower. He might bring a piece of wall down, and even cause a breach."

"He'll very likely try it; he'll know about it. I'm more afraid of an attack at dawn, at three points: the two points that he has already tried, and a third where he will mean to break in. He will try it at dawn tomorrow morning, if you ask me; he will know that the Big City army is on its way. He will surely try his big attack before it comes. But there are my two trumpeters; I must go."

We shook hands again; he moved across the Square to his two stolid-looking trumpeters, who were waiting for orders. I looked for Yvonne; she was not there. I saw the King speak to his men; they blew their calls, which were not like the soldiers' calls of Europe, but much more like the calls used on the great ranges, in blowing the cattle to salt or to milking. At the sound, I saw the horsemen mustering to their horses. Then, as I was hoping to see the cavalry move off, the light went off the houses, and the glow ceased in the sky. The night had begun to move in. A sharp voice, which I had come to loathe—it was a thin dry voice, without any oil in it, with no life in it—suddenly broke in upon me:

"I thought I sent you to tend cattle; what are you doing in the Square away from your cattle?"

"Oh, so it's you again?" I said. "I've been fighting the M'gai."

"You were drafted to the defaulters' squad. What are you doing away from it?"

"Fighting the M'gai," I said.

But my Plainsman cattle-herd appeared suddenly. He was no respecter of city men or soldiers.

"Come on here, Ned," he said. "I want you, now, with the cattle. Let this fellow stay and talk to himself."

I went off with the cowherd, while Sheep-Snake stamped with fury, and then stormed off to tell someone or find someone.

"That man is no good," the herd said to me. "However, I'll put you down with some mountain bulls; he'll never find you there. It'll be dark before he gets his escort to ram you into prison."

He led the way slowly down a lane which led to the south-east tower. I heard the horsemen in the Square moving off, or at least moving on the stones. I thought that I had not begun my life with the Kranois well. What was to be the end of it? I longed for the King to appear, saying: "Ned, you come with me; here's a horse for you," but had no such luck. I was hurt at the time, that he had not asked me. He told me later that he just had heard that some in the City Council were for using my guns, and that if this were so I had better be there to use them. My Plainsman stopped at a rather dark penthouse under the south-eastern wall. Here, strong pens kept the best of the bulls which had been saved. They stood in a row, uneasily shifting, all trying to get their heads from out of the beams which kept them penned; their horns kept rattling on the wood.

"These are our bulls," my man said. Together, we fed and watered them. "Don't heed that city fellow," my man went on. "I heard a fellow of his saying that, if ever they

got into battle together, he should get a crack sooner than
any M'gai. Don't heed him."

"I have to heed him," I said; "he has much authority
here. I'm only a foreigner."

"Authority, that fellow?" he repeated. "This is a war.
A man like that keeps no authority in a war. Nor is a useful man a foreigner. What are you at home? A soldier?"

I said, "No, a doctor, but I have had lessons in the use
of guns."

"I'd rather use these guns," he said, "than doctor people. I'd like to know doctoring, too; for it comes useful,
doctoring, with cattle, out on a range; the cattle may suddenly sicken, or your man is hurt, or bitten by a snake."

We talked of a good many things; presently he said,
"We'll go the rounds now of the Square, and then turn
in." So we went out, and found the cattle bedded down
for the night, while the night-tenders walked slowly round
the pens, singing to them. "Cattle like being sung to," my
man said. I think that it is true. Certainly, these cattle
were used to it, and took it as a part of the routine of rest.
The city was quiet enough, but for the drone of the song.
I heard the slow steps of sentries on the walls and below.
Now and then, a sentry hailed, or answered the hail of his
officer. The horses were gone from the horse lines: a man
told us that they had gone out, oh, about an hour after
sunset, and had not been attacked; they had ridden clear,
"and now let the M'gai look out."

I heard here and there at different points the familiar
crack of a stone whacking onto plaster from a sling, and
the rattle of the plaster as it fell. I knew now whether the
stone were round or flat, and whether it hit full or with

the edge. We went up to the northern parapet, and looked over the plain. The fires of the M'gai burned clearly, not in a complete circle, but round three sides of us. The fourth side was fenced by the river, and the falling-in of the two lesser rivers. "They won't camp there," my Plainsman said. "That waters'-meet is a bad place; there are devils there." I did not know what he meant; but it was clear to me that the M'gai did not like that quarter. Even in the daytime they had kept away from it. Probably they were right; devils might well be there; it was the sort of place a devil would choose. I wondered what the devils were or had been : crocodiles in the mud perhaps; or those snakes with the grey mouths, like dry silk; or some solitary mad cannibal, who drank fresh blood at the ford?

I would have said that the M'gai camps were quiet; very few figures moved in the light of the fires. I said to my friend, "It doesn't look as if they meant any trouble tonight."

"What is the likely thing?" he asked. "For them to wait till the Big City sends an army, or for them to attack before the army comes?"

"For them to attack," I said.

"And you are a doctor, not a soldier," he said.

His words gave me a thrill through the marrow. I envied him his courage. To him, it seemed part of life that there might be death before morning. He had lived on those terms all his days, out on the ranges, where the snake, the lion, the crazy steer, or the slipping pony might end the liveliest at any moment. I must say that I could not face it thus.

"So you expect the M'gai over the wall?" I said.

"I always expect savages to do the sensible thing," he said. "It's what I do myself."

"What will you do tonight, then?" I asked. "What is the sensible thing to do tonight?"

"Sleep soundly," he said, "and before sleeping have everything handy, and two things in especial."

"What are they?"

"A bottle full of water, and a piece of hard bread; be sure of those; and be sure never to use more than half of either, till you *know* you'll have more. It is not so easy to know, in war. But I'll see you fixed with those. We'll turn in now and forget it."

He had rigged himself a den or lair underneath the northern city wall. In this place he found for me a blanket, a string-covered bottle with a wooden stopper, and a bag to store my biscuit in.

"Now," he said, "you get down to the bull-pen, and sleep while you can. But first make sure that your bottle is filled at the spring."

I bade him good-night, and moved to the fountains near the temple. An oil-lamp in a shrine burned there all night long. I bent and drank, then filled my bottle, and stood a moment, listening to the singing of some women within the temple. They were singing some gentle hymn together, as part of a continual service of intercession proclaimed that morning. As I stood, wondering at the sweetness of the song, and the strangeness of my fate, that I was in a kind of Troy, in the heart of Africa, shut up, and to be killed, perhaps, before daylight, I heard a sound of people moving towards me, and made out that a party of women drew near. They were a relieving party, coming to take their turn of service. I moved aside as they went in. Presently the party who had been singing came down the steps. They went to the spring, lifted the running water in their hands and let it fall, speaking each some prayer aloud after the water had fallen. The last to speak was the one nearest to me. She was Yvonne.

After they had prayed, each knelt awhile on the stone lip sprinkled by the water. One by one they slipped away into the night. You might think that women would be scared to go through an unlit city in the night in wartime, with the wild Plainsmen and wilder cattle in the streets. These were not like European women; they knew that all within the city knew them as "the praying women," or "the singing women," who were sacred as the texts on the altar. Yvonne prayed after the others had gone. When she rose, she lifted the water in her hands once more, and said something in the ritual Kranois, which is a language never spoken save in prayers. Even then, she seemed loath to go, but at last with a little sob she turned to go. I said, very softly, "Yvonne, is that you?"

"Ah," she said. "I have not known where I could find you. I saw you in the drill this afternoon; then someone said that you had been hurt in the fight just after that."

"No, I wasn't hurt," I said, "but I was in the fight."

"Do you know that you are in deadly danger?" she asked.

"I?" I said. "Why, of course, I know that the whole city is."

"It is not the enemy outside," she said, "but the City Council. In these last hours, our friends have been seized;

the Council now is wholly of the Old Party. They are debating killing my grandfather and my brothers."

"But, Yvonne," I said, "whatever for?"

"For? To hide their own shortcomings. They themselves
have brought the war, by their folly. They have taken no
warning, and now seek a scapegoat. Anything to shew the
citizens that these foreigners have betrayed them. They
are now sending men about saying that the foreigners
brought the M'gai here, and even led them in."

"But, Yvonne," I said, "what rubbish! Your grandfather and brothers have been down at the Sixteen Peaks
in all these last weeks. The M'gai have been raiding nearer
and nearer for months."

"You do not know the parties here," she said. "I am
sure grandfather never told you; he speaks ill of no one;
but the Old Party now is snatching at a chance to get
power and break their enemies. They loathe grandfather,
because he opposed some of the old abuses here. They used
to hold cattle-ranges, which they let to others and never
visited. The subtenants made the Plainsmen almost their
slaves, there was so much abuse of power. Grandfather
caused it to be made unlawful not to manage the ranges
in person. The Plainsmen love him for that; the Old Party
have never forgiven him and never will. Now, with everybody scared, they say that the invasion is a plot, to bring
the Plainsmen into the city and presently with the help of
the M'gai to make the city and the Big City, too, subject
to the Plainsmen and the blacks. And now that the Plainsmen's horse have gone out of the city, now is their chance.
They mean to assert their power by making an example,
as they call it."

"But, good heaven," I said, "this is craziness."

"It may be. In war, everybody is somewhat crazy. And when people want to hurt somebody, and can't get at the enemy to hurt him, they will invent an enemy whom they can hurt. The people have been meaner and meaner to the foreigner, ever since the M'gai threatened and Raoul went to try to get the weapons. I heard men saying two hours ago that Raoul took our wealth, not to buy our weapons at all, but to stir up the M'gai against us."

We were now walking slowly backwards and forwards in the Square, in the open space just to the north of the cattle-lines. We had the city to ourselves pretty much. The cattle-herds were still quietly singing to their herds, or blowing a kind of tune from a little kind of pipe they played; it had a melancholy nasal note, wild, plaintive and attractive; I wish that I could hear it now; it was the product of the cattle ranges, and all who ever heard it there will long to hear it again. When we turned east, we heard the song of the praying women. When we turned west, we saw the sentries slowly pacing under the lamps at the City Council's doors. It was a clear night, very dark and starry.

"They have shut up grandfather and the others in there," she said, nodding towards the citadel above these doors. "By this time, they may even have killed them."

"No, no," I said, "you must not think that yet. Are you in danger?"

"I? No. I am one of the singing women; but I know they have been urging that no foreigner ought to be a singing woman, and that the spirits are angry because foreigners are allowed in to the shrines."

"Yes, they would say that," I said. "But I am sure that they will not harm you. And listen, your grandfather and brothers are safe for the present. I am sure I am right. The Council hope to attack the M'gai early on the day after tomorrow, when the army of the Big City will be here. Now, they expect to ruin the M'gai in that battle. When they have done that, they will be very well settled in command here. They will have great prestige, as the saviours of the city. Be sure that it is then that the danger will be. They will make their examples then, not before. If the battle does not go as they hope, then, too, I fear that there may be danger; they will want victims then, to screen themselves and to take the punishment due to their own incompetence.

"But victory will make for mercy, remember. If there be victory, they would hardly do extreme things. They might banish, they would not kill. If the foreigners were banished, what then? We might move to your Big City; they might take us. We might go to live on the plains; or down to the Sixteen Peaks. If there be defeat, there will be no need for them to kill the foreigners. The M'gai will do that for them. You see, it is only a partial defeat that you need dread, Yvonne."

"What do you think of our chances of defeat?" she asked.

"Yvonne, it is best to be prepared. How can men like your Chief, with undrilled, unarmed men, expect to beat men like the M'gai? With my guns and the King's horse they might, if the Big Army come up to expectation. How good is the Big City's army?"

"Better than ours; they have very good spearmen. But

do not despise our army. Our bowmen are often very good ; and the M'gai have no bows."

"Nor had the Greeks," I thought, "but they took Troy, that had." I did not say this but said, "We have no arrows, have we?"

"They say they have a thousand people making arrows since yesterday," she said.

"Who say?"

"Just 'they.' "

"The Old Party?"

"Well, yes."

I said nothing, having seen something of the city's efforts. I had seen very few making arrows, and disbelieved in this thousand. Still, of course, many may have been at work in their homes. I was pretty sure that, when the arrows were made, they would find that they had no bow-strings, or no bows, or no bowmen, for that matter.

"Another good point, much in our favour," I said, "is that we have horsemen and the M'gai none. Have the Big City people any horse?"

"Some : spearmen mainly."

"Yvonne," I said, "we may not be able to talk again like this. Could we possibly get at your grandfather and brothers? Could we help them to escape?"

"Not possibly," she said. "They are in the citadel there, which is the quarter of the Old Party; all the tribes of them are in that quarter—the Aies, as we call them, and the Golden Sheep and the Gold Fish ; the Chief is one of the Aies. I do not even know whereabouts their prisons are ; somewhere in that great black mass. All the body-guard are quartered there ; no one could pass in without a special seal, or somebody to vouch for him. And where could we escape to?"

"The Big City army," I suggested. The army was not yet there, and the danger was. "Tell me," I said, "you trust the King, surely. He is a friend of your people. Why has not the King helped them?"

"Because they have lied to him. They told him, they assured him, that grandfather and the boys were going to be in charge of the foreign weapons. Then, as soon as the King had left the town, of course, they put them all into prison."

"War is begotten of the devil, who is also the father of lies," I said. "Is there any place at all in which you could hide, or anyone who could hide you?"

"I am a praying woman," she said. "I will not hide. Even if I were to hide, who would not betray a foreigner suspected?"

"Is there any priest, or priestess, who could help you or help your people?"

"There is no priest at the moment; the head priest died while you were on your way. The priestess is the Chief's daughter, one of the Aies, a terrible woman."

"The King will help," I said. "He will be back in little more than a day now. He and his Plainsmen will defend you."

"I do not think he will be allowed back," she said. "We Quichets are in the nets. But I am so glad to warn you. You are in danger; you should hide, and can hide. The cattlemen will hide you."

A man on the northern tower now blew a melancholy horn.

"That is for the changing of the watch," she said. "People will be thronging here. I must go; so must you."

"Yvonne," I said, "will you be at the temple tomorrow night as you were this night? If you are, can we meet again, like this? I'll meet you at the spring then, if I am not a prisoner. Will you do that?"

"Yes," she said. "I will, if— But hide; get the Plainsmen to hide you all tomorrow. I must go."

She was gone from me into the darkness; men came stumbling up to relieve the guards. Some of the cattle rose hurriedly in their pens at the coming of so many.

I thought to myself that my lot grew worse and worse. I had been dead, quite dead, unconscious of anything in the world. From that peace, I had been dragged into this succession of dangers and confusions. In the *Albicore,* I had at least been a doctor, a member of a learned profession. Here among these Kranois I seemed to be nothing but a butt or a suspect, who would be put to herd cows on one day and to death on the next. Though the guards were soon changed, the cattle were uneasy, now that they had been roused. The tenders went round them, singing their songs, and now and then chiding them. As I did not want to be recognized, I slipped away to my corner near the bull-pens, and took my blanket for bed. Another Plainsman was camped near there; he was a farrier, or cattle-doctor; I had seen him during the day. He was half-asleep, but roused at my coming, and said,

"Is that Ned?"

I said, "Yes."

He drowsily growled out, "There was someone here, looking for you," and was asleep again.

"Someone was here, looking for me," I repeated to my-self. "Who was it? But only the cattle-tender knows that this is my den. It must have been he who came, or someone from him." Then, as I lay down, I wondered if it were so. Might it not be that the cattle-tender, being a Plainsman, was under suspicion? Might he not have been forced to say where Ned, the foreigner, who was in his company, had been put to sleep? Might it not be the Old Party's police who were after me? It might well be, I thought. What an odd coil life had prepared for me, with the *Hannibal*, the Admiral and Quichet and all of them, to bring me to this, to danger in the heart of Africa. How-ever, I was weary enough to sleep through earthquake. I slept soon enough; and forgot it all. As someone says somewhere, "Blessings on the man who invented sleep." Sailors are right : water and sleep are the two best things. I slept like a log for hours.

Every primitive sleeper, that is, every sleeper who is in the open or away from security, wakes before dawn, partly from cold, partly from fear. Then was the danger-time when man was young ; the lessons then learned are borne into all of us. I woke up with a start, knowing that something was about to happen. I sat up, and found the morning nearly on us. There was a cold and brisk breeze blowing about the town. It blew always, I think, for the place was as windy as Troy ; but being bitter cold before sunrise one only noticed it then. My first thought was, "What are the M'gai doing?" The question was usually settled by their war-cries and the rattle and clack of their sling-stones, neither of which came to my ears at the moment. My neighbour, the farrier, was asleep still. I got

to my feet and rubbed my hands. It was horridly cold.
Almost at once, the sentries on the north-east towers blew
the alarm horns, and roused the guards to the alert, and
at the same instant beautiful birds of fire sailed swiftly
over the parapets and swooped and settled down, to burn
brightly where they fell. "What on earth?" I said. But
others and others came. I knew then that it was the M'gai
attacking by fire-arrows, or wads of burning tow tied to
reeds. The alarm brought the watches up to the platform,
and as they reached it, the sling-stones began, that noise
that one despised yet dreaded, whish, whish, rattle, crack,
dribble, dribble, plot. The plaster began to fall and cries
came to shew that men were hurt, too. Then some of the
fire wads lodged in a reed-thatch not far from me, not in
my lane, but a neighbouring lane. The reeds were bone-
dry, the wind blew the fire; in an instant the roof was blazing, and at the glare of the blaze the M'gai war-cry rose,
and not near us, no, at the north-western tower. The attack was to be there, then. But as I turned towards the
north-west, there rose the devil's own racket at the south-
west end. Above all the noises, I heard an intermittent
thud, which was unlike any noise I had ever heard. "I
know what that is," I said aloud; "they've got battering-
rams of sorts onto that bulge where the wall's weak." At
that, I made up my mind that I would get my guns onto
them, if I had to do it all myself. I saw a spear. I ran with
it, along the wall, till I could see what was being done. The
sling-stones were coming over in dozens, from a couple
of hundred blithe young men who were enjoying themselves. In amongst the stones some fire wads came. I no
longer thought them beautiful.

Ye meaner beauties of the skies,
What are ye, when the moon shall rise?

Relays of M'gai had brought up the small carts of the
Kranois Plainsmen and market-gardeners. They had
mounted tree-trunks upon these, so as to make rude and
not very effective battering-rams. The young M'gai bucks
harnessed themselves to these, some ten or twelve men to
a trace, and with incredible dash and fury rushed with
them at the wall, and flung the ram against it. After the
blow, with the same speed and precision which took away
my breath whenever I saw it, they rushed the ram away,
to let another take its place. They had ten rams, and were
delivering quite five blows a minute at the bulged wall.
Nor was this all that they did. At the end of two minutes
or so, after every tenth ram-strike, they paused. Nimble
M'gai then darted forward, and with levers of hard
wood hove away the stones which had been dislodged, so
that the rams might continue. They had already made an
impression; they had started a slither of stone which
might become dangerous. By the time I reached the wall
above the breach, the Kranois had woken to the danger.
They were flinging stones at the ramming-parties. I called
out to them to bring up bowmen. "Bring bowmen and
shoot them," I shouted. One man said, "We're not to use
arrows on any account"; another said, "They've gone for
the pitch-pots." I should have said that the Kranois use a
black bitumen on the woodwork of their houses, as a safeguard against the ants. This stuff when heated in pots and
flung in a liquid state from metal ladles make a wicked
weapon. But as the Kranois had not prepared any, there

was what the seamen called "hell to pay and no pitch hot."
Two of them brought up a cold cauldron full of the solid
stuff, and then prepared to light a fire under it. I joined
the others at the wall, flinging stones. However, the M'gai
slingers were much more skilled than we. The stones came
at us from right and left, while the rammers dealt their
blows below us. "Fetch bowmen," I cried. "A few arrows
will stop these fellows." They repeated that no arrows
were to be used on any account until the battle.

Where were my guns, all this time? One cohorn only,
nay, one musketful of slugs or blunderbussful of gravel,
would have stopped all this battering at once.

I flung stones, I say, till there came a great rush of
smoke and a crackle and blaze of flame away to the east.
"Well," I said to myself, "I must find out where the waggons are before the fire gets to them. This city may be
blown sky-high otherwise." I ran off, peering right and
left for the waggons. I could see no waggons. A man came
down the lane towards me; I said, "Where are the waggons that were here yesterday?"

"Waggons?" he said. "What waggons? You don't want
waggons when the city's on fire."

He brushed past me and hurried on; he was a messenger for somebody to somebody; the man who sent him
wanted something, and the man to whom he was sent
could not be found, and another, I do not doubt, put the
messenger to look for someone else, who in his turn was
gone from his post, to find somebody who had gone from
his post. But whatever he was doing, he was wrong. When
a city is on fire, it is very important to find any waggon
full of gunpowder. However, I could not find this waggon.

I came instead to a house blazing fire, while men were
running aimlessly, although the water conduit was rushing brimful just beside them. There were buckets there,
too. Well, in a wild emergency, it is better to be doing
something than uselessly trying to do something that
can't be done. I snatched a bucket; they were the light
canvas buckets just stiffened with cane, which all the men
of the plain take with them. I dipped it into the conduit
and flung its contents swoosh into the blaze. It is astonishing what an effect water has in an emergency. Put it over
the head of the most dangerous politician, and it may save
a state. Dash it onto a swooning man, and he will stand up
and continue his task. Fling it with a fair aim onto a
blaze, and you will see an astonishing change; but when
a strong breeze is blowing and the fire has taken a hold,
the change is for an instant only. I repeated it. I called to
others, to seize buckets and put the fire out. As it happened, they were a good lot of young men, only wanting a
lead; they did as I bid, so that we put out the fire. We were
at this, I know not how long. While we were at it, I forgot
about the waggons, the guns and even the rams on the
south wall. We were hot and black when we had finished;
so was the house; we only saved the shell. We were rinsing
ourselves in the conduit, when we heard the devil's own
uproar from the north-western tower. At the same time, a
great flight of fire-wads came over near us and landed in
the ruin we had just quenched; some of them stuck in a
hot cleft in a rafter, which burst out into a blaze. However, that was nothing, or nothing much; the real attack
was behind us by the citadel. We took to our buckets again
and put out the blaze, while the yelling and racket behind

us grew louder and nearer. Men began to look anxiously towards the citadel. Then there came a yell close-to, and a sudden rush of hundreds of yellers: the M'gai were attacking the east wall. I, who helped to beat it off, can assure you that that was an attack indeed. People had said that the M'gai were only savages, who could not stand losses in war. Well, we were only white men, and stood them just as ill. People had said that the M'gai attacked with such fury that they could never maintain their attacks. Well, all that I can say is that they attacked with such economy, such thrift of men and such wise use of force, that they had always hundreds still fresh, to maintain what their twenties had won. In anything to do with war, they were ready, with something foreseen and already taught to their simple men, who perhaps could learn nothing else, but thoroughly learned this. I will not pretend to say how long this attack lasted. It seemed a long time, and at parts of it likely to be a fatal time. We kept them out. They were on and off the platform there, yet never got down into the city from us. Now and then, it looked as if they would; it was the Kranois feeling for the temples, close to our backs, which made the defence so good. Whenever they were at point to settle us, some Kranish lad would shout out something about the temples; then we would rally and heave them back. We had the immense advantage, of course, that we were on the wall. We learned, later, that they did not consider it an attack: it was only a diversion. Well, what's in a name?

When we were almost dead-beat with the struggle, suddenly, the attacking ceased; and almost on the instant a roaring blaze broke out near the south gate. I told you

that some men had brought pots of bitumen and had set
them to boil there. They forgot all about them, in the excitement of the day ; the pots all caught fire and set fire to
the houses near by; a glorious blaze they made. All worn
as we were from our fight, we had to run there to quench
the burning. We had to make a chain of bucket-passers,
then a double chain, then a triple chain, before we could
get it under. I do not know if anyone from headquarters
looked for Ned the foreigner that day. I judge that headquarters had enough to do that day. But I remember
thinking that headquarters had been divinely led to shift
the powder waggon. Had they left it where we had left it,
the south gate of the city would have been blown then
right clear of the walls and the southern wall would have
fallen.

After the fire was out, we fire-fighters were told to go
up to the north wall, "to relieve the poor devils there." We
set out, wondering why they should be poor devils to be
relieved : what were we? However, we found, soon, that
the north wall had had a fiercer struggle than ourselves,
and had let the M'gai get in. As we marched across the
Square we found dead M'gai there among dead cattle.
They had been right in. What had stopped them was
partly their fear of ambush, partly our Old Sword, brave
as a lion, cool as ice, smiling and cheerful, on his old white
pony. Old Sword had restored the battle there. When it
came to a body-to-body tussle, Old Sword was pretty good.

And yet we learned that, when the M'gai called off the
fight, they got away unharmed by us. Two thousand M'gai
withdrew from within arrow-shot and not one arrow was

sent at them. The arrows were to be saved for tomorrow's battle.

Well, the battle was over. The M'gai said, later, that they were scared of the city, which was so unlike anything they had known, with its painted walls and great houses, each a possible trap to them. They had done us much harm; and now we had the dead to bury. I was terrified of the many still-smouldering fire-wads, and my still undiscovered powder waggon. I made up a bucket party, with which I went through some lanes, quenching smouldering fire-wads. I did not find the powder, but I saw much of the town, and certainly quenched some fires. I did not meet one Kranish man who did not know that he had been beaten. What were our commanders thinking of, to let that spirit prevail? We had beaten the M'gai out of the town, yet all inside the walls felt and said that the M'gai had beaten us. They had come in when they chose, and had gone when it suited. Certainly, the M'gai thought this; they told us of it. Their young poets came out to sing about it. They were insolent young bucks, each in his regimental gear and shiny with oil. They came within earshot of us, and sang songs, which the Plainsmen translated to me. They were not cheerful hearing. This was the kind of thing:

"Is there any people liker hens than the Kranois?
 Can there be grown men more foolish with the spear?
 Many things are possible; that is not possible.
 We are the M'gai; our spears want blood.
 When we choose, we shall come into the town of the
   Kranois.

We shall perhaps eat their flesh, if they have any left.
They may not have any left, for we, the M'gai have shut
    them up.
We will take their girls and give the rest to Mimbo.
Mimbo is the god of the M'gai; Mimbo wants blood.
Mimbo shall have the blood of the Kranois.
That is, if they have any blood.
For there are no people liker hens than the Kranois.
We can go up their walls and down their walls.
Mimbo says, 'Bring out the cup. I will drink the blood of
    the Kranois,
'That is, if they have any blood, which I misdoubt.' "

We, in the town, let these fellows exult thus, while we
buried the dead and tore down the smoulderings in the
ruins.

Presently the sun went down, food was served out, and
we were able to prepare for the morrow.

Now word had gone about, for the past twenty-four
hours, that the army of the Big City, a drilled and disciplined body of spearmen, more than fifteen hundred
strong, was on its way to us. Shut up as we were, we were
in touch with this army. In the daytime, signals were
flashed to and from it. Beside these, carrier pigeons flew
in to the citadel, and at night, the adroit scouts of the
plain, or friendly natives, came through the M'gai lines
to the foot of certain walls, where they were looked for
and helped in. After dark that evening, three or four such
messengers came in at odd times, to tell us that the army
was making good progress. It was coming along behind
a screen of horsemen, quite unsuspected as yet by the
M'gai, who, indeed, had been pretty busy with us, all day

long. Soon after the coming-in of the last of these messengers, officers came round quietly to each ward, to say that everything was going according to plan; that the army would come in from the Big City just before dawn. It would attack the M'gai upon an arranged signal. The horse would hamper one wing of the M'gai from helping the other, and the whole strength of our own city would sally out, with spear and bows, to join the Big City army and end the war. The officers were quiet, well-spoken, elderly men, each with the same story, that the army of the Big City, with the horse, and steady well-disciplined spearmen, would surprise the M'gai before dawn, and that our task would be to join in and complete the victory. In a war, any confident talk of victory will cheer the heart. I know that I felt the difference made by these officers; the temper of the city rose with a bound; men became confident and began to long for the morning. After the food, all citizens received their orders; and men were busy with preparations, sharpening spears, drawing rations of hard bread, cheese and raisins, filling water-bottles, and then going to appointed positions. I had heard no word from any citizen of the foreigners in prison in the citadel; and from the silence judged that they were still alive. No man had come to arrest me. Yet when, after the food, I went to tend the cattle, my old Plainsman said to me,

"My lad, I fear they mean you no good."

"Who?" I asked.

He spread his hands abroad, and said, "The King ought to have taken you out of this; then you'd have been beyond their reach. There's little I can do to help in a trap like this city."

"But what is it they mean to do to me?" I asked.

However, at that moment, two guards from headquarters came up, to say that the foreigner, Ned, was wanted at headquarters.

"This is the man," they said.

I asked, "What am I wanted for?"

They said I should be told there; they only had to bring me.

I went with them, feeling that, indeed, they meant me no good, and wondering if this were to be the end. You will say that I might have run or fought, or done something. If you will go to a foreign city and be arrested by the police, tell me, later, will you, if you ran or fought, or did something? I went, and was taken to a lamp-lit room where two men were copying lists at a table. They looked at me, and then went on with their work, repeating the names on the lists and commenting on them. Then they looked hard at me, muttered something under their breath about me, watched me, as one might watch a snake, and returned to their writing. I gathered, from what I caught of their talk, that they were making lists of foreigners and Plainsmen not liked by the Old Party. They went through about a dozen names, with comment about some of them, who were not considered to be safe. The names were unknown to me, but I was struck by the knowledge they shewed of the characters and positions of the suspects. Then one of them mentioned the name Eevono, which made me listen with all my ears.

The other said, "She's a singing woman."

The first said, "No foreigner is to be that after midnight tonight. She will go with the rest."

The other said, "She's pretty, too."

The first said, "That will not count for much when the safety of the city's at stake."

After that, I listened with all my ears for a hint of what was being planned. I gathered that these foreigners or suspects would be arrested; but what did "go with the rest" mean? Were they to be put outside the city to the M'gai or put to death within the walls? I could not learn this. I remembered having read somewhere that it is difficult now to understand how high political passion ran in the packed cities of old time, in Troy, Athens, Byzantium and old London. In the close community, the mind ferments. I had no doubt that Eevono was Yvonne.

Presently, I became conscious that a noise, which was going on intermittently not far away, was the noise of digging. Men were digging somewhere quite close to me. I wondered what in the world they could be digging. I heard the unmistakable noise of spades on stones, and the falling of earth tossed aside. It went on for a long time; then Sheep-Snake and two others came in, took seats, and asked me a lot of questions: who I was; how long I had known the M'gai; what my position with the M'gai King was; what I meant by coming to the city. Had I planned to blow down the south gate with my foreign weapons? Was I to receive a grant of slaves for this, when the city had been taken? They were crazy questions, you will say; they made me understand something of my danger. When one of them had finished, another began, always with the preconceived idea that I was of the for-

eigners leagued with the Plainsmen and the M'gai to
bring the Old Party to an end.

Presently, when all had asked me questions to the
weariness of the soul, I was told I might go into the yard,
while they deliberated. One of the men opened a door for
me. I went out into a yard fairly well lit by a fire. In the
yard half-a-dozen depressed prisoners were wearily digging a trench of an odd shape. It was about five yards
long by two broad, and about three feet deep. They had
been at it a long time and were tired; a couple of spearmen watched them.

Now when I saw this trench, I knew that it was a grave,
and that it was meant for the suspects on the lists which
the men were preparing. It was almost deep enough, so
that it would soon be ready; if it were soon ready, doubtless it would soon be used. As I came out into the yard
there, the guards and the prisoners looked at me, not as
one looks at a foreigner, but as one looks at a doomed man.
Believe me, I know that look; it differs from all other
looks. Their looks said, "He's one that will lie here. This
earth will go on that face. After rain, this is where his
toes'll come through." One of the prisoners who were digging began to whistle a little tune, and another sang a line
of song to it: "A flower for my lady's garden." There was
no need to tell me that they were only prisoners; and that
I was condemned.

I suppose that I had been twenty seconds in this yard,
thinking these thoughts, when the alarm trumpets blew
from the tower just above us. These trumpets were followed by the violent ringing of a bell. When the bell
ceased, everybody in that quarter of the city waited for

the shouted orders which were quite certain to follow.
They followed at once. There was a general warning that
there was to be no rushing, no confusion, but that all citizens were to repair at once to their battle stations. "Go
quietly," the orders went, "and await further orders
when you reach your stations."

The prisoners near me ceased to dig, and looked at their
guards. Their guards looked at each other. One said,
"Well, we must go to our ward." They said to the prisoners, "You keep on with this grave, or you'll likely lie in it,"
and then, shouldering their spears, they set off to their
stations. All the city was full of people moving hither and
thither. As soon as the guards had gone, the prisoners put
down their spades, looked to see if the coast were clear
and went too. I had seen a door on the other side of the
bonfire; I slipped to that, unbolted it, and got away into
a lane, just as someone came into the yard for me. I did not
wait, but ran for it, and got into the Square. There was a
fine confusion there, of men going to stations, not knowing if it were a real alarm or a prelude to the morrow's
battle. It was a moonless night, and except for a few lanterns, some glowing ruins, and a bonfire or two there was
little light to go by. The cattle were up and inclined to
panic. I kept thinking, "These people will stop Yvonne,
probably, on her way to the temple tonight, before midnight. All the party of us will be in that grave before
dawn."

As the cattle were all in a stir, I knew that my friend,
the cattle-chief, would be with them. I came upon him,
as he strengthened a pen by beating in the hurdles.

"Let me give you a hint," he said, even before I spoke;

"I want no word from you." Seeing or judging that my need for a word might be extreme, he said, "Come on down the line a pace, till we see these pens secure. There's been blood shed here, and the cattle are all crazy tonight because of it. Now, son, what's the trouble?"

I said I thought we were all to be killed, including Yvonne.

"My mind misgave me you might not be too safe," he said. "You can't beat a city for wickedness, even in the country. You can't stay here. This is the first place they'll search for you. That crazy farrier has told them you slept at the bull-pens; you can't go there. And you can hear, wherever you turn, that they're mustering and learning where everybody is. Still, it's dark; I'll find you some place."

"I want a place for Yvonne. She'll be at the temple at twelve."

"You mean, she's a singing woman?" he said.

"Yes; but they're going to take her."

"In that case, come, now," he said. He plucked me by the arm and hurried me off towards the western end of the Square, and down a road unknown to me, to a lesser square. He explained to me, as we went, that the singing women were going in procession through the town, with one of the holy images, and would be mustering shortly. "Just another of the follies," he said, "when we want all roads clear for the men, for them to send these miaulers through the city. However, it's the Quichet girl, Edmond's grandchild : isn't that the one?"

"Yes," I said; "she's the one."

"Hold on, then, here," he said. "They're mustering in

the square here. And there's one of these madwomen letting fly. I know the girl you mean. She's been out at the
King's half-a-dozen times. I'll find a way to warn her, if
warning's any good. For yourself, I've a place here."

We were at the end of the road, where it debouched
upon the square. I could see ahead of me a number of very
smoky torches held by women, who were assembling
there. A crazy woman was rushing to and fro in front of
them, screaming, "Woe, woe; blood; blood. I see spears.
I see blood." I had seen two or three such during the day;
wars and revolutions produce them in numbers. This one
was more violent than most because the space was quieter
for her.

My friend opened a door for me and pushed me into a
house, where a lot of the Plainsmen were sheltering.

"See here," he said, to one of them, "this lad has had a
knock on the head from a stone. Take him up to the roof
and let no one come to him till I come myself. Let him
lie on the roof with the gear. Don't let anyone trouble
him; and don't let him talk. I'll come for him later."

The woman was his sister. They helped me up the steps
to the roof, which, being almost flat, had been used as a
store. They had rigged sheers, and had hoisted up some
thirty trusses of the sweet-smelling fodder. They told me
to lie there till they could contrive something; and then
left me. I crept to the edge of the roof to watch. I saw him
leave the house and move to the assembling women. Some
spearmen were trying to lead away the madwoman, and
presently succeeded. I lost sight of my man in the crowd
and movement; but I was sure that if Yvonne were there
still, if she had not already been taken, he would find her

and get her away. When, at last, the women began to sing, and came forward with the image, amidst the smoke of the torches, I could not see her among them. Either he had warned her and hidden her, or he had come too late; she had been arrested.

The procession passed just under me, and it was as well that I was there, for the burning fragments from the torches fell among the fodder and kindled little wisps of it; but for me, there might have been a fine blaze.

After that, I had to consider within myself that on the morrow, if I were not put to death first, there would be the battle. Possibly—who could tell?—I might get from the city to the King, and be a free Plainsman. I had found friends in these Plainsmen. What good fellows they were! It would be no bad life to live on the plains with the cattle among such men as those.

I lay down to rest among the fodder-bales, thinking of Yvonne, and my friends. The battle would be in a few hours. Though I was a most imperfect spearman, I should be engaged in the battle somehow; the cattlemen would all be engaged, of that I could be sure.

The city was at first noisy with men passing to stations or singing in companies; presently these became quiet. A few slingers from the enemy came out from time to time to scatter a few stones. These became scarcer as the night advanced. By about ten, all that I could hear of the enemy was the intoned calling of their sentries. I know not how they do it. It is a thing of great beauty. They have clear voices with the notes almost of bells. From their constant deep breathing of pure air, they have a power of dwelling upon a note which I have never

known equalled by any European. One sentry would
begin with some intoned fair phrase from far, far away
(from more than a mile away), so men told me. The notes
would strike in upon my ear, faintly, yet clearly, assuring
me, "The Kranois are liker hens than men, is it not so,
O warriors of the Umquilitzi?" As the note died away
(and it seemed to tremble on the air, as a bell-note will)
one of the warriors of the Umquilitzi regiment, who wore
the red plumes in their headdresses and at their spearheads, would take it up on another note, till the night
seemed full of it, and call aloud, "O Mimbo, who drinks
the blood from skulls, tomorrow, if the Kranois have any
blood, I will fill thee a skullful. Lo, I am the Stag of the
regiment of the Amalosa: thou knowest me, Mimbo."
Then from another quarter right over the city one would
cry upon another note, and answer the Stag, saying, "I
am Lion, of the regiment of the Nkombos; the Kranish
women shall bear my cubs." I did not know the tongue
in which these men communed across the night; men have
since told me what it was that they cried.

I was weary from the day: I slept heavily, in spite of
my danger. It seemed, in my sleep, that I heard horses
galloping: but I did not wake till my friend roused me in
the cold of the intense dark, to come up to the northern
wall, where some of the cattlemen were doing a turn of
guard. He said, "Don't ask about your friend: she'll do."
He had a helmet for me of an old type to cover my eyes:
this made a fine disguise for me. It had been a quiet night,
my comrades told me: no attack. They said that riders
had come to the western gates from the Big Army. This
had been the galloping that I had heard. Indeed, as I took

my place on the wall, a rider galloped up not very far
from me, and called something which I could not catch.
He waited there for an answer. Leaning at an embrasure.
I could see him, drawn up, close under the wall. However, on his repeating his call, some answer was given to
him, and he rode off, with what seemed expostulation,
slowly at first, then at a gallop.

I asked how they could ride up through the M'gai
sentries.

A Plainsman said, "The M'gai are afraid of horsemen.
Besides, they seldom attack one man; they think he may
be a herald, a wizard or a god. They would never attack
one of those."

I asked, "Do you know what this particular messenger
said?"

They told me, "Oh, something about the Big Army, I
suppose; a message for the Chief."

I asked, "Could they, with their Plainsmen's quick ears,
hear the Big Army?"

They said, "No; we saw the light of the camp last
night."

There was no light at the moment; all the M'gai campfires were out. Away to the east of the city there was one
little glow, from the ruin of a burnt house. But for that,
it was as dark an early morning as I could remember, and
cold enough to give the bone-ache and the cramp. The
native listeners, some black natives in the city's service,
said that they could hear the M'gai moving, "Oh, many,
many," and then assured us that they were moving away;
"Not come here; go there." They pointed at this to the

north-north-east somewhat. Some of the sentries, who were all city men, said that perhaps the M'gai had learned that the Big Army was near and had broken up the siege. I said, "Much more likely that they are gone to fight the Big Army on its way." They thought this a foolish remark; to me it seemed certain. I felt a misgiving, of a kind common to men before danger, that we should all be destroyed later in the day.

As to my own danger, it seemed for the nonce swallowed up in the danger threatening the city. What the time was, I cannot pretend to say. It was before the false dawn, or white light that shines there sometimes. A cock of the long-legged skinny kind that inhabits there, crowed a reedy crow and lapsed again to his dreams. It was pitch-dark and cruelly cold. As sleep was impossible, and as no M'gai were near the walls, we thought that we might be doing a good turn, if we went from the walls and set about the work of the cattle, so that the other watch might have less to do when roused. Beating our hands to warm them, we went down the steps and so forth to the Square to the cattle-pens. Here I found that a watchman was already at work bringing in forkfuls of fodder from the piles. Some cattle were already munching. I thought again that this clover-grass smelt like bean-blossom. It reminded me of a field near Cholsington, where I had walked with my father, on our way to the river. Now here I was in the heart of Africa, probably to be killed that day. I kept telling myself that. My body which had been such a curse to me was going to end: well, it had been a sad lot of trouble for nothing. I had always thought that I should be terrified before a battle: now I found that I had no terror, only a certainty that I should be killed, and that this was a melancholy but not a bad thing.

Our chief told us that we were to be the rear-guard when the army moved. "Well might they make us the rear-guard," he said. "They know we'll not let them run."

Men were moving about in the darkness of the Square: they were the callers of the companies, rousing the sleepers. All the Square was full of sleepers, who were lying there in their ranks, under arms. At the calls, they were waking wearily, stretching, then remembering that now was to come the battle, and so coming to their feet, and moving to fall in. I heard the wakers saying, "Quietly, now. No noise: keep quiet." I suppose that all thought that they were being quiet, but what with the calls, the oaths of the wakened men, the clink of weapons, and the frequent clang as a spear or helmet fell on the stones, the M'gai sentries must have known that large numbers of armed men were moving within the walls. As I came in among the throng, I found that food was being brought round; we cattlemen put ours aside till the cattle were fed. As in all wars, there was a great deal of confusion. Several companies, having roughly mustered, set off from the Square towards their appointed gates. They got into each other's way, blocked the roads and had to halt to let one or other get by. The darkness excused it, of course, but it was a part of the confusion which I had come to expect from the Old Party. As I moved about, I learned from the oaths that men from the eastern wards had been ordered to the western gates and vice versa: anything for complication. However, presently, there was a complete jam: no one moved; the companies stretched into the Square, where they stood patiently, leaning on their spears. As yet no one had gone out of gate. I wondered what was keeping them.

We were beforehand, as I said, in our getting to work among the cattle; and all this mustering, falling in, calling of rolls, and getting into each other's way took a long time. As we went to and fro with our clover we passed the same ranks standing in the same place, waiting for an order. They stood there on their spears and chaffed or cursed us, while we asked them when they were going to fight the M'gai—or had they thought better of it? They were waiting for the signal, they said. It was of no great matter to us while they stood in their ranks, but presently, after they had stood an hour in the intense cold and darkness, they took to sitting or lying down in rank, and this without order, or in despite of order. We had all said, "How well-ordered things are! Here are the men mustered and fed, and all fallen in, a good hour before they will march." But now we said, "How silly these orders have been! Here are the men roused an hour or two too early, and kept on their feet under arms, or wearied by being marched to the wrong gates and back, and dispirited by the want of decision in anything. Now they have got the Square, the central place in the town, in chaos, and when we want to move them, or to do anything, we shall not be able." Remember, too, that with the want of order, men out of rank, companies mixed, etc., men were growling and angry, asking why they were not marching, and why they had been roused all these hours too soon. Some of them started singing, so that presently there was real

uproar. The headquarters heralds had to blow their bugles
for silence, and shout from the walls that the ranks were
to keep silence. There was a moment's silence after that,
and in the silence, which may have lasted for twenty-five
seconds, we all distinctly heard a distant noise away to
the north of the city. It was a confused noise of shouting
and screaming; it came down the wind to us. Quite certainly, the noise was partly the war-crying of the M'gai.
I said, "That is clear. The M'gai are attacking the Big
Army. Why on earth aren't our men out of the gates and
marching?"

My old Plainsman called to an officer, "They're fighting there; why don't you move?"

He answered good-naturedly that the headquarters
men had gone up to the walls to watch for the signal; all
was waiting for that. It could not now be long.

My leader said, "If you ask me, it has gone long ago;
the Big Army is fighting now; any fool could tell that.
Get on out and set forward."

Indeed, a good many felt that that was so; the bugles
blew again from the walls, and the heralds shouted that
all were to fall in and stand to arms. This was a very good
order; but the effort to obey it made the chaos worse for
a while; however, the men did, in the main, fall in and
wait. We cattlemen mocked them again; but it was too
serious for mockery. Rumours floated down to us from the
walls that messengers had come to delay the marching;
then rumours came from the gates that they would be
open in a few minutes. Probably all the rumours were
false; one rumour was that a messenger had just come
on horseback to say that the M'gai were in full retreat.

This was believed and cheered; it was backed by a story which spread, I cannot think how, save as rumour does spread in war, that the Big Army had routed the M'gai already.

Though it was still dark, a streak of light rather high up in the east, which always lightened before sunrise, was aloft like a sign there. As it lightened, the armourers got to their forges; women came to their doors, and children slipped up and down the lanes to see the spearmen. Some headquarters officers came thrusting down from the walls and called that they had not had any signal yet, but expected one at any minute.

"Get the men fallen in, sergeants," they cried. "It can't be more than a minute or two now."

The sergeants called to the companies, and passed up and down and looked important. The ranks closed up, and stood again, waiting for an order, which still did not come. After about twenty minutes, there was a clamour of vexation from them. They knew well, or had been busily told, that the M'gai were easily routed if attacked before daylight; now the chances of a dawn surprise were gone, and that fine courage which had been in each one of them was gone, too. The oaths flew fast. "Why aren't we out? What is keeping us here? Why doesn't the old man move us?"

Then officers would call, "Silence, there. We're waiting for the north-west party to be out. They'll be on our flank. They have to be out before we can move."

Then one said, "Well, if that's so, why aren't they out? They haven't stirred. What's keeping them? I suppose they're waiting for us."

Then a sergeant would shout, "Less noise in the ranks, there. Less free with your jaws there. We're waiting for the signal. It'll be here any minute now. Keep your breath for fighting. You'll need all the breath you can get then, be very sure."

By this time, we cattle-hands had done our feeding and watering. We had filled our bottles and taken our spears (for some had come now). Our chief said that as soon as possible we should move back to the platform of the north wall. At this moment there came a stir in the Square, and some companies nearest to us with much difficulty set forward, not towards the north, but to the south. Anyhow, they went out of the Square, amid a good deal of mockery: did they think the enemy would be there? When they had at last filed away, in column of two, by the lanes to the south wall, we had a certain ease; there was room to turn. My old Plainsman called to all us cattlemen, "Come on now, boys; to the north wall. Set forward there. Come on, before they block the road again." At this, we left the cattle and moved northward across the Square, and so up the steps to the platform. As I was at my chief's side, I was one of the first in the group to move. I half saw, as I turned to go, the figure of a man in armour who seemed to step into our company. Someone near the eastern gate began to play upon a flute in what was called the ancient Kranish mode; a few, who knew the tune, sang to it; other flutes began. In that darkness at that tense time it was overwhelmingly beautiful. My heart beat quickly to the music. My chief said, "If they'd use their breath to fight, it might be more to the point. Not a man of them's outside the gates yet. Think of it." It did not bear thinking of.

When we reached the platform on the wall, we all craned over the parapet, hoping to see the long black lines of the Kranois moving out from both the eastern and the western gates, and merging to go on as one. We saw nothing of that kind; my chief was right; they were not yet out of gate. The night's darkness still held, but in such a way that all objects stood out against it with sharp edges, intensely black. The sky had begun to shew the faintest tints of primrose colour. I could see on my left, the gonfalon of the Commander-in-Chief upon the wall; its white swallowtail shewed clear, in the brisk, cold wind. My chief said, "Old Sword is up there, somewhere." Indeed, a moment later we saw him with his staff, not on the wall, but issuing from his quarters, and coming cheerily up the steps to the platform, laughing and joking. They passed along the platform, away from us. We could not hear what they said, only saw them taking post on the wall, and looking over the parapet.

I should have said that up there on the wall we could hear nothing more of the murmur and shouting of the Big Army. The wind, which is ever brisk there, had grown noisier. Up where we were we heard only the wind, which was everywhere, whistling and piping. It caught our garments and made them flap. Every shutter of the houses near by rattled and clacked. It came round every angle with some rush or swish, always bitterly cold. No M'gai were about; even across the city behind us their camp was quiet; no sentries, even, intoned their mockery. Generally, just before dawn, some of the M'gai sentries put fuel on the campfires or gave the embers a poke, so that the flames might burst, and perhaps make people think that the camps were alert. They were not doing that this morning; the change of routine seemed sinister to me. I could not see the eastern and south-eastern camps well. However, as I turned to look at them, I saw one fire catch the wind and blaze up for an instant.

"Well," my chief said, "it's broad day, now. What's the old fool thinking of, to be joking there?" He looked with bitterness towards the staff, then said, "He must know they're engaged. What's he waiting for?" Without waiting for my reply, he walked boldly across to the knot of men about the Commander. "What's keeping you, Sword?" he asked. "The Big Army's engaged there, can't you hear? Put in your men, man; the M'gai are all around them by this time."

One of the staff officers came between him and the Old Sword. "You must not try to speak to the Commander, nor come so close to him," he said. "Stand further away."

"Very good," my friend answered. "But tell him to send out at once."

"It is not for you to tell him, but for him to order you, which he does through me. Stand further back."

"I'll not. Let him send out." He turned to the waiting company of spearmen, mustered in the space under the wall just below him, and cried, "Open the gates and get to it. The Big Army's fighting there. Get out of this."

There was an angry murmur from several officers below. I heard, "What is he thinking of? Bang the fellow over the head; pitch him over the wall, the drunken Plainsman." But some voices cried, "The man's right: they *are* fighting. Let's get to it." Some cried, "Silence," and others, "We'll not silence." Then in the midst of it, while they were still abusing and quarrelling, we heard the galloping of hoofs in the plain below. We all dropped the quarrel at that sound, and turned to the parapet. Several horses were galloping to the foot of the wall. They had come over the western end of Fair Hillocks (the rise to our north) and were coming straight to where we stood. It was now fast growing light. I could see colour, a darkish blue-green, in a little thorny shrub which had grown into the wall close to me. The horsemen came at speed, straight to the point below the Chief's gonfalon. I could see that the leading horseman was the King. He was signalling with an active hand to the Chief, to come out.

"Come out," he shouted. "Bring out your men and fall on. What in fate are you waiting for?" He reined up a lathering horse just below us. He was white with excitement and fury. "Why aren't you engaged?" he shouted.

"Engaged?" Old Sword replied. "Engaged? We have had no signal. We have seen no signal. We are waiting for the prearranged sign."

"Sign and signal?" the King answered. "We have sent to you and sent to you. Why in the name of God have you not marched? Fall on; come out and fall on. I've sent six gallopers to you. They've told you this. Yet here you are still in the walls."

"Listen, young man," Old Sword said, when the murmuring of his staff died down. "The plans for this battle were that our movement is to depend upon a certain signal. I am not young enough to alter plans because an excited horseman tells me to. Keep your gallopers where you can use them. Don't send them with orders to me. I command here. And, being commander, I wait for the signal."

The King replied quietly, in his clear penetrating Plainsman's voice, "In that case you'll wait till the moon's purple."

The remark roused that staff officer who had told my cattle-tender friend to stand back, to say, "Sir, your insolence is that of a cub; that is no way to speak to our Commander."

"Look here, sir," the King said to the Old Sword, in the same calm, penetrating voice, "you'll get no signal. I've sent six times to tell you, as I now tell all of you, that we cannot reach the signalling point. We're engaged with the whole M'gai army, on the other side of Fair Hillocks, where you can't see. I've told you this six times by messenger. Now I've come to you myself. You have wasted the chance of ten thousand. Come out at least now and take them in the rear, before we're all killed."

His voice rang over the city. I suppose that in spite of the wind most of the men on the north wall heard him. What they heard passed at once down to the men in the ranks below. I suppose that Old Sword was stupefied at being so spoken to; perhaps his mind moved too slowly always to have a ready reply. The staff, stung to silence, looked at each other and at Old Sword: nothing was said.

The King, waiting for an answer as swift as his thrust, and getting nothing, cried, "Move, man; for very shame's sake, move."

The Old Sword moved slowly to the parapet, and turned to his left. "You there," he said to one of his officers, "tell them to open the west gate." As the officer moved, Old

Sword spoke to the King. "I've told them to open the west gate below there. Come you in by it, and make your report in a fitting manner."

"I've made my report," the King answered. "You act on it. My place now is with the fighters, where I can be of use. If you won't fight, at least shew yourselves, so that we may know you're there to fight for."

With that, he and his riders rode slowly off, nursing their horses, towards the Fair Hillocks. They did not look back at the city. Their eyes were roving along and across for M'gai lying in the grass to spear them as they went. Now that their backs were turned, I bit my nails with vexation that I had not seized one of the spy ropes secured to the parapet, gone down the wall and joined the King.

The staff officer said, "Sir, we will have that man before a soldiers' court."

Old Sword, who was ever one to bide his time, said, "Where is that Tali-Mali who killed the lion that time?"

The staff leapt at once into activity; the word was passed for Kleza, or M'Kleza, who was down in the headquarters somewhere. He was on the wall with us in twenty seconds; a big middle-aged savage.

"Kleza," Old Sword said, "what happens yonder?" He pointed to our north-north-east, in the direction of Fair Hillocks.

Now the wind was blowing, making much noise about us. This savage looked, bent an ear, took a deep smell of the wind and at once kindled all over. "Men fight," he said. "Many men fight."

"That will do, Kleza," Old Sword said. "That will do

for us, gentlemen. Send word at once. Prepare to march. Open east and west gates. Archers to cover the wings. Set forward."

There was now an almost full daylight; the men who had been waiting in the ranks for hours gave a cheer at the word to move. I heard the gates open; and almost instantly I saw some archers scatter out to cover the wings and stop any attack on the columns as they came out. All the troops were at once moving. The staff followed Old Sword from the wall. By this time, the King and his troopers had reached the top of the Fair Hillocks and turned over the crest out of sight. Some of the people in the Square cheered Old Sword as he went down to his old white pony, but it was not much of a cheer. As I turned to see him start, I found that man in armour, whom I had half seen in the Square, standing at my side. In earlier days, the Kranois had used defensive armour, made of metal or plates of metal, of which a few pieces are still preserved. It had then become the fashion to use quiltings of hide, and these in turn had given way to cotton quiltings, which were rather hot and when ill-made very heavy, but easily put on or off, and astonishingly good as defence. This man beside me wore the cotton armour of a lancer of the plain. A cuirass and back-piece covered his body; the helmet and throat-pieces made it hard to tell his age, for his visor was plucked down and the chin-piece plucked up. Some of these suits were little more shapely than shirts reaching to the knee. This one was a captain's suit, shaped to the body, and hung with the blue and white Kranois badge. Something about the figure made me catch my breath. The figure put out a hand and nudged me back to the parapet. All the others of our squad were at the stair-tops, watching the army moving out of the city.

"Don't you recognize Yvonne?" the figure said. "I was given this to wear. I'm hoping to reach the other camp. Are we to be shut here all day?"

"I hope not," I said. "Have you had any food?"

"Yes, and rest. And I've heard that our people aren't killed yet. You and I are both being looked for, but they won't search much till after this. What do you think is happening over there?"

"The M'gai have attacked the Big Army on its march. Our old fool ought to have foreseen that and prevented it by attacking in time."

"How do you think it is going?"

"I cannot tell. I only heard the noise of it once or twice in lulls of the wind or when the city was quiet. It was not further off when I heard it last, so I suppose there is no retreat yet. On the other hand, the King seemed anxious. If I were the Old Sword, I should feel scared though. These M'gai move like light; they seem able to break off any battle at an instant's notice. They are said to hate all battles which last long. Suppose they find the Big Army a hard task. Suppose they pluck all their regiments out of it and come in a rush on Old Sword. You can tell what is likely to happen then."

But at this point, my old Plainsman called, "Come on, boys; we're to leave this now; we of the gallant rear-guard. Come on to the east gate with you. See all your water-bottles full at the spring. War may be glorious or it may be damned, but it's always thirsty and usually full of lice."

We halted at the gate for some twenty minutes, while other odds and ends of armed men were gathered from different parts of the wall to make us somewhat stronger. It was, of course, full daylight now, and sunshine. Some cattlemen were turned back here, to be with the cattle in the Square.

The city was tense and scared. A few women, with very white faces, came to the doors for news, or to the springs for water. Some little boys who had formed themselves into companies came to the Square to drill with sticks; all the little girls seemed to have become women overnight. We being halted in the space below the walls could see nothing of what was happening outside; and hear little save some distant shouting, mostly orders of some sort. We could see old men on the walls, peering at what was happening outside. We all called to them from time to time, to ask how things were going. They could see very little except that the men were moving out; then that they had reached the Hillocks; that the M'gai were not to be seen; and that presently our army was over the rise and out of sight. We waited as we were for a long time; then an officer, an old man, with a singularly merry face, came up to us and said, "I'm just scraping up some archers. When I've got them, I'll move you out, and we'll see something of the fun."

Something in his face made me ask if I might not try to bring out the guns. He asked what they were, and seemed interested; then said, "Where are these things? Have you them here?" I had to say that they had been removed, but could not be far; a few enquiries would shew where. He said, "I'll ask about them." However, he had no luck, and had no time to make a real enquiry. He said to me, "I'm sorry not to use your things; they seem just what we need. But here come our bowmen : we must move now. We have to cover the right rear."

Some old bowmen came up to us from somewhere : they were to protect us from the lion's jaws. The gate was opened to us, the archers spread out in a fan formation in front of us, and so we passed out of the city. I had not loved my time within her; but still she was a city. Outside her walls, I had to reflect that only a few old bowmen stood between me and the M'gai. I assure you I longed for my guns. Yvonne at my side said, "There is the first step past : we are out of the city at least." Our captain led us in a somewhat loose order away to the east, straight towards the M'gai lines, now seemingly empty. Soon, I could see the enemy cattle-pens and the sites of old fires. As we went, I passed one or two hollows in the grass, like the forms of great hares, where M'gai sentries had passed the night. Presently, we were in the M'gai camp, such as it was. One of the Plainsmen with me said that this piece of it was the camp of a party of lads not yet allowed to sleep in huts; the main camp, of huts, lay south from us. No M'gai were there now. However, the Plainsman told me that no doubt half-a-dozen were watching us unseen. Our captain halted us, closed us upon our centre, and drew in the bowmen a little. We stood there, waiting and looking about for a few minutes. Then a small party of M'gai, with black and white plumes, appeared on the eastern end of the Fair Hillocks to north of us. They stood there for a time, looking at us; perhaps they were twenty strong. As they received no supports, and seemed uneasy at our pres-

ence, our captain said that he meant to clear them out of
that. The bowmen were told to go forward, in open order
twenty yards ahead of us; we followed in wedge formation, ready to receive the bowmen amongst us at an instant's notice. The M'gai watched our coming, without
trying to attack. As we came to a point that was almost
within bowshot of them, they slipped quietly back behind
the sky line out of sight. Our captain cheered, and said,
"They're running. Come on, boys, we'll hunt them."

My cattleman said, "Go slowly. That is only a trap.
They're falling back to draw you on. It is a rule with us,
never go over a sky line after M'gai."

Our captain disliked being checked, but said, "Perhaps
you're right." He called to the bowmen to come in within
our wedge; then we advanced again, up to the top of Fair
Hillocks, so that we could see the city behind and below
us on the one side, and the unknown world on the other. It
was no pleasant sight that we beheld. Coming up the slope
towards us, about three hundred yards away, was the
whole of our city's army in hollow wedge formation, beset
by a couple of hundred active young M'gai, who were
slinging it with stones. Men in the wedge were being hit
and were falling. Those near them picked them up and
made shift to carry them; they were carrying some sixty
already, at a rough guess. The body looked unwieldy,
baffled and beaten. I had seen drawings of bison in the
Americas beset by wolves. This floundering wedge seemed
like a bison so beset; it staggered along at the pace of the
men who bore the dead and hurt. Now and then, some
archers in the wedge drew bows and loosed arrows. Someone said, then, that Old Sword had refused to take many

archers, saying that the battle would be decided by spear-men. A few arrows were shot. The slingers danced about, and sometimes stood still to draw the arrows, which they parried with great skill with their scratch-sticks. They mocked the unwieldy wedge. Shocked as we all were at its appearance, we felt inclined to mock, too. Why was an army letting itself be pelted thus? Old Sword rode within the wedge on his white pony. He was certainly as brave as a man can be; but this was no way to fight M'gai. The thought came onto our hearts like a sledge-hammer, "What has come to the army of the Big City? Has it been destroyed?" Our army had not joined it. Where was it, then? Where were the M'gai?

We could not tell where the M'gai were. Parallel with the Fair Hillocks, about a mile in front of us, were other low rolling fair hillocks. I did not doubt that somewhere behind those the army of the Big City was in the lion's jaws of the whole M'gai army. What on earth was the Old Sword doing, to retreat thus before a couple of hundred slingers? The old merry captain who commanded us asked this. He at once told our bowmen to go on in open order and shoot the M'gai slingers. Now our archers were eld-erly men and good bowmen. I saw then, for the first time, what sort of weapon the bow is. I had read of Odysseus and of the English cloth-yard shaft, had wondered and had disbelieved. Now I saw the bow in use, and trembled at it. I saw our first arrow bring down a young M'gai, who had rashly paused to mock; then another and another fell. I saw then that the young M'gai at any rate were not disciplined to bear losses. They fell away from our side of the wedge, and left their dead, which the M'gai ever shrink from doing. By this time the wedge was pretty near to us. I could see the faces of the spearmen, all scared, humiliated, angry, white and sullen. Some of our men called, "Where's the Big Army?" But by this time I saw that a vast body of the M'gai were beginning to blacken the distant hillocks of which I have just spoken. Whatever had happened to the Big Army, the whole M'gai army was there between us and it. The question we asked was whether the M'gai had destroyed it. Anyhow, it was plain that our men had not joined it, but had been driven off. The wedge hove nearer and nearer; I could see the men looking back, and hear their mutinous growls. It was plain to me now that they were carrying far more than the sixty hurt of my first reckoning. They had been among harder knocks than sling-stones and had had the worst of it. Glancing back at the city, I saw the battlements of the north wall packed with watchers, all deadly still. I thought of Troy watching for the heroes returning from the field.

I said to Yvonne, "All will yet be well. Courage. We won't go back into the city till we must."

Like the wedge, we were all falling back thither. However, at this point we were all upon the ridge of the Fair Hillocks, and about to go down thence out of sight of the M'gai. It was at this point, that my friend the cattleman took command.

He said to our captain, "Keep all the bowmen out onto this ridge. No M'gai will rush over a sky line. You can hold them up there with twenty good archers."

My captain was a clever fellow, always ready to take a suggestion. As we dipped down the slope towards the city,

he called out the bowmen and told them that they were to
cover the retreat from that point. Something of the same
thought came to the Old Sword, for he, too, put out
archers. Now we were over the ridge, and going back to
the town. Almost at once a volley of sling-stones came
over, and an elderly bowman with a grizzled beard was
killed close beside me. I saw that he was dead. I jabbed my
spear into the ground and took his bow and quiver. I sent
an arrow at one of the young M'gai who had darted up to
sling. All this time we were outside the army, watching
its uncouth clumsy body heaving down towards the town,
and beginning to go dangerously quickly. Someone who
thought that the formation might break, began to sing
some slow-timed song, to steady the retreat. I have little
doubt that this was the Old Sword himself, who knew how
near to a panic his flounderers were. I sent another arrow
at another M'gai. Yvonne at my side handed me arrows.
Then in my rage for this old man beside me newly killed,
I shot at another and at another. Then almost before I
knew what was happening, there came a scream like
the end of the world and the M'gai were over the Fair
Hillocks, and were between us and the city, attacking the
wedge. It was the Black Regiment that was attacking.
They did not pay any attention to us archers. They went
straight at the wedge with an incredible raging, yelling,
screaming fury. I saw eyes turned up, shewing the whites,
and mouths foaming; the god Mimbo was in them, no
doubt to overflowing point. I shot arrows at them; so did
the archers with me. I don't think I hit anybody, but I
saw several men go charging on with two or three arrows
sticking in them. Then they got in upon the edge of the

wedge, and flowed round it and closed in. However, the wedge stood. I could see Old Sword upon his pony; he was the one happy man in the wedge, I judge; this was like his youth. This needed no brain, only cool courage in which he was supreme. Our position was not good, out there on the slope, with mad M'gai between us and the wedge, and possibly three thousand more M'gai about to leap over the sky line at us.

The wedge stood, for all the power of Mimbo; the first rush of M'gai drew back from it a little, and instantly the archers in the wedge shot and shot at them, so did we. I saw some M'gai biting the edges of their spears as they gathered for a new rush. A good many of them had fallen; some were dead; others were trying to worm their way along the grass into the wedge. At any instant, I expected to see the mad M'gai, the Red Regiment or the whole army, coming over the ridge to annihilate us. Our one thought was to shoot these of the Black Regiment till they sickened of their attack. If they had turned upon us they could have speared us all. We were only a handful, without any proper defence. What saved us was the fact that Mimbo is an animal passion or herd-madness, which blinds each of the herd to all other things than the herd-enemy. These fellows saw for the moment nothing but Old Sword's command. Well, they drew back an instant, and hurled spears into the wedge. They hurled with an energy that was appalling; as they hurled, they cried "Szaa," or some such noise, something between a hiss and a curse. Each man had two spears, one for hurling, the other never hurled. After the hurling, they bit their spear-edges and szaaed for a moment; then, as though one mind were in the regiment, they rushed again at the wedge, and again were held against the pikes, after receiving a flight of arrows. They thrust up against the pikes. I saw nothing of the wedge. It was all hidden from me by dark bodies and lifted dark arms. I shot and shot at this heaving mass, till I found no arrows handy. Yvonne snatched arrows from the ground; some of them had had their points snapped off, but I shot them. I saw that the wedge was moved as it were sideways by the weight of the M'gai against it, and said to myself that it would break; must break. Perhaps it would have broken. But then there came a roar and a thundering. I said, "Here comes the M'gai army." It was nothing of the sort. It was the King, with some three hundred horse, charging the M'gai from the west.

Now Mimbo, as I had seen, was a very good attacker; but he is a very imperfect soldier. He cannot change to the defensive. He can attack, but if attacked at that instant may give way. The M'gai were caught by surprise in the rear. The leading squadron were into them before they knew of their approach. They broke and fled in all directions, with the other squadrons after them. I suppose no battle has been more suddenly changed. What was so amazing was the change in the M'gai. They had been mad devils; then in one instant they were screaming runaways, throwing away their weapons and running like hares. However, it was not part of the King's plan to chase one scattered regiment over Africa, while four or five undefeated regiments might be just over the hillocks; besides, the horses had had a hard morning, and had the day still before them. Just as I was thinking that most charges of horse failed through the men going too far after the suc-

cess had been won, I heard a whistle blow, and saw the
squadrons rally to it. A loose horse stopped to graze just
beside me; I caught it and mounted Yvonne upon it. We
stood together there staring at the marvellous sight. The
wedge of the Kranish army was floundering back to the
city. I could see the Old Sword trying to stop it and turn
it, but he was not regarded; all those men were for getting
back within the walls. All the wall was strung with a kind
of beadwork of faces staring. I could see no bodies, only
lines of faces. This gave me a strange and haunting impression of being peopled only by souls, all anxious. The
M'gai being for the moment gone, we of the rear-guard began collecting arrows and spears with which the ground
was stuck thick.

I saw now that we had killed a good many of the enemy;
their bodies were scattered all about; most of them had
been killed by the lancers' charge; some by the pikemen of
the wedge; a few by arrows. Yvonne told me to be very
careful of these prone bodies, since some were only
wounded and others pretending to be dead, so as to have a
chance of striking any who ventured near. I saw one seemingly dead M'gai heave up, and stab an archer in the back,
then leap to his feet, curse us and fly for the M'gai camp.
An officer of the horse rode up to us, and called, "Come,
all of you. Leave the gear on the field. We want the M'gai
cattle and asses." He mustered us together, and set forth
with us towards the M'gai camp, and through this to the
old Kranish cattle-pens, in which they had stored their
booty of plundered cattle, and their supply-train of asses.
Some old women were tending the beasts in the pens. They
fled uphill from us as we approached and gathered to-

gether to curse and spit at us. The officer who had sum-
moned us to this work called out to get all the rope we
could to halter the asses together. I had the chance of an
instant of speech with him, and said, "I am not a Kranois.
I am a doctor and newly come to the city. When we drive
these beasts to the town, may I come with you to the King,
instead of going back into the city with them; my friend,
too?"

"These aren't going into the city," he said. "These are
the pedigree stock of the big plain-breeders. These are
coming with us to safety. Can you ride? Any of you men
who can ride, mount each his ass. So you're the man the
King was talking of. He must be somewhere. Did you ever
see a pretty chance worse spoiled?"

To be brief, we gathered the plunder, and then set forward to drive it to the camp of the Big Army. We of the
city were wondering what had happened. This Plainsman
told us everything. There had been a bitter fight from
before dawn, some miles from where we were. The M'gai
had attacked the Big Army on its march, and had had
many losses and not much success; they had then been
unexpectedly charged by the horse, of which they were
much scared, and had had a severe setback. If the city
forces had but marched out on the alarm, they might have
been annihilated; instead of that, they had marched out
when the Big Army, despairing of their moving at all,
had returned to camp. Seeing them returning, the M'gai
had plucked up courage and had followed them. The M'gai
regiment left behind to guard the rear had attacked the
city army when it appeared, the city army had floundered
about, and seeing no other Kranish army about had re-

treated, and had only been saved from destruction by the King's timely charge.

We had met the wedge of our men unable to beat off the M'gai slingers. This was the fault of Old Sword, who had insisted that his force should march with "the real old Kranish weapon, the spear": he had allowed few archers to come with him, and had limited those to five arrows apiece. The slingers had thereupon made life a burden to everyone in the wedge, and set the whole force floundering back towards home. That had been the situation when I met it.

When I had first seen the M'gai upon the plain, my heart had beaten high from a sense of adventure and the knowledge that I could cope with it. Then, almost as soon as I had entered the city, there had come humiliation, danger and the fear of death. Now, as I rode on the wide plain (on a donkey, it is true, but with my love beside me) my heart again beat high. I had found no friends in the city; I had found them at once among the Plainsmen; and with the feeling that I was out of the city came the knowledge that I might save Quichet, and help to beat back the M'gai. It is difficult to define the feeling of power. A man may face an audience, and say suddenly to himself, "I can sway this audience." He may see suddenly some scheme for work or building, and say on the instant, "I can do this thing." I saw presently, as we rode, the great black mass of the M'gai army, watching us as we drove our plunder. No doubt there were five thousand of them and we were but a handful, riding with our booty, and the horse out on the flanks, yet I knew instinctively that the M'gai would not attack. I had their measure now, and no

longer feared them. As a doctor, I knew that their way of
attack, under the madness of Mimbo, is extraordinarily
exhausting, and cannot readily nor swiftly be repeated. I
could now see, also, that they were afraid of attacks by
horses and horsemen, and had not yet devised a tactic for
dealing with them. All the same, it was not wise to defy
them too far. We should have time to deal with them properly; the war had changed. With the horsemen which they
did not like, and the guns which they would not like, I
knew that in a little while we should be able to beat the
M'gai. I had Yvonne beside me, too. That was another
reason for joy. Our talk as we rode was how to save the
Quichets.

Debating this point, we came in time to the camp of the
Big Army, as I have called it. This was on a low hill above
a little river. A clump of trees was on the hilltop; a ridge
from each end of the hill stretched out and fenced a grassy
level where the cattle could both be grazed and be guarded.
It was a beautiful place, impossible to surprise, having
this open rolling land on all sides of it. When I saw it, I
knew that the war had changed for the better; here were
people who knew what to do.

Long before we entered the camp, I saw that this was
not under the command of men like Old Sword and his
friends. Here all was order, forethought and design. Here
there was knowledge to support the native stubbornness.
Vedettes were out, a watchtower had been built and
manned; all approaches were either trenched or fenced
or both.

My officer friend, who had taken me under his wing, said
that, as I had this woman with me, I had better go straight

to the headquarters on the hilltop, as very likely I would
find the King there, if he had come in from the field. Many
of the horsemen had come in; the horses were being rubbed
down and dressed in the lower camp. Probably the King
would be up in the main guard.

Sometimes in my past, I had known from the looks of
the faces that all was lost for me. I went up the slope of
the hill to the headquarters wondering whether I should
feel all to be lost when I entered. I need not have troubled
myself. I came into the headquarters as into a new world.
It was not what I had expected headquarters to look like.
It was a level space on a hilltop, partly fenced with rolls
of blanket, which would presently be the general's bedding. A spear with a scarlet bannerol was stuck near it
as a guide. Food was about to be served; and the staff
officers were coming in for their meal, which was being
cooked for them at two little native stoves near by. Three
of the main officers lay on their faces on the ground having
their knees kneaded and pounded in the Kranish manner
after their long hours in the saddle. I saw at once that one
of these men was the King, so I called out to him:

"King, I am Ned, whom you met in the city. Can you
do something for Quichet and his grandsons? They have
got them all shut up and may put them to death."

He rolled over at once on hearing what I said; like most
Plainsmen, he had a very swift decision when anything
had to be done.

"Is not that just the thing these people would do?" he
said. "They cannot govern; they cannot foresee or meet
the unforeseen, yet they unite to destroy the men who can
do both. You must see the Chief. He will be here in a mo-

ment; he has only gone to speak to the galloper. In fact, here he comes. Chief, here is the young Englishman, the doctor, of whom I told you."

I had had some experience now of Kranish soldiers, and thought that I knew what to expect. I was not prepared for the man who entered. To begin with, he was a very young man, not more than twenty-five; he had a face of indescribable beauty and charm, with a smile and a bodily grace which made him irresistible. I had not expected youth in a leader, nor beauty and grace in a soldier, since Alexanders are rare. I knew at once that this man was of the stamp of Alexander and of those other young commanders who carry all before them. We, in our time, have known one such who has flamed across Europe. Here was one set upon a small stage, and without disfiguring ambition or purpose unworthy of his genius, who within his orbit could carry all with him, against any odds, to any success upon which his mind was bent. I knew that this man was already great, and at once my heart leapt within me, to think that now we might beat back the M'gai. This was the saviour of the Kranois.

He greeted me and welcomed me to the Kranish camp.

"He has bad news about Quichet," the King said.

It is usually held that fierce indignation is a righteous thing. It has to be honest indignation, untouched with any personal greed or self-interest; then it becomes the very voice of God within one. I had Yvonne there; her brothers and grandfather depended on me: now I spoke out.

"Sir," I said, "the leaders in the city yonder are going to kill the Quichets. What can you do to help?"

The young Commander, whom all called "Golden," asked, "What, do you think, can be done?"

"The only means," I said, "is to supplant the Old Party. If you leave them in power there, for only a few hours more, they may have killed these men."

"They may have done that, already," the King said.

"We think not; but, granted that they have," I answered, "they have not beaten the M'gai; and you can supplant them on the plea that they are ruining the Kranish cause."

Golden smiled and said, "They were not very helpful this morning. I'm surprised at Old Sword. Still, you cannot expect a man of impulse to be a man of intellect. So you think we ought to supplant the Old Party?"

"Well, I am only a foreigner. But how else are you to make proper use of the little city's strength?"

"It will be said," the King said, "that the Plainsmen made a war to lose their cattle and then made a revolution to save them; we shall be less loved than ever."

"You will," I said. "But if you beat the M'gai the city will see that you have saved her, and at present she knows pretty well that Old Sword and his friends have brought her to the brink. What help do you expect tomorrow or next week, or next year for that matter, from such a set?"

"The King has told me about some weapons you brought. Would you pledge your faith that these weapons of yours are sure to help to beat the M'gai?" Golden asked me this question in a way which made me feel that he was on my side.

"I know that they will," I said. "But remember, the weapons have been removed somewhere. I know not

where they are now. Some of the things are very dangerous when brought near fire; the M'gai use fire in their attacks, and may at any moment have the luck to fire these
things. Then, too, remember, that some of these things
can be very dangerous if handled carelessly. They may
kill some of your own side. But give me a fair chance, and
a few careful men, and I pledge you my faith and my
head that I will shock the M'gai. No savage race has with-
stood firearms yet. They kill at great distances. and with
loud noises; they are terrifying."

"You told me something of the sort," Golden said to the
King. He turned, then, to Yvonne, and said, "These
camps are no places for you women. We will try to find
a shelter for you here. Could you guide us about in the
recesses of the citadel, if we came into the city tonight?"

"No," she said. "I have never been in the citadel. But I
know that the temple on the west wall has a door leading
to it."

"That is something," Golden said. "I suppose the people are shut up in the citadel?"

"If they are alive at all," the King said, "they will be
in the prison there, somewhere deep down, where I have
never been. I know some of the upper citadel: it's a great
rambling place. Old Sword and his men will be in the
quarters there up above. So much is sure."

"About this door into the citadel," Golden said, "—this
door from the temple. It is hardly likely to be open?"

"No," Yvonne said, very white. "You may put me to
death for sacrilege afterwards, but I know where the
priestess leaves the keys."

Golden looked at her with his charming smile. "Come,

come," he said, "I don't think we shall have to ask you to betray any trust. I hoped that perhaps you had been allowed to visit your people in prison, and knew whereabouts they are shut."

"I know nothing whatever," she said.

"Well, we must find out," he said. "Now here is food; after that, we will find a shelter for Yvona, and then set to plans."

After food, that is what we did. When Yvonne had gone from us, Golden said, "As leader here, I can supersede Old Sword, which will break his old heart, I suppose."

"He'll break the hearts of his city if he's left there long," I said.

"That is true," Golden said, "but I could find it in my heart to spare him all I can; there's something fine about him."

"I know that," I said. "War is the test. He is superb when fighting. But his party is less fine; his party did not come into the fighting. It was deep down at dirty work, down in the citadel."

"And you, King, what do you think?"

"I'm not much loved at his headquarters," the King said. "I'm a Plainsman, and I have spoken my mind very freely to him. The trouble is that I must be something like what he was when he was my age. I think you can only save these lives by superseding him; that is, of course, assuming that the lives can be saved."

"Would this be possible?" I asked. "Could you, as Leader, send for him, to confer with you; then, when he has come, keep him here, while a party enters the city to save the prisoners?"

"He would never leave the city," Golden said. "He is as vain and as ticklish on the points of procedure as man can be. He would say that he was placed in charge of the city, and could not leave it save with the city's army, and then only if he thought the situation asked it."

"He would consider any order an insult," the King said.

"But surely, you as Leader of the Big City's army, could demand it."

"I could," Golden said, "but he wouldn't come."

"Then, could you, as Commander, enter his city for a conference?"

"Only if invited," he said. "He is the ruler there."

"Rules are made by men and have to be broken by men," I said. "I am a doctor, and see the case as a doctor might. Sometimes in a body you have a clot somewhere, inhibiting function everywhere. Often, we cannot tell just where the clot is. In this case we can. If you remove this clot, the Old Sword, the body will function. As far as I can learn, the Old Party has no other man so able. After today's battle, when he risked the whole Kranish cause, from stupidity, you have every excuse for breaking all precedent. If you enter the city, secure him and the few about him, and explain that it is done for the city's salvation, you will have everybody with you in what you do. He himself will never lack admirers. He was superb, both in the Square and out in the wedge; but he is a public danger where he is; and his party is both a public and a private danger."

I was hot from injured vanity; the King was hot as a

stallion might be from the rein; the Commander tried to keep the matter in the way of wisdom.

"It will soon be too late to send a pigeon into the city," he said. "I will send one now. I shall say that I am coming to confer with him at three tomorrow morning, and that it is most important that he should overlook the irregularity; and at the same time keep the meeting secret, even from his staff. I shall ask him to flash an answer back to our outposts as soon as it is dark enough and to repeat the assurance that he understands, and that I may come, not less than twice, at intervals of half-an-hour."

"You will not be able to explain your reasons by pigeon," the King said.

"I shall not try," Golden said. "I shall put my mark, that it is very important. I will go down to the pigeon-house and have that sent at once."

He went off at that.

"What chance will there be of the pigeon reaching the city?" the King asked. "It is already late in the day for a pigeon to go."

Indeed, the day had drifted from us, as these busy wild days do drift. I had seen carrier pigeons in England, and knew something of their speed.

"What will he do, if Old Sword refuses to see him?" I asked.

"I think he will go to see the Old Sword," the King said.

We went together to the entry to the headquarters, just in time to see two pigeons loosed from the pigeon tent. They whirled up and round and away on a wild wing. Golden came back to us.

"The message has gone," he said. "You, King, warn the fourth and fifth companies that we shall be starting one hour after midnight. It's a pity to take the fresh horses, but you see, Mr. Ned, I am believing in these guns of yours. You are a doctor, you say. Did it strike you that Old Sword is vain?"

"Very vain, even for old age," I said, with the cruelty of youth.

"I'm afraid it comes with grey hair," he said. "The thin old blood needs sugar—is not that so?"

"Perhaps," I said, "the second childhood in us cries for its second mother and cannot find."

The King had gone out to warn the companies; I was alone with this wonderful youth, and thought that perhaps Leonidas had looked so before Thermopylae, or the young Arthur when he plucked the sword from the stone.

"Tell me, Doctor Ned," he said, "did you often remove clots, as you call them, in your country?"

"Not quite this sort of clot," I said.

The sun, which had been sinking fast, now dipped to the jagged trees on the sky line and went out. As we could not now expect a pigeon from the city, we went to the watchtower and climbed to the platform. They had signallers there, watching for the flash-messages. Up there, in the cold, under the stars, I could see the twinkling lights in the city towers; presently, among them, a brighter light began to flash at intervals.

"There it is," the King said. "That is the Attention. Now we shall have the answer."

The signallers spelled it out: "The Commander in the City sees no need for a conference. His mind has been

made quite clear. He will march his men out before daybreak next morning on receiving the signal arranged for
this morning. Is he to expect that signal, yes or no? He
waited in vain for a signal this morning. He will not fa-
tigue his troops again unless certain that others will keep
to plans carefully laid. Will you give that signal tomorrow morning? Reply."

The King sent out a reply: "Please expect and admit
trusted officers at three."

After about an hour, when this had been repeated
twice, an answer came: "Will neither expect nor admit."
After this, the messages stopped. Our signallers tried
two or three times more to make Old Sword give an inter-
view, but now no answer came, nor sign that the message
had been seen.

At last Golden said, "It is useless; he has gone to bed
or to feast, and has sent his signallers to bed."

I said, "They are about to do some iniquity, and dare
not let you in. They are going to kill their foreigners at
dawn."

"How do you know that?" Golden asked.

"Why else would they refuse your entrance? He knows
that you would support the foreigners. He is going to put
them out of the way before you see him. He'll do it tomorrow at dawn, with some word to the citizens later that he
had surprised a plot against the city itself."

"Old Sword wouldn't do a thing like that," Golden
said.

"He would let his party do it," the King said. "Ned has
a very clear eye."

We were now back at headquarters with Yvonne.

"Yvonne," I said, "we aren't to be allowed into the city."

"That means that they are going to kill the foreigners," she said at once.

"That's exactly what I fear it does mean," I said. "We can't get in to help."

"Yes, we can," she said. "Some of us can get in, two or three. There's a secret way in to the inner shrine of the goddess, from right outside the walls. I am not supposed to know it; but I do know it. I heard the priestess tell it to one of the priests of your city; he was her lover. They would have killed me if they had found me listening. I was there and heard. It's a hidden entrance among the rocks near the north wall. It looks like an old ruin, but some of the stones move. I heard how. Then you crawl on hands and knees, till you come to the cave where the water runs. It is all a holy path, where the goddess walks. It comes out in the shrine—"

"Where they'll be singing," the King said.

"Yes, but I can take you to a side door. The singers need not see."

"That is good enough," I said. "If two or three of us can get in, we can get the cattlemen to help and open a gate to the horse. When the horse are in, we will seize Old Sword and his staff and have the Quichet party out of danger."

"What then?" Golden asked.

"You shall supersede these rulers and get to the task of the war. Give me a day or two with the young men; I will then have my guns for you; then we can fight our battle and break these M'gai."

"One thing puzzles me, Yvona," Golden said. "The entrance to this passage is out by the north wall, you say? At some little distance from the wall, perhaps? You understand that M'gai listeners and scouts will be in that rocky patch all night, every night. Then, it will be a dark night. How can you expect to reach the spot in the dark? Perhaps, too, it will be near enough to the walls for you to be shot from them."

"The place is found by getting certain buildings in line," she said. "You will see those buildings on the darkest night; some by the temples, some to the west."

"How long ago did you learn this secret?" the King asked. "It may have ceased to be a passage."

"No, no. I heard this two months ago. The two used the passage till the raids began, only three weeks ago."

"Ah," Golden said, "I think I know which priest is the one. But since the raids perhaps your priestess has barred the passage. She would hardly leave it for any chance M'gai to find. The city might be surprised through it."

"It could not be found by chance," she said. "Two things must be done at once to open the mouth; then it closes of itself, and only one can pass at a time."

"We will try it," Golden said, "if you will explain carefully all the marks."

"No," she said, "I will come. I know how to use the stones. I went out on several nights when my brothers were away in the boats. I tried them for myself and know how they work."

"Can you get out of the city by that way?"

"I cannot. I do not know how to open the mouth from

inside. When I tried it, I had to leave the city by the gates.
I could come in by the passage."

"What was the passage, and what is all this about the
goddess walking?" Golden asked.

"The goddess used to appear," Yvonne said. "There
was a most holy old shrine under the springs where she
appeared."

"Most holy, I do not doubt," Golden said. "You shall
guide us, if you will. But those outlying rocks are just the
places for outlying scouts."

"We will take the horse over them first," the King said.
"Any scouts lying there will get away back to camp if the
horse come near. You see, a horse would see any scout
even if his rider didn't."

It was agreed that we should set forth, so as to be at
the rocks at half-past two or so; and that Yvonne, the
King and I should try the passage. If we got in, we were
to call the cattlemen in the Square and proceed to the
least well-guarded gate, which by all accounts seemed to
be the south gate. This the King would order to be
opened, to admit the horse, who would be outside it, we
hoped, waiting to enter. After that, if the horse were once
inside, we should proceed at once to headquarters and
seize the leaders of the Old Party. At dawn, if we had
been successful, Golden, with the other squadrons of
horse, would enter, and the city would be under his command. If we were not successful Golden would demand
that we be sent back to him, with our friends. But if we
were not successful I judged that we should all be in the
long grave which I had seen dug in the courtyard. We

were putting our lives on a throw; well, in Newgate, I
had not had a throw.

Having decided thus, we were going to rest, when an
officer came in to say that some scouts had come in with a
party of Matablancos. Now I had had dealings with Matablancos, and knew that they were in feud with the
M'gai; so I asked if I might see them. I knew a few
phrases of their tongue. So we went down to the lower
camp, and there found these Matas under guard. Now to
my surprise I found that two of them were men who had
been slaves in the *Albicore,* and one of the two was my
friend Deray. Now I had not done much for these Matas
in the *Albicore,* but I had done a little, and had at least
shewn that I wished to do more. I was not prepared for
the extravagant gratitude with which they overwhelmed
me. Men have told me since then that slaves will ever remember gratefully one who does even a little for them. I,
who had been in Newgate, should have known this. For a
few minutes I was treated as though I had saved their
lives seven times over.

The news they brought was important. The Matas were
in force, expecting to attack the M'gai, but not while the
moon was small; that was against their luck. They had
heard of the Kranish war with the M'gai and wished to
share in it as allies of the Kranois. They had all the three
full regiments of the Blood-Drinkers of the Matas ready
to help us, if we could wait for one week, till the moon was
friendly. These were lying now between the Kranois and
the land of the Indoto, and had a full supply from the
Indoto country. They would move up to attack when and
where we asked. Golden was not well-pleased with the

news of more savages moving up towards the Kranish
lands. However, I told him that these haunted near the
Coast, and were in feud with the M'gai. If they would
help us against the M'gai, any reasonable policy would
keep them friendly to the Kranois thenceforward. I said
that two thousand Matas coming in upon the M'gai rear,
or moving against their supplies, would be decisive helps
to us. The Matas had an ill name for treachery. I saw that
Golden distrusted them as being possible allies of the
M'gai. But I assured him that I knew for certain that
they were in an implacable blood-feud with them. In the
end, I won them over to my view: the Matas were accepted as our allies. I persuaded Golden to let Deray
come with us on our expedition.

Presently, we set forth to fling our throw. Ah, that
night, which needs a book, almost, to itself; that was my
night—mine in invention, mine in the doing. We went out
in the swift dark night, and came to the blackness of the
city, lit only in the towers and in lonely rooms far from
the walls. The horse and the Matas scouted through the
rocks for us; then we of the forlorn hope, with Deray,
who would not leave us, came to the ruins, where we
found the moving stones and so crept into the dark pit on
hands and knees. We had rushlights, which we managed
to light; and, holding these, crawled on into the darkness
till presently we came to the passage cut in the stone,
"where the goddess walked," where we could go stooping.
Presently, the noise of water told us that we were near
the springs. After that, we were in a most strange place,
no doubt holy for its uncanniness; it was part narrow
cavern, part a sort of crypt. As we went, I felt that

strange rites, of an intense kind, had been practised there; no doubt the goddess had walked. Presently, we were in earshot of the singing women, and then slipped aside to an aisle of the temple, and so, by the temple door, into the Market Square. We were in the city; now, if we failed, we should probably never get out of it alive.

We went into the Market Square, I say, and so to the cattle. I scouted ahead and found an old chief of the Plainsmen asleep in his little den in the north wall. The King roused him quietly and bade him call down some of his men from their sentry duty; this he did.

With these, we walked through the city to the south gate; it was dead still, cold darkness; the city worn out and asleep; the night outside full, seemingly of a myriad of horse, trampling and jingling. The King called, "Where is the Captain of the South Gate?" and on being told that he had been killed an hour before with a sling-stone, said, "Very good, then; open up here. The horse are to come in." The sergeant, seeing the gold on the King's chest, opened up, not doubting; and a hundred picked men filed in, picketed their horses in the Square and prepared for what we meant to do.

What that was, we did. It was my thought, my deed. We will not, therefore, speak of it. Someone has told us that revolutions are caused by vanity. Think, therefore, that this of mine was wrought from vanity; partly it was; but partly, too, by love of Yvonne, by love of the Quichets, who stood for Europe and thought against these clotted and cruddled Old Swords; and partly by the Newgate in me, which loathes that element in Man which shuts a soul in prison and sends her out on Monday. We did it;

we took the city of the Kranois, we freed our friends, and
had Old Sword out of it, with his staff, on their way to
the Big City, long before the sun rose.

You must not think that I shall blow my trumpet
louder and longer. I had found what I could do. I could
work with Golden and the King, Yvonne and the Quichets. We had saved them from death, now we could
work with them to save the city. I found the waggons in
the citadel yard. We had the guns out, and mounted during that morning. I had a couple of hundred Kranish lads
drilled in the cannon exercises within three days; nay, I
made those lads into light artillery, able to drag and ma-
nœuvre their pieces, almost like horse artillery. They
had not fired; we dared not use our scanty powder nor
lose the surprise we planned. We fired and surprised the
M'gai when the day came, be sure.

There is a phrase in a letter from some old soldier of
our Civil War: "Our horse had the execution of them almost to their camp." Our horse, on that day of battle,
broke the M'gai, but the Matablancos had the execution
of them. I am a doctor, and hate war and the killing of
men; this great killing was largely my work. The Matas
came in as I had bidden, and broke the Amalosa and the
Umquilitzi, and brought the red and the black plumes
into Kranish dust forever. There is a song sung by the
M'gai widows:

"Great are the Kranois, who ate the pride of our hearts."

It was a devilish deed, perhaps. It was my deed; and by it
I broke the power of devils. You can settle the rights of

it. I still glow with the gleam of the joy I felt on that day, when I looked on the victory and knew that we young men had broken the M'gai in pieces.

Five minutes after that triumph, intense as it was, I was saying to Edmond Quichet, "Now the real test comes. Now we have to remake the Kranish state."

I married Yvonne when I came back to the city with the army. I remade my state at least.

You will understand, for you have now seen, how hard it is to rule men after a war. While the danger lasts, the herd draws together for safety and acts as a herd, that is, with less intelligence than that of any individual in it. After the danger has gone, then each individual shakes himself from the restraints, and asserts himself, by striking out at those nearest. So it was with us in the city, when the M'gai had gone and the Matablancos had withdrawn. I suppose that the herd is the basis or common foundation of society, from which the angels and devils of self strike forth in all directions.

The war was over; and all admitted that we, the foreigners and Plainsmen, had won it, and gave us our due. At the same time, they became free to say that we were foreigners and Plainsmen who had taken liberties with the city's elected rulers. You, who have any knowledge of men in communities, will know what was said, repeated, enlarged upon and misrepresented. All this, I will say, went on for years.

I will not weary you with all this. Politics, even those at home, are sorry affairs. It is now a long time since these little squabbles in a small city in a distant part of the world in an unimportant continent in a small planet of one of the smaller suns took place. I triumphed, partly through my own skill; since I had medical skill, useful to everyone, and unique at that time in the land of the Kranois; and partly through the wisdom of Yvonne. But though I prospered and was happy, two things pressed upon me. One was that I wished, as Quichet had wished, to open intercourse with Europe; and another, that I longed, as Yvonne did, to clear my name in England and receive the Royal Pardon for the crime I never committed. I know that unless we opened up an intercourse with Europe in the ways of dignity and civility, it would be opened for us brutally by the slave-traders. The Coast was already feeling the influence of the French wars; the slavers were assuming the control of the trade there with even greater brutality of greed than formerly. Competition being checked in the business, the monopolists began to push their success. It was clear to me that the Kranois might expect an armed attack in force by the slave-traders and their allies, which could only end in the enslavement of the citizens. I knew from my talks with the slavers how white niggers were prized in the Indies, for their cleverness, and for their beauty as mistresses. I knew with what relish the slave merchants would carry a thousand Kranois to the west, and sell them at seventy pounds a head or more. These white Kranois were so many bank-notes waiting to be passed. This matter was one on which we of the Quichet faction debated long and eagerly.

We decided that we must open up an intercourse, above the heads of the slavers; an envoy would have to go to Gabo and thence to London. So much was clear. Of the possible envoys, I was the one appointed by Providence itself. I unfortunately was a condemned felon, under capital sentence, quite certain to be hanged if caught. And yet, now that the first years of terror had passed, now that I had become another man, I could face that danger, and did face it, with a kind of anger of determination to crush the Fate that had so nearly crushed me. Time had passed, which makes so much clear. It was possible that augurs and understood relations had brought forth the secret, of who had killed the Admiral. Someone, by this time, might have let fall words, might have raised a doubt, might have set going an enquiry. My friends, Dr. Copshrews and the others, all shrewd men, might have been busy on my account. Fate, too, the blind thing, which works with such apparent clumsiness, yet with such certainty, She, too, might have reckoned that the evil had had its hour, and that now evil should go down, and the wronged one be righted. And yet, I was cynical enough about that, too. I had been in Newgate, and took the Newgate view, that there is a lot more law than justice in this world. I knew with what joy what passed for law would fasten on me if it could. I knew how skilled, and how merciless, the thief-takers were, and how dangerous my coming to London might be. Yet I longed to try it, and to dare it. And yet, it was a good deal to dare. First, the long road to Gabo, with its dangers from slavers. Then, the almost certain delay at Gabo, before I could ship to London. Then, the uncertainty, the danger, the enquiry into my antecedents, which would so surely be made. What was I to pass as, or pose as? If as an Englishman, what? If as a Frenchan, how? We might well be at war with France. I might pass at once to a prison as suspect. But long before that happened, I might be enslaved, or pressed into the fleet, by that real Britain which sang all the time that Britons never would be slaves. One thing was in my favour: if I went at all, I should not go alone. I should go with the younger Quichets and with some considerable wealth, for the city had a wealth of amethysts and of some other jewels. With these, I might be securer. With these, I could bribe or trade. Still, going was no little risk to run.

And, having reached England safely, how was I to proceed to clear my name? It was like to be no easy nor safe matter, to go raking into that mystery, or setting others to rake. Many men and all women are full of curiosity, and are set going by a mystery. I knew what would be said. "Who can this stranger from Africa be, who is prying into the murder of Admiral Cringle? Why should a mysterious stranger be interested in that question? Who is this stranger? He has medical knowledge; he is like the young doctor, who was hanged for the crime; it was said by some that he was not hanged but spirited away. What if he be the man returned?" From that point it would be easy for them to go further. Letters of denunciation would be written to magistrates. Perhaps most would be neglected, but some would be attended to. If I were taken and confronted, many would arise to shew that I was I. There might be changes indeed. I had grown a beard and looked older, much older; I had suffered. I might be able to browbeat some of them and confuse others. I could not hope to persuade a jury that I was not I. And I had a horrid fear that possibly my friends, who had brought me

back to life, had been had into question about it, and perhaps been hanged for it. Though the Law was supine and
corrupt enough in many ways, in all questions of property it was deadly. Life ranked as property; anyone who
snatched a life from the Law was hanged as surely as if
it had been five shillings. If my friends had suffered, then,
of course, all would regard me as their murderer, and
would pursue me with fury, as the virtuous mob in every
country will.

The way seemed thorny to me. And yet, the thought
that I might seize my enemy by the throat and crush him
was strong upon me. I did not know who the killer of the
Admiral was. He was my enemy, for had he not killed
me? I had often and often gone over in my mind that
glimpse or quarter-seen glance of a man disappearing.
But no amount of effort could make it more than it was
or more precise than it was. It was a glimpse; the certainty that someone had passed. I had built in fancy a
body and mind to that disappearing leg and coat-skirt. I
judged that it had been one of the types of my antipathy;
one of the swell-mob, as they are called in Newgate; one
of the dangerous criminals who have insolence, some dis-
play of manner and of clothing, perhaps even some tincture of letters and breeding, or more than a tincture, and
with these gifts a selfishness that will kill rather than
want. There must have been half-a-dozen such in Cholsington on that day of the Fair. I had seen two that day:
one in the crowd; one at the inn. The thought of those
two, the one of them crafty and sneering, the other bold
and brutal, had often been in my mind. Then, Henery had
been in my mind, too. He had hated me from the first, and

had pursued me to the end. Why? Well, who shall define and lay bare the springs of hatred? Few can tell the reasons why they dislike Dr. Fell, that elegant man. I had as surely hated Henery as he me. And of course, at the inquest, suspicion had for an instant turned upon him. He had been thankful when the tide had turned upon myself. But then, I asked, why had he pursued me, as it were, beyond the grave? Well, hatred was sufficient cause. Apart from that, I judged that a show of zeal against me might well help to clear himself of suspicion. He and his wife had been very near the scene of the crime at the very time it was done. They had need to be zealous to clear themselves. And yet, when I thought over all those awful days, and my last sight of the man, I shuddered to think how hot he had been upon my trail; and how nearly he had caught me.

Something that I had heard in Newgate was a comfort to me, that you could not hang a man for murder, unless you had a body to shew that a murder had been done. So, I supposed that they could not have hanged my friends for saving me from the gallows until they had me in person to shew that I had been saved. Well, I must not weary you with all these thoughts. You know now how I was placed, and may judge the kinds of worry constant in my mind. But on the whole the worry was less than the longing to be done with it. I had faced the armed array of the M'gai and had beaten them; I wanted to do the same by my old enemies, Murder, ill-luck, and that brutal rectitude, the Law, which might be wrong.

After long talk, we decided that an attempt should be made to open negotiations with England. But first there was the question of beginning. You here write a letter, which the post bears, so that in a few days you have an answer. But we in the Kranois country a thousand miles from Gabo could not expect to get an answer to a letter for three or four months, according to the state of the river, the shipping and the wind. For bearers, whom had we? We had friendly blacks, who could take the letters into the wilderness, to some tribes who would take them further and perhaps lose them or throw them away upon the road. We began the business by going down the river to Sixteen Peaks and going from thence to Gabo Amarilho. Edmond Quichet came with us to the Peaks.

"It is the third time," he said. "Twice my coming here has given my enemies power."

I said, "The third time brings men glory. This time, you shall triumph."

It shall serve, if I say that I came to Gabo in state, with my rowers, with a blaze of new gold-leaf on my railings, and with my blue and white Kranish colours trailing from my flagstaff. As I drew in, I fired a salute to the Governor and dipped my colours to the Flag. When the Government boat came out to give me pratique, I sent in gifts of fruit and asked for an audience. An English frigate lay in the outer road, rolling a good deal. I looked at her through the glass, but could not read her name. She had her upper spars struck, on account of the rolling, which was often excessive there. I waited with much anxiety, as you may imagine, for a reply. Presently, I was sent for by the Governor's coxswain, and went ashore to wait upon him. He received me in the cool, white-

washed windward room of the Castle quarters, with the
surf on the rocks seemingly just below, and the patio on
the other side all screened with awnings and sprinkled
by a little fountain. He was a very weary, white-faced
man, from whom the climate had taken all vitality. He
had a charming, limp manner.

"So, sir," he said, coming to me, and touching my hand
with the wet rag of his own hand, "so, sir—Mr. —"

"Mansell," I said.

"Ah, yes," he said. "I have to thank you for this letter,
and for the gift of fruits. You say, in your letter, that you
come from the cities of white people of whom tales sometimes come. You state that you have products with you
and that you can open a profitable trade with England.
That is very much the desire of our Government at the
moment. Can you now satisfy me as to the nature of the
trade?"

This I proceeded to do, for the next hour. His garrison
commander came in from time to time, and listened a
little. I shewed my specimens, and pleaded my cause and
made my necessary points, that the Kranois were to be
protected from the slavers. He was interested and impressed by what I said. At the end, he said, "The best
thing that I can do is to send you home in the *Hannibal,*
there, the frigate in the road. She is sailing for home the
day after tomorrow. Captain Culham will give you and
your wife a passage. I will give you a letter to the Secretary; you will have no difficulty in getting to him to state
your case; he happens to be my brother."

I said that there was another difficulty. "We carry

great wealth, indeed, but have no money; and need a considerable sum, to fit ourselves. We must appear in a fitting state in London."

"That will be easy to arrange," he said. "We here need no money and do not use it, or hardly use it. I can appoint you our Trade Commissioner for the Interior, and give you abundant credits, or, if that might seem to prejudice you with these white people, your friends, I can have some of your jewels valued here, and a credit given against them."

Most commercial matters could be arranged at Gabo. I received for a few jewels a sum of money and letters of credit in England. As to equipment for England, and European clothing, the *Hannibal* was to visit Vigo on her way, where we could buy clothes in which to land. So here I was received and honoured, sent forward with a letter to a Secretary of State, in a King's ship. How differently had I reached the Coast in the *Albicore!*

It was strange indeed to me to know that the ship that was to take us was the *Hannibal;* one of the earlier *Hannibals* was bound up with my life, in ways too deep to be told. To be brief, we went aboard the *Hannibal,* Captain Culham, and were given the state apartments, and then, after a rolling in the road, saw the anchor weighed and the Coast slowly draw away from us as we stole to the windward. In no long time, we were in the Channel, and so by degrees came to Portsmouth, where we took post-chaise for London and presented our letters.

It was a strange moment for me, when I saw again the scenes of my old unhappiness. The journey had been by the usual routes; I changed the last stage of all, so that I could drive through Colsington and look at some of the scenes known to me. They say that nothing is ever really forgotten by the mind; probably nothing is. As we drove, I would shut my eyes, tell myself what lay round each bend before we came to it, then open my eyes to see the familiar scene unfold.

I had last looked upon those fields in the autumn; now I saw them in early May with so little foliage on the trees that the growth was not marked; few things seemed changed except myself. There was the big house among its elms; there was the bend near which I had routed the footpads when they had attacked the Admiral; up there, to my left, was Hannibal House, and somewhere beyond it was the house where my father had died. Perhaps Dennis was there; perhaps my mother's portrait was still there. Yvonne watched me, knowing that I was deeply moved by my thoughts. Soon, we were going past the church, with that open space in front of it where I had bought the knife of Jane Jollycok. We went rather slowly past this place; it seemed not changed at all; the sign of Watkins, Clock-maker, a gilt hand pointing to a clock dial, was still there. Watkins himself came to the door as he had so often come in the past, to peer at the piece of work in the light. He had changed; he wasn't the man he had been; well, nor was I. From outside his shop, the road swung somewhat to the east for London town; before me, for all that I knew, lay my old friend and master Dr. Copshrews. I longed to see him. "Oh," I thought, "if I can only see Dr. Copshrews alive, to thank him in person for what he did for me, and to let Yvonne thank him, then I shall die happy. I can ask no more from life."

In front of me now was all my old life, with the danger that going back to it entailed. I knew, too, very sharply, that there was danger. It was at that point that a strange thing happened. I do not pretend to explain it, but on the right of the road as we drove, I saw a woman in a black dress who was somehow familiar to me; walk and bearing alike suggested my mother, so that I leaned forward sharply to see her. She was lost on the instant, but on the same instant I had the most vivid sense that it was my mother, and that she had entered the carriage and had taken my hand. The feeling was so vivid, of her presence, that I said to Yvonne, "My mother is here."

Yvonne answered, "That is what I think."

After a time, I said, "There was a painting of her. Oh, if I might find it!"

Presently we were at the lodgings that had been commanded for us.

They were in the square in which I had lived with my parents, not one hundred yards from the door, though upon another side of the square. When I looked out from our sitting-room window, I could see the door, to my left. Workmen were busy upon it at that moment, painting it blue and the iron railings near it white. I took this insistence on the Kranish colours as a good omen. I was there with Yvonne, and had much cause for gladness. I had also cause for alarm and for caution. I had brought Charles Pierre and three other Kranois with me. These all spoke French, and a fair English. I had been warned that there was sometimes a good deal of feeling in London against the French, owing to the excesses in Paris and the war. I had, therefore, cautioned all four to be careful not to draw attention upon themselves, but to live very quietly in the house with us, as my secretaries and servants. Now that I was fairly back in London, I began to see clearly some of the dangers round myself. I knew now that I had become again a condemned felon, who might be denounced at any moment. I was a stranger, with wealth about me, and with associates who spoke French : curiosity would be focussed on me. How soon would the blow fall?

Well, blow or none, I had tasks to do.

My first task was to find if Dr. Copshrews still lived. I could hope to discover this without running a risk of recognition. Still, I reflected that my every movement in England made me run a risk; one or two more could hardly count. I had changed much since my troubles. Trial, travel and the tropics will alter all men a good deal ; then, I thought, after all, most people who remember me at all will wish to forget me, and will know, too, that I am dead. They will say, "He is like that fellow who was hanged for the murder that time." I meant to run no unnecessary risk, but to go to some tavern, and ask for a list of doctors in the district ; that would be one way. Another way would be to drive through the street in which he lived and look at the house. His brass-plate of attendance hours would be there, if he lived ; that would be a good way. Then I thought, "His church, of which he was so long a warden, will have his name in its printed list of wardens within its door ; that will be a sure guide." Then the reflection followed, "Someone at the church might remember me ; I was there often and often, and was known to all the parish ; that will never do." It was a Sunday afternoon. In the end, I decided to drive, first, to the street in which the Doctor had lived, to go through it, past the Doctor's door; after that, if necessary, I could go on to the church or to the tavern. I was scared, of course, though I kept telling myself that my known death was my safeguard, and boldness my shield. I sent for a glass-coach, or hackney-carriage as it would now be called, and in this drove off alone through a part of London once very well-known to me. I had steeled myself to drive back past St. Sepulchre's and Newgate over my Via Dolorosa. We had gone along Holborn towards Snow Hill when I noticed that the driver turned out of his way. I hailed him, "Why are you not going down to Newgate?"

He said, "I'd never get through, sir. There is such a crowd at the prison."

I asked, "Why?"

He said, "I suppose you are a stranger, sir, to ask that. There is always a crowd on Sundays in Assizes, sir, to see the hangings on Monday. There are seven of 'em to go tomorrow, including the murder cases."

I boldly said, "I have been out of England. I thought they hanged at Tyburn."

"Yes, sir, they did," he said, "but they've took to this way now, sir; it's more convenient to have it near the gaol."

Indeed, I could see that a mob of people blocked the way. Some hawkers were crying broadsides, and there were the usual hangers-on, of thimble-riggers, pickpocket-boys and their allies. Even after we had turned into the side street, to make the detour, I noticed that all feet turned towards Newgate; everybody was going there. My driver leaned back to me, and said,

"They're all going to the prison, sir. They won't be able to get anywheres near it, but they'll like to say they saw the crowd. There'll be thousands in the streets all night; you see, sir, it's the murder cases. People don't often have the chance of seeing a case like that hung."

I said I hoped not. After that we drove quietly till we were in the familiar street, and my eyes were fixed on the Doctor's house.

I saw at once that his notice or placard was gone; we went past the familiar door, which had been new-painted. Usually at that time in the afternoon our dispensary door had been thronged by the evening patients coming for our four to seven treatments. No patients were there now; the place was no longer a doctor's home. I called to the driver to drive me on to a tavern, to which I had never been, but of which I knew, well enough, down at the end of Cheapside, where I could make enquiries. I left my driver, telling him to wait for me, as I might well be half an hour. Going in to the coffee-room, I called for something, and presently fell to talking with the waiter about trade, the French war, and the prospects of peace. He asked if I were staying the night on the chance of seeing the hangings.

I said, "No. Nothing would shock me more than to see a hanging."

He said, "Ah, but tomorrow, sir, it is not like ordinary. It's not a Man's Justice that you'll see tomorrow; it's God's Justice."

I said that I could not but pity a condemned man, whatever he had done or been accused of.

I asked if there were any doctors near by, who could

supply me with some tincture for my throat. He said there was a list of doctors in the bar, in case of the guests needing one. He went forth to find it and presently handed it to me. As I feared, the name of Copshrews was not upon it; and never had been; but I noted one of the names and addresses (unknown to me of old) and said that I would go to him and then return. So I went out, and did visit the physician's house for a simple remedy, and while it was preparing walked on to the church where Dr. Copshrews had attended worship with me, so many times. It was a fair Sunday afternoon, still too early for many people to be about, their Sunday afternoon nap being not yet over. The people at that end of the town were civil good citizens with their families, often with servants attending them. They were not shewing that longing to see God's Justice done which moved so many towards Newgate. I wore horn spectacles, with smoked glasses, and was not recognized by anyone. London renews itself quickly; people often remove; and in the city the movement is swifter than on the fringes. I, for my part, did not see any old acquaintance, till I was entering the church, when I passed Mr. Northfield, the antiquary, who wrote the book on Roman London. He had been a churchwarden with Dr. Copshrews, and also a patient; we had attended his family for years. He did not recognize me in the darkness of the porch, but brushed swiftly by, in his swift dark way, with some mutter of apology. In the porch of the church, I read the parish announcements; they were not signed by Josiah Copshrews, but by Nathaniel Clutterbuck, Rector, and by Ebenezer Trustagod and Jermyn Northfield, churchwardens. My heart sank, I own, when I found the name no

longer there. I had hardly expected it to be there, but hope
had persuaded me that it might be. I pushed through the
heavy inner door into the dark church, wondering sadly
if I had brought his venerable head to the grave in misery.
I sat down in a pew, and bowed my head as though in
worship. Two or three old women were there, praying or
contemplating. My eyes soon grew accustomed to the
gloom, and presently a verger came to the nave and drew
up the sun-blinds from two of the windows, so that one
could see. They had always drawn down the sun-blinds, I
remembered, to keep the sun from the handsome new
scarlet cushions on which the Bible and Prayer-Book
rested. Alas, the cushions had faded, in spite of this care,
though the care continued. The light from the window
near me streamed across the church to a memorial marble
on the church wall. It was an elegant work. On a grey-
blue oval stone, a sculptor had placed a white marble design in relievo. It represented a weary traveller sitting on
a bench but drooped forward, so that his head was reclin-
ing on a table on his bent left arm. His scrip and staff were
on the ground at his feet; his little hound licked his right
hand which had fallen at his side. Underneath was an inscription in Latin, to say that immediately beneath that
wall, in a grave beneath the floor of the church, lay the
body of Josiah Copshrews, physician and churchwarden
of this parish. He had died on November the twelfth, the
year before, deeply loved and respected. I had expected
something of the kind, of course, but I was deeply moved.
I had so hoped to see him again and to thank him for all
that he had done for me and to shew him that it had not
been done in vain. If only he might have lived on the few

months which parted us! I looked at the tablet for a long
time, and then moved, so that I might see the grave. It
was covered with a smooth, hard, bluish stone, of a kind
then much in use for memorial tablets, because the incised
lettering upon it shewed up whitish against it, with a good
effect. The stone bore the inscription that here lay the
mortal parts of Josiah Copshrews, Physician, awaiting a
joyful resurrection, with the statement that he was the
son of Josiah Copshrews, of Copshrews House, in Berk-
shire. There followed some verses:

> Here lies the Friend to whom the Wretch in Pain,
> Or Soul in Sorrow, never cried in vain,
> Whose Courage in Distress and Human Skill
> Bore countless Thousands Healthward out of Ill;
> Here the beloved Physician lies at rest,
> His Spirit shines in Heav'n, a wedding-guest.

On the grave, placed there by somebody that morning, for
the flowers were still very fresh, was a coronal of twisted
sprays of apple-blossom. I remembered how he had ever
loved the apple-blossom of early May, as one of the most
beautiful of all things. Someone had borne that in mind.
The verger, seeing my interest in the tomb, looked at me
curiously. I had looked at him, be sure, not less curiously,
yet without recognition. He was not one known to me. He
came up to me and said,

"I see you admire our new Tomb, sir. It is much admired. Many have come to see it from the far end of the
Town; it is by Wolcot, sir, the great Wolcot, from a de-

sign by the great Baxter. It is very tender, sir, the weary Traveller. Lots of the tender sex can hardly restrain their tears."

I said, "It is very affecting. Did you, by any chance, know the gentleman, the Doctor?"

"No, sir," he said. "I'm a newcomer here, sir. I came in with Mr. Clutterbuck, the new Rector, after the gentleman had given up the wardenship. But I was here for his burial. It was like the burying of Royalty, sir; not a dry eye in the parish. He was a physician to the poor, sir. I suppose ten thousand persons came to the service. The Lord Mayor had to call out the trained bands to keep them passing along. And the memorial was all subscribed for, sir, by grateful patients, as you will read, sir, better than I, in the Latin. And Mr. Wolcot refused to take any payment for his memorial, sir; he said that Art would ever be proud to commemorate Virtue. His letter's in the Vestry about it, if you would care to see, sir."

I went into the Vestry, not that I much wished to read the letter. In the grateful gloom of the place (the blinds were down, and there was much dark woodwork, against which the surplices hung like linen put out to blanch), I asked if this Doctor were famous or loved for anything but his skill as a physician.

He said, "No, sir; that and his kindness in attending people."

I was anxious to know if he had ever been in question about my escape, so I said, "It is happy to think that such a man should live to a good old age and be loved to the last."

"Yes, sir," the verger said; "he was happy in his life and in his death, which they say we might all be, if we were as good as he."

I asked if he had left any family.

He said, "No, sir, I believe not, sir. His son died before him. They say, sir, he had a venture in Jamaica, I think it was, and died of the climate. We've a memorial to the son, too, sir, on the other wall, though it isn't to be compared with Wolcot."

I was plunged more deeply into gloom by this, for I had counted on Dick's being alive. But, no; he had engaged in an enterprise in Myngsville, Jamaica, for the furtherance of British commerce and had there succumbed to the climate fortified by the sincerest Christian principles. Dick was dead, too; and this memorial had been put up by his sorrowing father more than a year before the father had ceased to sorrow. I had liked Dick; he had been very very good to me. I could only say that it was sad that so good a man had left no son. I gave the verger a shilling and went out. He asked if I were going to be a parishioner. I said, "No." I was a traveller from Africa, and had only come in by chance, and, having missed the morning service, felt the need for a quiet moment in a holy place.

I went out, sad at heart, to find two of my helpers dead, never to be thanked or praised. At least, they had not suffered through me. I could thank God for that. But when I was out in the street the tears ran down my cheeks, not for Dr. Copshrews—he was with God—but for poor Dick. I had longed to see Dick again. He had been more than trebly good to me. What was this venture in Jamaica? I judged that it was some happy effort of friends, gay, charming and not very prudent. They had gone out, no doubt with every hope, and had been the joy of the mess with which they sailed, and welcome recruits to the planters ashore. Then, after a merry meal or two, alas, the climate. I thought that perhaps he had looked out for me there. He might have asked, "Has any word come of a young doctor named Torrance?" The young doctor might have helped him through the climate, perhaps.

I walked westward slowly, with my head bent. I thought of the ten thousand people who had thronged those streets when Dr. Copshrews had been buried. "Not a dry eye in the parish," the man had said. Well, that was much. Still, more than ten thousand were gathering to see these murderers. On the morrow, there might be ten times that number. I remembered how many had come to see me in my misery, and how I had longed that staring man might have but the one face, so that I might spit in it. Here was the tide setting to Newgate, all feet were turned that way, and of all of the myriads only one had thought of Josiah Copshrews and remembered that he had loved the apple-blossom. Still, that one was worth the rest. So thinking and feeling, I found that I was again in the street where Dr. Copshrews had wrought. At the end of the street, I saw the sign of the Sponge and Rammer Inn, under which I had so often passed on my way to visit patients. Then I looked across the road and saw what I believed to be an old friend; certainly, my heart stood still.

Just before my troubles, a patient had given Dr. Copshrews a small and somewhat shaggy little dog, with silky hair of a sandy colour. He was a clever little beast. Dr. Copshrews had named him, for his sagacity, Polumekan,

after Odysseus; this name had shortened down to Polly
or Pollymac. He had been a great pet, and had shewn a
fondness for myself, who often took him on some of my
rounds. Now, as I looked about me, I saw what I took to
be Pollymac looking at me on the other side of the road.
He had winded me, I suppose, and had remembered. He
was a sad-looking little dog now; he had come down in
the world since the Doctor had died. But, being sure that
he was he, I called him with my old whistle and cry of
"Polly, Polly, Poll." This decided him; he came over to
me, and plainly knew me; there was no doubt that he
knew me; he welcomed me with a frisk and jumps and a
great wagging of the tail. A loutish man, who had gone
on towards the Sponge and Rammer, now turned and
watched us. He came over to us.

"So you know the dog, sir," he said.

"Was he not the Doctor's dog?" I asked.

"Yes," he said; "and when the Doctor died, he went to
the country to a place, ninety-odd miles, they say, from
London; but back he came within the week, to cry at the
empty house. Three times he did that, but after the third
time Mrs. Spiggott of the Sponge here said she would give
him a home; but it isn't much of a home, really, that an
inn can give—no one can take him about, the way the
Doctor could."

I was relieved to find that the man did not recognize me;
he was a stranger.

"If the dog would follow me," I said, "I could give him
a home and plenty of movement; but perhaps Mrs. Spiggott would not care to part with him?"

"She's be glad to part with him, sir," he said.

I was turning over my memories for the name Spiggott;
Mrs. Jones, a Welsh lady, had had the inn in my time; I
was not eager to find Mrs. Jones, whom I had often treated
for a recurring trouble in the wrist. If she had married
Mr. Spiggott since my death, and were now Mrs. Spiggott,
she would be sure to recognize me; she was quick and
shrewd. Then I thought, "No. The inn is under new man-
agement; it is not Mrs. Jones' inn any longer." So I said,
"Of course, the dog may not follow me; he seems to like
this place too well."

"A good many like the Sponge and Rammer too well,"
he said. "But you'd find Mrs. Spiggott in her parlour, it
being Sunday."

I thanked him, and called the dog after me to the inn,
where I found Mrs. Spiggott friendly and kind. She was
willing for the dog to go. "But he's a hold dog, sir," she
said, "and a hold dog is attached to places. I doubt he'll
not stay with you." I doubted it, myself, but was willing to
try. I led the way back, calling the dog, who followed with
every symptom of joy. I went a little way to the west on
foot, but was soon in the presence of the crowd flocking to
Newgate. I should be engulfed there, and should certainly
lose Pollymac, if I went further, so I turned, and took my
glass-coach again and so drove home with the dog to my
lodgings.

We had to go a long way out of our way, by the new
road to the north, to avoid the crowds.

"They are all going to Newgate, sir," my driver said.
"There's nothing like a good hanging to bring 'em all out;
they'll sit up all night, the most of 'em, or stand where

they are, rather than miss it. They've fine weather for it, but cold for the time of year; still, if it was snow, they'd stay, in a case like this. I suppose you've read it and followed it, sir?"

I said, "No. I've only just landed and know nothing about it."

"Oh, sir," he said, "you'd ought to ask the house where you're staying to let you have the papers about it. They're said to be in a good frame of mind, the murderers; one can't help pitying them."

"I pity any man who has the whole of society against him," I said. "At the same time, Law is a protection, of a sort."

"British Law is," he said. "I wouldn't say much for foreign law."

"British Law is like British kindness to animals," I said. "Very like a fox-hunt. All the same, it's the question that puzzles the wisest. What is justice?"

"The man who sheds man's blood," the driver said, "he ceases to be one of the citizens. He has to be cut off."

"Are you always sure that the man you cut off did shed the blood?" I asked.

"Yes, sir, under God," he said.

"It's a grand thing, to be sure," I said. "But I think I'd forgive any murderer rather than hang him."

"Well, sir," he said, "you must excuse me; I'm all for the rope, myself. I'd hang the murderer, then I'd be sure of my throat at nights. I've a weakness for my throat, sir."

"Cherish it," I said; and at that we parted.

After I had gone to the landlady and arranged for a kennel, food and water for the little dog, I went upstairs to my rooms. It was early in May, and fair enough weather; but to us fresh from the Coast it seemed cruelly cold. I asked the maid if we might have tea and a fire. She said she would prepare the tray at once and would send up Harry with the firing. I braced myself against Harry; for though I had been out of London a long time, I had been known to a great many as Dr. Copshrews' assistant. What if he should come up all eager to see the foreign gentleman, and at once recognize me as one who had poulticed his cut or bound his fracture? Harry came in with the firing, which he proceeded to lay and then to light. He had one or two glances at me as he worked. He was a smiling, good-humoured sort of man, of about thirty as I judge.

"Yes, sir," he said, "I'll just add a blob of taller to make sure it burns up well. There's nothing like a bit of fire of an evening to cheer things up, is there, sir? And could I bring up some more cushions for Madame, sir? London comes very cold, we always say, to them as aren't used to it."

I thanked him and asked if he were used to it.

"Yes, sir," he said, "I'm getting used to it, but it's full of surprises, London; everyone has to admit that."

I asked what the latest surprises were, since I had only just arrived from a far country.

"Why," he said, "why, sir, have you not seen an English paper?"

I said, "No."

"Why then," he said, "you've not seen that he's confessed?"

I said, "I have heard hardly any news, save the foreign
news, and that only as it affects the Navy and African
trade."

"You must excuse me, then, sir," he said. "A treat is in
store for you. I'll bring you in the set. I've got them all
laid by. It is one of the surprises of my life."

By this time, the blob of taller had kindled the fire,
which burned brightly. The maid brought in the tea-tray,
and as we settled to our tea Harry brought the *Intelligencer* for the past few weeks: "in case you should like
to glance at them after your cup of tea, sir."

We drank our tea; when Yvonne had gone to unpack, I
took up the copies of the *Intelligencer*. It was a small
weekly sheet, with some little engravings in the letter-
press here and there as illustrations. It seemed to me that
the engravings were fifty years old, and had done duty
often before. There were advertisements of horses lost or
stolen, and of a black servant, Juba Manasseh, who had
disappeared wearing his master's suit of livery. A tiny
cut shewed the packet *Ruby*, about to sail for Port Royal
from Falmouth. I skimmed an account of a prize-fight
between English Ben and the Dutch Windmill, and then
lighted on something which made me leap out of my skin.

Harry had laid these papers for me in order, the oldest
on the top; they had made his reading, perhaps his only
reading, for some time, and had been a good deal worn.
What I had lighted on had been the exordium, or *avant-
scène,* of his delight. The date was several weeks before. I
read as follows:

## STRANGE CASE AT CHOLSINGTON.

A case which is likely to cause some sensation in the near future was brought before the magistrates during the last few days. On Saturday, Mr. Dennis Rackage, of Hannibal House, in Cholsington, accompanied the Rector to the house of Sir ——————, the Magistrate, where he made a voluntary statement so extraordinary that at first his sanity was doubted. He persisted in his story with such confidence that Sir —————— had no alternative, but to call in his brethren of the Bench for consultation. They agreed that the case was too important to be neglected and took the necessary steps with the result that Henery, Mr. Rackage's confidential servant, was taken into custody for examination. To be brief, such a tale of villainy was unfolded as has seldom been listened to, and such as fully justified the closest investigation. As the case is still sub judice, it would be of the highest impropriety to comment further; but we promise our readers that next week's issue will provide them with a full account of this astounding case.

Here was indeed matter to make me thrilled. I remembered the crowds outside Newgate and thought, "Can it be that those crowds are gathered to see them hanged?" I felt faint for a moment, to think that somehow those two had been the murderers of the Admiral. I put down the first sheet and took up the second, dated a week later. It went as follows:

Last week at the time of going to press, we promised our readers a full account of the astounding case at Cholsington. We thought then that the case would prove to be of an unusual interest, but had no least idea that we should be privileged to tell them of a case perhaps unique in all the murky annals of crime. To those who by some mischance missed the opening scenes of this drama, let us say that it began by the appearance of Mr. Dennis Rackage, at one time well-known in sporting circles, but latterly less frequent in his attendance among the elite of the knowing, before Sir ———— with a confession implicating his one-time servant Henery in systematic blackmail, and himself in the double crime of murder and permitting an innocent man to suffer for his crime.

It may not be beyond the memory of most of our readers to recall the murder of Admiral Cringle, late of Hannibal House, in Cholsington. The Admiral was a crotchety bachelor, supposed to have a sum of gold in his house. He had taken a fancy to a young doctor, of the name of Mansell, who had saved his life from footpads, and in gratitude for this valorous act had made the young man his heir. It chanced that this Dr. Mansell was related by marriage to Mr. Dennis Rackage, whose widowed mother had married Dr. Mansell, père. It will be remembered that the Admiral was found murdered at his house in the afternoon of the Cholsington Fair some years ago. Suspicion pointed to the young Dr. Mansell as the murderer, who was charged with the crime, and convicted for it at the next Assizes, and though he persisted in declaring his innocence, and in spite of many protests by his friends, was hanged for it at Tyburn. It was suspected by some that these friends contrived to restore him to life after hanging the appointed time, but an investigation shewed the fallacy of this belief. It is, however, certain that body-snatchers rifled his dishonoured grave on the night of his burial.

Mr. Dennis Rackage startled the magistrates by declaring, and with convincing proofs, that it was he, not
the young doctor, who had murdered the Admiral. He
had done the deed, hoping to lay his hands on the large
sum of gold said to be secreted in the house. He did the
deed, but failed to find the hoard. He surprised and broke
open a secret cupboard, but found in it only papers; and
was prevented in a further, and perhaps more successful,
search by the sound of footsteps. He decamped at once,
and left the house unobserved. The steps heard by him
were, by an unhappy chance, those of young Dr. Mansell,
who was afterwards hanged for the crime. Hannibal
House, being devised to Dr. Mansell, was confiscated to
the Crown on his conviction. Being the property of the
Crown, it was put up to auction, yet none would buy. It
was true that wealth was reported to lie hidden in it, but
report soon went abroad that it was haunted by the ghost
of the Admiral and by that of his unhappy heir. However, after it had lain deserted for a year, it was bought
for a song by Mr. Dennis Rackage, who had at that time
lately sold his estate of the neighbouring Manor to the
man Henery, sometime steward to the estate. To be brief,
he moved into Hannibal House, apparently undisturbed
by the fear of the ghosts of his victims. Being in, he began
a systematic search for the buried wealth, although the
Crown agents had sought in the likeliest places, and had
expressed themselves sceptical as to its existence.

After a little while, it was noticed that the man Henery
was frequently at Hannibal House, and that his coming
was the signal for the locking of all gates and doors. It
was supposed that the two were searching together. Certainly evidence of digging and destruction accumulated
in the gardens outside the house. It was noticed, too, that

Mr. Rackage became less and less the dashing blood that had once startled London. It was said that the curse of the house had fallen on him, and that he had succumbed to the lust for gold to the neglect of all other considerations. A householder of Cholsington told us that he had seen Mr. Rackage, all white and sweating, digging in the garden far into the summer night. Others have said that he gradually gave up all intercourse with his fellows, and developed every symptom of that miserliness which is so difficult to distinguish from aberration. He ceased to be particular in his dress. Gone were the buckles and mohairs that had once been the envy of Tats and the delight of the Cyprians of the Bath House. Instead, he appeared, if at all, in his shirt-sleeves often soiled with the dirt of the garden clay. He would not enter Cholsington, even to purchase the few necessaries such as bread, beer and onions which made the bulk of his diet. At the same time it was noticed that his one-time servant Henery became more and more a figure in the world, drove his equipage, and dressed in an extreme of fashion, besides venturing with much acumen in the brick and gravel industry. It was easy to see that master and man had changed places. This state of things continued a long time, till it was at last understood that Mr. Rackage had disposed even of Hannibal House, and now worked there as his steward's servant; indeed, some reckoned that the relation was more truly that of master and slave.

But it is a well-known maxim that murder will out and that the worm will turn. It transpired that in one of his recent diggings Mr. Rackage, to give him the title to which his birth entitles him, found in the garden a few pieces of gold, with which he planned to make his escape into the Americas. Judge then his chagrin to find, when he set forth to put this plot in execution, that he had been observed, and anticipated. One with whom we have talked assures us that on finding himself checked in his plan of escape the unhappy creature wept. However, it was not for long. Dissembling for a brief while, he shewed a timely compliance with his tyrant, only to confound him more completely. On seeing Mr. Henery off to the tendering for the new bridge at Coles' Eyt, he determined to endure his conscience and his servitude no longer. He went, therefore, to the Rector of his parish and made a full confession. The Rector advised him that such a thing must be communicated to the magistrates, and urged him to come at once to repeat the dreadful tale before the justice of the peace. This the unhappy creature offered to do and promptly did. He said that shortly after the perpetration of the crime, and after the inquest held upon the body, it became known to him that the man Henery had seen him near Hannibal House before the crime was consummated. He had been filled at first with terror lest the crime should be fastened upon him, but the trial of Mansell followed swiftly upon the inquest and Henery still held his peace. It was not till after the execution of Mansell that Henery shewed that he knew who had done the murder and was determined to be paid for his silence. In the shaken condition of nerves to which blood-guiltiness had reduced him, he weakly paid for the man's silence and surrendered himself to years of an extortion, at first not unreasonable, but growing with each fresh demand until all that he had had gone into the leech's maw. He said, no doubt truly, that since the execution of Mansell he had known no single moment free from alarm and misery, till the happy day when the Rector urged him to come before the Justice.

As the readers will by this time be aware, the man Henery was laid for on his return from the tendering for the construction of the new bridge, where he had had the satisfaction of knowing his tender accepted. On his return, full of satisfaction, knowing that the new venture would bring him wealth and consolidate his importance, he was met at the door of the Manor House by Mr. Fetterer of Bow Street, who conveyed to him the dreadful tidings that he was awaited by the magistrates who wished to ask him a few questions. It says much for the acumen of the law-officers that no suspicion of the purport of the questions crossed Henery's mind till he was within the toils and charged with being an accessory after the fact in the murder of Admiral Cringle. Being a ready as well as a resolute rogue he at first tried to brazen it out, with the expected defence, that the man Rackage was a poor creature not far above imbecility and not to be accepted as a witness, that besides, the crime of the Admiral's murder had been proven to have been done by Dr. Mansell in a fit of anger mingled with greed, and that it was well known that no one doubted the guilt of Mansell. It was, however, retorted upon him that his wife, who some months before had gone out of her mind, had confessed to friends that Henery knew more of the Admiral's death than he let on to know at the inquest and the trial. This fact had so lain at her heart that it no doubt occasioned her unhappy insanity. From this point, the law was able to proceed by little and by little, with testimony from one and another to prove that Henery had obtained power over his late master by the possession of a secret and had used this power to extort from him what he wished. Evidence accumulated, and enough existed without it to cause the committal of both prisoners for trial. As the Assizes are on, there can be no doubt that it will soon be possible to sift this extraordinary case to the bottom.

The next copy of the paper gave a long account of the trial, which had roused the country thoroughly. I suppose all nations are alike in thinking that their legal institutions are the best in the world. I had had occasion to suffer from ours, and did not share the popular view of them. The writer shewed that even our magnificent system might sometimes err. It had erred, but was now going to exact full measure. It was a lesson to Guilt in general that, though Crime might long pass undetected, the hour of evil was a brief one; sooner or later it passed, leaving the terrible deed displayed and the wicked head in the dust. The Judge had said something like this, it seems, and the editor repeated it, with comments of his own. The two criminals had been found guilty and sentenced to be hanged. The most recent of the papers said, "The man Henery has made a full confession."

Since my day there had come to be changes in the system (perfect as it seemed); criminals were no longer hanged within a few hours of sentence, nor taken to Tyburn to suffer. They were given some days for repentance, and to fit themselves for death. These two, even after this, had had this time extended, "because of their exemplary behaviour." I felt that this was unjust. I who had been innocent had not been "exemplary," far from it. I had been stubborn, and had shewn no sense of my iniquity. These two, who were full of iniquity, had "closely followed their religious exercises" (as the phrase went), and were given a full week more of life. I knew what a full week more of life would have meant to us wretches in the Hold; it would have seemed an eternity of mercy. I was glad to think that they had that mercy. As to the rest of the revelation, it was so unexpected, so complete, that I knew not well what to do first. But after a time it seemed to me that the thing that I must do was to visit Newgate and somehow assure the two that they had not my blood upon their hands. I had always supposed that Henery had known of my escape from death, and had followed me to Liverpool. From what I now read, it seemed certain that both men thought that I was dead through their action. They were to die in a short while. I could perhaps get to the prison, and have access to them and assure them that that at least was not so. There was danger to myself in doing this; it might lead to my arrest. It would certainly imperil my cause on behalf of the Kranois, and perhaps leave Yvonne in a terrible situation in a foreign land. It was pleasant enough to have the people on one's side, welcoming the stranger, and smoothing the path. It would be a very different thing to be a felon; held up to shame as a returned convict, with all his property confiscate. What though the confession of the men cleared me and amply cleared me, the old conviction held; and I knew enough of the Law to know that it was slow enough to move, slower to admit error, slowest of all to disgorge. It had gathered to itself a booty through my conviction: was it likely to welcome one who would demand restitution? Was it not far more likely to hang me out of hand as a condemned felon, and seize upon whatever I had at the moment as a further payment for the trouble I had put them to? I did not trust our justice an inch. Still, I determined to get at these men, if it were possible. If I could get word to the gaolers that for a few words with the Chaplain a man would pay two guineas down and three more after the talk, then, perhaps something could be done. It would probably cost a guinea or two to get the offer to the gaolers or turnkeys, and who would bear the message? Who could? I judged that the potboys or the keeper of the tavern near the gate would be the only people likely to be able to get the message through. And how could I hope to get at them? I waited for a while; then, towards sunset, I went out and turned towards the city, down the hill up which I had once driven to my death.

I had felt sure that the coming of dusk would have taken half the sight-seers home from the prison precincts, but as I went on, I found three hurrying towards the city, for every one turning away; long before I was in sound of St. Sepulchre's bells, which I could tell from every other bell in Christendom, I saw that all that approach would be choked and blocked by sight-seers. As there was no reaching the prison that way, I turned off to my right, and after a time reached Ludgate Hill, which I found choked and jammed like the other approach. I drew out of the press, and asked a decent fellow how one could get to the prison.

"Have you a ticket?" he asked.

I did not know well what he meant, but said, "No."

"Ah," he said, "I thought you couldn't have a ticket; you've left it so late. The ticket-holders got there the first thing after church this morning; otherwise they'd have had no getting in and lose what they paid. They pay for windows," he added, with some pity in his voice for this stranger who knew so little. "They pay to see the show."

I asked if he could tell me how to get a word to the Chaplain of the prison.

"Why," he said, "you couldn't do it from this side at all, not if his salvation depended on it. But is it something for the prisoners you want?"

I said, "Yes. It is something which might be a comfort, even a very great comfort to one of the prisoners to know. If I could see the Chaplain, he would tell them, I'm sure."

"Well, you see for yourself, sir," the man said. "No man could pass these streets unless a troop of Horse-Guards rode along first and cleared the way. But if it's the Chaplain you want, on what they call an errand of mercy, I tell you what you might try. The turnkeys have their club at the Goat and Oboe, that's in Goat Alley, which opens off Shackle Lane. That's at the back of the prison. You might try from there. You'll have to go round by St. Paul's, and I doubt that even there you'll find the ways blocked; but if you do get to the Goat, it's ten to one you'll find someone there belonging to the prison, who would pass the word to the wicket-gate, if that's not beset, too; for this is not the usual thing at all. I've never seen it like this; never."

I thanked him and was for moving off, when he said, "Excuse me, sir, for mentioning it. These Newgate turn-keys and so forth : they've got the taker's itch, if you know what I mean. The inside of their hands wants scratching; and on a day like this, well, sir, it's in a sense their market day; they would want a good deal for a very little.

They'll be entertaining their friends and that; some of the greatest in the land may be at the Goat, at their regale, as they call it."

"What would you think would be fair," I asked, "for a message to be sent to the Chaplain?"

"They're a very haughty set of men, the Newgate men," he said. "They set a lot on theirselves. I wouldn't expect one of 'em to do much on his market-day, in a case like this, for under two or three guineas. They have themselves to consider. They have to wait long sometimes, to get where they are; it's only a very little time they have to feather their nests. And it's only human nature to shrink from the condemned holds; there's always the risk of the gaol-fever."

I thanked the man for all his help, and set forth to fetch a compass for the Goat and Oboe, wondering which of the highest in the land would be at the regale, and whether it was now, perhaps, to fall to me to visit Dennis in the Hold where he had visited me. I reflected that it was a market-day of an unusual kind, and that I must not expect to be privileged, like the highest in the land, to gaze on Newgate's choicest flowers. Statesmen, jockeys, prize-fighters and Peers of the Realm might well claim the precedence. But I had lost my tide, I found. Had I gone to the Goat that afternoon, when I was going to the Sponge and Rammer, it is possible that I might have arrived, and done my errand. But I found in a few minutes that the entire prison was surrounded. Throngs were filling all the lanes at the back of the prison quite as closely as they filled those on the west. The lane they called Poll Maggot's Lane, from some female friend of

Dick Sheppard, was jammed with people. A man told me that a noble lord who had gone along had had to fight for it and had had his head broken by a porter. What the crowds hoped to achieve by being where they were, I could not think. Some may have been bent on reaching the turnkeys' regale, perhaps. A good many were pickpockets and snatch-thieves, who were there for business. A few were hawkers selling or trying to sell broadsides and confessions, oranges, eel-pies, jellies and wisps of snuff. The main bulk of the company was made up of average, stupid men. They had been moved by the story of the crime, they had read the case closely, they had seen, perhaps, the strangeness of the working of the justice to this end, and wished to be near the centre of the tumult. They could not hope to see anything or anyone even remotely linked with the events. They would stand all night, jammed in a pack in a land, perhaps rained on, perhaps chilled by the cold north wind then blowing and unable to defend themselves if set upon by the gangs of thieves, who were already gathering to the prey. In the morning, if they could endure so long, they would at the most hear the tollings of St. Sepulchre's and the horrible little bell of the prison, and might hear the yellings of the crowd stilled as the victims appeared. After this, they would be free to disentangle themselves from the mobs and make their ways to work. Yet they would be able to say that they had been at the execution. Years later, when a famous rogue would hang, they would say, "Ah, I was at the hangings of Henery and Rackage. That *was* a hanging. You couldn't get nearer to Newgate than the Fleet Ditch, there was such a crowd." I had to give up my plan of reaching the Goat and Oboe. Somewhere in the snuggery there, no doubt, the head turnkey or gaoler stirred the punch at his regale, and did the honours of Newgate to the bloods and sporting peers before taking them in for a peep at his conservatory. At that moment, as I heard later, the regale was in full flow; a certain grand lady, dressed as a young man, was with her brother there; both afterwards were admitted to the Hold, to speak with Dennis. It became known, somehow; and I am glad to think that it was the cause of some horror even in the set they moved among.

I moved out of the crowd, and then from the movement of people, who were coming only to see the crowd. I supposed that I might perhaps find the sheriff and from him have leave to visit the Hold, and perhaps an escort to take me there. He and his javelin-men would be present the next morning doubtless, and would have a means of clearing a path thither. But by this time it was getting to be night. I had been thrusting and pushing in the crowd and was weary, as well as eager not to leave Yvonne longer alone. I retraced my steps, and by good luck found a coach to take me on my way. The driver wanted to know if I had been to the prison.

I said, "I could not get near it."

"No," he said. "If you'd got near it, you'd be there now; you couldn't a got away. Besides, no man who'd got near it would come away on an occasion like this. This is one you'd not see the like of, not perhaps in a hundred years."

I reached home too weary to do more that night. I suppose that Dr. Copshrews would have found the sheriff, obtained an escort, seen the Chaplain and given comfort to the dying. I thought of what he had done for me in a like case, and was sad to come so far short of a Christian's effort. I sat for a while looking out of the window at my old home. Lights were on in the windows. I wondered who was living there, and what they talked of. If they were talking at all, I knew that they would be talking of Henery and Rackage. I wondered if they knew that one of their victims had lived and been happy in their house.

As always that day, the thought of my mother was much in my mind; she seemed very near to me. During the night, I wondered much about her portrait, which had been in the Rackage Manor when my father died. I supposed that it had been destroyed by my stepmother. If not—and there was a chance that that foolish woman might not have gone to such lengths of violence—it had come into the power of Dennis, who might conceivably still have it. Portraits by the fashionable painters of thirty years ago do not fetch much money, if sold. Possibly, the portrait would now be in one of the lumber-rooms at the Manor, in the dry, fusty air of such places, near the chair with the leg gone and the bureau with the handles broken. It might well be there; quite possibly, I might see it again. I lay awake for a long time that night, thinking, "Perhaps I shall find it."

But I thought, too, that if it had ever come to Henery, he would have kicked it through and burned it; or (in his hatred of me) sold it to the rag-picker. It might now be over the seas or on the seas; who could tell? And yet, even so, search will find most things; he who follows a track, and asks and seeks, he will find. In the end I felt that perhaps I might trace the picture, and so at last fell asleep, to dream of the Hold in Newgate and the tolling of the bell across the road. If any man treads through the horror of Newgate its nightmare will dog his soul till he dies; there is no doubt of that. Its dye is in grain, and comes not out for any washing.

I had meant to rise early, to pray for those two; but, lo, when I woke, it was after eight and they had trodden all the road that I had gone. The old Newgate phrase returned to me, "We'll be out of it by Monday." Here it was Monday and past the hanging time. By this time, they must have ended, poor wretches, beyond any hope of a revival such as had come to me.

However, I was wrong about this. When I came to breakfast, Harry and the maid were both bursting with the news, that the two had been reprieved for three days on the urgent recommendation of the Chaplain, who felt that they were not quite prepared for their fate. The officers charged with the reprieve had had the utmost difficulty in reaching the prison in time, but had done so as the prisoners moved to the scaffold, after their irons had been knocked off. There was now a riot at the gaol, Harry said; people were so mad with disappointment at not seeing them hanged, after stopping up all night. Five had been hanged, but not these two. It was very much like waiting up to see Garrick act and then, after waiting all day and part of the night, finding that he would not act for three days. Going out presently, I saw some of the flood of rascality setting back from the gallows, and did not marvel that the soldiers were drawn out from the barracks till the streets were quiet. I thought, "Tomorrow, I will go to Newgate to see those two."

As my Secretary of State could not yet see me, I took coach and drove to Cholsington. I wore my horn glasses, lest someone there might recognize me, yet I was growing careless, too, or shall we say confident. I had begun to think that the danger was less than I had feared. Still, no one can want a second taste of Newgate Hold. I told my driver to drive to the Cholsington Manor, saying that passers-by would tell him the way, if he did not know it.

"Oh, sir," he said, "I know the way to Cholsington Manor, and to Hannibal. I've driven a full score people there in these last days. The place is as well known as Vauxhall. They all go to see the places where any deed's been done. You'll find fifty people there, I don't doubt."

I asked, "Can people go into the houses?"

"It isn't supposed to be allowed," he said. "But, of course, they get in. I took a gentleman on Saturday, who went into both, though I suppose he paid for the privilege. There's nothing to see at the Manor, sir; the most of it is shut up."

I said that I would like to see it, even if shut up, and asked, "Is it far from here?"

He said, "No, only a few miles, and the good road most of the way."

Presently, I was in the lane that led to it, and found myself in a long stream of carriages and carts of all sorts, all heading in the same direction, all full of the sight-seers come to see the place where so much evil had dwelled. As the stream moved slowly, I got out and walked, telling my man to pull up beyond the house for me. Soon, I came to the house, from which I had been flung. At the sight of it,

I knew how frightful a wound that day had dealt me. I shook my fist at the building.

"Yes, sir," a man said, seeing my gesture, "it is hard not to want to do that. This is a house of iniquity. There's been dark doings plotted here, sir."

I said, "I fear so."

I saw that some of the callers were going up the steps and into the house. I asked a man who seemed to have some post of authority there, and yet was not one of the men of the estate, if it were possible to see the house.

He said, "Of course, sir, people aren't supposed to see it. It's Crown property, being in a sense confiscated under the Act; but, of course, sir, the interest being so great, exceptions have sometimes to be made. Did you wish to see over it, sir?"

I said, "Yes."

He said, "If you'll excuse me, sir, I'll speak to the caretaker, and ask him."

He returned soon to say that the caretaker would be very pleased to shew me the house, and led the way to where the caretaker was shewing out my predecessor. I went up the steps down which I had come with such ignominy. Henery and Dennis had both stood to mock me there; now they lay in the condemned Hold, and I was going into their den as one of the sight-seers.

I was somewhat scared as I went up those steps. Some of the servants might be there. I had found that those with no memories for books have often quick memories for life, and do not forget either faces or those physical tricks which are less easy to disguise. I was subject to a good deal of scrutiny by the little company near the door. A good many were there, either watching the carriages and their occupants or idly staring at the house where a terrible man had lived. I went in out of the fine May weather into a shuttered house. The caretaker said to myself and another who was to see the sights, "Come straight through, gents; there are no steps." So we went straight through, to a part of the house where I had seldom been. It was all shuttered on that floor except a smallish room to which the man led us. "It is here, gents," he said, "that the man had his office as he called it. He lived mostly here after his wife went mad. This is where he did his calculations and put on what he called his screws." It had been Henery's office, where he had done his estate accounts in the old days. The room had a big desk, which had been there in my day, and some shelves ranged with ticketed bundles of paper. I recognized the man's rather bold handwriting. The fireplace had been altered and enlarged, so that cooking might be done upon it. Water had been led to a sink at one side. "He lived here," the guide went on; "after his wife went mad, he did all his own cooking and lived here. There are his pots and pans and his last loaf of bread, all cut for toast, as when he was taken. He was something of a miser and watched every mouthful and every penny."

I asked if the house were full of beautiful furniture and paintings.

He said, "He always kept one room as a state-room, for when he received the great. I'll shew you that, sir, in one minute."

I looked at the room in which we were. It had been panelled with wood, and the wood painted a leaden grey colour. A strange chair with an iron frame, and a cover of black quilted leather from which padding exuded in cracks and slits, was beside the fire. "That is his easy-chair," the guide said. "He pulled it out at this end, and lowered the back, so; then it made a bed. 'A chair by day, an easy bed by night,' as our Shakespeare says. His blankets are still rolled up in the cupboard there." I marvelled at the meanness of the life. To what end had all this discipline tended? Monks, as I knew, would give up all things for the love of God, or for the hope of access to Truth, but this man was living like a rat in order to be a rat trap. I asked if the house were his.

"Yes, sir," he said, "he had it all from his master; it was all his, and all the things in it. But now, gents, as there'll be others wanting to see, I'll take you to the state-room, which is back this way." There was no sign of any painting in the office, of course. The furniture was the old desk with a wooden chair, the iron easy-chair, a box or two, a big scuttle for coal and a little round table where the creature had eaten his meals. These things, a kettle and a saucepan were almost the only things there.

"He grudged his victual," the guide said. "Gruel was his main regale. But this is the state-room."

He led the way back to what had been the dining-room, and going to the window opened a leaf of a shutter. "This is the other room he used," he said. "He only used the two rooms: the office and this. This is the state-room, as he called it."

It was the Rackage dining-room, much as it had ever been. My mother's portrait was not there. The other portraits which I remembered of old were there; Mrs. Rack-

age as Flora, and the other. The chairs were not the dining-room chairs. They were the tall, handsome chairs with
painted and gilded backs which had once been in the
drawing-room across the hall.

"This is his state-room," our guide said. "It was
here that he received the great, when he had his meet-
ings."

"What great were these?" my fellow sight-seer asked.

"The great he lent money to, or persuaded money out
of, for his schemes," the guide said. "He had fingers in a
many great pies. It was thought he was putting in to be a
lord himself."

"You say that he only lived in these two rooms?" I said.
"Are the other rooms shut up? Could I see them? It was
told me that they are full of lovely things, but perhaps
that isn't quite true."

"It isn't true at all, sir," the man said. "The other
rooms are empty. There's not a stick in the rest of the
house."

"Nor any books?" I asked.

"Nor any books except what you saw in the office, them
*Ramblers* as they call them."

Two odd volumes of the *Rambler* had lain on the desk
in the office. One of them, which I had glanced at, had
been used as a memorandum book, of expenses made on
a journey to Stamford and back.

"Yes, sir," the guide continued, "these were the only
two rooms he used; all the rest are empty. And this room
you are in is the one he used to receive the lords in, when
he had any little scheme to put through. It is thought
by some that he was bribing the very greatest. He was out

for a coronet: if not for strawberry-blossom, what comes above coronets."

I asked if he had found the house full of things from his late master.

"It's not for me to say, yes or no, sir," the man said. "But the tale goes that not much was left here by his master; most of the stuff that would fetch money had gone before ever the man became the master. The dealers and the frippery men had bought all that. But that was before my time. I'm only here since the Crown took possession. You would find people in the garden to tell you that; down to your right, sir, at the cottage: the gardener's cottage."

He had been, as it were, shooing us towards the door, with an eye on the newcomers, who were already on the threshold, and yet with an eye upon our hands, to see if we were going to make it worth his while, and at the same time with a caution in his look, which shewed us that he knew that it might not be good to be seen taking "what we might be pleased to offer," and that, therefore, he had better see what sort of men these newcomers might be. He took our offerings and dismissed us.

My fellow sight-seer said, "I think I'll come with you, sir, to the gardener's cottage, for I feel, with you, that a little memento of such a house would be worth having, to leave to one's children. Depend upon it, sir, such a thing will fetch money in years to come."

I said, "That is what I've been thinking."

"Sir," the man replied, "I'm grateful to you really, for putting it into my mind. Without your saying that just now, it would not have occurred to me."

As we neared the gardener, I made some excuse of having a pebble in my shoe, to give my companion a chance
to speak to him first, while I made sure that he was a
man I could approach with safety. As I stooped, I saw
that he was not. He was one who had been there as a useful hand in the old days. I could not remember his name,
but I had seen him about, with the pigs or in the stables.
He was a rough red-haired man, with a rude authoritative
way. He was said to have come from northern Ireland.
He was the sort of man who might well remember me;
he was a good deal cleverer than most of the men on the
estate. As I took off my shoe and shook out the supposed
pebble, I heard my companion begin:

"Can you tell me who had all the furniture of the house
when it was sold?"

"Mebbe I can."

"Who had it, please?"

"Who wants to know?"

"I do, and this gentleman here."

"For what would ye want to know ut?"

"So as to buy something from it."

"Hold on till I ask."

He gave me a swift look, but did not recognize me;
indeed, I was getting confidence every moment now, from
the certainty that all knew that Ned was dead, past all
possibility of return. He went across the kitchen-garden
to what had been the pigman's cottage, near the sties,
where another man was supervising some digging. This
supervisor seemed to be some person in authority, as
we could plainly perceive, for the gardener asked him if

he were to give us the information we wanted. The supervisor looked shrewdly at us, and with some misgivings. It
flashed into my mind that all these people, all the work-
ers on the estate and all the visitors, had some wild belief that treasure was buried somewhere; that Henery
had gotten the Admiral's treasure, or that Dennis had
found it and conveyed it away somewhere with the sold
furniture to some safe place. This man in charge of the
digging was no doubt an officer of the Crown, following
some clue; now it fell to him to find out if we, who were
anxious to trace the furniture, had some clue, too, and
what it amounted to. He was a pleasant-looking man,
with a look of honesty and pertinacity.

He came towards us, looking at us and asked, "What
is it you want, gentlemen?"

I said, "We would like to buy some small memento of
the house, but they tell me that all the furniture, except
from two of the rooms, was sold some time ago. Could
you possibly tell us who had it? It probably was sold to
some dealer."

He seemed to suspect that all was not quite fair, for he
looked at us both with an air at once innocent and determined to prevent guilt.

"The things were sold some time ago," he said. "They
would all be scattered far and wide by this time. Which
things did you wish to purchase?"

I said, "No things in particular, but little objects to
keep, in memory of a strange event."

He seemed convinced from this that we were suspicious
people, eager to get hold of particular things which might

give clues of importance. It did not seem right to him that any sane person should wish to own relics of a horrible house and its inhabitants.

"Well," he said, "I'm not at liberty to tell anyone anything, but if you care to give me your names and addresses, I will make enquiries and let you know if I can hear of anything."

By this time, three or four men and women had appeared about us, to hear what might be heard.

I said that it was of no importance at all; we had only asked in case the things might be easily had. It was not our wish to go to any trouble or put anybody else to trouble. The idea had come to us that the things might still be in the parish. With this, I bade him good morning and turned away towards the lane. The little party broke up. A young woman who had been in the party came shyly up to us, when we were in the lane, and asked,

"Was you asking about the things sold from the house?"

I said, "Yes. Do you happen to know who bought them?"

She said, "A Mr. Wittenham bought them, sir, oh, a long time ago. Wittenham was the name, a long gentleman."

My companion asked, "Did Mr. Wittenham buy them from Rackage, the murderer?"

"No, sir," the woman said; "Mr. Rackage lost them all at cards to another gentleman. Mr. Wittenham was the gentleman who bought them from the other gentleman. He took them all away in waggons, Mr. Wittenham."

"Where to?"

"I'd have to ask my mother that, sir, down at the cottage. She did say, but I forget the name; it's somewhere in the country."

My companion said, "Well, since I've gone so far, I may as well come down to the cottage to ask that. Where is your mother's cottage?"

"Just down the lane, sir, at the corner."

I remembered the cottage as the home of a comely woman, a Mrs. Smith. This young woman must be one of the little children whom I remembered as playing about the cottage. Mrs. Smith might recognize me, of course; but then I was so dead. So we went to the cottage, and the girl asked, "Mother, could you tell the gentlemen where the Mr. Wittenham lived who bought the things from the Manor?"

She came out from her cooking, wiping her hands upon a cloth, and peered at us both; her cottage was dark and we were in the sunlight. "Mr. Wittenham lived at a place called Condicote," she said. "It is a long way from here. He was setting up house at the time; a very tall gentleman. But it was a long time ago. He took all the things away in waggons, if it's the things you want. It took him days to get everything away."

We thanked her. I said something to a plump little girl who was playing near, and asked if that were her dolly in the corner? Something in my voice, or in my manner, made Mrs. Smith look at me strangely; but no, Ned was dead. I thanked her and her daughter and returned to my hackney coach, where I parted from my new acquaintance.

"I shall not go on my chase any further," he said. "Redshire's too far for me."

I told the driver to go on slowly by the lane, so as to pass Hannibal House. We soon came in sight of it. A crowd was about its gates, as when I last entered there. The place looked bare, mean and as though pillaged. The figurehead was gone; there were no little guns or piles of shot near the door. The garden was seamed with trenches and cuttings where Dennis or the Crown had been digging for treasure. Mud from boots was thick on the walks which had once been so trim. The creepers, shrubs and trees had all been neglected. Being May, the nettles were in full push. The windows were shuttered, and the shutters in need of paint. The place looked evil. Of old it had looked so trim.

The driver leaned back and hailed me through the little opening. "This is Hannibal House, sir," he said. "This is the place. You can see, sir, where he dug to find the treasure. The room where he did the deed is the one above the big window, sir, in a room in there. He's said to have pulled most of the walls to pieces looking for his victim's gold; it's only the shell that is left. I'm afraid you won't get into this, sir. It's too well guarded."

I told him to stop a moment, while I had a good look.

"Yes, sir," he said. "You must take a good look. You won't see such a place, I dare well say, sir, not twice in a life."

"I hope not, I'm sure," I said.

I did take a good look. I looked, so as to conquer the dread and horror of it that I had felt for all these weary times. I found that looking at it was like grappling a snake that had twined right round me twice and was heaving me dead. It seemed to me to be a terrible place.

As I looked, the people in the lane came all about me. "Last dying speech and confession," they cried. "Buy a relic of the crime, sir. Last dying speech of Edward Mansell, hanged for the murder of Admiral Cringle. This is the true account, sir. Read how the murderer confessed, sir. Henery's statement." Each of the men had some printed sheet held out to me. "Buy this one, sir: all about young Dr. Mansell, falsely hanged." "Buy what Rackage told the magistrates. Read the ravings of Henery's wife in Bedlam: all about Blood, sir."

My old misfortunes had been raked into the light again; here were the accounts of my trial and death, my hardened, unrepentant death. I bought two of them, but dispensed with the accounts of Dennis and Henery. I wished to get away from these hawkers of horror, so I told the driver to push ahead. When we were out of the press, I stopped him and got down, so that I might look at the house from the point from which I had approached it on the day of the murder. That view of it had not changed, I thought, except that the ivy on one of the walls had been stripped, perhaps in the treasure hunt. No smoke was rising from the kitchen chimney. I wondered where the Admiral's servants were now. I supposed that they had been ruined by the murder. I was the heir. I had promised to look after them after the Admiral's death. It was likely that the Admiral had made no other provisions for them than my word; then, when the Admiral was killed, and the heir hanged, the property was confiscate. Who had allowed for their long service and expectations? What had become of them, then? What had become of the relics of the *Hannibal* and of Quichet's drawings and the

painting? As I knew now that my driver was a mine of
knowledge of all connected with the house and crime, I
spoke to him:

"You say, that the Admiral was killed here. Do you
know what became of his things? Are they in the house
still?"

"I was asked that by other gentlemen, sir," he said. "I
can tell you the answer. When the murder took place, the
property went to the Crown. There was a sale of the furniture at the house itself. It was all sold. Then the house
and grounds were sold, and this Mr. Rackage bought
them, hoping to find the treasure, which everyone said
was buried there."

"Why should it be there?" I asked. "Why should the
Admiral, or any sensible man, bury money or valuables?"

"Well, sir," the driver said, "it's often safer than a
strong-box or a bank. And they do say, sir, that when the
Crown took over the property they found that he ought
to have had not twenty but thirty thousand pounds more
than could be accounted for. Where was it, sir, if not hidden?"

"Where?" I said. "Why, of course, the man who was
hanged for the murder, the young doctor, had it given to
him. Or this Dennis had it, and dared not admit it. Or
Henery had it and, being a secret man and a miser, never
let on that he had it."

The driver shook his head. "No, sir, if you'll excuse me,"
he said. "I don't think any of them had it. It's my belief
it's still there, if one had the luck to hit the place."

"Listen," I said. "The Crown, you say, went into the
question of the property thoroughly, and learned that

thirty thousand pounds was missing. They knew at least
that the Admiral had had thirty thousand pounds and
hadn't left it. If the Crown knew that it was missing, and
might be in the house or on the grounds, why did they
sell the grounds and house? Why did they not continue
to search? They gave up search. Surely, they must have
known that the money wasn't here. Why, they may even
have invented the whole story, to persuade people to
offer for the property; since without some attraction of
the kind, few would care to bid for a house in which a
murder had been done."

"No, sir," he said stubbornly. "I think it must be there."

"It's well hidden, then," I said. "But someone was saying that the Admiral had a lot of houses in London. Why
should he not have hidden it in one of them?"

"That I never thought of, I'm sure, sir," he said. "But
they say he wasn't often away from here, and never slept
out of this house."

"Well," I said, "whoever finds the treasure, wherever
it may be, I hope he will share it with us."

"I'm sure I hope so too, sir," he said.

With that we drove on past the great house where I
had called the Coroner to my undoing, and so round the
bend and back to London.

The newspapers were full of self-righteousness, that
day, for the Christian kindness that had granted reprieves
to the two criminals, "on whom the thoughts of all must
have dwelt during yesterday's religious exercises"; they
also said that such mercy is a recent grace in us (I agreed,
very recent), and added that though they could never
disapprove of mercy they felt that if ever it had been

misapplied it may have been so here, in a case of such
hardened heinousness. I wondered whether the two poor
wretches in the Hold were not tortured the longer by the
mercy. They must have made up their minds to die on
Monday morning, and may even have contrived a stupefy-
ing drunkenness to that end. When a man was reprieved,
he always hoped for a second reprieve or alteration of
sentence. These two could hardly expect that, and yet, a
lot of people were saying that they were both men of
some education and ability, who might yet do good if
transported to the new settlement. They would cling to
these hopes, no doubt, and be frantic with hope, as I had
been, and then the hours would run and the hopes would
dim, the bells would strike the horrible hours and the
clergyman would tell us to hope for mercy. Mercy. When
you at last know that you are not to have mercy in this
world, you hope for annihilation or a chance for revenge
in the next. It isn't mercy you want. I was sick with
memories of my misery when I thought of those two there
in the Hold. Going out to enquire if there were any letters
for me, I heard Harry saying that he had been down to
the Prison in his dinner hour, and that there was a big
crowd, but that soldiers were keeping people moving. He
had the news that the gallows had not been taken down;
it was there still. "So they will go out of it on Thursday,
sure to, or they wouldn't leave it up." The opinion of the
maid was that the two ought not to have been reprieved,
but Harry said that death was a great change, and people were the better prepared for it. She retorted that
they hadn't given their victims much time to prepare.

In the afternoon, I went to an address in Whitehall,

to speak with a Naval officer, a relation of Captain Culham. Quite by chance, I asked if he happened to know a
place called Condicote.

He said, "Yes, well; I lived there as a boy."

I asked, "Do you know a tall Mr. Wittenham?"

He said, "Yes. He was my cousin. He died of this cholera
morbus that went about last summer. Why? Did you
know him?"

I said, "No, but I was told this morning that he had
bought the furniture once belonging to the mother of
Rackage the murderer."

"Did he, indeed!" the man said. "Well, he hasn't got
it now, that's sure; nor do I know who has. His things
were sold there at his home."

My heart sank a little at this, but I determined to go to
Condicote, as soon as I could, to follow the portrait further.

While we were at breakfast the next morning, some
men came shouting about the square, as they often did
when there was terrible news. The maid was sure from
their cries that the French had landed, but this seemed
improbable. The yells of the men were like the cries of
wild beasts, but I made out the words "Escape from Newgate," and at once guessed that Dennis had somehow
bribed his gaolers to let him get away. As these men
seemed to be selling newspapers, I went out to buy one.
One of the hawkers saw me come from the house and
waited for me. I asked him his price. He said, "Sixpence
for this, sir." I thought it a monstrous price, but gave it.
He said, familiarly, "It has come with a clap, sir. I
thought when they granted the reprieve, there was some-

thing stirring. Money does everything in the Newgate world the same as in any other."

"Not quite everything," I said. "But how did they get away?"

"It's all in the paper, sir; if you'll excuse me, there are some wanting a copy."

I opened the still damp sheet and read:

### DARING ESCAPE OF RACKAGE AND HENERY.

During the hours of darkness last night, the two prisoners who were to expiate their crimes on Thursday morning, contrived to make a daring escape. It is thought that the prisoner Henery received from some friend or sympathiser a set of files and picklocks concealed in a Bible sent in to him. It is learned that a Bible left in the Condemned Hold was ingeniously contrived as a box within which such articles may have been easily secreted. The escape must have taken place after the Last Rounds (at about 9 P.M.) of the Gaolers, who say that the prisoners then were quiet and securely ironed. Between that time and the morning visit the prisoners had ample time to remove their irons and pick the locks which stood between them and freedom. The prison officials preserve strict reticence as to the way by which the two left the prison. The fact remains, that they have escaped, and are now at liberty. Be on your guard. Two murderers are now at large, and are not likely to have attempted to leave London.

That was the sheet; I have it still. I cannot begin to tell you what a storm was roused by the escape. Harry and the maid were both sure that the head gaolers had received five hundred pounds each to let the men go. Money was everything in Newgate, they said; "Nobody with money ever suffers." They said that it was well known that the rich could get away. I said that that was not so, as many rich men had suffered death from Newgate; and added that the only man who had twice escaped from Newgate was the penniless house-breaker Jack Sheppard. It was said that "the Government," that vague body which receives the blame in England when a more visible culprit fails, had connived at the escape on condition that they received news of where the treasure was buried. This and more fantastic rumours spread over the town from mouth to mouth. The newspapers and catchpenny printers printed sheet after sheet which were hawked about and eagerly read. I had never till then, and have never since, known the nation so deeply stirred about anything. They were said to have been deeply moved when the French King was beheaded, when the famous ratting terrier, Trigger, was run over, when the black man beat the white English boxing champion, and when the horse, Eclipse, died. But I am sure that the escape of Dennis and Henery moved London more than any of these things. The city had gloated over the crime and the working of justice; it had panted for the blood of both miscreants, and now the two had contrived to get away. There was a cry for vengeance on somebody. Someone had thwarted them, that someone should be found and made to suffer. The matter concerned me more closely than anybody, and I read all that I could find about it. I have since then made many enquiries. The facts seem to be that Henery received the means of getting out. Who provided them was a point never cleared up. Strong suspicion was on two of the prison officers, that is, an almost certainty, but no real proof. He had received these means of escape, the picklocks and files, and doubtless had not meant to help Dennis, but to escape alone. It was said in some of the prints that he had even arranged to drug some rum so that Dennis might be senseless while he made his way out. However, it was thought that Dennis in his preparation for death had abjured drink, and refused the drugged rum, so that Henery had no option but to take his companion with him. The popular prints said that Dennis had said that he would raise the prison, if he were not taken, too. How they proceeded after they had come out of the Hold was much debated; the public feeling was that someone in the prison must have made their way smooth for them. They got out of the prison easily enough at last, by means of some builders' ladders on the roof at the back. Here again, someone in the prison must have helped for money down. Henery was rich, of course, and could have procured a good deal from some hidden source, even though his main having had been confiscated. Who had helped them? There was an angry outcry everywhere, companies gathered at the prison, and many shouted at the gaolers, "Who murdered the Poggses?" The Poggses, husband and wife, had been hanged on the Monday, when Dennis and Henery had been reprieved. The point of the cry was that, if the Poggses had been rich, they, too, could have bribed and escaped. The prison had to be guarded by troops, for in those days popular cries were much dreaded; an attack on a prison had been the beginning of much civil commotion in France.

I cannot begin to tell you the terror that hung over London from the knowledge that the two murderers were at large there. Their descriptions were put about at once. To me, who knew both men, the descriptions seemed perfect, cut, build, colour and little ways. I will not repeat these to you, for they were bad men, and you will not do well to fill your mind with their idea. I well remember how men in the street looked at all passers-by, and how women who opened doors to callers put on the chains before they opened even a chink. The "Government," or people responsible, at once offered a reward of a hundred pounds to any man giving such information as would lead to the taking of either man. The papers said that undoubtedly both men were hiding in London, that they could not have dared to make for the open country, that they had probably ample funds, and faithful friends. Much was made of a young Quaker woman who had brought the Bible to Henery in his cell. She had been reading the Bible to other prisoners for some days before she had asked if she might visit the Hold. It was now thought that she was not a woman at all, but a stirring young man. The Society of Friends said that no member of their Society had visited the prison on those days. The gaolers now remembered that they had thought at the time that this young woman had had a deep voice for a woman. One paper brought in the story now of a post-chaise seen loitering in Maggot's Lane at the back of the prison between one and two on the Tuesday morning. They who told this story said that with fast horses, and relays, the prisoners might be thirty miles from London, completely disguised, before daylight. After that, all sorts of stories spread ; how on one road a

post-chaise had gone through Chingford at four on that
morning, with two old Frenchwomen unable to speak
English, and how on other roads named a Greek and his
wife, who knew no English, had passed, and on another
two very suspicious cases of whooping-cough might well
have been the two. Another paper said that it was considered unlikely by the thief-takers that the criminals
had left London. The city held purlieus and dens in which
fugitives from justice might lie quietly perhaps for years.
It might take some time for the thief-takers to obtain
the necessary information (this paper said), but there
was no doubt that the word would pass and the men be
brought back to justice. This paper said that the two
would infallibly keep together, and make use of various
disguises for their mutual aid. This was a theory pleasant
to the public, that two men who had hated each other
to the death should cling to each other as friends now
that both were fugitives. To myself this theory was absurd. I judged that Henery had planned the escape for
both of them, because he could not leave the Hold alone.
I was sure that he meant to get clear from Dennis; but
that, if he could not, he would denounce him to the thief-
takers. This might well bring him a pardon, for the State
wanted Dennis's blood. In that mood of the public mind,
any man who denounced Dennis, even if he were a murderer himself, would be rewarded by a grateful country;
he would be sent abroad or to the hulks, not hung.

Meanwhile, men talked of nothing else; clue followed
clue, and rumour followed fable; dread of those two escaped murderers was everywhere. England was terrified
of them. There was no need to say who "they" were: "Have

you seen them?" or "Have you had any news of them?" were words spoken by all, in those fateful days.

London never goes to bed, I suppose. A crowd, of sorts, will gather at all hours of the day or night, from nowhere, in any street. Yet it seemed that these two men had passed into the quiet streets at the back of the prison in the small hours of the morning unseen by anyone. There is little real darkness in early May; the milkmen must have been up and the bakers busy at the time; but the two had gone, and London had swallowed them up. I wondered whether they were not hidden by the conniving gaoler in some disused part of the gaol, or in some den close to the prison. There were dens enough within a quarter-mile of that foul spot. It is the fashion to call them rookeries. But a rookery is a fair place builded in the tops of elms. The rookery blows about with the airs of heaven, swaying yet sure; its inhabitants look down on the world, or sail above it crying their joy. A city den is very unlike that kind of rookery. It is built near to the earth and shut from all air; and from its foulness the creatures come to see their brothers hanged. I suppose there were a thousand or two waterless, filthy lairs on the city side of the Fleet Ditch, where the men could harbour. Yet I did not think that they would be there, because every inhabitant in those Alsatias would sell his best friend for a case of Hollands.

However, during that morning I received a letter from my Secretary, to tell me that he would be in London again in one week from then and would be happy to see me at his office in Whitehall upon such a day. As I had ten days to wait, I proposed to Yvonne that we should go into the

country, to Condicote, to look for the portrait of my
mother. It was fair spring weather, with England at her
fairest, so we set out together by one of the famous coaches
to Oxford and then away beyond to countries that Yvonne
had never dreamed of, and all of them a wonder to her.
Years before when I was flying from England, I had had
a loathsome moment of terror at an inn where I took
coach. I was within touch of a master thief-taker, who
ought to have recognized me and did not. This man was
famous in the prison world and a terror to it. It was said
of him that he had brought more men to the gallows than
any three judges on the Bench. He was supposed to have
uncanny powers, and in a way, I do not doubt that he
had. He had a marvellous memory for faces and for scraps
of information. He talked with every criminal and remembered all that was said. He would piece bit to bit and
draw his conclusions, and another wretch went out on
Monday.

Now this man was well-known to me, who saw him in
Newgate daily while I was there. I suppose that no one
once pursued by him, or in danger from him, ever forgot
or could forget him. His face with its inhuman mask of
indifference was like a cat's face; it had the same sort of
smile of cruelty and of power. Nor had I forgotten him.
I had thought of him often and often; he had been in
my nightmares and my terrors for months together. Now,
when I came to the coach-office to take our places for the
west, he was there in the yard. He was coming with us
in the coach. Luckily, I had a view of him before we came
face to face; I braced myself for meeting him and speaking with him, hardened my heart and told myself, "Now

for it. This man will remember, if anyone can remember; some flash of association may bring it all back to him, and I may be lost." I braced myself, but could not face the danger. All my resolution was knocked out of me by the suddenness of the shock. I asked the landlady if I might have a post-chaise as far as Brentford, to see some tombs in the church there, and then pick up the Oxford coach that evening. As it chanced, this could be arranged; so I took Yvonne to a sitting-room while the chaise was made ready, and saw the coach drive off, with this thief-taker riding outside. He was booked through, to a distant place. I wondered what crime took him so far from his usual haunts.

In the course of the next days we drove on, mostly by post-chaise, to the town of Condicote, where we put up at an inn, and went forth to see the town. We had been told that the most remarkable sight of the town was the prior's house near what had been a house of monks. Not much of the house of monks remained, but the prior's house was perfect, with strange painting and plaster-work in some of its rooms, including a Vine of Life, wrought in plaster on the walls and ceiling, and then coloured, as heralds say, "proper" in its natural colours. We went to this, and admired. I asked the keeper about Mr. Wittenham; he said that Mr. Wittenham had lived just the other side the churchyard from there, where the peacocks were crying, and that Mr. Dorchester lived there now. He said that Mr. Wittenham's things had been sold soon after the death, and bought here and there by people in the district. He did not think that there were many pictures, but I gathered that by pictures he meant his-

torical pieces or tapestries; he was sure at least that Mr.
Dorchester had none of them. I asked what had caused
the death of Mr. Wittenham, who was still a young man.
He said, "He never got over the fire there was, when one
wing of the house was burned; he got a chill from that,
which left him weak and presently turned to the bowels."
The medical history interested me. I had the impression
of a very tall, not very robust man, who had to let himself
out of a window in his nightgown on a night of frost and
wild east wind. How the chill had turned to where it did
was another matter. I preferred "cholera morbus" for
that. I asked if any auctioneer there might know where
the things had gone. He said, "Yes. Mr. Chaffinch would
that." He did all that kind of work, and I should find him
at his office near my inn. Somehow, I felt that Mr. Chaffinch would not help very much, but I went there and
asked. He said, "I had better let you see the books, sir.
They have a list of the things with the prices paid and
who bought them." He produced some ledgers, and turned
to the account Wittenham. He said, "If it's pictures you
ask for, they were on the first of the two days." He turned
the pages for me, so that I could read:

A sett of the Triumph of Flora, engr, French taste.
                                 Mr. Sporteau. 7gns.
Hagar and Ishmael or the Piteous Mother.
                                 Mrs. Godlie. 11gns.
Landscape after Poussin. Mr. Wouldbe. 5 gns.
     do.      do.      do.           do.
     do.      do.      do. with Rape of Europa.
                                 do. 13gns.
     do.      do.      do.      do.      of Ganymede.
                                 do.

Italian Scene after Claude. Miss Languish. 5gns.
A sett of Neptune's Progress, engr, French taste.
Mr. Sporteau. 7gns.
Still Life by Huyghens. Mr. Corporal. 24gns.
Gent and lady companion pictures by de Zoest.
2gns. ea. Miss Wittenham.
Gent in red, by Lely. 2gns.
Gentleman in armour. 30/-.
Gentleman with truncheon, Italian taste. 25/-.
Mr. Mudde.
Portrait of gent. 10/-.
Old portrait. 5/-.

Those were all the paintings. Some of them I recognized as having been Mrs. Rackage's. The engravings, the "Gent in red" by Lely and the four Poussins had been hers, I thought. I could not be sure of the others. The "Still Life" may once have been my father's. The "Old portrait, 5 shillings" was the only one that could be my mother. I could not bear to think that that lovely thing had gone at that price under that description. I asked Mr. Chaffinch about it.

"What was this 'Old portrait, 5 shillings'?"

He said, "I can't properly remember now, sir. I see so many. I think it was an old thing done upon wood, of a Bishop."

It came into my mind that the fire which had been Mr. Wittenham's undoing had destroyed my mother's portrait, too.

I said, "I'm afraid that the pictures I look for are not among these. Perhaps they were destroyed in the fire?"

"Very like, sir," he said. "The wing was burned out. The fire caught downstairs, where it was panelled, and

was all one blaze at once. When Mr. Wittenham wakened
the place was lost; he had to escape as he could."

I asked if I could see the ruins of the burned wing. He
said no. Mr. Dorchester had builded it all up at once.

That was all that could be learned from Mr. Chaffinch.
Probably the portrait was burned. I went back to the inn
sad at my heart that I should not see that image again;
it was gone. I had not expected to find it there; yet the
hope had been strong, and my disappointment was keen.

We had planned to stay that night in the inn and take
post-chaise in the morning, and go by easy stages of fifty
miles in a day back to town. The day was hot and op-
pressive, likely to thunder, as it seemed; the clouds had
the silvery brightness and boldness of form which fore-
tell thunder. We ate a midday meal and then thought that
we would go out to take the air. We wandered up a road
which seemed to promise freshness. A brook ran by its
side, and toadflax grew in the wall above it. After a quarter of a mile the sky became so overcast that I spoke of
returning to the inn. However, we had delayed too long,
the rain began; we, therefore, took shelter under some
trees near a small house with thatched roof. Lightning
warned us that a thunderstorm would break upon us; it
shortly did. The rain worsened, and the thunder drew
nearer. We, therefore, left the trees and hurried across
the road and stood under a wall close to the little house.
We had not been there twenty seconds when a woman
ran out of the house with two sacks, crying to Yvonne
to come in or she would be drowned. She wrapped Yvonne
in a sack and motioned her indoors; so we ran indoors
and had just shut ourselves within when a crash of thun-

der came from just overhead, and the rain pelted as in
the tropics. It became also so dark that I could not see
my hand before me. The woman who had rescued us was
a little oldish woman with something amiss in her mouth;
she had either lost her teeth, or had some deficiency in
her palate. Some letters she could not pronounce. "Oh, it
do cud dowd," she said. "Oo was ell outa at" she meant
"It does come down. You are well out of that." I said that
it was a very severe rain, and it was most kind of her to
take us in when we might have been soaked or blasted. She
said to Yvonne, "Oo cud id to de harlour" and led the
way out of the darkness to a little room. She drew a cur-
tain so that we could see the streams of rain falling in
cataracts in front of the glass. A cataract was spouting
down the wall over the window. "Oh!" she cried. "At is de
arrow's nest. I tode Dabez to clear it; he iddn't do it." She
meant that the flood was due to a sparrow's nest in the
guttering, which James ought to have cleared and had
not. The lightning blazed across heaven; the thunder
roared and all the road where we had lately stood seemed
a running brook. "Oh, it do cud dowd!" our hostess said.
It did indeed "cud dowd." There is a joy in watching rain.
All the excesses of nature are our pastimes.

The little room in which we were had not been aired,
used or opened for many days. It smelt of all the smells
which had crept into its darkness to die. Even when un-
curtained it was dark. The little old woman had a duster;
she dusted two chairs and set them for us, with the cour-
tesy that one cannot sufficiently praise or thank in simple people all the world over. Often those who have least
will give the most generously. She would not perhaps

have been thus to many, but she had seen Yvonne's young profile and had loved it, and had at once run to shelter and mother her. She said that now she must leave us a moment if we would excuse her. She went back to her kitchen where we heard her moving about, talking to herself or to somebody; probably a cat, I supposed. "No, Keren," she was saying. "Oo ought to think of Dod and not o ad." Why a cat should think of God and not go mad was not so clear; but it is sound advice for all living things. We sat in the window there, looking out at the pouring of the rain, which held our eyes. We were looking thus when I saw a figure coming down the road towards the house. He was huddled against the rain, which streamed from him, but with it he had an assumed air of not minding and indeed enjoying it. I would have known him in an instant anywhere. He was Henery. I thought that he was going to turn on to the little town by the road we had come. Instead of that, he came straight to the door of the house, past the window where we sat. As he stepped a little wide to dodge the spout from the gutter, he did not notice us, passed to the door and knocked upon it. The little old woman went to the door, asking, "Hooey dere?" When she recognized Henery, she said, with a little scream, "No, no no. Oo not cud here. Oo drove Keren ad. Now oo go."

"Hark to me," Henery said. "I'm wet and I'm cold. I must come in."

"No, no," she said; then dropping her voice she said, "There are eople ere, an ann and ooman; eltering."

"Who are they?" he said. I could tell that he tried to peer in, but could not.

"Eople in ee rain," she said.

"Well, I can come in to the kitchen," he said.

"No, no," she said. "Oo drove Keren ad. Oo wicked, wicked. Oo not cud id or I call out. Jayes is id de ack. Oo not cud id here." He seemed to grasp that James was about at the back of the house somewhere; still, his need for something was great. I did not doubt that he had money. What he wanted, I judged, would be for this woman to buy him some disguise or dry clothing. Who was she? Well, it was easy to guess that she was Mrs. Henery's sister. He had driven Keren, that was Mrs. Henery, mad; this lady who minded that so cruelly must be related or linked to Keren; she was perhaps a little mad herself, from thinking of it. "Where is James?" Henery asked. "Just at de ack," she said. "Go you and see. I don't want him spying here," he said. "No," she answered. "Oo go and see. Oo not cud id here."

"I've got to talk to you about Keren," he said. "Come, now, Kezie. Only you can help Keren now. You've got to listen." At that he stepped in to the door, reached swiftly across the little passage and shut to the door of the parlour where we sat. Our hostess gave a little cry of terror, but Henery checked her probably by clutching her wrist; we heard them pass to the back of the house and close a door behind them. I turned to Yvonne and told her swiftly that the man was one of the two escaped felons, and had been a part of my past; that if he had seen me in the past he would have recognized and denounced me, but that now he was nearly desperate and with a price upon his head. Still, I did not wish him to recognize me; he bore me ill-will. The storm passed over at that moment; the sunlight came into the room in which we were and filled it with a glow of surpassing beauty. Over the road, we saw the purple darkness of the storm with a rainbow upon it; the room was made radiant. On the wall opposite the window was the portrait of my mother by Baxter, just as it had been in the past. It was almost as though my mother had come out of the light to bring light. "Look, Yvonne," I said. "This is the portrait of my mother. How it came here, I cannot think." How could it have come there? Meanwhile, Henery was in the house only a few yards away, probably in some extreme of need; he was not likely to leave that house. Shelter and his other wants could be had there. You will say that I had but to walk into the town and tell a magistrate that I believed the felon Henery to be hiding in a cottage up the road. Straight the magistrate would have called his men, and Henery would have been taken. All this I could have done, you will say, without any least risk to myself. It is true. I could have done that. Perhaps the magistrate in the excitement of taking Henery would not so much as ask the name of him who brought the news. I could have done this. All the little town, as all the rest of England, was talking of the escape. But two things kept me from doing my duty by Henery. One was that I had a fear of being denounced and taken too. The other was that I had been in Newgate; I believe that any man who has been in Newgate, belongs to Newgate thenceforward and is on Newgate's side against anything that is called the Law.

Well, there we were. I did not want to leave till Henery had gone; he did not want to leave till the two strangers had gone. The two were still talking in the inner room. Henery was urging; she was protesting. I heard his voice become threatening, and felt that he might proceed to violence. I had listened for James, and had heard no sound of him. I had begun to believe that James was a fiction. The little old woman was probably far from any help. I walked across to the room within which the two were talking. Opening the door a half-inch or so, I said, "Miss Kezia." Henery stopped talking. The little old woman said "I'll cud now, sir." She came out confusedly, much shaken, breathing hard and weeping but with a game-cock look that told me that she was not going to give in. I said, "Miss Kezia, I do not know your name. My wife and I would like to know it, for you have been so kind to us and have saved us from a wetting. But will you tell me how you came to have that painting?"

She turned as white as a sheet, and sat down on one of the two chairs. She looked at me with the hopeless look that I had seen in Newgate when lads came in under guard after being committed. I did not think that she had stolen it, yet she looked guilty enough. "I orgot ee icture," she said, meaning probably that in her wish to help us she had forgotten that the painting was in the room. Then she rose up and said, "It was Hosea had the icture, at the tie of the ire." If she had not been shaken by Henery, she might not have been so forthcoming, but she told us then that her brother Hosea had once lived there with her; he was James's father. He had since died, which was why the room was never used. It was Hosea's room. When the fire broke out at the Hall, in that wild winter night she and Hosea had gone up in the glare to see if they could help. People were darting into the burning house at different points and flinging out anything that they could find onto the grass or into the flowerbeds. A great many things were saved thus, and lay there unregarded or were taken piecemeal to barns and such places. Hosea had brought in one or two things from the garden, this picture among them. He had put it upon the wall and left it there, meaning no harm. Mr. Wittenham had died, nobody had asked about the picture, and Hosea had fallen ill at that time and had done nothing about it. It had stayed there ever since. She had left it, as she had not liked to disturb anything that had been in Hosea's room. She had not looked at it much, because she had some notion that pictures were idols; she did not know whom it represented; she did not know whose it was, now that Mr. Wittenham was dead and all his things sold. She was all shaken by Henery's presence, and by the fear, lest she should be had in question about it. I said in a low voice, for I did not wish Henery to overhear, that I would pay her ten pounds present money for her care of the painting, and would undertake to restore it to Mr. Wittenham's heirs, if any, or to pay them a fair price for it through Mr. Chaffinch. I said that I well knew who the lady was, and knew her son very well, and knew that he would be rejoiced to have her portrait. She was shaken, as I say, and afraid, and eager for us to be gone. She said that that would be the best, if I would do that. So I took the picture from the peg on which it hung, and paid to her ten pounds, which I feared might soon pass into the property of Henery. We thanked her for her kindness and then set out, carrying the painting. We did not meet more than three people, even as we passed through the town to the inn-door. I suppose that those who saw us wondered a little who we were and what I was doing with that thing I carried, that idol or Dagon. I carried it up to our room and sponged it over, and then gazed long at it, remembering how I had seen it in the past and compared it with the original. It was a happy afternoon for me.

It must have been an hour after my return to the inn that I looked out into the inn-yard. It was like every other big inn-yard at that time. It horsed the up and down mail each day, each way, over one stage. It had therefore always a big and busy stabling and a strong smell of stable. The yard was busy with cocks and hens picking and scratching, ostlers passing with hay or straw, men polishing boots or harness, and now and then doing something to the feet of horses, or pulling out some trap, cart or chaise to wash its wheels. All this was being done all day long, and made a busy scene of English country life, of intense interest to Yvonne. When I looked out upon it now, I saw the famous thief-taker in talk with two who I supposed were sheriff's officers. They had some horsemen with them, waiting on their pleasure, and a glass-coach was being prepared for them. Word of something had gone abroad, for they were being watched by a little crowd, which was increasing. I had ever a terror when I saw this man, lest he should be after me. He was not after me. It occurred to me at once that he was after Henery. He had learned, no doubt, that Henery's wife had a sister in the country here, and had made sure that Henery would make for this place for shelter and help.

He had come down here and had waited for the fox to run into the trap. All the same, I had a sinking in the heart to think that this thief-taker whom I had done my best to avoid had come to the very place to which I had come and may well have been staying in the inn there with me, unsuspected by me; yet making all enquiries as to who I was and what I did there. He may have had many a good look at me, and must no doubt have thought, "He looks very like that young doctor we dealt with, the murder-case, the man they thought got spirited away; however, this fellow is said to be a foreigner, married to a French wife. He seems to be here about some paintings; probably, he's only a foreigner." However, there he was, talking quietly to these two men, giving them last instructions. Soon, all three of them moved over to a window ledge at the side, and loaded and primed their short pocket pistols. This last task was watched with intense interest by the little crowd. When the pistols were loaded, the three turned and walked with decision to the coach and climbed in; the door slammed fast on them, the coachman called up his team and they drove out of the yard under the arch into the street, followed by the attendant horsemen, who led a spare horse or two. As soon as the horsemen had passed, the little crowd turned after them and followed, running. I went down to the inn-office and asked what the disturbance was. "It's the murderer," the girl said. "They think the murderer's come here." From the inn-office, I could see through greenish window panes the street of the town. All who could run were running after the horsemen, those who could not run were gathering at the crossroads to discuss. I thought that, if I

were a more active man, I might still get to Henery across
the fields sooner than these takers by the road. I could
by great exertion just reach him in time to warn him. I
took the Newgate view, you see, much as I loathed the
fellow, that bad as he was he didn't deserve Newgate,
nobody could.

I was shocked for him. He must have thought that he
had come unobserved and unsuspected, that all would
be well at Kezia's, and that he could lie there and get
new disguises and outfits there, before making for a port
to take ship. Kezia was not making it easy, but no doubt
he had talked or scared Kezia over. Now, just as the
trouble seemed a little easy this horrible surprise would
burst upon him. And I felt that I had better not exult too
much, for a similar surprise might at any moment burst
on me. Well, as to warning Henery, that was out of the
question, but I felt that I would not be about when the
thief-taker returned to the inn with his victim. It would
be wise for me to get away while the interest was on
someone else; so I bespoke my chaise, and went round
to Mr. Chaffinch to explain about the portrait that certainly had belonged to me, may have belonged to Mr.
Wittenham and should supposedly be now the property
of Mr. Wittenham's heir. Mr. Chaffinch, who was used
to appraising paintings, said that he always reckoned
two guineas for a gent (three if he were in armour, four
if on horseback) and three guineas for a lady, if still
young; but of course more, if she were classic, with a
swan and that. He said that no one bid ever for a portrait
of anyone who wasn't in the family, unless it was just
to cover the walls. He thought that he would recommend

Mr. Wittenham's heir to accept three guineas for it, and in the meantime he was sure that I could take the picture with me till he could let me know the heir's decision. The heir had sold all the other paintings, and certainly would not wish to keep this. At that we parted; I returned to pack and make ready. But being ready in a few minutes, I had still to wait for the post-chaise driver. He had been ordered to be ready to start with me, but it was soon plain that he had gone to see the taking of the murderer. He had been seen going out in that direction, and though the girl in the office said that she was sure he would be back in a moment, for she had never known him late before, it was clear that he would not be back till the adventure was finished. I asked if there were no other driver. She said she was very sorry, but the other driver, who might have taken his seat, had gone with him. I thought of going over to another inn to get a driver there but judged that the driver there would have gone to see the fun, and that it would not do to seem too anxious to get away. So there I stayed while the time passed, and I chafed, thinking that now I should set off right under the eyes of Henery and the thief-taker. At last, being very indignant at the delay, I sent to the other inn, to ask if they could drive me, and had word at once that they could, and would send a chaise at once. The chaise came, much to the chagrin of the innkeeper, who said he had never been so treated before. I told him that, if he treated his guests in that way, he soon would be so treated again. There was some bitterness of feeling about our going.

Just as we started off, we saw surging round the corner towards us a running shouting mob of boys and young men, with some frightened or excited women among them, swept up probably by the crowd's approach and unable to get away. With these came the glass coach, with the outriders on each side of it. They were coming pretty fast; our driver had to pull to a side and stop to let them by. They came surging and whooping past us. I had a glimpse of Henery wild-eyed and white sitting next to that impassive awful man, whose face was a cat's face. I imagine that Henery was handcuffed to him, and the cat was smiling at having caught his mouse. I have often wondered at the man. He was born with this aptitude of following trails and catching people; he was not more virtuous, probably, than the men he brought to the gallows; but chanced to be born on the right side of the prison bars; he was the son of a turnkey; he was born against the mice and had continued in that way. He was not to be corrupted by his victims, further than was then the custom. He made them pay for privilege, as everyone in the prison world did, but no one ever bought an escape from him. He is now dead. As the saying goes, "he cut up very warm." What with rewards and payment for privilege, he did well; such men do. But I have often thought that the men who make vice seem pleasant do a lot less harm than those who make virtue stink in the nostrils; well, he was past in a flash, staring, smiling, straight ahead of him, thinking of his triumph at the Newgate regale, and the payment of the reward; his calculations had come off, he had perhaps won some side bets as well as the reward. He went past the victim who might have won him a little more glory. Ah, if he had but looked at me with recognition at that instant, what a triumph his had been! How-

ever, he was looking ahead, smiling at himself; and in an
instant he was past and round the bend upon the directest
road to London. The boys and young men called and
booed at us, in their noisy way, and then we were through
them and away. I thought it would be kind to see Kezia;
so we stopped there, and found her weeping, poor soul.
She had a black eye, poor soul, which Henery had given
her in the course of their talk, after we had gone. James,
who was a pleasant lad, with clever, bright eyes and good
manners, said that Henery had done nothing but harm
to them and had broken the heart and mind of his wife
by all his ways. He had come down upon them that afternoon for money and shelter, hoping presently to work
back to one of the seaports and get away to America. His
sister-in-law, Kezia, had refused to help him or to have
him about; he had therefore struck her and had gone on
to a lair in the ruins a little further on. He had known
the place from of old when he had come down there with
Keren in summer time; he had been caught in the lair
by the thief-taker. His tracks in the long May grass all
wet from the rain had been too plain to miss. We did
what we could to comfort the two, and to thank them for
their kindness to us. I shewed them what Mr. Chaffinch
had said about the painting; then we went on to our next
stage. I was wondering how it came about that Henery
had parted from Dennis. No word of Dennis was in the
paper or came from Kezia. Could it be that Dennis had
given him the slip? It seemed more likely that Dennis
had turned upon him and tried to kill him. Henery had
good reason to be afraid of Dennis.

At Oxford, the next day, we had a London paper that

told us that Dennis had been taken. He had, it seems, set
fire to Hannibal House, in some crazy hope of finding
the hidden treasure in the ruins. The house had burned
to the ground and he himself had been taken while digging in the ruins with a stick ; he had been recognized and
pointed out by a woman called Jollycok, who had been
attending the Fair at the neighbouring village of Smith
St. Emlins, and had come to see the site of the house. No
treasure had been found, the paper said. We delayed at
Oxford a little while, and then returned to our London
lodgings, where we learned of the safe arrival of both prisoners in Newgate. They had been carried before the magistrates for formal evidence of identity : after which, both
had been very heavily ironed and taken to the Hold, where
it was made impossible for them to escape again. They
were to be hanged next morning. There had been some
little delay, it seemed, for the man Henery had offered
to reveal some important fact if his life might be spared.
What the fact was, he would not say ; but he let it appear
that it had to do with the bringing of somebody to justice.
This staggered me, for I was in an uneasy position. I
know very well how swift and flashing a perception may
be in times of distress. What if Henery had had glimpses
of me at Kezia's house, or even as I drove past in the road.
He may have recognized me, and at once known that I
was a returned felon. What was more likely than that he
had seen the picture on Kezia's wall, on some former
visit, and known too well who the lady was. He knew the
picture, and it was in some way due to him, no doubt, that
the picture had gone there from the Rackage home. Who
would recognize the picture but a friend of the doctor's

whom he loathed? Who would wish to buy it but the son
of the woman? I was scared, I own, and yet, what had I
to fear, you will ask? I had everything to fear. I was a
condemned man. I had been hanged once for a crime I
didn't do, and could be hanged under that sentence until
I was dead, and had no doubt that I should be so hanged,
even though another man had confessed to the crime, and
a witness had brought evidence to confirm the confession.
I had had enough of our justice to know that it was pretty
merciless and by no means likely to examine into my
case. I should be hanged out of hand and enquired about
later. You say that this was crazy of me. Well, wait till
you have been in Newgate: then you may know a little.
These thoughts filled me, I assure you, as we drove out of
Oxford upon the London Road, with my mother's picture
beside me, and the lovely country flitting past. I was sick
with anxiety, I confess, and cursed my fate that I should
have been blasted thus. What had my soul done in some
past life, that I should be beset thus? Had I accused anyone falsely? Had I sent someone unjustly to the gallows?
Why otherwise should I now be punished? I had been
innocent. It had made me cynical. I had loved people.
It had made me loathe my countrymen and shun my fellow man. And there was to be no escape from it. Possibly
even now, a trap was set for me into which I should fall
to my death. So I drove on to London, sick at heart at
what I was to bring to Yvonne.

As we turned into the Square, we were delayed for
perhaps twenty seconds by a carriage in front of us,
which, after making the turn, stopped to set down a passenger. In the little halt, I looked out idly on the pave-

ment, and saw two men standing at the corner, both looking into my carriage. They were mean and shady-looking
men, with looks at once furtive and resolute. As I looked,
I saw one of them nudge the other with his elbow, and
make a sort of signal with a jerk of his thumb to a third
man standing further into the Square. It was after sunset, but the light was full and glowing. I thought idly
that the men might be snatch-thieves, who came to arriv-
ing coaches, and under cover of helping to unload would
pass some package to a confederate. I said something to
Yvonne about London having always its pickers and
stealers, then we set forth again and drew up at our
door.

As the horses stepped, the maid and Harry came across
the pavement to us, opened the door and helped Yvonne
down. The maid went in with Yvonne; Harry took my
mails and the portrait; and I stood for a moment to pay
the driver and to thank him. I had not thought of the two
men at the corner but I now saw them coming swiftly to
me from the one side, while the third man came from my
right. I looked at them sharply. The two men were not
known to me, but the third man was the thief-taker, the
cat-faced man, whom I had seen so recently sitting smiling
beside Henery in the road of that country town. He said,
"You must excuse me, Dr. Mansell. I have my duty to
perform. I must ask you to come with me."

"Certainly," I said, with my heart all gone to water.
"But come where, and why?"

"To the Bailey, sir," he said, "if you please."

The blow had fallen. I was caught. And I had done a

foolish thing. I had left my poisons in my room upstairs
in the lodgings.

"Can I get some things from my room?" I asked.

"You won't want them, sir," he said. "Indeed, you won't
find them. I've removed them, will you please come?"

I was stunned and without defence or wit. I had a
glimpse of Harry staring from the door of the house, and
one or two people staring. I think they thought that I was
a young debtor caught by sheriff's officers. A glass-coach
appeared and I was in an instant in it, and we were moving off: I have no recollection of getting in or being pushed
into this carriage. I know that there I was, with the cat-
faced man beside me, and one of the other men opposite
to me inside, staring hard at me, "learning my face," as
they called it, in case I should ever escape. The third man
was on the box with the driver. They had been very quick
with me. I had a dreadful minute thinking of Yvonne.

"Mrs. Mansell will be all right, sir," the man said
kindly. "We arranged for her to be seen to."

"Seen to": what amount of seeing to would help a
widow in a strange land? For the first few minutes of the
drive, I suffered as I suppose few can have suffered from
the blackest of grief and despair. We were driving very
fast, and nothing was said. I was in no condition to speak.
I became conscious of many people in the street and of the
cat-faced man calling to the driver through the hatch to
give up the thought of it and get in by Poll Maggot's, so
we turned into some byroad or lane, and so by lane and
lane till we were in a dark alley at the back of the prison.
I suppose no daylight could ever get into the lane even in
summer. It was in dark twilight when we stopped; two or

three men were loitering in the lane, seemingly waiting
for our arrival; our driver whistled and they closed in.
At the same time a door opened and sent a great glow of
light onto the pavement. The place seemed full of light
and people; I heard laughter and the clinking of glass.
This was no doubt the warders' regale before the famous
hanging; they were entertaining the great, no doubt;
turnkey and title alternating with song and sentiment.
But it was not quite that. A great gentleman, somewhat
flushed from his punch was coming towards me. "Dr.
Mansell," he said, "you have nothing to fear. We know all
about you. Come in and join the party. We are going to
repair the wrong done to you. You'll get your pardon tomorrow, for the crime you never did. Now here are all the
warders; some of them remember you, and the rest are all
your friends. Now we all want you to shake hands."

I was in the room of the regale. It smelled very strongly
of punch; there were fourteen or fifteen people there, and
they were at their second or third bowl. They had all risen,
who could rise at all, to greet me, and shake hands. I said
something like "Am I not a prisoner, then?" The cat-
faced man said, "No, sir." The great gentleman said,
"Now, gentlemen, we have got Dr. Mansell here. Charge
your glasses, and let's drink to him." They were all unsteady and uproarious, except those who had come in
with me. The great gentleman said, "You may think we're
Bedlam, but nothing of the kind; absooty nothing of the
kind." I said, "I must ask to be allowed to go back, to
reassure my wife."

"That is done. My wife is there to do that," the man said.
"I've been asked by the Ordinary to bring you here. He

begs that you will have the charity to see the prisoner, Dennis Rackage. He was the main cause of all your trouble of course, but he asks to speak with you."

"I will see him," I said. "But tell me the truth. You are not going to shut me in the Hold?"

"No," he said. "On honour, no. Let me explain though. You were recognized at the coach-office by our friend here, who followed the case when you were supposed to have escaped that time. Our friend here, as it happens, suspected that you were innocent from the first. He believed that Rackage and Henery between them had put the Admiral away. He had his eyes upon them for a long time before he could deal with them. When he saw you at the coach-office he let me know. You will have your pardon tomorrow, and no further trouble at all. I understand that you will be with Mr. Secretary tomorrow. But come now to the Ordinary; you shall be off home as soon as you have seen the prisoner."

I hardly knew if I were living or dreaming. I was not sure that I was not a prisoner, and that these men were too drunk to be sure of it. However, there was an Ordinary, whom I well remembered. "Dr. Mansell," he said, "you did not care for what I offered in the past, but perhaps you may reflect, after tonight, that the case for guidance is stronger than you supposed."

The prison smell was as before. The stone corridors stank and echoed in just the same way. The old terror of that awful place stuck in my throat as we trod towards the Hold. In the darkness of the night outside, a church bell struck an hour. It was St. Sepulchre's. No need to tell me what that bell was. Near the Hold I heard again the

loud mad whimpering of the despairing women who were
under sentence and the yelling of the main prison from all
the men who had the fortune to be drunk. It was terrible
to smell the Newgate stink and hear the Newgate snarl
and yell. The great locks clicked and the heavy doors
rolled back. The Ordinary whispered that they had put
the two in separate cells, lest they should destroy each
other. It seemed to me that they had done that completely
as it was, but the mercies of Newgate were ever odd to me.
"Mr. Rackage," the Orderly said, "I've brought Dr. Mansell to you."

I believe that the Ordinary had not seen Dennis for
some hours. In the interval some kind warder had brought
a can of brandy; Dennis was by this time pretty drunk.

"This is Dr. Mansell," the Ordinary said. "You wanted
so much to see him, to tell him something."

Dennis stared through the fog of the prison brandy at
me, and asked, "Who is he?"

"Dr. Mansell," the Ordinary replied. "Young Dr. Mansell."

"Tell that to the godly," Dennis said. "Don't tell it to
me, for I'm an unbeliever. See?"

"Come, come," the Ordinary said, in pleading tones.
"Come, Mr. Rackage; recollect yourself, and where you
are presently to appear. You were going to tell Dr. Mansell something; something that might be of value to him."

"What was it?" Dennis said, supping his brandy.
"What was I going to tell him?"

"Something perhaps about money," the Ordinary said.

"Money?" Dennis said. "If I'd money I wouldn't be
here. What does a man of your cloth want with money in

this carnal world? I've done with money. The only comfort money's been to me is this. With this I can forget.
This time tomorrow I'll be given a golden harp and set to
sing. Any harp that's given to me I'll pop for brandy any
time, and so I give you warning. Have a sup with me for
old sake's sake."

He held out the brandy to the clergyman. He was
heavily ironed, so that even a simple movement needed an
effort.

"Mr. Rackage," the Ordinary said, "will you not put
aside this brandy? Come, let me take it away. Here is Dr.
Mansell, come to shake hands with you and if possible set
you at peace."

"Peace," Dennis said. "This is the place for peace, isn't
it?"

"Rackage," I said, "I am Edward Mansell. You came to
see me here in this very place. Whatever bitterness has
been between us, let us put an end to it now for God's sake.
Let us shake hands and be done with that. I am grieved
indeed that we were not better friends in the past."

"Friendship goes by destiny, my joker," Dennis said.
"But as long as I've got a spot of brandy left I'm not going
to complain about that. You say you are Ned Mansell as
your filthy father called you. Well, you always were a
fool and won't mend that by keeping. You put in to make
yourself heir with the Admiral. You played a clever game,
didn't you? Your father thought he'd cut out Dennis from
his inheritance, didn't he? I knew a trick worth two of
those. But for you and your filthy father cutting in, I
might have had the Admiral's blunt; all of it. I was as
good as his heir. He liked me. He saw that I was a gen-

tleman, not an upstart doctor's apprentice smelling of
squills. He liked a man to dress, did the Admiral. All the
same, you came along and put my nose out of joint, or
thought you did. You thought you did. See here, you who
are come to see this Christian die, this fellow, if he's Ned
Mansell, thought he'd done for me with the Admiral;
thought he'd feathered his nest; got the old boy to make
him his heir. So he had done, and got me put off the course;
all his way was as smooth as soap; he'd only to keep tread-
ing water and he'd have been in the Admiral's shoes, house
and lands and blunt. He'd as good as landed his fish. Then
what happened? Little Dennis stepped in. He thought he'd
done with Dennis, and done for him; but it wasn't so. No,
it wasn't so. I had my eye on him all the time, if he didn't
think it. I had it, and I watched my tip. He was always a
soft fool and always will be. He had a row with his Admiral. I heard it. I heard lots of what went on. So I
thought, this is the chance. This is the time. A wise man
has only one chance only one time. He has to take or lose
it. I had only to go in and stick a jemmy in the panel and
out the gold would fall, or so I thought. I was wrong
about that; only papers were in the panel and the Admiral
came in as I was making sure. That was the silliest thing
the old cock ever did. I banged him with this poor fool's
stocking, I stuck him with this poor fool's knife, the one
he'd just bought as a fairing. He didn't take a second
stick, only one was needed; down he went and out went
his candle. And then in came this Edward Mansell the
heir by the back door. In he came. I was above looking for
Mr.'s keys, when in came the loved one's footsteps down
below and it was time for me to be off. Off I went. I hadn't

got the blunt, I'd done something that was as good. I'd killed off Ned's benefactor with Ned's knife, and Ned was in the house as I went out and saw me and never recognized me. That was the real joy. I got out of the gate. He saw me go and never knew it was me and never guessed it was me." Here he turned to me and added, "If you ever have the spunk to kill a man, outside your doctoring, do it when there are fools about; then they'll be hung instead of you." He took more brandy and began to sing a low song. "I came in to this prison afterwards," he went on, "to see this Ned Mansell, the night before he went out. I thought he'd blab where the blunt lay, but not a blab out of him. Now he comes to exult over me, and thinks I'll tell where the blunt is. He has some odd ideas if he thinks that, the silly swine."

"Rackage," the Ordinary said, "we have the man Henery here. We want you both to shake hands with Dr. Mansell and with each other. You both stand in need of forgiveness. You both are going to the fount of all forgiveness. Will you not clear yourself of this mood and go hence with forgiveness?"

"Am I going to be forgiven, old cock?" he asked. "You know quite well I'm not. I'm for the public show to-morrow. Hark at the audience already, the dirty dogs. That's the measure of forgiveness you're giving me. Don't think that I'll give you, or anyone, a penny better love than you give me. As for that dog Henery, I've squirmed under him all these years paying for his silence; I'd like to bite his throat open with these teeth."

"I'm here, Master Dennis," Henery said. They had brought him there from the next cell at the Ordinary's request. "I'm here, Master Denn, and I want you to forgive me, so as I may come to God forgiven."

"Forgive you!" Dennis said. "No, you come to the wrong shop for forgiveness, my cock. No. You come to me for exultation. You thought you'd set up for being a Lord Henery, Baron Cholsington, no less, and to that end you rode me like the Dick's Bay Horse; ah, you leech and suckblood! But the worm turned and bit you dead at last, didn't he? You won't be Baron, just yet, I gather. Ah, and when we were here together all bound for the cold-meat cart, who put you up to making an escape and bribing a way out? Little Dennis Rackage, that was. And when we were out, who thought of being King's evidence and getting a pardon? Henery, that was, but little Denn got the better of him. I saw your game, my twister, and I put the cross on it. I got away and I left the office where you'd go. I knew where your wife's sister lived. I knew where you'd make for, as soon as leg would get you there. I might get away or I might not, but you weren't going to get away. I had you watched for, you great looby, and in you walked to the trap, you so smart and so cocky. I didn't get far myself, but I had my run for my money. I burned your baronial hall down, and I know where the money is. I don't much care that I don't get it, as long as I know you won't. You'd have been Baron Cholsington but for me; now you won't be. I'm drunk now, drunk and dying. And I'll be drunk till I'm dead now, but I'll not be so drunk as not to know I've done for you. The rope's all knotted for me; so's yours, my Lord, and I'll see you in it, drunk as I'll be. And now, brothers, give us a song. I've done all the talking and I'm sick of it. But this Baron Cholsington,

Lord Henery Hannibal, is sicker than I. Yes, my Lord. I
settled you. I, whom you squeezed dry, have got you so
you'll be squeezed dead.

> "So follow the fortunes of clever Tom Pinch
> Who died like a hero and never would flinch.

You, Ordinary, if you want to do a Christian deed, you get
these gaolers to supply real brandy to prisoners, not gin
done up with red pepper and vitriol."

He lapsed into an outrageous song, so loudly that the
men outside the prison in the lane heard it and laughed
and joined in it. There must have been twenty thousand
men outside the prison, all somewhat touched with drink;
they sang the filthy tale to its end with disgrace notes of
howls and cat-calls. Dennis, who became drunker mo-
mently, sang with them and swayed to the sound. It was
pretty dark there; they had a lantern in the yard outside
the Hold, and a couple of lanterns, one a small one brought
by the Ordinary, where we were. Dennis swayed as he
sat, being ironed to the floor. Henery stood with the irons
hanging from him, like draperies on a bronze. Henery was
weeping with grief, rage, fear and misery. I was weeping
from the thought that I was freed from my terrors, and
from the knowledge that Yvonne was free, and that I had
been in that Hold, expecting Death remediless, and that
by miracle I had been brought out of it to life; the Ordinary was weeping, from the thought that the hours would
soon strike, and that those souls, but for him, might fall
to a fearful fate. When the song died away into yells,
screams and howlings, the crying of fried fish and eel

jelly, the shouts of encouragement and obscenity, Henery said to me, "I hope, Mr. Mansell, that you found the picture of the late Mrs. Mansell?"

I said, "Yes, thank you. I saw you at the cottage there, but I had nothing to do with your being taken. I don't think even I could be quite such an iron thing as to send anyone here, after being here myself."

"No, sir," he said, in his servant's voice. "No, sir; I suppose not, sir."

"Tell me," I said. "But first let us shake hands, if we may."

I held out my hands to him, and the poor creature put out his ironed hands to me and caught them. In the half-dark my hands caught on the wrist-iron of one of his wrists. I slid my finger on it. Near the bolt was a little Z-shaped irregularity on the iron surface. I had run my finger along it countless times. It was the iron once put on my left wrist. I shook his hands and said, "Tell me; can't I do anything outside for you?"

"I daren't ask it, sir," he said. "I've hated you too cruel."

"That's done," I said. "I've not liked you, but that's done, God knows. What can I do?"

"There's my poor wife in Bedlam, sir," he said. "I've let her go in on the poor side, to save expense. But the keepers stir them up for sixpence on the poor side, to make them rave to visitors. If she could be put on the paying side, where they are all spared that, or are said to be, sir, it couldn't be for very long."

"I will see to that, I promise," I said. "Could I do anything for Kezia?"

He ground his teeth at the thought. "You can tell her," he said, with an effort, "that you saw me where she always said I'd be. I wish I'd smashed her praying jaws on her."

The Ordinary here put in, to remind him that it was supposed that he had some money put away, and that if he declared where it lay, no doubt the Crown might order that some of it should be disposed for the maintenance of dependents and relatives. "You've no doubt, haven't you?" Henery answered. "Nor have I. What the lawyers get their fangs on, they keep. Doubtless they'd like to know where my savings are. Well, they won't, from me, nor from the present keeper."

Dennis at this, with a great effort, flung his empty can at Henery's face. He missed his aim, owing to his irons. "Your savings!" he said. "Your thievings from me and mine, you mean."

The great gentleman (I call him this, because that was his position, if not his nature) whispered to the Ordinary that we had better go from there. I think that he needed more punch. The warder motioned Henery back to his den.

"Time to go home," he said.

"Goodbye, Henery, and God bless you," I said.

"Time to go home," he muttered bitterly. He seemed to droop down into his irons and shuffled and clanked into his lair.

Dennis had forgotten that he had flung his can. He had forgotten all things except perhaps that there was no more brandy, and even that he was too stupid to feel acutely. He, too, was collapsed into his irons, and was repeating some nonsense to himself; I have thought since that it was the jargon of some gambling card-game of a kind simple enough for him to follow. He was repeating.

"Spider, fly—fly—fly. Spider, fly, web, web."

"You had better come away, sir," the Ordinary said. "I will return to him later when he is in more of a mood to listen. I thank you, sir, for coming to them."

"Goodbye, Dennis," I said. "Goodbye."

"Don't interrupt the dealer," he said savagely.

They were plucking me by the sleeve to go; I was eager to be gone. In a moment the door had snicked to with that clickety-clock of the well-oiled, beautifully made great door-lock, that triumph of skill which helped to end what man had neglected till too late. I was outside the Hold, and he was shut up within it. I saw a glare above the wall, from the lights outside where people were yelling their wares, of last dying speech and confessions and the like. I found myself with the turnkey following the party.

"Look here" I said. "Will you promise to do something for those two men?"

"Yes, sir," he said, "on the usual terms."

"Well, then," I said, "here are two guineas. Promise that you will get to them as much brandy as will make them both senseless, if they wish that, before they go out."

"I'll promise that," he said, "but the brandy'll be a guinea extra."

"Here it is, then. God help you if you fail," I said.

"We never fail, sir, where the money doesn't fail."

"I believe that's true," I said.

"For the poor," he said, "we sometimes have our failings, I don't deny; but any gent that is a gent, why, sir, we like to treat him *as* a gent."

"One of you must have made a pretty penny by letting them out," I said.

"So it is supposed, sir," he said.

But by this time we were at the regale and about to leave the prison. My great gentleman had some runners to clear the way to his coach, which was waiting to take us home. Some thieves were hanging about there as we came out. They edged up when they saw us coming, thinking that we were drunken gentlemen coming from the regale. One of our runners called to them, in their slang, "Come and nab the nickers, bowmen." One of them laughed and said, "Keep inside, George. Don't spoil our market-day." George laughed and said, "We'll have plenty on the roads tomorrow looking out for you." So we passed on, and came to the coach waiting in the quiet, with the coachman under a lamp, with the light shining on his tarred cape. He was talking to a married couple, about the man Henery and Mr. Rackage.

The carriage brought me home to Yvonne. The house was brightly lit; the great gentleman had sent his wife there to comfort Yvonne, during the hour of my absence. She swept out, gracious and glittering, as our carriage drew up, and was swept into the carriage as I came out of it. She looked at me but did not speak to me. I knew that this was because I had been hanged. That would not be forgiven me, whatever pardon might come.

"You will hear from us tomorrow," the man said, "and he is expecting you at Whitehall at eleven." The carriage drove on.

What more shall I say? Those two went out of it the next morning, as you may read, if you wish, in their last dying speeches and confessions, and in the good Ordinary's report. Such a scene of rascality, blackguardism and bestiality had never been seen at any execution in the memory of man; but all the reports note that "both prisoners seemed unaware of their condition." My turnkey kept faith, it seems.

At eleven I was at Whitehall, arranging that the land of the Kranois should begin a trade with us. This has continued ever since, with good and evil fortune. One good thing has come from it, that the slave-trade has been shut from that part of Africa. My pardon was handed to me before our business talks began. The Lord who handed it to me said that of course no one, and no thing, could atone to me for what I had suffered. What reparation could be made, would be made; the site of Hannibal House would be mine, and some sum would be offered for the Admiral's house-property, now long since sold, and not to be recovered. He said that life was full of strangeness, but that sometimes one seemed to perceive a plan, or at least a justice. He said that all had agreed, and perhaps I should agree, that the matter should be kept quiet; he was sure that both I myself and my wife would prefer that. He was a man of charming manners; he began then to talk about the weather, and about the possible origins of the Kranish people, of the importance of English trade in that part of the world, and of the beauty of the new theory of disease which had been put forward in a remarkable book. He said that he was empowered to add that if I wished to practice medicine no obstacle would be placed; far from it; a diploma would be granted.

I said that I would not practice medicine; my task was

to try to preserve a valiant and pleasant people from the savagery and slavery which threatened them from blacks and whites. I thanked him for all that he had said and done for me and for the Kranois. I hoped that he would persuade his colleagues to visit Africa, and judge the land for themselves. He said that my wife had given such an impression of Kranish beauty, that no English lady would permit her husband to visit a land where such beauty lived. After that, with some more compliment and the expression of obligation, he left me, with my pardon and my title deeds and a note of money.

So Fortune that had deserted me returned, bringing with her more than I had lost and infinitely more than I had ever had. The past was cleared from me and need not now trouble me. I should not be much in England, and if I were, who would remember, or connect the stranger from Africa with Dead Ned? Not many, I judged. Already the few friends whom I had had were dead or scattered.

The Fortune who gives is ever prodigal. Some time later, when we were about to sail for Sixteen Peaks, Yvonne and I went out to Cholsington, to look at the site of Hannibal House. It was a fair summer day. Since the fire, the place had been deserted. Being now full summer, the weeds had taken charge in such strength that even the curious had ceased to trespass there; a few boys after birds' nests, perhaps, no others; the blackened walls partly stood. The roof had collapsed into the shell, all the windows had gone; the starlings, which once nested in such strength in the roof, now nested in the ruin—they were very busy, whistling, chuckling and bringing food. Two strangers, who seemed more intent upon each other than upon the ruins, were looking through the gate at what had been the front of the house. Yvonne caught my arm as one of them, the man, partly turned to us. She said, "Ned, that's my brother Raoul." I was intent upon the woman, whose exquisite hair and attitude I would have recognized anywhere; she was Patty Morsoe, to whom I had once been, not a slave perhaps, but a devoted lover. "Raoul," Yvonne cried. "You remember Yvonne? How have you come here?"

The disturbances and wars had brought him there, after long wandering east and west, unable to reach France, unable to go back to the cities of the Kranois. He had tried planting in the West Indies, and had then turned trader and agent. He had married Patty in Kingston two years before that. There we four should meet again.

I went alone into the garden, leaving the others to talk. The ruin of the house was all thickly grown with nettle, some of it four feet high. Going round, I came to the track made by some animal. My little dog, that had once been Dr. Copshrews', at this point came rushing. He yapped at something; a rabbit or cat disappeared into the ruin, with the little dog after it. I followed, with difficulty, beating down the nettles, till I was inside the house, by what had been the back door, through which I had been taken to Newgate. The door was gone of course; I clambered over fallen roof and wreck to where the little dog was scuffling and snuffling. He was in the central part of the house now, scratching at a rabbit-burrow. The floor had been burned or stolen; I was on the earth on which the house had been reared, in what had been once the dining-room, a very beautiful room, where the Coroner had once committed me for trial for murder. It flashed into my mind that the little dog was scuffling just where I had stood to hear my fate. The Rector had stood there; the Coroner had sat yonder; the Henerys had snuffled and gone white over there; I myself had been in that very place and now stood there again; if, indeed, I was I and here was here.

The little dog paused from his scuffling, put his head upon the ground and tried to clear the moist clay from his nostrils. As he could not do this, he put up his nose for me to do it for him, which I did. Bending down there, I thought that I saw something in the burrow and, putting down my hand, touched metal. Something hard was stuck in the earth there—some post or column of iron, it seemed; I could not budge it. It flashed into my mind that it might be the Admiral's treasure chamber, and so it proved to be.

How anyone had reached it before the house was burned I could not tell; probably by some simple and cunning contrivance of the Admiral's own. In a narrow space he had contrived to pack, muzzle up, nine of the small guns which had been the armament of the *Hannibal*. He had used each one as a strong box. Eight were full to the muzzle with notes and golden guineas, the ninth half full. Each was carefully stoppered with a metal tompion, puttied in. Being muzzle up, they had taken little space. As the giving of wealth depends on fortune, this wealth had been kept from all till my little dog led me to it.

So there I was, with wife, friends and fortune, the Rose revived, Ned Alive and the bright road clear before me.